Dear Reader,

Thirty years ago I began my career by writing romances under several pseudonyms. These were stories of women and men who meet, fall in love, despite the odds against them, and endure the heartache and joy that is unique to that experience.

These stories reflect those classic themes, which have engaged and entertained audiences since storytelling first became a popular pastime. They have been reissued at your request and for your enjoyment. I hope you have as much fun reading them as I did writing them.

As in all romance novels, expect a happy ending....

Sandra Brown

# SANDRA BROWN

## The Thrill of Victory and Tomorrow's Promise

Previously published under the pseudonym Erin St. Claire

ISBN-13: 978-0-7783-1606-0

THE THRILL OF VICTORY
AND TOMORROW'S PROMISE

Copyright © 2014 by Harlequin Books S.A.

The publisher acknowledges the copyright holder of the individual works as follows:

THE THRILL OF VICTORY
Copyright © 1989 by Erin St. Claire

TOMORROW'S PROMISE
Copyright © 1983 by Sandra Brown

Recycling programs for this product may not exist in your area.

Printed in U.S.A.

# CONTENTS

# The Thrill of Victory

# Prologue

"Ramsey is out for your butt, Mackie."

The gopher, who had met the star sportswriter of the *Dallas Tribune* at the elevator, fell into step behind him as he walked toward the city room of Dallas's largest newspaper. Judd Mackie was unfazed by the threat of being out of favor with the *Tribune*'s managing editor. He made a beeline for the coffee machine. Its brew was so viscous, so black, he'd often joked that they used the leftovers to fill in the cracks on North Central Expressway.

"Mackie, did you hear me?"

"I heard you, I heard you, Addison. Got a quarter?"

The pockets of his slacks—expensive, but hopelessly wrinkled—hadn't produced the correct amount of change for the vending machine. He was notorious for never carrying money. It was ludicrous that he was bumming from a guy whose age and income were a fraction of his.

"Ramsey's fit to be tied," the gopher said in an ominous undertone as he passed his idol a handful of coins.

"He usually is." Mackie watched a foam cup fill with

coffee whose only virtue was that it was scalding and as darkly opaque as the sunglasses he still had on, though he'd been inside the building a full five minutes.

As he sipped barely diluted caffeine from the disposable cup, the lenses of his glasses fogged over, reminding him they were there. He took them off and dropped them into the breast pocket of his jacket, which wasn't any more dapper than his slacks. His eyelids were puffy; the whites of his eyes were rivered with red.

"He told me to catch you at the elevator and personally escort you to his office."

"He must really be steamed. What'd I do this time?" Judd asked with disinterest. Michael Ramsey was perpetually steamed at him. From one day to the next the extent of his wrath was only a matter of degree.

"I'll let him tell you. You coming peaceably?" the gopher asked worriedly.

Judd took pity on him. "Lead on."

Addison Somethingorother was an intern who worked part-time between his journalism classes at Southern Methodist University. During the boy's first day on the job, Judd had passed him a rumpled handkerchief he'd fished from an even more rumpled pocket and jokingly suggested that the eager student use it to dry behind his ears. But when Addison had looked wounded, Judd had slapped him on the back, said he'd meant no offense, and offered the best advice he could give someone who aspired to a journalistic career, which was to reconsider.

"The hours are long, the pay lousy, the working conditions abysmal and the best you can hope for is that whatever you've written gets read before the dog chews it up or the bird craps on it or the housewife wraps chicken guts in it."

Addison was still around, so apparently he hadn't taken the jaded sports reporter's words to heart. Judd would have continued to rebuke Addison's idealism if he hadn't remembered a time when he himself had had stars in his eyes about a career.

The stars had gone out long ago, but on occasion, usually when he was deep into his cups, he remembered what it felt like to have a burning ambition for greatness. So he let the cub go on dreaming his dreams. He'd find out for himself that life played dirty tricks.

It was midmorning and the city room was a bee-hive of activity. Reporters at word-processing terminals clicked away on their keyboards. Some had telephone receivers tucked beneath their chins. Messengers hustled among the desks, which were already stacked with packages and mail as yet unopened.

Then there were those individuals simply hanging out, smoking, sipping canned drinks or coffee, waiting for something newsworthy to happen or, short of that, divine inspiration.

"…the Arabs. But then Israel—hi, Judd—wouldn't do…"

"So I said to her, 'Look, I want my keys back.' Hi, Judd. To which she said…"

"…me a quote. Hi, Judd. Somebody's got to stick his neck out and go on the record about this thing."

Popular with his cohorts, he nodded greetings as he followed Addison through the maze of desks, then down a carpeted hallway toward the managing editor's office.

"There you are," his secretary said in exasperation. "Since we don't have a militia, he was about to send me

in search of you. Thanks, Addison. You can get back
to whatever you were doing before Mr. Ramsey summoned you."

The gopher seemed reluctant to leave just when the
fireworks were about to start. But Ramsey's secretary
was almost as indomitable as the boss himself. He ambled away.

"Hi, doll. What's up?" Judd tossed his empty cup
into the nearest wastepaper basket. "Pour me a cup of
the real stuff, will you?"

Propping her fists on her hips, the secretary asked,
"Do I look like a waitress?"

Judd winked and gave her the leisurely, miss-noth-
ing once-over that rarely failed to make points toward
a big score. "You look like a million bucks." He saun-
tered through the connecting door before she could re-
taliate against either his blatant sexism or ingratiating
compliment.

Inside the door, Judd was greeted by the noxious
fumes left by the first two of the four packs of cigarettes Michael Ramsey would smoke that day. He had
one cigarette smoldering in an ashtray and another in
his mouth when Judd strolled in.

"It's about time." His face was florid with rage.

Judd flopped into a leather chair and crossed his ankles in front of him. "For what?"

"Don't get cute with me, Mackie. You've really
blown it this time."

Ramsey's secretary came in bearing the requested
cup of coffee, brewed in her personal coffeemaker. Judd
thanked her with a smile and another suggestive glance
that she knew, and regretted, was meaningless.

After she withdrew, Ramsey exhaled a veritable

thundercloud of acrid smoke. "You missed the biggest tennis story of the year."

Judd burned his tongue on the coffee and choked on a laugh. "Tennis! You're all red in the face over a tennis story? Geez, as high as your blood pressure is, I thought the Cowboys must've declared bankruptcy. What happened, did McEnroe call the line judge a naughty name?"

"Stevie Corbett collapsed during her morning match at Lobo Blanco."

Judd's grin fell. His attention and his mirth were instantly arrested. He held the coffee cup, real china, against his lips and gazed at Ramsey over the patterned rim. Ramsey ground out the cigarette in the ashtray, took a final drag on the one presently in his mouth, then haphazardly flicked the ashes toward the overflowing ceramic bowl on his desk.

"What do you mean collapsed?"

"Well, now that's what we don't know because we didn't have anybody out there covering the story," Ramsey replied sweetly. "Our overpaid star reporter was sleeping in this morning."

"Cut the sarcasm, alright? So I overslept. Big deal. What'd Miss Corbett do, trip and fall over her braid?"

"No, she didn't trip. Thankfully the photographer showed up even if you didn't. He said she 'collapsed.'"

"Like fainted?"

"Like dropped down and folded up into a little heap on the court."

"Terrible phraseology."

Ramsey's face went darker red. "If you'd been there, you could have phrased it yourself."

"It wasn't necessary for me to be there," Judd said

in his own defense. "Corbett was a cinch to beat that Italian girl."

"Well, she didn't. She had to forfeit the match. She's out of the tournament."

"On the heels of her winning the French Open, this one was a shoo-in. She was playing more as a courtesy than anything. I was going to catch some of the more interesting matches this afternoon."

"When you came to terms with your hangover," Ramsey said balefully. "As it is, you missed reporting on Stevie Corbett's collapse in front of a huge hometown crowd that got up early and fought rush-hour traffic to watch her play while you were still tucked in."

"What's the word on the street?"

"Nothing. Her manager read a statement to the press. It amounted to three sentences that don't tell us a damn thing."

"Which hospital is she in?" Judd was already mentally compiling a list of reliable sources in the medical community who would squeal on their own mothers if the money was green enough.

"She isn't."

"Isn't in the hospital?" The adrenaline rushing through his system ebbed. His quick brain applied the brakes and threw everything into Reverse. He coughed another rough laugh and took another drink of the coffee he'd set aside and forgotten. "Leave it to you to blow this all out of proportion, Mike. Cute little Stevie probably had a rough night. As I did."

Ramsey shook his head adamantly. "She had to be carried off the court. This was more than a rough night." He pinned Judd to the chair with a hard stare. "You're going to find out what it was...*before* anyone else does.

And you're going to be playing catch-up ball because the story has already been reported on the radio. Didn't you hear it while you were driving in?"

Judd shook his head. "I didn't turn on the radio. Headache."

"Figures. Here." Ramsey took a tin of aspirin out of the lap drawer of his desk and tossed it to his most intuitive, incisive reporter, who also happened to be the most exasperating. He kept the stock of aspirin for Judd alone.

"Take three of them, all of them, whatever it takes to get yourself in shape and on the phone or out beating the bushes, but find out what brought on Stevie Corbett's collapse." He jabbed the space between them with his current cigarette. "I want your story in time for the evening edition."

Judd glanced at his watch. "I kinda had this lunch, uh, thing, set up."

"Cancel."

"No," Judd drawled as he lazily rolled out of the chair, "that won't be necessary. I'll just call the young lady and move our date to midafternoon. By then I'll have this Corbett story sewn up and ready to go to press."

At the door, he gave Ramsey a mocking salute. "You know, Mike, if you don't calm down, you're going to die young."

He left the door standing open. Everyone in the city room heard Mike Ramsey call Judd a name that flattered neither him nor his mother.

# One

"Oh, my Lord, *you*."

Stevie Corbett slumped against her front door, which she had just pulled open. She was wearing a short kimono-style robe that overlapped across her chest and was tied with a self-belt at her waist. The light green silk looked as cool and fresh as a ripe honeydew melon.

The details of her attire were noticed by the sportswriter, her nemesis, and the last person on earth she wanted to talk to at that moment.

"I thought you were somebody else," she said.

"Obviously. Who's the lucky dog you were expecting?" His voice was heavily spiced with insinuation.

"My doctor is sending over some medication. I thought you were the delivery boy."

"That's what peepholes are for," Judd reminded her, tapping the small round hole in the door.

"I didn't think to look."

"Got your mind on other things, huh?"

She glanced beyond his wide shoulders, hoping for a glimpse of the expected pharmaceutical delivery. "Yes."

"Like making a fool of yourself at Lobo Blanco Tennis Center this morning."

Her eyes snapped back to his. "As usual, Mr. Mackie, your choice of words is inflammatory and incorrect."

"Not from the way I hear it."

"The way you *hear* it? You weren't there?" She drew a sad face. "What a pity. You would have tremendously enjoyed my humiliation."

He smiled and the lines in his tanned face deepened. "I'm graciously volunteering my shoulder for you to cry on. Why don't you invite me in and tell me all about it?"

"Why don't you go straight to hell?" In contrast to her words, her smile was positively angelic. "You can read about my ignominious fall in your competitor's column."

"I don't have a competitor."

"Nor do you have any modesty, or scruples, or talent, or taste."

He whistled. "That tumble you took this morning did nothing to improve your rotten disposition."

"I have a lovely disposition around everybody except you. And why should I? I'm not a hypocrite. Why should I be pleasant to the columnist who writes scathing articles about me?"

"My readership expects me to be acerbic," he said blandly. "My acid wit is my trademark just like this single long, blond braid is yours." He reached out and ran his fingers over the plaited strands, starting at her shoulder and following it down to the curve of her breast.

Stevie slapped his hand away and tossed the heavy, thick braid over her shoulder. "I ducked the press today. How did you slip past?"

"I know who to bribe for home addresses and such. Why are you ducking the press?"

"I don't feel well, Mr. Mackie. I certainly don't feel like swapping insults with you. If I'd known you were on the other side of my door, I certainly would never have opened it. Please leave."

"One question?"

"No."

"Why did you faint?"

"Goodbye."

She slammed the door in his face, almost catching the hem of his jacket in the crack. For a moment, she rested her forehead against the wood. Judd Mackie of all people! Only yesterday his column had made snide mention of her playing in the tournament at Lobo Blanco.

"This writer can only wonder what the fashion-conscious Ms. Corbett, who recently got lucky at the French Open, will wear to dazzle her adoring hometown fans," he had written. "If only her backhand had as much swing as her cute little skirts."

For years, since she'd become a top-seeded player, Mackie had taken potshots like that at her. If she won, he credited luck for the victory. If she lost, he cruelly elaborated on the reasons why.

Sometimes he was painfully correct in his observations. Those were the times she resented his columns most. He never had a charitable word to say about her either as a person or as an athlete.

Lately, however, she hadn't given his poison pen much room to maneuver. She'd been winning—most recently The French Open, which had put her halfway to getting the Grand Slam. Next, Wimbledon. Wimbledon?

Where the very word usually generated expectation and excitement, it now evoked foreboding. Right now, Judd Mackie was the least of her problems.

Absently she laid her hand over her abdomen and headed toward the kitchen to brew herself a cup of tea. Sometimes drinking something warm made her feel better.

No sooner had she filled the kettle again and set it on the heating burner than her doorbell rang again. This time she wisely used the peephole, but saw through it only the distorted, fish-eye view of a prescription bottle. She opened the door.

Judd Mackie was still lounging against the door-jamb, idly shaking the brown plastic bottle of pills in front of the peephole.

Stevie uttered an exclamation of outrage and surprise. "How did you manage that?"

"With a five-dollar bill and my sincere promise to hand-deliver the prescription. I passed myself off as your concerned brother."

"And he believed you?"

"I have no idea. He took the money and ran. Smart fellow. *Now* are you going to ask me in?"

Sighing with resignation, she stepped aside. For several moments after the door closed behind him, they stood regarding each other closely. For all the name-calling and backbiting that had gone on between them over the years, this was the first time they'd ever been alone together.

Well, there had been that one time years ago in Stockholm, but they hadn't exactly been alone and Stevie doubted that he even remembered.

He was taller than he looked from a distance, she re-

alized. Their paths often crossed at local sporting or so-
cial or charity events. Sometimes he even waved at her
from afar, cheerfully waggling his fingers in a smart-
alecky manner that never failed to set her teeth on edge.

Perhaps it was his clothing, which could be described
as "casual" at best, that made him appear shorter. With
him standing this close, however, she was surprised to
discover that her eyes were on a level with his collarbone. She hadn't remembered until he removed his sunglasses that his eyes were hazel—heavy on the gray.

She reached for the bottle of pills. He held them
above his head of unruly chestnut hair and out of her
reach. "Mr. Mackie!"

"Ms. Corbett!"

The teakettle suddenly whistled shrilly as though
ending a round on an impasse. She turned on her bare
heel and marched toward the kitchen. He followed her
through the wide, airy rooms of her condominium.

"Nice place."

"For a writer that's extremely trite," she said, pouring boiling water over the tea bag in the mug. "Would
you like some herbal tea and honey?"

He winced with disgust. "How about a Bloody
Mary?"

"I'm fresh out of Bloody Marys."

"A Coke?"

"Diet?"

"Fine. Thanks."

She spooned honey into her tea and took a couple of
sips before fixing his cold drink. When she passed it to
him, he asked, "Tummy ache?"

"No, why?"

"My mother used to make me drink tea whenever

I was recovering from a pukey bout with a stomach virus."

"*You* have a mother?"

He sternly lowered one eyebrow. "That had as much sting as that serve that aced Martina last month."

"As I recall you failed to mention that ace in your column, which said that Martina just had an off day."

"You read my column?"

"You watch my matches?"

Smiling with enjoyment over their verbal sparring, he took a drink from his glass and lowered himself onto a bar stool with a bentwood back. Stevie thrust out her hand. "May I have my pills now, please?"

He scanned the label on the small bottle. "These are pain pills."

"That's right."

"Toothache?"

She bared her front teeth, exposing them for his examination. "Want to see my molars?"

"Your molars look fine from here," he drawled, his eyelids lowering a fraction.

Stevie gave him a contemptuous glance. "The pills?"

"Muscular injury? Tennis elbow? Sprained shoulder? Stress fracture?"

"None of the above. Will you please give me the medicine now and stop behaving like a jerk?" With a shrug, he set the bottle on the bar and slid it across to her. "Thank you."

"You're welcome. You look like you need them."

"How can you tell?"

"Tension around your mouth." He touched one corner of her lips, then the other.

Stevie yanked her head away and quickly turned her

back. She filled a small juice glass with tap water and swallowed two tablets. Retrieving her cup of tea, she sat down on the bar stool next to his.

She drank most of her tea in silence. He studied her every move. Obviously the adage that "if you ignored something long enough it would go away" didn't apply to him.

"What are you doing here, Mackie?" she asked wearily.

"I'm on assignment."

"Isn't there a ball game of some sort you could be writing about this afternoon? A golf tournament? Other matches at Lobo Blanco?"

"You're the big sports story of the day, like it or not."

She averted her eyes and muttered beneath her breath, "I don't like it."

Judd set his elbow on the bar and propped his cheek in his hand. "Why did you collapse out there this morning? It couldn't have been the heat. It wasn't that hot."

"No. It was a perfect day for tennis."

"Stay up past your bedtime last night?"

She gave his dishevelment a critical glance, her disapproval coming through loud and clear. "I never carouse the night before a match."

"Might do your game some good if you did," he said with a crooked smile.

Wryly she shook her head. "You're hopeless, Mackie."

"So I've been told."

"Look, I'm very tired. I was on my way to bed when you showed up the first time. Now that I've taken the medication, I'd like to get some rest. Doctor's orders."

"Your doctor recommended bed rest?"

"Yes."

"Hmm," he said, taking a sip of his drink. "That could mean anything. But I guess if you were drying out or going through drug rehab, you'd be hospitalized."

"You think I've been on alcohol or drugs?" she demanded indignantly, her sagging posture improving dramatically.

He leaned closer and, pulling down her lower eyelids, examined her eyes. "Guess not. No dilation. I doubt you're chemically dependent. You've got good skin tones, no needle tracks, clear eyes."

She angled her head away from his touch. "Yours certainly wouldn't stand up to close scrutiny."

Undaunted, he gave the rest of her an appraisal. "No, come to think of it, you look too healthy to be dependent on anything except low cholesterol, high-fiber foods. Get hold of a bad batch of bean curd?"

She dropped her forehead into her palm. "Would you please just go away?" She was disheartened on several counts. Chief among them was that she needed to be with someone right now, anyone, and Judd Mackie was the only one around. As much as it cost her to admit it, his obnoxious presence was preferable to solitude.

"That narrows down the possibilities considerably," he remarked.

"To what?" In spite of herself she was curious to hear his hypothesis.

"Publicity."

"Give me a break," she moaned. "I don't need it."

"Right," he admitted grudgingly, "you're already hyping enough products to keep your face smiling out of magazines and TV screens for years."

Narrowing his eyes, he assessed her through a screen

of thick, spiky lashes. "Are you sure you didn't just fake a fainting spell to get out of playing that match?"

"Why would I do something like that?"

"That Italian broad is supposed to be good."

"But I'm better," Stevie staunchly exclaimed.

"You've *been* good," he conceded reluctantly, "but you're getting up there in age. What is it now, thirty-one?"

He had struck a sore spot and she lashed out, "This has been my best year. You know that, Mackie. I'm on my way to getting a Grand Slam."

"You've still got to win Wimbledon."

"I won it last year."

"But your younger competition is breathing down your neck, players with a hundred times more talent and stamina."

"I'm noted for my stamina."

"Yeah, yeah, along with your saucy braid. You're not an athlete."

"As much as any football player in the NFL."

"You don't look like an athlete. You're not even built like one."

Stevie, angered over his sneering accusation, followed the direction of his gaze down to her chest. Her robe was gaping open, revealing the smooth, pale slope of one breast. She hurriedly gathered the fabric together in her fist and stood up. "It's past time for me to throw you out."

Unperturbed, he continued smoothly. "Maybe your collapse was brought on by anxiety, pure and simple."

Stevie was seething, but said nothing. She wouldn't honor his ridiculous theories with a response. Her expression remained impassive.

"You've always known, deep down, that you don't have what it takes to be a real champion. You're one bowl of Wheaties short," he said tauntingly. "You're a flash in the pan."

"Hardly that, Mackie. I've been on the pro tour for twelve years."

"But you didn't do anything significant until about five years ago."

"So, I'm improving, not declining, with age."

"Not according to what happened this morning."

"My age has nothing to do with why I—"

He sprang to his feet and bore down on her. "Come on, give, Stevie. Why did you faint?"

"None of your damn business!" she shouted.

"Cramps? Hmm? Is all this hullabaloo over a case of cramps?"

"No! Definitely not cramps."

"Ah." Judd released the word slowly. Tilting his head to one side, he let his eyes slide down her body again, searching for a telltale sign he might have previously missed. "Is there any particular reason why it's 'definitely not cramps'?" he asked in a lilting voice. "Like a b-a-b-y perhaps?"

Her eyes rounded. "You're crazy."

"And you're pregnant," he concluded bluntly. Drawing his face into a stern frown, he demanded, "Whose is it? That Scandinavian cobbler who designed your special tennis shoes?"

*"I'm not pregnant."*

"Or is the happy father that polo player from Bermuda?"

"It's Brazil!"

"Brazil, then. The guy with all those chains on his chest and at least four dozen teeth."

"Stop right there."

"Or don't you know whose it is?"

*"Stop it!"* she screamed, folding her arms across her abdomen. "There is no baby!" She repeated it more softly, more tearfully. "There is no baby."

Tears began to roll down her pale cheeks. "And before long there probably won't be anything else there, either. Because when they take out the tumors, they'll probably have to take out everything."

# *Two*

Her outcry took Judd completely by surprise. He made a little hiccuping sound when he sharply sucked in his breath. It was a reaction foreign to his character, as he was usually indifferent to even the most appalling pieces of information. This was one time he couldn't shrug and go on his uncaring way.

Stevie turned her back on him. The long blond braid hanging down her back no longer looked saucy, as it did swishing behind her on a tennis court. It looked heavy and burdensome. Or was it that she suddenly seemed so small and defenseless?

Her narrow shoulders shook with her sobs. She was crying openly, making heartrending, strangling sounds that penetrated his cynicism and prompted him to touch her.

"Shh, shh." He took those shuddering shoulders between his hands and turned her to face him. Disregarding her resistance, he pulled her against him and wrapped his arms around her. "I'm sorry. If I'd known it was anything that serious, I wouldn't have badgered you."

He doubted that she would believe him. He could hardly believe himself. He rarely apologized for anything. Almost never to a woman.

For a woman sobbing her heart out, all he usually felt was contempt and impatience to escape her clutching hands. But when Stevie Corbett's fingers curled inward toward his chest in a silent plea for help and support, it didn't occur to him to get the hell out before coming involved. Instead he drew her closer and turned his head, resting his cheek on the crown of her blond hair.

He held her while she cried. That in itself was an oddity. When he held a woman, it was strictly for prurient purposes. When he held one wearing a short kimono that did great things for her bare legs, they were as good as in bed. When he held one wearing a short kimono with nothing underneath it except panties, his hands were usually inside it, not stroking her back consolingly.

Those comparisons no doubt accounted for how differently this embrace felt from any other in his recent, or even distant, memory.

His trained eye would have had to go blind to miss the details of her bralessness, the attraction of her smooth thighs, the delightful faint outline of bikini panties beneath the robe, but he didn't follow through on any sexual impulses.

To do so would have made him a real heel. He *was* a heel, but so far, he hadn't stooped that low. Or maybe guilt was keeping his caresses platonic and circumspect. After all, he'd unwittingly induced this emotional breakdown. Unlike the other women he had reduced to tears during his career as a bastard, Stevie Corbett had a helluva good reason for needing to cry.

Eventually her sobs turned into soft, catchy, moist little breaths that he felt through the cloth of his shirt. "Shouldn't you be in bed?" he asked softly.

She nodded and stepped away from him, making ineffectual swipes at her eyes. They were still leaking tears and leaving muddy mascara trails down her cheeks.

He had a hot broad waiting to feed him a cold lunch. Mentally he kissed them both goodbye. Surprising himself even more than he surprised Stevie, he bent slightly at the knees and lifted her into his arms.

"This isn't necessary, Mackie. I can walk."

"Which way?"

She hesitated, then raised her arm and pointed. She had great muscle tone, which at any other time would have warranted leisurely exploration with fingertips and lips. On the other hand, she was so light that he could carry her for a hundred miles and not break a sweat, at least not from exertion. Holding her against him for any extended period of time without doing anything about it might make him perspire.

"In there."

He carried her into a spacious bedroom filled with natural light and an overabundance of potted plants. "Didn't they film a Tarzan movie here once?" he wisecracked.

"These plants are my pets. It's cheaper to have them taken care of while I'm away than it is to board a dog or cat. Besides, they can't miss me."

He deposited her on the edge of the bed. "Lie down."

"I'll bet you say that to all the girls," she remarked drolly.

"I'm not kidding around. And neither should you be. Lie down."

She reclined on the heap of eyelet-covered pillows. By her expression, Judd knew it felt good to her, though she'd probably never admit it.

"Sorry about your shirt."

"Huh?" He glanced down and noticed that it was damp and smudged with makeup. "It'll wash," he said negligently.

He shook out a light, puffy, quilted comforter, which was folded at the foot of the bed, and covered her with it. He then sat down on the edge of the mattress, his hips even with hers.

"Talk."

"Not to you, Mackie."

"My name is Judd."

"I know that. I've seen it on your byline."

"Forget the column for a minute, will you?"

"Have you?" she shot up at him.

"Yes!"

During the ensuing silence, he watched tears fill her eyes again—light brown eyes the color of very expensive scotch. "Stevie," he said gently, "this is off-the-record. I think you need to talk to someone."

"Yes, I do, but…" She sniffed wetly; he popped a Kleenex out of the box on the nightstand and held it to her nose.

"Blow." She did. He tossed that Kleenex in the wastebasket and used a fresh one to dab at her eyes. "You need a sounding board, right?"

"I just don't feel natural talking to you like this."

"Well," he said, shaking his head ruefully, "this is a highly unnatural situation for me, too. Usually when

I'm on a bed with a half-naked broad, the last thing on my mind is conversation. And she would be using her mouth for something besides spilling out her problems."

"Mackie!"

"Judd. Now talk. When did you find out about these tumors?"

"This morning," she said huskily.

"Before your match?" She nodded. "Whose bright idea was it to tell you before a match?"

"Mine."

"Figures."

She frowned up at him. "I'd had some tests done. I wanted to know the results. *Had* to know."

Her gaze drifted to the window where a box of paperwhites were blooming on the sill. "I guess I wasn't really expecting the worst, though. I'd told myself I was prepared to hear it, but..." She looked back at him. "You were right. I collapsed from anxiety."

"Justifiably so."

He rubbed his hands together, studying them intently, as though he'd never noticed his blunt nails, the sprinkling of hair across the backs of his knuckles, the thick wrists that should have belonged to a professional baseball player and didn't.

"These tumors, they're, uh..."

"On my female organs," she told him, glancing away again. "I'd been having some pain, more than ordinary."

He cleared his throat uncomfortably. He was learning that where the female body was concerned, he had a teenage boy's mentality. He liked to look and touch and have sex with it. He thought the variations among individual women were intriguing and considered himself a connoisseur of the finest. He had never been faithful to one in particular. He had enjoyed more than his fair share of them, more than he was proud to admit in this age of safe sex.

Yet, this was the first time he'd ever thought of a female body from an objective standpoint. He considered what it meant to the owner instead of what it meant to him. It contained a person. It wasn't just a soft, beautiful instrument of pleasure.

He didn't like himself very much at that moment and would have found it hard to meet his own eyes in a mirror.

"So they're going to operate and take them out," she was telling him softly. "It'll take months for me to recover and regain my strength, *if* the tumors are benign."

"You mean they might not be?"

"No, they might not be." They shared a long stare, a heavy, ponderous stare full of implication.

"But there's a good chance they are," Stevie continued briskly. "If that's the case, the surgery can be delayed until a more convenient time. Either way, they'll probably have to do a complete hysterectomy."

Judd came to his feet and began pacing the length of the bed. He glanced down at her angrily. "Why in hell are you lying on your butt here? Why aren't you in the hospital and on your way to the operating room?"

"I can't have surgery now," she exclaimed. "Wimbledon is barely a month away."

"So?"

Her lips narrowed with vexation over his obtuseness. "So I've got to play."

"It's not going anywhere. There's always next year."

"As you so unkindly pointed out earlier, I'm not getting any younger. I'm playing better than ever, but for how long?"

Shaking her head adamantly, she continued. "This is my year. My time. If I don't get that Grand Slam now, I'll never have another opportunity, no matter what the surgeons find when they operate. Maybe, if I were ten years younger, I could come back. As it is, it would take months, possibly longer. Even then, I'd never be as strong as I am now."

"What if those tumors are malignant?"

"Naturally that makes things more complicated," she replied evasively.

"How complicated?" She refused to answer. Testily he repeated, "How complicated?"

"If they're malignant, delaying surgery for several weeks could be fatal."

Judd propped his fists on his hips and looked down at her with consternation. "You're crazy, lady."

"You can't judge me because you don't know what you'd do in this situation."

"Does your gynecologist have an opinion?"

"He wants to do the surgery immediately, but he says two weeks won't make much difference."

"Immediately gets my vote."

"You don't get a vote."

"What about your manager?"

"He sees both sides and has left the decision strictly up to me. But he says if I play Wimbledon, I can only have two weeks to make up my mind."

"Meanwhile, you're in pain."

"It's not constant. It comes and goes. Naturally he wants what's best for me."

"He wants what's best for his business interests in you."

"That's unfair."

"What about your parents?"

"They're deceased."

"Lovers?"

"There's no one else to consult." She glared up at him. "Not the 'Scandinavian cobbler' who, by the way, happens to be approaching seventy and has countless grandchildren."

"What about the bare-chested Brazilian with the Ipana smile?"

"I loathe that lecher. Whoever leaked the story of our so-called affair must have graduated from the same school of yellow journalism that you did."

He ignored the gibe. "So you're all alone in this."

"Until you splash it across the sports page. Then everybody will know and have an opinion."

"This conversation is off-the-record, remember?"

"I just wondered if you did."

"I won't print the story, but it'll get out the minute you check into the hospital."

"I'm not sure when that will be."

"Yeah? Well I think you're nuts for not having this taken care of pronto."

"Have you ever had surgery, Mr. Mackie?"

He hesitated before answering. "Not abdominal surgery."

"Then who are you to be giving me advice? Unsolicited advice, I might add."

"Look," he said impatiently, "you're not just screwing around with a career here. We're talking about your *life*."

"Tennis is my life."

"Now who's being trite?"

She tossed her head and gave him a lofty glance. "I've got a lot to think about, Mr. Mackie, and you're a disruptive element. Now that you've got the sensational story you came after, kindly leave."

"Okay. Maybe I'll go back to my office and start working on your obit."

She sprang into a sitting position. The comforter slid to her waist. "You can't possibly understand how difficult a decision this is for me."

"Life and death? That's a difficult decision?"

"It's hardly that simple. I don't know that the tumors are malignant. I don't know that delaying the surgery will be fatal. What I *do* know is that if I have an operation now, my career will be over. That's the only certainty I've got right now and the only one I can base my decision on."

She pulled in a deep breath, a reloading procedure as it were. "You can't judge me, Mackie, because you've never had to sacrifice your life's dream. Your dreams don't extend beyond the next easy woman and double highball."

He couldn't argue with her observation since it so accurately described the life he was currently leading, but it made him mad as hell that she'd pegged him correctly. Intentionally or not, she had vocalized his secret opinion of himself. He couldn't deny her allegations. He wasn't about to leave, however, without getting in a parting shot.

"Before I go, there's something you probably should know, Miss Corbett."

"Well?" she demanded.

"Your robe is open."

"Yes, I'm feeling much better, thank you."

It was hours later and Stevie was speaking with her gynecologist by telephone. "The medication helped relax me. I took a long nap."

Her sleep had been interrupted only by dreams of Judd Mackie's handsome, leering face, looking exactly as it had when he had nodded down at her chest and called attention to her exposed breasts. He was despicable and she rightfully despised him.

"It was just a silly fainting spell, brought on by anxiety over the test results."

The doctor took issue with her blasé attitude and urged her to let him schedule surgery right away.

"You agreed, doctor, that two weeks wouldn't be critical one way or another," she reminded him. "I need that much time to weigh my options and think this through."

She hung up moments later. He had urged her to seek a second opinion. She didn't tell him she already had. And a third. The tumors were definitely there on her uterus and ovaries. Whether or not they were malignant could only be determined by surgery.

On that dismal thought, Stevie padded into the living room and switched on the television. She was just in time to catch the sportscast on the local evening news. There she was, sprawled on the green tennis court like a rag doll while the hushed crowd looked on.

Her collapse had resulted in a mad scrambling of media and tournament officials. Blessedly she'd been unconscious during the mayhem. She didn't remember anything after walking onto the court, wondering if that tournament would be her last.

At the time of her collapse, she'd had her opponent down by two games. Her playing must have been instinctual, mechanical. She remembered nothing of it.

"...can only speculate on the nature of Ms. Corbett's illness," the sportscaster was saying. "A statement issued by her manager merely stated that her condition isn't serious and that she is resting in an undisclosed location. And now we're going live to Ranger Stadium where the—"

She switched off the set flippantly, "A few tumors. Nothing serious. My career will probably come to an end, and I'll never be able to have children, but it's really nothing at all."

She went into the kitchen, more out of habit than because she was actually hungry. Spying the glass that Judd Mackie had drunk from, she placed it in the dishwasher. "Out of sight, out of mind."

But he wasn't out of mind, and that was galling. He was very much on her mind. Why? Perhaps because she hadn't expected him to treat her so kindly when she started crying. Or maybe because she'd won his promise not to leak her story. She supposed that when she did make a final decision, she should call him with the story first. For behaving so honorably today, he deserved that consideration.

She ate a bowl of granola and fresh strawberries— out of spite for his sardonic comment about her healthy diet—and retired again to her bedroom.

Unplaiting her braid, she was again reminded of Judd. He'd touched her hair, the corners of her lips.

He'd held her in his arms, apparently in no hurry for her to stop crying.

He had even carried her in his arms. It disturbed her that she could so clearly remember the feel of his sleeve against the backs of her bare thighs and the strength of his chest beneath her rib cage.

He was her mortal enemy who constantly attacked her with his vicious pen. Yet, now that she was alone and no one could read her mind, she confessed that his touch had elicited unexpected physical reactions: a fluttering in her breasts, a tightening in her belly, a sensation of swelling and fever between her thighs.

Slouching on the bar stool in her kitchen, he had looked rumpled and crumpled and comfortable. His dark brown hair was worn long, not because he consciously chose a longer style but because he neglected to have it cut regularly.

He was attractive in a disheveled, disreputable, range-wolf way. Debonair he was not. But he was sexy. The chip he carried on his shoulder only added to his appeal. So did his arrogance. To a woman with sensitivity, he would be lethal. Stevie pitied any who might fall in love with Judd Mackie.

As she brushed out her hair, she chided herself for letting him arouse her temper. She had been foolish to engage in a shouting match with him. No one could understand her dilemma, especially not him. What did he know of denied ambitions? He'd never had aspirations to rise above the level of mediocrity. He was an elegant bum, content with half measures.

One thing he did know was women, Stevie conceded. He had known that his departing line would be a zinger she wouldn't easily forget.

She finished brushing her hair and got into bed. She slept on her side because lying on her back and pulling her stomach taut often caused her discomfort. Stacking her hands beneath her cheek, she stared beyond the hem of her pillowcase into the darkened room and thought about Judd. Involuntarily she recalled the drowsy appraisal he'd given her breasts. Had he noticed that her silk kimono had deliciously abraded her nipples to tautness?

Even as she fell asleep, she was blushing over the possibility that he had.

# Three

"Hello," Judd mumbled into his telephone. "This better be damned important," he added after consulting the digital clock on his nightstand.

"Oh, it is, it is."

"Mike, for godsake, why're you calling so early?"

"To fire you."

Exasperated, Judd blew out a gust of breath and buried his head back into the pillow. "You did that already last week."

"This time it sticks."

"You say that every time."

"You lazy, no-account bastard, I mean it this time. Have you seen the morning papers?"

"I haven't even seen the morning."

"Well, let me be the first to inform you that your competitor got the story you were supposed to get and didn't."

"Huh?"

"While you were clacking out that less-than-inspiring piece about the Rangers' new Mexican rookie catcher, our friends over at the *Morning News* were scooping you about Stevie Corbett. She's got cancer."

Judd swung his legs over the side of the bed, cursing the twisted sheets that restrained him, and damning his splintering headache and furry mouth. He and some cronies had gone to a topless joint after the Ranger game the night before. There'd been a lot of beer and a lot of bare breasts. He had swilled down beer after beer, in the vain hope that out of the plethora of bobbing breasts he would see something as sexily enticing as an angry Stevie Corbett with her robe gaping open. He hadn't, so he'd kept drinking.

"What the hell are you talking about, Mike? And you don't have to shout."

"I thought you said you talked to Corbett yesterday."

"I did."

"You also said there was no story there."

"In my opinion there wasn't."

"You don't think the fact she's got ovarian cancer is a story?" the editor bellowed.

"She doesn't have cancer!" Judd shouted right back, though it intensified his headache. "She's got a few tumors that might or might not be malignant. How'd they find out about it over at the *News*?"

For the span of several seconds there was a taut silence. Judd didn't notice. He had left the bed and carried the cordless phone into the bathroom with him. His reflection in the mirror over the basin confirmed what his headache had already suggested: the night before had been a bitch.

"You knew about this? You *knew*?" Mike Ramsey roared. "And you gave me tripe for last night's edition?"

Judd didn't have to hold the telephone against his ear

to hear the forthcoming tirade. He had it memorized anyway. So he propped the instrument on the edge of his bathroom sink and commenced to shave.

"You're no journalist," Mike shouted over the sound of running water. "You wouldn't even have a column if you didn't carouse in the taverns where players and fans hang out. You're not a reporter, you're a stenographer. All you do is regurgitate boozy conversations and call it creative journalism."

Judd had finished shaving. He picked up the phone long enough to sputter through a mouthful of toothpaste foam, "The readers eat it like candy, lap it up like ice cream. What would your sports page be without my column? Nothing, Ramsey, and you know it."

"I'm willing to find out what it would be. You've just written your last column for me. You got that, Mackie?"

"Yeah, yeah."

"I mean it this time. You're fired! I'll have Addison clean out that rat's nest you call a desk. You can pick up the contents at the receptionist's desk on the first floor. Don't let me see your booze-bloated face in the city room again."

The next sound coming from the telephone was a dial tone. Unperturbed, Judd stepped into the shower. Before he got out, he'd already forgotten Ramsey's call. He got fired half a dozen times a month. It never stuck.

Even if it did, it might be the best thing that could happen to him. Because Ramsey was right in one respect: his column *was* just transcriptions of what he overheard after sporting events, garnished with a few witticisms that didn't tax his imagination any longer than it took him to type them. For the past year or so, he'd been telling himself that his readers didn't know his column came that easily for him and that it wouldn't matter to them if they did.

But it mattered to him. He knew that what he was writing wasn't worth the paper it was printed on. He was grossly overpaid for the amount of work required of him to produce the daily column. Fooling his editor, the man who signed his paycheck, and his reading audience no longer gave him any satisfaction. It got harder each day to laugh up his sleeve about it.

That's why he boozed it up and slept with women he didn't care about and let the days of his life tick by without anything to show for them. He had nothing to care about, nothing to work toward, nothing to get up in the morning for. His life was a big fat zero in the productivity department. Even though he was the only one who realized it, the fact was hard to live with.

He needed a creative challenge, but was afraid that whatever literary talent he had once possessed had been squandered, never to be regained. So what? He was too old now to think seriously about a career change.

His future, however, wasn't his main concern right now. Stevie Corbett's was. Where had his rival columnist heard about her illness? And how did she feel about the most intimate aspects of her life providing fodder for the sports page?

It didn't take him long to find out.

She exhibited her famous forehand, aiming the tennis racquet directly at his head.

"What the—"

"You bastard!"

He had ducked her first swing at him, then caught the handle of the racquet as she executed an arcing backhand. They wrestled over the racquet. "What the hell's wrong with you?" he shouted.

"You leaked the story. You told me our conversation was off-the-record. You liar! You—"

"I did no such thing."

"Oh, yes you did," she ground out. "You were the only one who knew."

He yanked the racquet out of her hands and threw it to the floor. "Do you think I'd feed the story to my competition? *I* didn't write the piece. It was printed in another newspaper. I haven't even read the damn article yet."

Stevie curbed her frustration and fury and thought about that for a second. Why would he give the story to someone else? It didn't make sense. But not much in her life did these days.

"Then how did you know about the article?" she asked suspiciously. "And how did you get past the police?"

Since early morning, her yard had been crawling with reporters. Her manager had finally called the police, requesting that they cordon off her condominium.

"One of the patrolmen on duty owed me a favor."

"For what?"

"It has to do with his sister."

She rubbed her forehead. "I don't think I want to know."

"I don't think you do, either. Suffice it to say she sneaked into a locker room one night after a big game and served as hostess for a spontaneous victory celebration."

Stevie stared up at him, shaking her head in dismay. "I believe you. Why would you make up such a sordid tale?"

He took her by the shoulders and guided her back onto the bar stool in the kitchen, where she'd been sitting when he picked the lock on her back door and slipped through. That's when she had begun hurling insults at him and taking well-placed swats at his head with the racquet she had helped design.

"How did that columnist find out about me, Mackie?"

"I don't know. But I intend to learn." He reached for her kitchen extension and punched out a number. He asked for the sportswriter by name. Apparently they were friendly rivals.

"Hey, Mackie here. Congrats on your story about the Corbett broad." Stevie shot him a fulminating look, which he ignored. "How'd you manage to sweet-talk her into revealing the intimate details of her life? Or should a gentleman ask?" Stevie's mouth dropped open. Judd covered it with his hand. "Oh, no? She didn't tell you? Hmm. Her manager maybe?"

Stevie shoved his hand away from her mouth and adamantly shook her head.

"Okay, I give. Uncle. Who talked? Come on, the cat's already out of the bag so you might as well tell me." Stevie watched his brows pull together into a steep frown. "Look, you ornery cuss, I busted my buns yesterday trying to track down the reason for her collapse and came up empty. Just tell me who I missed."

He listened for a moment. His frown smoothed out, but he didn't look any happier. "I see. Well, you pulled a fast one on me this time, pal. Don't let it happen again." She overheard the vulgarity that was offered in a friendly, harmless manner. "Same to you. Have a nice day," Judd finished in a singsong voice.

"Well?" she asked as he replaced the receiver.

"A technician at Mitchell Laboratories."

"Where I had the sonargram done," she wailed softly. "I knew no one in my doctor's office would talk. I never thought of someone at the lab."

"Don't be naive. Anybody'll talk if you bait the trap right. Coffee cups?"

"Second cabinet, second shelf."

"Want some?"

"No thanks. I've had plenty."

He poured himself a cup and carried it back with him to the bar. He sat down on the bar stool beside her, exactly as they'd been the day before.

"How'd you sleep?" he asked.

"Fine."

"The circles under your eyes say otherwise."

She had avoided looking directly at him for fear that he'd see she hadn't slept well at all. The truth was that she'd had a very restless night filled with dreams that fluctuated from strange to erotic to terrifying. He'd played a rolle in all of them. She was exhausted. But it irked her that he had so tactlessly pointed out how bad she looked.

"Well you look worse for wear, too," she retaliated snidely.

"It was a helluvan evening."

"Then what are you doing here? Why aren't you wherever you call home sleeping it off? Or did you come to gloat?"

She noted the tensing around his mouth, indicating his irritation, but he calmly sipped his coffee. "I might be gloating if I'd written the article. I didn't. If I had, I would have gotten the facts straight."

The starch went out of her then. Gloomily she said, "The way this article reads, I'm finished as a player, and all but dead and buried."

Judd came off the stool so quickly and cursed so viciously that she started in reaction. "Don't say anything like that again. It gives me the creeps."

"Well, I'm sorry I offended your sensibilities," she snapped. "But they happen to be my tumors and I'll talk about them any way I damn well please. If you don't like it, you can leave. Which isn't a bad idea."

It *was* a bad idea. The idea of his leaving didn't appeal to her at all. Now that she knew he was innocent of the crime and no longer felt like murdering him, she was really glad to have him around. At least when he was with her, she had to keep her mental reflexes sharpened. That exercised her mind and kept it from dwelling on dismal thoughts.

To safeguard against his knowing how badly she wanted him to stay, she assumed an aloof and hostile expression. "There's nothing you can do here except further aggravate me, so you might just as well go."

"I came to drive you to the hospital."

"I'm not going to the hospital. I told you that yesterday. I've got two weeks—"

"Look, Stevie—"

"No, *you* look, Mackie. This is my life, my decision, and nobody—"

The doorbell rang. "Ms. Corbett!" Someone began shouting through the door. "How do you feel about having cancer and giving up professional tennis?"

"Oh," she cried, "why don't they leave me alone?"

Nerves already frazzled, she ducked her head and covered it with her arms.

Eventually the persistent reporter gave up or was hauled away by one of the policemen who were supposed to be guarding against such intrusions. The house fell silent again. She flinched when Judd laid his hands on her shoulders.

"At least let me get you away from here for a few hours." He swiveled her bar stool around, separating his legs and positioning her knees between them.

"Why would you want to do that?"

"To make up for being such a jackal and sniffing out blood yesterday."

"But you didn't write the story."

"In a way, though, I still feel responsible." She made a scoffing sound. "I know you think I'm a sorry excuse for a journalist," he said, "just like I think you're a sorry excuse for an athlete. I drink too much, party too hard and have a great capacity for self-indulgence. I'm unreliable and sarcastic. But basically, underneath this ruggedly handsome exterior, I'm a nice guy."

"Oh, sure."

His face broke into a roguish grin that made her tummy flutter. "Give me today and I'll prove you wrong."

She wanted to consent, but hesitated. For all his charm, he might still be working on a story about her. Maybe he was planning an in-depth character profile that would portray her as the shallow "deb of the tennis courts," as he had once dubbed her.

"I don't think that's a very good idea, Mackie. I'll take my chances here."

Almost simultaneously her telephone started ringing and the doorbell pealed again. "Did you plan that?" she accused.

He chuckled, delighted with those unexpected endorsements of his idea. "Providence is on my side. Go get whatever you might need during the day. We won't be back until after dark tonight." The instructions were given as though the matter had been settled to his satisfaction.

"Mackie, even if I wanted to spend the day out on the town with you, which I don't, it wouldn't work anyway. We're both too well-known. We couldn't go anywhere in the city without being recognized and hounded."

"That's why we're going *out* of the city."

"Out of the city? Where?"

"You'll see."

"How do you plan to sneak past all those reporters?"

"Will you quit stalling and go get your things?" he asked impatiently.

Stevie warily studied his face. It looked no more trustworthy than a pirate's. They would probably spend the day quarreling. But the alternative of being held under siege in her own house was even more gruesome.

Mind made up, she spread wide the short skirt of her white cotton culottes, which she had on with a T-shirt and sandals. "Can I go like this?"

"Sure can. Get your purse."

In under five minutes, she reentered the kitchen carrying a canvas tote bag into which she had stuffed everything she might conceivably need. Judd was at the sink, rinsing out the coffeepot.

"You make yourself right at home, don't you?"

"Hmm." He unhurriedly dried his hands on a dish towel, then tossed it aside. "I do."

He stepped forward, slid his arms around her waist, pulled her against him, angled his head to one side and settled his lips upon hers.

Stevie was caught so totally unaware that she didn't put up a struggle or utter a single sound of protest. He kissed her lightly, gently bouncing his lips against hers, until they rested there.

On its way up to her neck, his hand grazed her breast. It brushed against the tip and caused it to bead. His touch couldn't even be counted as a bonafide caress, but Stevie's reaction was very real. A sudden infusion of heat spread through her middle. Its intensity heightened when he readjusted their bodies, fitting his into the notch of her thighs.

As his fingers closed around her neck, his tongue playfully probed at the seam of her lips, lazily, half-heartedly, as though he didn't give a damn whether she parted them or not. If she did, fine. He would kiss her. If not, fine. He would be amused, not angry or disappointed.

Stevie parted them.

Then his tongue, warm and wet, entered her mouth and leisurely explored. At least the kiss started off leisurely. The change came on so gradually that it wasn't noticeable until the thrusts of his tongue went deeper, the strokes became faster, and the suction of his mouth grew hungrier. The whole character of the kiss altered. Likewise, so did their responses to it.

When Judd's response became so obvious it could be felt through their clothing, he quickly set her away. She gazed up at him with a mix of desire and bewilderment.

"Why did you kiss me like that?"

"Curiosity." He croaked the word, cleared his throat

and repeated it. "We've both been thinking about it, right? Ever since I saw your breasts yesterday, we've been wondering what it would be like to be together. Now that our curiosity has been satisfied, we can relax around each other and enjoy the day. Right?"

Stevie knew that if she became anymore relaxed, she would melt into a puddle of wanting woman on the kitchen floor. But she nodded wordlessly.

Going along with this idea of his would probably end up being a big mistake.

# *Four*

❧━━━◉⊙◉⊙◉━━━❧

"**Y**ou missed your calling." They were underway. Stevie spoke to him over the thrum of his sports car's engine as he weaved it through traffic. "You should have been a criminal."

His plan of escape had called for her to create a diversion at the front door of her condominium by poking her head outside just long enough for the reporters and film crews to think she might be prepared to give them a statement. Then while they were clambering across her lawn toward the entrance, Judd and she had slipped out the back, jogged down the alley and, undetected, got into his car, which he'd left parked on the next street.

"I thought about going into grand larceny," he said expansively, "but figured that it required too much ambition and hard work."

Smiling, Stevie settled comfortably into the leather upholstery. The moment they had left her condominium, a sense of freedom had stolen over her. The break from her normal disciplined routine was in itself a luxury. Most mornings by this time, she had already put in hours of physical conditioning and practice. She remarked on her delinquency to Judd.

"When did you start playing tennis?" Glancing over his shoulder to make sure the lane was clear, he took a ramp onto the interstate highway and headed east, leaving Dallas behind.

"I was twelve."

"Late for most players who get as far as you have," he observed.

"A little, but I can hardly remember a time when I haven't intimately known the feel of a racquet in my hand." She thought back to the night she had first expressed an interest in playing the sport. "Out of the blue, I told my parents that I wanted to try out for the junior-high tennis team." She had made that startling announcement over supper. "Mother and Daddy looked at me as though I'd said I wanted to move to Mars."

*"Tennis?"*

*"Yes, sir."*

*"That's a rich kid's sport,"* her father had said, returning to his meal. *"Pass the potatoes."*

"What did they have against tennis?" Judd asked.

"Nothing really. It's just that they couldn't relate to it. My mother had no interest in athletics whatsoever. Daddy only liked sports like football and basketball and, of course, those were for boys."

She had been an only child, a *female* only child, who knew that her gender was a vast disappointment to the gruff stranger she called Daddy.

"So how did you get their permission to play?"

"After dinner, I broached the subject with Mother while we were doing the dishes. I explained that the school had racquets and balls I could use. I wouldn't have to buy anything. She said okay."

Stevie went on to tell Judd that by the time she reached high school she had a passion for the sport. She saved baby-sitting money to finance the lessons she took at an exclusive club in north Dallas.

"We weren't members. Any member's bar bill might exceed what my dad earned in a month." There was no rancor in her tone. She'd never been bitter over her family's modest economic level, only impatient with her parents' disinclination to improve it.

"I was playing in a tournament on the club team when I met Presley Foster."

*"You're wearing your shoes a size too large. Your backhand stinks and your forehand isn't much better, though you've got good, basic strokes. You show off for the spectators more than you concentrate on your strategy. If you get two points behind, you automatically sacrifice the game. Your serves are hard and fast, but inconsistently so. You don't put forth any effort unless you have to, and that's a damn bad habit to get into."*

She paraphrased Presley Foster's first words to her. Judd whistled. "Geez."

She could look back on it now and laugh. "I felt like all but the very top of my head had been hammered into the ground. Then he said, 'But you've got talent. I can refine it, make you a world-class player. You'll hate me before we're finished. I need two years.'"

One week after her high-school graduation, she had left with the famous coach for his camp in Florida. Her decision had been incomprehensible to her parents. Tennis was no job. Tennis was a game. She went despite their objections. She might have no future in tennis, but she certainly had none by staying at home and stagnating with them.

"I didn't know what hard work was until I came under Presley's tutelage," she told Judd with a wry smile.

She had been dreadfully outclassed by the players who had begun tournament training in grade school and had attended Foster's tennis summer camps. Most of them had played tennis to the exclusion of everything else. Some had had no childhood at all. Tennis was everything.

"I was nineteen before I went on the circuit." She gazed out the window at the landscape whizzing by. Judd drove competently, but fast. "I was playing a tournament in Savannah, Georgia, when I received word that my parents' house had been destroyed by a tornado and they'd been killed."

"They died in that storm? The one that tore up half of east Dallas?"

"Yes. Practically the whole neighborhood was destroyed. I was lying face down on my bed in the motel room in Savannah, crying, when Presley stormed in and demanded to know why I wasn't on the court warming up for my scheduled match."

*"My parents are dead. You don't expect me to play today, do you?"*

*"I damn sure do! It's times like this that a player shows the stuff she's made of."*

She had played. She had won. She'd flown to Dallas after the match to arrange her parents' funeral.

"Six months later," she said, speaking to Judd in a reflective, faraway voice, "Presley was in midsentence when he gripped his chest and, without another sound, died of a heart attack. I played a scorching match the following day. He would have expected me to."

Neither her parents nor her mentor had lived to see her become the top-seeded woman player in professional tennis. This year she was on her way to getting the Grand Slam. Then she would retire, knowing she had proved her father wrong. Tennis wasn't just a rich kid's sport. It was a demanding and jealous master, one for which she'd sacrificed a college education, romance, marriage, family—everything.

Now that she was so close to mastering it, she couldn't let anything, *anything*, stand in her way.

Becoming aware that Judd was watching her closely, she unclenched her jaw and her fists and forced a tepid smile. "What about you? Did you always aspire to become a sportswriter who uses his victims' blood for ink?"

He made a face and shivered. "God, you make me sound horrible."

"You've written some horrible things about me in your articles. Why should I spare your feelings?"

"I guess a few blows below the belt are fair." He winked at her wickedly. "Come to think of it, a few blows below the belt might even be fun."

She ignored his sexual insinuation. Thinking about the kiss they'd shared—and there was no sense in fooling herself into believing that she hadn't participated— could prove hazardous. The safest tactic was to pretend that it hadn't happened.

Judd Mackie was a reputed lady-killer. She had been victimized by his scathing prose many times. She wasn't going to fall victim to him in another area as well.

"Just out of curiosity, Mackie, why me?" She turned

toward him, crooking her knee and tucking her foot beneath her hips. "Why have you singled me out to throw poison darts at?"

"Why should you care? You've got the rest of the world's population eating out of your hand. What difference does it make to you if this burned out, bummed out sportswriter gets his kicks by taking shots at you in his tacky column?"

"It's annoying."

"Not to my readers. Ever since that first article years ago—"

"For which I demanded a retraction."

He gave her a smug smile. "I printed several paragraphs of your letter, remember? Readers loved it. I got so much play out of it, I deliberately cultivated the antagonism between us."

"Why?"

"It makes for good copy."

"What did I ever do to deserve your contempt in the first place?"

"It's not so much what you've done or haven't done. It's what you are. What you…"

"Well?" she prompted when he left the sentence unfinished.

"It's what you look like."

That admission stunned her into silence. Finally she said, "Which is?"

"Cute. I find it very hard to take you seriously as an athlete when you look like a Barbie doll wearing a tennis dress."

"That's chauvinistic!"

"Unabashedly."

"How I look is totally irrelevant to how I play."

"Probably, but that's a chauvinistic pig for you," he quipped with an unapologetic grin.

"And if I had a wart on the end of my nose, would that make me a better tennis player in your estimation?"

"We'll never know, will we? But probably. At least I'd be less inclined to write snide things about you."

Leaning against the car door, she gazed at him with patent dismay. "For all these years I've wondered what I did to incur your wrath. And it really has nothing to do with me at all. What it boils down to is your own reverse snobbery and sexist prejudice."

"That's a broad generalization…forgive me for saying no pun intended. I'm not prejudiced against women athletes at all."

"Just me. Is there anything I can do to change your mind?"

"You could get ugly."

"Or get cancer."

Taking an off ramp, he came to an abrupt halt at the stop sign. Turning his head toward her, he said, "That's another of those blows beneath the belt, Stevie. But I'll overlook it on one condition."

"What?"

"Tell me you can cook."

"Cook?"

"Cook. You know, in a kitchen on a stove. Putting food products into pots and pans and making them edible."

"I can cook."

"Good," he replied, slipping the car into first gear and turning onto the intersecting, two-lane highway. "But nothing with a sauce. I don't like sauces, except for cream gravy on chicken-fried steak. Sauces are for sissies."

"Oh, please," she groaned. But she was smiling.

At the next crossroad, he pulled up in front of a combination grocery store and filling station. "Let's go shopping."

A half hour later, he pulled the car onto a narrow country road. The trees growing on either side of it formed a dense green canopy overhead. The hardwoods were intermingled with tall, straight pines.

"Where in the world are we going?"

The town where they'd made their purchases hardly deserved that designation. Besides the grocery store-filling station, it had only a feed and hardware store, a post office, a fire station, a Dairy Queen, a school and three Protestant churches.

"To my grandparents' house." He laughed at the astonishment she registered. "That's right. Not only do I have a mother, but I have a father. Or did. This farm belonged to his parents. They willed it to him. When he died a few years ago, the property was handed down to me. I sold off the pastureland, but kept the twenty acres surrounding the house."

"Twenty very beautiful acres," she noted.

"Thanks."

The house was another surprise. It was situated in a clearing surrounded by massive pecan trees that were just coming into full leaf. There was a windmill, a detached garage and a barn. All were painted white and trimmed in green. All could have used a facelift. The flower beds bordering the porch were overgrown with weeds. There was an air of desolation and neglect about the place.

"It needs some work," he remarked, understating the obvious. "It looks better on the inside, I promise."

"It's charming," Stevie said graciously. She alighted from the car, then had to duck under a spider web that had been spun from one tree to another.

Judd unlocked the front door with a key he took from beneath the welcome mat and ushered her inside. They were greeted by the dim, hushed, musty atmosphere of a house left vacant for a long time.

Standing in the wide hallway, his voice slightly echoing, he said, "Initially this was meant to be a weekend getaway, but I can rarely leave town on the weekends because so many sporting events are going on. And it's just not practical to come during the middle of the week. As a result, I don't get over here as often as I'd like or as often as the place deserves."

"What's that?" Stevie asked, nodding at the room behind him.

He pivoted on his heels. "That's a dining room with one card table, one folding chair and one portable typewriter in it." She gave him an inquiring look. "The dining-room furniture is now at my mother's house."

"Oh." That wasn't the question Stevie had in mind, but she let his explanation pass for the time being. Apparently he had done some writing here. "Upstairs?"

"Three bedrooms, one bathroom. There's also a powder room tucked behind the staircase if you're feeling the urge. No?" he said when she shook her head. "Then let's get these things into the kitchen."

She followed him past a spacious living room. All the furniture was covered with dust cloths. They took a right turn at the end of the central hallway and entered the kitchen. Judd set the sacks of groceries on the round oak table.

"This looks like a grandma's house," Stevie commented wistfully as she ran her hand over the carved back of one of the dining chairs. "I never got to know either set of my grandparents. They died before I could really remember them."

"Whew!" Judd was at the refrigerator, lifting out something that was curled and black and, as a result, unidentifiable. He carried the foul-smelling thing at arm's length to the back door and threw it out. "Glad Grandma isn't here to see that. She'd have a fit."

He opened the windows to let in fresh air while Stevie built them sandwiches out of the cold cuts and cheeses they had bought. As she was doing it, she felt one of the twinges in her lower abdomen that she had come to recognize, almost anticipate. Strange, though, she hadn't thought much about her illness since leaving Dallas. She guessed she had Judd Mackie to thank for diverting her mind.

Only two days ago, she would have thought that if she were left alone with the columnist for any length of time, she would slowly strangle him and derive a great deal of pleasure from watching his eyeballs bulge out of his skull as she did.

It was surprising that she found his droll sense of humor so comforting. He didn't mollycoddle or pity her, which she would have found untenable. He didn't play the clown, forcing laughter when it would have been inappropriate.

She would never have guessed that getting along with him would be so effortless. He was being the friend she needed right now, entertaining, but easy to talk to. She

was glad he had come along when she needed someone who was detached, objective and uncomplicated.
But she would rather have her tongue cut out than tell
him so.

"Lunch is ready."

He washed his hands, then joined her at the table.
"Hey, this looks great," he said enthusiastically as he
straddled the seat of his chair.

Stevie took a bite of her sandwich. Through the
mouthful, she asked, "What are we going to do after
lunch?"

And through his mouthful of sandwich, he replied,
"Make love."

# Five

Stevie swallowed her bite whole and gaped at Judd who calmly swallowed and blotted his mouth with a paper napkin. "Just a suggestion, of course," he said.

In a flash, she was out of her chair and headed for the door. "I should have known better than to trust you, you... Oh! When I think how gullible I was to believe that you— Ouch!" As she sailed past his chair, he had reached out and grabbed the swishing end of her braid. Using it, he reeled her in. "Stop that!" she cried. "Let me go."

"Sit down." He tried to sound stern, but she saw that he was having difficulty keeping a straight face. "Can't you take a joke?"

"That was a joke?"

"Sure, what did you think? That I was serious?"

"Of course not!" she snapped.

"Well, then, why didn't you just laugh?"

"It wasn't funny."

"I thought so. But not near as funny as the expression on your face." He mimicked it, and if she had looked anywhere near that idiotic, she wanted to vaporize. "Kind of like you'd been hit in the face with-—"

"I get the picture," she interrupted crossly as she sat down and took a savage bite out of her sandwich. "It would have been in perfect character for you to lure me here under false pretenses, then try to seduce me."

Rather than being insulted, he seemed flattered. "How do you know it would have been in character for me to seduce you?"

"I said *try* to seduce me."

"Okay. How do you know it would have been in character for me to try to seduce you?"

"One hears things," she said snootily.

"Oh, really? Like what? What have you heard about me?"

"Never mind."

"You're not referring to that story going around about me and the redheaded triplets, are you? Listen, that was a damn lie."

"Triplets?" she repeated thinly.

"They might be the most outstanding contortionists in the world, but even so..."

She eyed him suspiciously. "Are you putting me on?"

"Yeah, I'm putting you on." He resumed eating, but his smile remained insufferably com-placent and amused. "Well, we know that Grandma's beds are safe from us, don't we?"

"We certainly do."

"I mean, when we kissed, nothing happened, right?"

"R-right."

"The earth didn't tremble, stars didn't pop out, fireworks didn't explode. I didn't feel much, did you?"

"No."

"No surge of lust."

"Definitely not."

He shrugged eloquently. "We tried it out and found it lacking, so you've got nothing to worry about. Now, back to your original question about what we're going to do this afternoon."

Stevie barely listened. She had been relieved to know that he was teasing about an afternoon of lovemaking, but her ego was stung. Why had he found the possibility so absurd? When they kissed, hadn't he felt even slightly feverish? Lust was a strong word to describe the tingles she'd felt in all her erogenous zones when his tongue had softly engaged hers in a mating rite, but at least she'd tingled.

He'd come away from the kiss totally unaffected. Was kissing her so unexciting that even a renowned and seemingly indiscriminate womanizer like him could come through it without feeling *something*?

"...you don't have to."

"Don't have to what?" she asked, realizing that he'd been talking all this time.

"Don't have to help," he said, looking at her strangely. "Haven't you been listening?"

"No. My mind was on something else."

His brows frowned steeply. "You're not in pain, are you?"

"No, nothing like that."

"Good." He studied her for a moment as though he wasn't convinced that she was telling the truth. When he was satisfied, he summarized what he'd been saying earlier. "I've got some chores to do around here. While I'm at it, you can relax in one of the bedrooms upstairs."

"I'd rather be outdoors. The woods are so pretty."

"Suit yourself," he said, getting up out of his chair and carrying his empty plate to the sink. "There are books on the living-room shelves. Feel free to browse if you get bored."

"Thanks."

"I brought along some work clothes. As soon as I change, I'm going to start working outside. Holler if you need anything."

"I will."

He left the kitchen. Feeling slightly dejected and deserted, Stevie turned toward the sink.

"Oh, Stevie?"

"Yes?" she said, coming around quickly.

He was peering around the edge of the door, only his head visible. "I felt a *little* surge of lust." Then, lightly slapping the doorjamb and giving her a quick wink, he vanished.

Stevie muttered foul imprecations to the empty spot where his grinning face had been.

"What the hell are you doing?"

Stevie, sitting back on her heels in the dirt, glanced over her shoulder. She almost did a double take, but caught herself just in time.

Judd was looming above her wearing nothing but a pair of dirty Levi's and a frown. In the couple of hours since she had seen him, he'd worked up a sweat. Little rivers of perspiration trickled through his plentiful chest hair. He was using a rake as a prop, one elbow resting atop the handle, his hip thrown off center.

She could see straight up into his armpit, but it seemed an invasion of his privacy to stare at that as much as it did to visually track the beads of sweat sliding down the center of his belly into the low waistband of his jeans.

Something sweet and elemental pierced through Stevie's femininity, reminding her of the twinges of pain she had been experiencing recently. But these were different. These twinges brought pleasure, not dread and doubt. But like the others, she pushed conscious thoughts of them aside because they left her feeling ambivalent and afraid.

"What does it look like I'm doing? I'm weeding this flower bed." She turned back to the task that had hopelessly soiled her white culottes and caked her hands with fertile loam. She was sweaty. Her braid was lying heavily on her damp shirt, which was clinging to her back.

She felt wonderful. It was as though this sweat was healthier than that which she worked up on the tennis court.

"You're supposed to be relaxing," Judd told her.

"This is relaxing. I enjoy tending to plants and these have been so badly neglected." She turned her head to give him a reproving look, but quickly glanced away. He was crouching behind her. Up close, his face was grimy, streaked with sweat, and more handsome than ever. She could smell his skin and knew that his lips would taste salty if he chose to kiss her just then.

Swallowing hard, she said, "There's a pitcher of ice water on the porch."

"Thanks." He eased up, groaning slightly when his knees popped, and moved up the steps to the porch. "These old bones needed the exercise, but I probably won't be able to get out of bed in the morning." He poured himself a glass of ice water. After he'd drained it, he asked, "Did you do something up here?"

"I swept. The porch was littered with leaves and pine needles. It was a disgrace."

"A regular little busy bee, aren't you?"

"It feels good to be doing honest-to-goodness work. Besides, staying busy keeps my mind occupied."

He loped down the steps and gave her long braid a playful yank. "Just don't wear yourself out."

"I won't."


"You look worn out."

The sun had already slipped behind the tops of the trees, which in turn cast slanted shadows across the clearing in front of the house. Stevie was sprawled in a bench swing suspended from the branch of a mighty pecan tree. She was idly pushing the swing with her bare foot.

Before she'd sat down in it, she'd hosed it off and swept cobwebs off the chains. They needed oil, but she rather liked the pleasant squeaking sound they made as they rocked forward and back. They were in harmony with the perpetual creaking of the windmill.

The swing had been just one of the many projects she had assigned herself during the course of the afternoon while Judd nailed up dislocated shutters, used a weed sling on the clearing, and did some major cleanup around the barn and garage.

Now, as he spoke his semichastening statement, he dropped onto the ground in front of the swing and lay on his back in the recently mowed grass.

He had put his shirt back on but left it unbuttoned. It fell open, baring his impressive chest and tantalizing stomach, which for all his carousing was flat and taut and lightly shadowed with dark hair. Stevie kept her eyes studiously averted, but it wasn't easy. It hadn't been easy to keep her eyes off him all afternoon.

"I am tired," she conceded, "but deliciously so. I don't remember when I've watched the sun sinking behind leafy trees. The dappled light, the shadows, the shades of gold and green. It's all beautiful. And the sounds—rustling forest sounds that you never hear in the city. Yet it's quiet."

He rolled to his side and rested his cheek in his palm as he gazed up at her. "Do you always rhapsodize?"

"Only when I get this tired," she said with a smile, which he returned. "I enjoyed today. It's a shame we have to go back and inhale carbon monoxide and diesel exhaust instead of resin and wildflowers."

"Do we?"

She braked the swing with her heel and lifted her head off the thick chain, on which it had been resting. "Do we what?"

"Do we have to go back?"

Her eyes narrowed on him. "What are you up to now, Mackie?"

"God, you have a suspicious nature."

"I'm not suspicious. It's just that I don't trust you as far as I can throw you," she said sweetly. "Now what do you mean by asking if we have to go back to Dallas? Of course we do."

"Why?"

"Obligations."

"To whom?"

"Well, for one, you've got an obligation to the *Tribune*."

"Not as of this morning."

"What do you mean?"

"I got fired."

She looked at him with amazement. "Fired? They *fired* you?"

"Yep."

"Why?"

"Because I let our rival newspaper scoop me on the Stevie Corbett story."

Her lips parted in surprise. For several moments she only stared at him, but could find nothing in his open expression to indicate that he was lying. She had hoped he was.

"You got fired on account of me?"

He made a negligent answer. "Don't worry about it. Firing me is one of the few things my boss enjoys. I wouldn't think of going straight and depriving him of that occasional pleasure."

His joking didn't make her smile. "But...but you could have written a dilly of a story. You're the only one who knew the truth."

"That would have made me a real son of a bitch, wouldn't it? You might find this hard to believe, but I do have some ethics, and when I say a conversation is off-the-record, it's off-the-record."

He came to his feet and moved toward the swing. Stevie was sitting at an angle, one of her legs stretched along the length of the swing. He encircled her ankle with a firm grip and lifted her leg, then sat down in the swing and laid her leg across his lap.

"You've got a blister on your foot," he observed.

"That's what I get for wearing sandals instead of tennis shoes and socks."

He rubbed the raised, red skin with the pad of his thumb. Stevie's initial plan was to pull her foot away from his massaging hand, but she reconsidered. She was afraid to move it for fear that when she did, her heel would come in contact with the bulge behind the frayed fly of his jeans. Better safe than sorry, although she wouldn't call having her foot anywhere near *that* very safe.

"We'd better get going before it gets dark," she suggested huskily.

"I meant what I said." He turned his head and speared her with his eyes. "Let's stay."

"We can't."

She wished he'd remove his hand from around her foot. He was drawing patterns in her high arch with his thumb. It was difficult not to squirm and almost impossible to keep from purring with pleasure, especially when the look he was giving her was so disarming.

"How come?"

How come? She couldn't think of a single reason. "Because."

"Good reason." He flashed her a grin, but instantly reverted to seriousness. "You need time alone to think, Stevie. What better place than here? There's no telephone, no distractions, no snoopy reporters. No one to pressure you. Just me."

Little did he know that he was the main deterrent. But because the idea held such appeal, she hedged from giving him a definite no. "You're going to sit and watch me think through my dilemma? Is that what you're proposing?"

"No, I'm going to work on my novel."

"Novel? What novel?"

"The one I'm going to start tomorrow morning. If

we stay, that is. If we don't, the great American novel will never be written and everybody'll be blaming you."

"Oh, thanks. So now your career is my responsibility."

"Well, I *did* get fired because of you," he reminded her gently.

"You just said—"

"I know what I said," he said grumpily. "Look, let's stay. You can putter in the flower bed and around the house, cook and clean, and I'll write."

"Free maid service, that's what you want." She pulled her foot from his warm grasp, hoping for the best. Her heel grazed the button fly on his jeans, but she didn't let her mind dwell on the solid fullness she felt beneath it. "You want a housekeeper at your beck and call while you're playing John Steinbeck. You're a con, Mackie, a big con. The most manipulative—"

"You can lie in bed the livelong day for all I care," he said loudly, overriding her protests. "*You* are the one who said you wanted to stay busy to keep your mind off..." His eyes skittered down toward her lap. "You know."

Then he lifted his eyes to hers. One look into her hostile gaze and he blew out a disgusted breath. "Okay, forget I mentioned it. Bad idea. I thought both of us could use some time away from the grind to think, reassess, plan, that kind of thing. This seemed the perfect place for it. Obviously I was wrong on all accounts."

He left the swing. It rocked crazily. Stevie steadied it with her foot. "Where would we sleep?" she asked his retreating back.

He came to an abrupt halt and for several seconds

didn't move. When he did, he came around slowly. "'Where would *we* sleep'?"

"Where would *I* sleep?"

"You get first pick of the bedrooms."

"Where would you sleep?"

"In one of the other bedrooms." He propped his hands on his hips. "Is *that* what you're thinking, that I have an ulterior motive? A combined housekeeper and mistress." She remained stonily silent and accusatory. "I thought we'd already established that there's no sexual chemistry between us," he said. "Look, I meant this to be a purely platonic setup. Right now both our lives are in upheaval. Why would we want any additional complications?"

"Exactly."

"I don't see any sparks arcing between us, do you?"

"No."

"Would you go around all dirty and sweaty and generally looking like hell if you were trying to tempt me into being your lover?"

"No," Stevie said stiffly, wanting very badly to slap him.

"So fine. Neither would I. If I wanted you in my bed, I'd come right out and say so. Geez," he breathed, raking his fingers through his hair. "Now that that's understood, do we go or stay?"

# Six

"I thought it would be nice to eat out here."

Stevie gestured awkwardly at the card table she had brought from the dining room onto the front porch. She'd gathered a colorful bouquet of wildflowers and placed it in the center of the table. A raid of closets and cupboards had produced a tablecloth, linen napkins, even a candle, which, with the help of melted wax, she'd managed to stand in a saucer. The light flickered onto Judd's shadowed face.

"Great idea, but you went to too much trouble."

"I enjoyed it."

As promised, he had given her first pick of the bedrooms. She had chosen the one facing east because she was accustomed to waking up early. Her choice pleased him because he admitted that the last thing he wanted to see in the morning was sunlight pouring through the shutters.

Moving from the bedroom, he had showed her into the bathroom. It had a pedestal sink and an old-fashioned claw-footed tub.

"At least seven feet long and suitable for reclining

if you're in the mood for a long soak," he had said with the nasal accent of a snake-oil vendor.

They had found towels and sheets, along with a few odds and ends of clothing, in the upstairs linen closet. Judd had looked skeptically at the clothes. "Think you can find something to wear until we get into town?"

"I'll manage. Who did these clothes belong to?" she asked, holding a full skirt up against her.

"Assorted cousins I guess." There was a mix of men's and women's apparel. Judd took a shirt and pair of shorts. "Just because I'm such a nice guy, I'll let you go first in the bathroom. If it's okay with you, we'll cook those steaks I bought today for dinner." Her stomach had rumbled as though on cue. He made a scrubbing motion against it with his knuckles. "Guess that means you approve."

Stevie had tightened her stomach muscles in defense against his touch and tried to pretend that she still had sufficient breath. But for all her efforts, her voice still sounded unnaturally soprano when she said, "Steak sounds wonderful."

"Okay, I'll go start the charcoal while you're bathing. I found granddad's grill in the garage and scrubbed it clean today. There was even a sack of charcoal."

A half hour later, she had met him coming up as she was returning downstairs. She was fresh and clean, her hair still damp. He was dirtier than ever. Besides the grime he'd collected during the day, he'd added an overall dusting of charcoal powder.

"The water comes out rusty," she had told him. "But if you let it run a second or two it clears up."

"Thanks for the warning," he had replied as he trudged past her.

Now, they faced each other over the candlelit table. The night sounds coming from the surrounding woods were loud and distinct, the smell of cooking steaks mouth-watering, the breeze balmy.

Stevie, feeling foolishly nervous and self-conscious, groped for something to say. "The coals were just right."

"Good."

"I went ahead and put the steaks on the grill, but you might want to check them."

She was plagued by a sudden shyness and couldn't imagine where it had originated. Maybe the peasant blouse had been a poor choice; it was making her feel foolishly feminine. It was a size too large. The neckline was wide and kept slipping off one shoulder. If her clothes hadn't been so dirty, she would have put them back on after her bath.

As it was, she was standing before a man who could joke about bedding triplet contortionists, feeling ridiculously gauche and vulnerable.

He surveyed it all: the candle, the flowers, the table setting, her. Especially her. He left his eyes on her for a long, ponderously quiet moment. "Trying to impress me, Stevie? Maybe I should warn you before your heart gets broken that I'm not the marrying kind."

The sensual bubble burst. "You conceited jerk!" she cried indignantly, planting her hands on her hips. "I didn't do this for you. I did it for me. I rarely get to entertain and when I do, I usually take my guests out to dinner. This was a rare— What are you laughing at?"

"You. You can't take a joke worth a damn, but you're cuter than ever when you get riled."

Stevie stood there stewing while he moved to the grill, which he'd set up in one corner of the porch. She vacillated over whether or not to finish giving him a piece of her mind, but decided to leave well enough alone. Invariably their verbal skirmishes came out in his favor.

Over his shoulder, he said, "Five more minutes and the steaks will be perfect."

Stevie used that five minutes to carry out the green salad she had made, a loaf of French bread she had buttered and left warming in the oven and a pitcher of iced tea she had garnished with fresh mint she had discovered growing on either side of the back porch.

Judd sipped from his tall, icy glass and smacked his lips with appreciation. "The mint in the tea really reminds me of summers I spent here on the farm with my grandparents." For a moment he stared reflectively into space.

"What?" Stevie asked softly.

He focused on her and snorted a self-derisive laugh. "I just realized that happy hour has come and gone and I hadn't even missed it." He saluted her with his glass of tea. "Must be your company."

She basked in the warm glow coming from his eyes and began eating. A few moments later she said, "The steak is delicious, Judd."

"Well, don't get too excited. This about exhausts my culinary talents."

They resumed eating in silence. To make conversation, Stevie asked, "What's your novel about?"

"Writers never talk about the pieces they're currently working on."

"You haven't started working on it yet."

"Same rules apply to an idea."

"Why don't you talk about it?"

"Because talking about the story dilutes the compulsion to write it down."

"Oh." She returned to her food, but her mind stayed on that track. "I can understand that, I think. Before an important match, I don't like to talk about it. I don't want to discuss my strategy or the odds either against or in my favor. I'm immersed in my own thoughts. Sharing them would jinx the match."

"You're superstitious," he accused, pointing the tines of his fork at her.

"I didn't think so until now. But maybe so." She finished her food and pushed the plate aside. "I take my game very seriously. That's why your column has always been such a bone of contention, Mr. Mackie. You poke fun at me."

"It sells newspapers. I realize you take your game seriously. Maybe you take it too seriously."

"There's no such thing."

"Isn't there?" he asked, propping his elbows on the table and leaning closer to the burning candle. The flame flickered across his features, softening them, but enhancing their masculinity. "Where's the husband, the kids, the house?"

"If I were a man would you be asking me those questions?"

"Probably not," he admitted. "But then…" His eyes lowered to the neckline of the white peasant blouse. "You're not a man."

While she'd been busy eating, she had forgotten to give her neckline an upward tug every so often. It had dipped to cleavage level. The shadows cast by the single wavering candle made the valley between her breasts look velvety and mysterious.

Stevie, feeling threatened by his hot gaze and the personal slant their conversation had taken, immediately threw up a defensive wall and went back to their generic topic. "Everything, even success, comes with a price tag attached. You can't have it all."

"Some do. But not you. You don't have anything but your game."

"A damned good game," she said testily.

"Granted. But I bet if you polled most sportswriters, *male* sportswriters, and asked them what Stevie Corbett's finest contribution to tennis is, they wouldn't say, 'Her backhand.' If they were being honest, they'd more than likely say, 'Her backside.' It's just that I've got the guts to say, or write, what the rest of them are thinking."

She scooted back her chair and stood up quickly. "You're incorrigible, Mackie."

"So I've been told by everybody from my nursery-school teacher to Mike Ramsey as recently as this morning. He said—Stevie?" Judd slid out of his chair and rounded the corners of the table in one motion. "What's the matter?"

"Nothing."

"Dammit," he swore, "don't tell me nothing. Are you in pain?"

She took several swift, shallow breaths. "Sometimes, whenever I move too suddenly, like just then, it hurts a little."

Judd pressed his hand against her lower abdomen. "Do you need your pain pills? Sit down, goddammit. I'll go get them."

"No, it's fine. Much better." When she glanced up at him, her smile was tentative, but brave. "It leaves as fast as it comes. I'm all right now."

His fingers pressed into her abdomen, kneading her through the skirt. "You sure?"

She was sure of only one thing, and that was that if he didn't take his hand away and stop doing with it what he was doing, her desire-weakened knees were going to buckle and her mouth would reach for a taste of his.

"I'm sure," she replied thickly.

He searched her eyes, seemingly reluctant to believe her, but several heartbeats later, he withdrew his hand and stepped away. "You'd better go upstairs and lie down."

"Nonsense. It was just a twinge."

"Twinges don't make your lips go white."

"Kindly step aside so I can start clearing the table."

"Hell, no. Leave the dishes until tomorrow morning."

"I wouldn't think of it. Your grandmother would never forgive me. Now move."

He did so, but grudgingly, while he muttered curses beneath his breath. "How often do these twinges strike you?" he asked as he followed her into the house, bearing a tray of dirty dishes.

"Maybe once, twice a day. Really they're nothing to worry about." She filled the sink with soapy water. Each time she tried to move in any direction, she nearly stepped on him. "You're underfoot, Mackie. Why don't you be a good boy and go outside and play? Or work on your novel."

He slammed out of the kitchen, mumbling beneath his breath as he went through the shadowed rooms of the house. He knew pain when he saw it, and Stevie had been in pain. Did she think he was stupid enough to fall for her glib dismissal of it?

"A 'twinge,' my ass," he thought out loud.

She had downplayed that reminder of her illness the way he was currently de-emphasizing the swelling behind his fly. He wouldn't dare call it what it was. But what else could it be?

Stevie Corbett had been the warmest, softest thing he'd ever touched. Removing his hand from the folds of her skirt had been the hardest thing he'd ever had to do. He didn't know how he'd kept from touching her breasts just to see if they felt as fantastic as they looked.

To take his mind off how good she smelled and how badly he wanted to kiss her again and how much he ached, he carried the card table back into the dining room and set it up.

He positioned the lamp just so, adjusting the cheap lamp shade for maximum light. He replaced the typewriter and the ream of paper, stacking it and restacking it until all the edges were as straight as a knife blade. He checked the typewriter ribbon and made certain that pencils and erasers were within reach.

Then he just stood there, staring down at the card table, flexing his fingers at his sides.

"What are you doing?"

He spun around. Stevie was watching him curiously from the arched doorway.

"I'm setting up," he answered cantankerously. "You don't just jump into writing without setting up, you know. It takes lots of preparation."

"Oh. It looked like you were just standing there, shivering in your shoes, knees knocking, afraid to start."

"Well I wasn't."

"Okay, okay." She took a step backward as though she had roused an ill-tempered wild beast, which wasn't too far from the truth. "I'm going into the living room to read."

"Fine. Don't make any racket, will ya?"

"I won't."

"Say, wait!" He went after her when she turned away. "I didn't mean to snap at you like that. This is our first night here. The country is making me jittery, I guess."

"No city noise."

"Something like that. I've got it!" He snapped his fingers. "Want to play cards? I'm sure I can find a deck around here somewhere."

"I'm tired, Judd. Maybe another night."

"Trivia? We'll make up our own questions. You can choose the categories."

"I'd rather just read."

"Okay. That's fine. I'll help you select a book."

But as he went past her, she grabbed his arm and hauled him back. "I'll find my own book. Quit stalling, Mackie."

"Stalling?"

"Stalling. You're stalling like a kid at bedtime. That novel isn't going to write itself."

"Is that what you think I'm doing? Stalling to keep from starting on my book?"

"Yes."

"Geez, no wonder you never got married," he grumbled, as he turned back toward the dining room. "Who would want to marry you? You're no fun. No fun at all."

Stevie caught herself nodding off. She finally admitted defeat and laid her book on the end table. Earlier that day she'd uncovered all the furniture in the living room. It was basic Early American, constructed largely of maple, nothing she would have decorated with herself, but in perfect keeping with the rest of the house.

She switched off the lamp and retrieved her sandals from the floor, carrying them as she crossed the wide hallway. Judd was prowling the dining room, rolling his head around his shoulders and flexing the muscles of his arms. There were several models of paper airplanes scattered about the floor. One had crashed into the drapery cornice.

"How's it coming?" She moved toward the table, glanced down at the paper in the typewriter and read what he'd written so far. "'Chapter One.' Very insightful."

"Very cute."

"You're a long way from a Pulitzer, Mackie."

"And you're a long way from a Grand Slam."

His words extinguished the teasing light in her eyes and caused her smile to collapse. "You're right. I am."

He swore liberally as he plowed all his fingers through his hair. "I'm sorry. I didn't mean…I didn't think…I wasn't referring to—"

"I knew what you meant. No harm done. What's the matter with your shoulders?"

"Nothing."

"You're wincing every time you move."

"Too much of the weed sling, I guess."

"Really?" Pulling a worried face, she moved toward him and dropped her sandals onto the floor. She lifted her hands to his shoulders and squeezed the muscles lightly.

He yelped. "Ouch, damn, they hurt enough without you digging into them like that."

"You're as cranky as an old bear."

"Yeah? Well that's what I feel like. The first morning after hibernation."

"Come on upstairs. I'll give you a rubdown with this stuff that I'm never without."

She picked up her sandals again; he turned out the lamp. Together they started upstairs. "What kind of stuff?" he asked warily.

"A lotion. A sports injury specialist developed it. It's guaranteed to get rid of all stiffness and swelling."

She was several steps ahead of him. He caught the hem of her skirt and pulled her up short. She turned inquisitively.

"If it's guaranteed to do that," he drawled, "you gotta promise not to rub it on any parts I haven't okayed first."

# *Seven*

~∽⊙⊙∼~

Snatching her skirt out of his hand, Stevie shot him a quelling look and continued upstairs. After getting the bottle of lotion from the tote bag she'd brought along, she went to his bedroom door. "Knock, knock."

"Come in."

She did…just as he was peeling off his T-shirt. With his arms stretched high over his head, standing beneath the overhead light fixture, he was granting Stevie an unrestricted view of his body: the broad shoulders, wide chest, trim torso, narrow hips, scarred leg.

*Scarred leg?*

The T-shirt cleared his head. As he lowered his arms, he caught her staring at the jagged, purple scars that crisscrossed his left shin. He balled the T-shirt into a wad and, with a hook shot, tossed it into the easy chair near the bed.

"It's not polite to stare."

The chip on his shoulder had doubled in size since she'd entered the room. She could hear the insolence in his voice, an overcompensating sarcasm. Maybe she had accidentally happened upon Judd Mackie's one spot of vulnerability.

It would be ludicrous to pretend she hadn't seen the scars. Even if she could pull off such an act, he wouldn't fall for it and would resent her attempt. Her curiosity wasn't morbid, but sympathetic. There was no better way to deal with the awkward situation than to be straightforward.

"What happened to your leg, Judd?"

"Compound fracture of the tibia."

Worse than she had thought. She didn't even try to hide her grimace. "How?"

"Waterskiing accident."

"When?"

"A long time ago," he answered with a mix of bitterness and sadness. He moved toward her. She followed the progress of the scarred limb, lowering her eyes as he came closer in order to keep it in view. Judd placed his finger beneath her chin and tilted it up. "If you keep gawking, you're going to give me a complex."

"I'm sorry," she said, meaning it. "It's just that you've been wearing shorts all night and I didn't notice the scars until just now." It had been dark on the porch and his legs had been beneath the table while they ate. The angles hadn't been right at any other time. "It came as a shock, that's all. I wasn't prepared, didn't expect it."

"Most women find that leg incredibly sexy."

Now that she'd seen it, been stunned by it, he wanted to tease her shock away. That was fine with her. She would play along for now and ruminate later on the injury that had healed, but which remained a supersensitive spot to the seemingly invincible sportswriter.

"Oh, it's sexy alright," she told him with an impish grin. "Devilishly so. Almost as good as the hairy chest."

"No lie?"

"No lie. My mouth's watering."

"Hmm."

He lowered his eyes to her lips. His intense gaze was as stirring and provocative as his scathing prose, though in an entirely different way. The bottom seemed to drop out of Stevie's stomach. Before she became hopelessly trapped by his stare, which seemed to be drawing her closer to him like a powerful magnet, she turned away from him and began vigorously shaking the bottle of lotion.

"Where do you want to do this?"

"I don't know," he answered in a low voice. "How well are we going to get to know each other?"

She spun around to find him standing very close behind her, looking hungrily at her exposed neck while he played with the end of her braid. As he rubbed the silky strands between his fingers, he whispered, "There's the chair. Or there's the bed."

She flicked his hand away. "Do you want a rub-down or not?"

"I do."

"Then sit down and let's get it over with."

"I guess that means the chair," he said dryly, making an effort to keep from smiling. He pulled a straight chair from beneath a desk and straddled the seat, folding his arms over the back of it. "Have at me."

Stevie moved to stand behind him. She filled one palm with the lotion, then rubbed it against the other. However, when it came time to actually touch him, she hesitated. He had his chin propped on his stacked hands. Eventually her hesitation brought his head around.

"What's the matter?"

"Nothing."

"This isn't going to burn or anything, is it?"

"Chicken?"

"When it comes to my hide, you bet your ass."

"Do you think I'd smear it on my own hands if it burned?" she asked crossly.

"I don't know. You might. I've written some rotten things about you. This might be your way of getting revenge."

"Which you sorely deserve."

The conversation had given her time to bolster her courage. She laid her hands on his naked shoulders and began massaging in the healing lotion.

"Hmm," he moaned pleasurably after several moments. "Not bad, Stevie."

"Thanks. I've had lots of practice."

"On whom?"

"Other players on the tour."

"Men?"

"Sometimes."

"Oh, yeah? Is there material for a column here? 'Locker Room Lechery'?"

"That sounds like you. Low, mean, base."

"'Tennis Court Courtship'?"

"Ghastly headline."

"'Racquets and Romance'? 'Overhands, Or Head Over Heels?'?"

The freckles that dotted the ridge of his shoulders were adorable. They begged to have kisses pecked on them. The skin beneath Stevie's slippery fingers was taut, the muscles supple.

She wanted to slide her hands down his sides and over the corrugated rib cage. The fuzziness in his armpits intrigued her. With her eyes, she followed his spine into the waistband of his shorts. Touching him hadn't satisfied a building curiosity. It had only heightened it.

"Well, how 'bout it?" His mouth was pressed against his hands so the words came out mumbled. Her massage was lulling him. His eyes were closed. For such a tough guy, his eyelashes were ridiculously thick.

"How about what?"

"Romance. Ever had to use your racquet to beat off the circuit Romeos?"

"Never."

"Not your style, huh?"

"What is my style?" she asked.

"To give an unwanted suitor one of those cool, condescending stares of yours. That would chill most men to the bone."

"So far it hasn't worked on you, Mackie."

"As you said, I'm incorrigible. If I'd taken every woman's first no as final, I'd still be a virgin." He sighed. "Keep this up, Stevie, and you can have your way with me."

"Don't play so hard to get."

Even though he didn't open his eyes, they crinkled at the corners when he smiled. His eyebrows were as dense as his lashes. They were the eyebrows of a man with integrity, although integrity was a term she would never have applied to Judd Mackie. Not until yesterday, when, out of respect for her dilemma, he had let another sportswriter scoop him on a big story.

That unselfish decision had gotten him fired from the *Tribune*. Didn't that indicate that under that tough, bad-boy veneer, there was a man of honor?

"Do my arms, too."

"My fingers are getting tired," she complained. "This massage business is hard work."

"Just do it."

Her complaint had been a token one. She was deriving as much pleasure from the massage as he. His biceps were as firm as green apples and as finely shaped. She squeezed them hard, watching the deep impressions her fingers made in his flesh. When she let go, white stripes were left on the tanned skin. He grunted with animal pleasure.

"You accused me of missing my calling," he said. "I think I just figured out what you should have been."

Stevie realized then that Judd wasn't the only one being stimulated by the massage. She had moved closer to him, until her middle was lightly grinding against his back with each motion of her hands.

Realizing that, she suddenly withdrew them. "That's all I can do," she said, silently adding, "Without making a fool of myself."

Reluctantly he raised his head and pivoted his bottom until he was sitting correctly in the chair. He spread his knees wide, placed his hands around her waist and drew her between his legs.

"Mackie?" she said breathlessly.

"Hmm?"

"What are we doing?"

"Doing? Nothing."

He laid his hand on her abdomen again, with his fingers pointed up toward her breasts. "Any more pain?"

He applied pressure to her lower body with the heel of his hand.

Unable to speak, she shook her head no.

"Positive?" His fingers curled into the softness of her belly, then relaxed again.

"Positive."

"Good." He'd been watching the movement of his own hand. Now his eyes scaled up her body until they connected with hers. "You'd tell me, wouldn't you?"

The demand was disguised in the form of a polite question. "Yes. I'd tell you."

Keeping his gaze locked with hers, he slid his hand up the center of her body until it covered her heart, which was beating heavily.

"You smell good." He leaned forward and nuzzled her breasts, bumping them with his nose. "Where'd you find the perfume?"

"I brought my own." Stevie was barely able to form the words while his head was moving from one side of her body to the other and his hand was catching each of her drumming heartbeats.

"I like it."

"Thank you."

"You're welcome."

She whimpered when his lips touched the bare skin of her chest just above the slipping neckline of the peasant blouse. Briefly his lips brushed across her cleavage. Gradually, slowly, he kissed his way up her chest and throat as he came out of the chair.

When he was standing, feet still widespread, he encircled her waist with one arm and pulled her against him. His lips covered hers as his hand curved around her breast.

"Mackie...?"

"Judd."

"Judd...?"

"Go with it, Stevie."

His lips parted, so did hers. When they met again, their tongues touched and each released a low, satisfied, and conversely hungry sound. His mouth was as warmly possessive as his hand upon her breast, which he reshaped with his gently flexing fingers. Her nipple became hard and flushed beneath the idle sweeping motions of his thumb.

He dipped his head and kissed her through the blouse, leaving a damp, sheer spot on the soft cloth. Noticing that as he raised his head, he molded the wet fabric around her nipple until it clung, delineated, made visible.

His nostrils flared slightly and he muttered irreverently and arousingly. When his lips returned to hers, he kissed her with more depth and urgency and wildness.

"Stevie, don't worry, baby," he rasped against her lips, "you're more than enough woman for any man."

When the words registered, a wildfire of a different sort rampaged through Stevie's already burning body. She tore her mouth from beneath his and sent him sprawling across the hardwood floor when she pushed him away.

"So that's it!" She was seething, angrier than she'd ever been in her life, angrier than she'd ever been over a rotten line call or a lousy draw. "That's why you're being so nice to me. That's what all the sexual innuendos and pawing are about. You feel sorry for me."

"Huh?" Judd blinked his eyes back into focus. "What the hell are you talking about?"

"Your kindness and concern, your unselfish invitation to share this rural refuge with you, your flattery and sly come-ons." Clenching her teeth, she slapped her hands against the sides of her thighs. "Lord, I can't believe I was stupid enough to fall for it."

"Does this tirade have a point?"

He was looking up at her darkly, obviously none too pleased that she'd cut their party short. But his anger didn't come close to the level of hers.

"I don't need your pity, Mr. Mackie," she said heatedly.

"*Pity?* Pity didn't put this here," he said, briefly touching his fly.

"Then if your motivation isn't pity, that makes you even more despicable. You're manipulative. You figured I'd be easy to get into bed because I was panicked over losing my womanhood."

He released a series of creative curses. Aiming a finger at her, he said, "You should be the one writing the novel. You've got the imagination for it."

Stevie was pacing the width of the room. "While you were at it, you thought you would soften me up, get me to talk about every private aspect of my life. Then, when we returned to Dallas, you planned to write a really bang-up story that would ingratiate you with your boss again, sell newspapers, and leave the competitor who scooped you with egg on his face because you got the *real* story."

"I don't believe this." Still sitting on the floor, he laughed softly and shook his head.

"Let me tell you something." She stood above him, quaking with fury. "I don't need a Neanderthal like you to restore my faith in my femininity. Even if the surgeon does have to take everything out, I'll be more a woman than you are a man. A real man doesn't have to resort to the lowest, sneakiest form of trickery to get a woman into bed with him."

"That's the highest pile of crap I've come up against in a long time." He came to his feet so that they were standing toe to toe. "I'm not about to honor it with a comment, much less a denial."

"No matter what you said now, I wouldn't believe you."

"That's why I won't waste my breath."

"You're a lying con man. Your writing stinks. Your column is a joke. Being in your company makes me sick, and I've eaten much better steaks!" She tossed her braid over her shoulder and took a calming breath. "I want to leave. Right now. Drive me back to Dallas."

"Forget it."

"*Now* I said."

"*No* I said. You can stand there and fume all night if you want to, but I did the work of ten men today. I'm tired. I'm going to bed."

He unfastened the shorts. They dropped to the floor and he stepped out of them. Then he peeled off his briefs. Nonchalantly he moved toward the bed, flung back the covers, hit the wall switch of the overhead light and got into bed.

"G'night."

Stevie was sitting at the kitchen table the following morning when he came sauntering in. He was idly scratching his bare chest and yawning broadly.

"Ah, coffee, good." He took a cup out of the cabinet

and filled it, then leaned against the drain board to drink the brew. "Got your bags all packed, I see."

Wearing an amused expression, he nodded toward the large canvas tote bag she'd brought with her the day before. It was propped against her chair. She was dressed in her own clothes. They were filthy, but her bearing was one of superiority.

"Sleep well?" he asked guilelessly.

"No."

"Gee, that's too bad. I slept better than I have in months, maybe years. What was your problem, bed too soft?"

She gave him her iciest stare. "I guess I should thank you for putting on some shorts before coming downstairs." That was all he had on, but more than he'd been wearing the last time she'd seen him.

"Actually I enjoy drinking my first cup of the morning in the buff, so the shorts are a real concession in your honor." He executed a quick, little bow.

"Go to hell."

He laughed. "Come on, Stevie, lighten up. If we're going to be staying here together—"

"We're not. I'm going back to Dallas. If you won't drive me, I'll take a bus."

"There is no bus."

"Then I'll hitchhike."

"I'd pay to watch that."

"I'll find a way home," she shouted.

"Are you still mad at me? Look, you know that everything you said last night is garbage. Taking pity on you and getting you here under my roof just so I could bed you while you're in a vulnerable state of mind is all hogwash."

"Is it? I don't think so."

"Believe me, baby, the only reason I ever kiss a woman is because I want to. Pity has never extended that far."

"You said yesterday that you wanted this arrangement to be platonic, that seduction wasn't what you had in mind."

"Okay, so I told a fib. It was a tiny one." She didn't return his beatific smile. He tilted his head down and peered up at her from beneath his eyebrows. "I think you're madder at yourself than you are at me."

"Why would I be mad at myself?"

His grin was egotistical and knowledgeable. "You didn't want to enjoy kissing me, but you did."

"You…you…"

"No need to get huffy. I was enjoying it, too," he said, raising his hands helplessly. "I couldn't very well hide the fact, could I?"

She quickly averted her eyes. "I don't know what you're talking about."

"The hell you don't. See, Stevie, that's what happens to a man when he caresses a woman's breast. Even kissing it through her blouse is a real turn-on." His voice lowered an octave.

"And your nipple wouldn't have been so easy to find through your blouse if you hadn't been as aroused as I was. So what are you going to do, shoot me for behaving and responding normally? If so, you're gonna have to shoot yourself, too. That's only fair."

Her cheeks were flaming. Her whole body was as hot as a furnace. All her extremities were throbbing. His words had evoked stirrings within her she wished she could forget. But after unsuccessfully battling them all night, it didn't seem likely that they would simply vanish over breakfast, especially with Judd fanning the coals of her recollection.

"I want to go home," she said sternly. "You put on a sincere dog-and-pony show yesterday, but you brought me here for self-serving reasons."

"Nope, Stevie, that's not why you're angry." He set his empty coffee cup on the countertop and moved toward her. "You're not even mad because I stripped down in front of you."

She inclined away from him, until she was at risk of falling out of her chair. "Of course that's why I'm mad."

"Then why didn't you take the car and strike out for Dallas on your own?"

"I thought of it!"

"Well?"

"It was late," she said, hoping he couldn't tell that she was grasping at straws.

In fact, she hadn't thought of leaving by herself. After seeing him naked, all she had thought about was distancing herself from him before she did something really foolish, like follow him into bed.

She'd gone to her room, got into her own bed and lain as stiff as a board, afraid to move for fear that her churning body would prompt her into committing a rash and regrettable act. For all his swaggering this morning, she might just as well have.

If he were this disgustingly arrogant when she resisted, imagine how obnoxious he would be if she ever gave in. It didn't bear thinking about.

He was waiting for a plausible answer. She said the first thing that popped into her head. "I wasn't sure I could find my way along these country roads back to the interstate."

He gave her a smug look that told her at once he knew she was lying. "Uh-huh." Bracing his arms on the table, he leaned over her. "You got upset because last night reminded you of Stockholm."

# *Eight*

If his goal had been to knock the props out from under her, he had succeeded. She made several vain attempts to speak, opening and closing her mouth like the dummy of a ventriloquist with laryngitis. Finally she was able to croak, "I didn't think you remembered."

"I do."

"You were drunk."

"Not that drunk."

Leaving the chair, she ducked under one of his imprisoning arms. The coffeepot shook in her hand as she refilled her cup. She sipped it for fortification and to give her eyes something to look at besides the triumphant gleam in Judd's.

He thought he had her at a disadvantage. He did. The only way she was going to save face was to brazen it out. She assumed a haughty, indifferent air.

"Stockholm happened a long time ago, Mackie. Ten or eleven years, for heaven's sake. It wasn't any big deal."

"Oh, no?" He sprawled in one of the kitchen chairs, thrusting his bare feet out in front of him and crossing them at the ankles. "The shindig at that place was one of the best damn parties I've ever been to."

"You crashed it."

He chuckled. "See, that's the beauty of party crashing. You get to choose the very best ones to go to."

"You and your pals bribed—"

"Charmed."

"—your way inside. You upset—"

"Entertained."

"—everybody. The hosts were mortified—"

"—Amused."

Stevie sighed with annoyance. "I see we remember it differently."

"Admit it. My group livened things up considerably."

"That much I will admit." Her lips ached to surrender to the smile tugging at the corners of them. "Until you showed up, it was a stuffy and boring affair."

"After the hubbub we created had died down a bit, my well-trained radar system homed in on the prettiest woman there." His eyes found hers across the homey kitchen, just as they had across the ballroom of a Swedish palace so many years earlier. "You."

"Thank you. But I was also the youngest."

"I was young, too," he remarked introspectively. "I didn't realize how young. That was before I got the job at the *Tribune*. I was working for a news service, covering sports in Europe. My leg…"

He shook his head, clearing it of that unhappy thought. "I had a helluva good time over there, hanging out with all the sports celebrities, hobnobbing with royalty, going to parties, eating free food, drinking free booze."

"Picking up free women."

"The job definitely had its perks." He flashed his most unrepentant smile.

"I was so naive," she said in a reflective tone that echoed his. "That was my first year on the tour. I hadn't been warned against predatory media wolves like you."

"That was a stroke of good fortune for me."

Stevie snapped to attention and said with emphasis, "Nothing happened."

"That's not the way I remember it."

"Okay, we danced. You rudely cut in on my other partner."

"After you gave me that smoldering come-hither look."

"Smoldering? Come-hither? Boy, is your memory warped."

"And I didn't cut in, I just sort of nudged your partner out of my way. Besides, his dancing reminded me of a goose flapping its wings."

She smiled at the memory of her partner and Judd's unflattering, but accurate, description. "No, he couldn't dance very well."

But Judd could. Oh, he could. He had ignored the gyrating couples surrounding them on the dance floor and had pulled her into his arms.

*Hi.*

That's all he had said. That single Americanism. But there had been something totally captivating in the way he'd said it, softly, confidentially, as though they were meeting in a hushed, remote place instead of in a gigantic ballroom seething with laughter and deafening rock music.

He had mesmerized her with his compelling tone of voice and the possessive way his hands had settled on either side of her waist and pulled her swaying hips directly against his.

He had been everything she wasn't: sophisticated, cocky, self-assured, arrogant, undisciplined. He was out to enjoy life, make friends, have a good time.

She thought of little except her tennis game. Her constant companion was Presley Foster. Their conversations revolved solely around tennis and how tough the competition was and how far she had to go to get into the big bucks and the big time. She was self-disciplined to a fault. Even attending a party and staying out that late had been a rarity.

The handsome sports journalist was fascinating—and dangerous. He danced close enough for her to feel his breath on her face, held her in a manner that wasn't decorous, looked at her suggestively and moved his lithe body against hers with blatant symbolism. He had made dedicated, disciplined Stevie Corbett feel deliciously reckless.

"And after we danced, you went upstairs with me."

"You're dreaming, Mackie." Stevie wished her voice sounded stronger, more derisive. Instead it sounded hoarse and emotional. "I went into the garden and you followed."

"You ran."

"I needed air!"

"You were scared!"

She was scared. Scared of him and of her responses to him. Scared of the sensual awakening he had orchestrated. Scared because for the first time in many years, tennis was the last thing on her mind.

"I guess now you're going to ungallantly remind me that you kissed me."

Judd's steady gaze didn't waver. "You kissed me back."

She cleared her throat and made an offhanded gesture. "It was…pleasant."

"I'll say. Damned pleasant. Pleasant and wet and hot and sexy."

"All right," she flared, "so we kissed."

"French kissed."

"French kissed."

"And I put my hand inside your dress. I touched you."

"An outrageous thing to do," she whispered.

"Was it?" He rolled off his spine and came to his feet. He didn't stop moving forward until he had her backed against the countertop. "You were soft and very sweet, Stevie. Your heart was beating so fast. Just like it was last night." He laid his hand against her chest. "Just like it is right now."

"Nothing happened."

He dropped his hand and stepped back. "Because Presley Foster bore down on me and threatened me with castration if I didn't get my hands off you."

Stevie covered her face with her hands, feeling again all the embarrassment she had at that black moment in her life. She had wanted the earth to swallow her whole, so she wouldn't have to endure her coach's censorious glare, Judd's contemptuous smirk or her own scalding humiliation.

"Presley was doing what he thought was best for me," she said miserably. "He was protecting me from getting hurt."

"Were you sleeping with him?"

She lowered her hands and gaped at Judd with horror, her face pale and stricken. "Are you crazy?"

"Were you?"

*"No!"* She gulped reflexively. "Is that what you've thought all this time, that I was sleeping with my coach?"

"It crossed my mind."

"You're sick."

He shook his head ruefully. "Just realistic. I've known of kinkier relationships."

"Then you've been around people I never want to meet."

"Indubitably."

Staring into space, she organized her thoughts. "Well, this conversation explains a lot. No wonder you've taken potshots at me in your column. Either you took me for a slut with a lover older than her father. Or I'm just one that got away. Either way, your phenomenal ego couldn't handle my choosing Presley over you that night, so you carved me to bits in your columns as vengeance."

"One has nothing to do with the other."

"I'll bet," she said bitterly.

He grabbed her upper arm. "It was years before I connected the champion player Stevie Corbett with that wide-eyed kid I met at a party in Stockholm."

"When you did, I bet you had a good laugh." Angrily she pulled her arm from his grip.

"Not really," he surprised her by saying. "When I think back to that night, it's with poignancy, not derision. Want to know one of my deepest, darkest secrets? Even if Foster hadn't stopped it, I doubt it would have gone much further than it had."

"Why not?"

"You were so damned young. Innocent. Fresh. And I...well, I wasn't."

She was almost hypnotized by the sadness in his expression. However, in the nick of time, she narrowed her eyes suspiciously and asked, "If you knew I was innocent and fresh, then why'd you just ask me if I was sleeping with Presley?"

"Oh, I knew you weren't sleeping with him then. You were a virgin in Stockholm, right?" She opened her mouth to speak, but again discovered that she was too flabbergasted to utter a peep. "But I wanted to know if you had *ever* slept with him and were still carrying a torch. Now I know you didn't and you aren't."

Propping her hands on her hips, she glared up at him. "You sneaky lowlife, underhanded sonofa—"

"Before you launch into another round of name calling, could you fix me some breakfast? This country air has given me a roaring appetite."

"Fix your breakfast?" she screeched.

"That was part of our deal, remember? You cook, I—"

"The deal is off, Mackie. What makes you think I'd stay here with you now?"

"Why is now any different from yesterday when you agreed?"

Last night for one, she thought. And for another, their reminiscent conversation about a shared experience she had hoped he'd forgotten. She wasn't, however, going to cite those reasons.

"There's been too much water under the bridge. This is never going to work. One of us will end up murdering the other."

"Again, you're demonstrating a real flair for creativity, Stevie. If I get writer's block, I plan on consulting you first." He inspected the refrigerator. "For right now, juice, toast and coffee will do. When we go to the store later today, remind me to buy bacon and eggs."

*"Mackie?"*

He came around. "What? And for future reference, you don't have to shout. I'm not hard of hearing."

"And I'm not staying."

He studied her for a moment, a picture of exasperation. "Fine. The keys to the car are on the hall table. Be careful driving. But before you go, consider this."

He held up his index finger. "One. Your condo will probably still be staked out by the media. The public will be panting to know whether or not you're going after the Grand Slam. Will you play Wimbledon in three weeks or not? Will you have surgery right away or won't you? What are the consequences if you don't? What's your prognosis if you do?

"Can you give them answers to those questions, Stevie? No. Because those are the questions you're still grappling with yourself. What better place to arrive at some answers than the peace and quiet of the country, far away from the news hounds and unsolicited advisers?"

Another finger went up. "Two. You look like you need a vacation. You've still got unattractive dark circles under your eyes." His ring finger joined the first two. "Three. I got fired on account of you. The least you could do is cook a few meals for me while I try to hack out a rough draft for a novel. Selling it for publication may be my only hope of supporting myself in the future." His pinkie sprang up. "And four, nothing infuriates me more than somebody who goes back on his word."

His reasons made sense, especially the first one, but Stevie glared at him mutinously, still not prepared to surrender unconditionally. "I need to practice. Do you realize how rusty I'll get if I don't play some tennis at least once every day?"

"Valid point." Gnawing the inside of his cheek, he considered their alternatives. "When we drive into town, we'll check the public school. If memory serves me, it's got a tennis court. And since I'm the only famous or near-famous person from around here," he said with a conceited grin, "I think I can finagle permission to use it."

"If you can do that, I'll stay."

"Thank heaven that's settled," he muttered, turning to pour himself a fresh cup of coffee. "I'll be in the dining room writing. You can bring me my juice and toast in there. I like it lightly browned and heavy on the butter."

"The juice or the toast?"

He was almost to the door when he turned and scowled. "Try and not make any distracting noise."

She was tempted to go after him and deliver a good swift kick to his taut, narrow buttocks.

But she didn't.

One evening over dinner, Stevie contentedly remarked that these were halcyon days. Judd gave her a reproving look and said, "You'll never make a writer if you resort to clichés like that."

Despite his teasing, that was the adjective that best described their days. She awoke early and puttered around in the yard. The mint growing near the back porch was thriving. She'd carefully weeded around long neglected, but stalwart, periwinkles, which were now profusely blooming in shades of pinks and purples in front of the house.

On one of their trips into town, she'd bought a package of zinnia seeds. They'd been planted and were already sprouting. She enjoyed watching the vibrant green shoots grow, thriving in the rich east Texas soil. Stevie regretted that she wouldn't be around to enjoy their brilliant blossoms.

Judd was a late and grumpy riser. Each morning he stumbled into the kitchen and poured himself coffee she had brewed. It took at least three cups to make him civil. He then retired to the dining room to work on his novel. Later she would take him toast or cereal, but as often as not when she silently checked from the archway, it was still on the tray, untouched.

After lunch, Judd would return to his typewriter. Stevie napped or read in the afternoons. She studiously avoided thinking about her illness or what she was going to do about it. That was the purpose behind this respite from her normal schedule, but she couldn't bring herself to dwell on it.

At dusk they drove to the public school campus and played low impact tennis, wearing inexpensive shorts they'd bought in the only dry-goods store in town, where they had also purchased other clothing. Her new wardrobe had little merit beyond keeping her decently covered, but she had had more fun shopping for it with Judd than she ever remembered having on a buying spree.

They took drives through the countryside in the cool

of the evening, or sat together in the bench swing beneath the pecan tree, or played cards on the porch. Judd cheated unconscionably and sulked when he didn't win, blaming his losses on everything from the weak porch light to the racket made by the cicadas in the trees.

One evening he had disgustedly tossed down a losing hand and said, "Let's play strip poker and the winner has to take off all her clothes."

Gloating, Stevie had raked in her mountain of match sticks. "Such a sore loser."

"That's a game I wouldn't mind losing."

His back was propped against one of the posts supporting the roof over the porch. He was lazily wagging his knee back and forth. Even in the faint glow of the porch light, Stevie could see the intensity of his gaze and sensed that he was no longer teasing.

With clumsy hands, she quickly reshuffled the deck and dealt a new hand. "Maybe if you try playing fair instead of cheating, you'll win this hand."

She didn't acknowledge either his suggestion or the fire in his eyes. Doing so could prove dangerous. She had been dancing close to the flame since agreeing to stay alone with him. So far, she had been singed, not burned. She wanted to keep it that way. There were undercurrents between her and Judd that she couldn't cope with. It was easier to pretend they didn't exist.

One afternoon they bought an edition of the *Tribune* at the grocery store. Stevie was crushed when she read the sports page. One of her rivals had won the Lobo Blanco tournament. "They're saying she might replace me as the top-seeded player," she told Judd glumly.

"Ready to go back and face the music?"

She raised her head and stared into his eyes for a

moment, seeing in them the same reluctance she felt toward his suggestion. "No. Not yet."

"Me, either." Unable to mask his relief, he playfully jerked the newspaper out of her hands. After a moment of reading, he said, "Look, here's a letter to the editor from a reader asking about me."

"How does the management respond?"

"That I'm taking a 'few weeks off.'"

"They don't come right out and say that you're fired," she said, reading over his shoulder. "That must mean they want you back. Should you call them?"

"No way." He refolded the paper and tossed it aside. "Let Ramsey sweat."

The next morning, the postman delivered a letter to Stevie as she was working in the flower bed. It was addressed to Judd. Wiping her hands on the seat of her shorts, she went inside.

"I hate to disturb you, but a letter just came." She entered the dining room. Judd, she noticed, not for the first time, typed with his index fingers only.

He finished his sentence, then rolled the paper out of the machine and laid it face down on the card table. He had refused to discuss his plot, characters or anything else about his book with her. He never gave her a glimpse of what he'd written and had forbidden her to pick up the wastepaper that littered the floor every morning.

He read the letterhead and muttered scoffingly, "Ramsey." Judd scanned the brief letter, crammed it into a ball and tossed it onto the floor where his other rejections were strewn.

"Well," Stevie asked impatiently, "is he sweating yet?"

"Like a pig. But he hasn't got to the begging stage."

"He has to beg?"

"Sure he has to beg. I want him to get as low as a slug and then grovel."

She laughed. "I take it that means you're not ready to go back."

"What I'm ready for," he said as he came to his feet, "is lunch." He placed his arms around her, clapped his hands on her bottom, gave the firm flesh a hard squeeze and soundly kissed her. "Fetch my food, woman."

She slipped out of his arms, asking saucily, "Or what?"

His eyes became drowsy and as sultry as the summer weather. "Or I'll show you what else I'm ready for."

She fetched his food.

# Nine

"You're awfully quiet tonight. Is something wrong?"

Stevie, who had been staring vacantly over their dinner table, blinked Judd into focus. "No, nothing. I'm sorry I'm not better company."

"You're not having any pain, are you?"

She shook her head. "Just tired I think."

"No wonder. You waxed me today on the tennis court."

She smiled, but it was a fainthearted attempt. "You still gave me a good workout."

Watching her closely, Judd played with his spoon, turning it end over end. "It's more than fatigue, isn't it, Stevie?"

"Maybe. I don't know. I've got a lot on my mind."

"It was seeing that couple."

She looked at him sharply, then tried unsuccessfully to hide her spontaneous reaction by innocently repeating, "Couple?"

"The young couple we saw in the grocery store this afternoon. The couple with the baby."

She looked away, which was as good as a signed confession.

"Up till then we'd been having a great time," Judd said. "You beat me soundly in three sets, but I lost gracefully. We were joking, wrestling over the last bite of Hershey bar, doing our grocery shopping.

"Then you caught sight of those two attractive young people wheeling their basket down the store aisle, cooing to the kid and smiling goosily at each other over the top of his curly, blond head. After that, you clammed up and have had the personality of a turnip ever since."

"I didn't know that my duties as cook extended to being a court jester, too," she said caustically. "Maybe you should have specified that."

He dropped the spoon onto the table with a clatter and held up his hands in a gesture of surrender. "Touchy, touchy. It's *you* I'm worried about."

"Well, don't be."

"Too late. I already am."

Stevie gauged his expression. It appeared to be sincere. She wanted, and needed, to believe that it was. With a short, self-derisive laugh, she said, "I suppose you think I'm the one who's goosey."

"Actually that living portrait of matrimonial bliss and domestic harmony left me a little choked up, too."

"I'll bet," she said drolly.

"It did. I haven't always been a surly, cynical jerk, you know. The owners of this house, my grandparents, instilled in my father some basic values. He, along with my mother, instilled a few in me."

"What happened to them?"

"They got dashed against the rocky shore of outrageous fortune."

"I hope you're not putting that in your novel. It's terrible."

His lips tilted into a half smile. "Not in those exact words, but they sort of capture the gist of the theme."

She lifted her shoulders, then let them drop as she released a heavy sigh. "Okay, as long as we're being open and honest, I'll admit that seeing that poignant little scene got to me. I was envious."

"Envious?" he asked incredulously. "How could you be envious of these rural folk? You've traveled the world several times over, been introduced to royalty, earned a helluva lot of prize money in addition to what you make on endorsements. You couldn't possibly build a trophy room large enough to hold all that you've received."

"None of which I can confide my troubles to. I can't curl up with a trophy on cold nights. Or even have a healthy fight with one."

"Know what this sounds like to me? Whining."

"That's exactly what it is," she retorted crossly.

He let a moment go by before asking, "Are you regretting some decisions, Stevie?"

"Yes. No. I don't know, Judd. It's just that…" She paused, trying to convert her random thoughts into understandable language.

"For the past three years, the Grand Slam has eluded me by one tournament. Once I had got it, I planned to slow down. I would have had to anyway in a year or two because of my advancing age, but I had already decided that if I got the Grand Slam I wouldn't ask for more. I'd retire on top, with dignity and a very respectable career behind me."

Pensively she continued, "But I didn't think much beyond that. Now that the inevitable future is here, it seems so bleak, so empty. There's nothing in it. There's *nobody* in it."

"No baby."

"No baby," she repeated emotionally. "And probably no chance of having one. Ever."

"Do you wish you had had a child sooner?"

"Maybe. But hindsight is twenty-twenty, isn't it?"

"With whom, Stevie?"

She laughed mirthlessly. "Good question. With whom? I never took the time to fall in love, get married, develop a meaningful relationship. I'm not even certain what that catch phrase means or how it applies to me and members of the opposite sex."

"Now that you've got the time to find out, you might not get the opportunity. Is that what's bothering you?"

"In a nutshell, yes."

Each fell silent. Judd was the first to speak. "Sometimes our decisions are forced on us."

"Mine weren't. I freely made my choice years ago. I chose tennis. At all costs, I wanted to be the number one player in the world."

"You are."

"I know. I also know I have no reason to complain. It's all been wonderful." She gave him a bleak smile. "It's just that every once in a while, like today, I'm reminded of everything I sacrificed and start feeling sorry for myself. Now that my career is coming to an end, I'm asking myself, 'now what?' And I don't have any answers."

She took a deep breath. "In my estimation, self-pity is the most wicked of sins. It's also a big waste of time, unless it's within one's power to bring about a change. In my case," she concluded, laying a hand on her tummy, "I don't have control over the situation. That's the bitterest pill to swallow."

They had finished their meal. Judd helped her clean up the dishes. In that respect, he wasn't nearly as chauvinistic as he pretended to be.

"I'm going on up to bed," she told him as soon as they'd finished the chore.

"To brood?"

"No, because melancholia is exhausting."

He smiled crookedly. "Personally I think there are a lot of sins far more wicked than self-pity. Want me to enumerate a few I've engaged in, just so you'll feel better?"

"Thank you, no. I'll pass."

He pressed her shoulders between his hands and dropped a quick kiss on her forehead. "Say your prayers. And close your door so the typewriter won't bother you."

"It doesn't bother me."

She stood looking up at him, feeling lost and lonely. She wished for something. For what exactly, she wasn't sure. For starters she wished that his good-night kiss had been placed on her mouth rather than her forehead. She wished it had been deep and lingering instead of light and quick. She wished his caress hadn't been so fraternal and that he hadn't removed his hands from her shoulders so soon.

She was seized by a strange and powerful yearning that she couldn't put a name to. It was silent and internal, but as strong and overwhelming as a waterfall. She longed to rest her cheek against Judd's chest and feel the safe sanctuary of his arms closing around her. She wanted to hear his husky voice whispering encouragement into her ear, even if all he gave her were platitudes.

Before she submitted to the impulses tugging at her, she needed to put space between herself and Judd. He might mistake her unnamed need for weakness. "Good night."

"G'night, Stevie."

She couldn't sleep. The day had been cloudy and muggy. Ordinarily her room was cool enough, thanks to the droning oscillating fan that stirred the evening air. She hadn't missed air conditioning a bit. Indeed, she liked watching the sheer curtains on the open windows billow and float on the breeze.

But tonight the curtains were hanging limply in the windows. There was no breeze. Even if the curtains had been doing their entrancing dance, she doubted it could have lulled her to sleep. She was restless. Her body needed sleep, but her mind wouldn't cooperate and let it come.

Suddenly it occurred to her why she couldn't sleep. Judd's typewriter wasn't clacking. Contrary to what he thought, the sound of its metallic tapping didn't keep her awake when he worked well into the early morning hours. It had become a reassuring sound, an indication that for once she wasn't spending the night alone in an otherwise empty house.

Throwing off the light muslin sheet, she padded over to her bedroom door, which was always kept open to allow the air to circulate through the house—a lesson she had learned from Judd, one which he remembered from spending summers on the farm with his grandparents when he was a boy. She listened. Nothing.

A quick peek into his bedroom revealed that he hadn't gone to bed yet. She moved to the head of the staircase and looked down. The light was burning in the dining room. He was still up, probably just taking a break. But she waited for several minutes, and he didn't resume typing.

Curious, and somewhat worried, she crept down the stairs and silently approached the dining room.

She caught him deep in thought. His pose was what she considered to be very "authoresque." He sat, staring at the page in his typewriter, his hands folded over his mouth, elbows propped on the card table.

The sleeves of his white T-shirt had been cut out, though it looked more like they'd been chewed out. The armholes were ragged. He was wearing a pair of navy blue shorts.

His hair looked as though it had been combed with the yard rake she used in the flower beds around the house. One damp, dark lock had fallen over his brow. His feet, in laceless tennis shoes, were resting on the lowest rung of the straight chair. His spine was bowed.

Not wanting to disturb him, she backed away and turned toward the stairs without making a single sound.

"Stevie?"

She came up short and stepped back into the light of the open archway. "I'm sorry. I didn't mean to distract you."

"Obviously you didn't."

"The muses aren't being kind tonight?"

"Those bitches." With his hair falling across his forehead, his face shadowed from above by the lamp on the table and below by his sprouting beard, he epitomized disreputability.

He looked temperamental and dangerous and... gorgeous. Something deep inside Stevie stirred and stretched, like a seed that had been planted in fertile soil and was now on the brink of germination.

"Why aren't you asleep?" He took a slurp of coffee she knew must be stone cold.

"I don't know." She lifted her hands awkwardly, then let them drop back to her sides. "I think I missed the sound of the typewriter. And the humidity is oppressive. As long as I'm up, I'll be glad to make some fresh coffee."

"No thanks. I've had enough." He looked her up and down. "You okay?"

"Yes."

"No problems?"

"No."

"I don't believe you. If you were okay, you'd be asleep."

She came farther into the room. Her nightgown had been one of the purchases she'd made in the dry goods store. It was sleeveless, had a tucked-and-pleated lace-trimmed bodice, and was modest enough for a nun. Although a nun probably wouldn't have worn a nightgown made of cotton that was so soft and sheer that light could shine through it.

Unaware that her body was silhouetted against the fabric, she extended her arms at her sides. "See? I'm fine."

"Well, I'm not," he muttered grouchily. "Sit down and keep me company for a while."

She glanced around. "There's no place to sit."

"Sure there is." He swiveled his legs from beneath the table, reached for her hand and pulled her onto his lap.

She felt his bare thighs against the backs of hers. The contrast was so thrilling she uttered a soft cry. "Judd!"

Nuzzling her neck, he snarled, "Did I ever tell you that white cotton nighties make me as horny as hell?"

"No!"

"Well, they don't. I just wondered if I ever told you that."

"Oh, you!" she remonstrated, giving his shoulder a push.

Chuckling, he raised his head, but loosely linked his hands around her waist. His eyes moved over her. "I couldn't seduce you now even if you'd let me."

"Why?"

"Because you look about twelve-years-old, that's why. With your hair down and wearing your sweet, prim nightie."

Smiling, he ran his index finger down the row of tiny buttons until it came up against a neatly tied satin bow between her breasts. By then, he was no longer smiling. He lifted his eyes to hers. Their gaze melded.

Stevie's pulse was pounding in her ears. He had already teased her once about her rapidly beating heart, and she wondered if he could feel it now. She could scarcely breathe.

Before things got out of hand, she had to bring the subject back around to his writing. "Is it terribly hard?"

"It's getting there," he replied roughly.

"How long will it be?"

"Long enough, baby."

"What's it about?"

"Huh?"

"Your book."

"Book? Oh, my book. We're talking about my book."

He dropped his head forward and blew out a pent-up breath. For several moments he breathed deeply with his eyes shut. When he raised his head again, there were lines of strain around his mouth.

"'Book' is a polite euphemism for 'pile of crap.'" He nodded toward the pages turned facedown on the table.

"I'll bet it's not crap at all. You've been working so diligently, it can't be all bad."

"Hopefully not." He took her hand in his and studied it. Turning it palm up, he ran his thumb across the calluses left by her tennis racquet. His touch was a further aggravation to her already chaotic system and increased her awareness of the warmth emanating from his lap up through her thighs.

Hastily she withdrew her hand and made to stand. His arms tightened around her. "Where are you going?"

"Back to bed."

"I thought you were going to talk to me."

"You're not talking."

"You want to know what the book is about?" he asked moodily. "All right, I'll tell you."

"I—"

"Hush. You keep bugging me to know, so now you'll know. Be quiet and listen."

Ordinarily Stevie would have protested this gross inaccuracy. Since she had first asked him about his novel and he'd told her that writers didn't discuss their current projects, she had refrained from asking specific questions about it. She usually referred to what he did in the vacant dining room, as his "work."

Now, however, she could tell that he was bursting to discuss certain aspects of it. Obediently she sat silently on his lap and listened.

"It starts out when the protagonist is just a kid, see?"

"Male or female?"

"Male."

"Figures."

"He had a very ordinary—"

"Does he have a name?"

"Not yet. Are you going to keep interrupting? Because if you are—"

"I won't say another word."

"Thank you." He took a deep breath, opened his mouth, then looked at her blankly. "Where was I?"

"May I speak?" His glare threatened murder. She quoted, "'He had a very ordinary…'"

"Oh, yeah. He had a very ordinary childhood. Mom, Dad, typical suburban-America upbringing. He'd always been good at sports. All sports. But in high school, he concentrated on baseball. By his senior year, he'd won the attention of many notable universities, all vying for him. He picked one and got a scholarship in exchange for playing baseball on the varsity team.

"During his sophomore year of college, a minor league talent scout approached him and offered him a contract to go pro. It was as tempting as hell. Although his coaches, everybody, had told him that he had what it took to make the major leagues, he decided that he had better decline—much as he wanted to play—and go ahead and finish college, just in case this career in baseball didn't pan out.

"So he stayed in school, which, as the story progresses, turned out to be one of the wisest decisions he ever made. Since he wasn't particularly interested in any other field, he tried to find the path of least resistance to get through college. He'd never been much of a scholar, too busy with athletics, you see.

"Science and math courses were a hassle for him, and he barely squeaked by. But he aced classes like English and history where he could b.s. his way through an exam. Friends told him that he had a way with words and a knack for turning a clever phrase. So, it seemed logical that he major in English and minor in journalism.

"By the time he graduated from college, he had an agent negotiating with three major-league teams. Under the misconception that he was invulnerable, he behaved recklessly, thinking that his future was one big bright solar system that revolved around him, its sun. He partied a lot. There were lots of women, good times, fun and frolic."

Judd fell silent for a moment and stared reflectively at the blank sheet of paper in the typewriter.

"One of those seven-figure, five-year deals that dreams are made of came through for this clown. He was celebrating it with a group of friends. They decided to spend a weekend waterskiing."

Stevie rolled her lips inward, wishing she didn't have to listen to the rest of the story. But dynamite couldn't have blasted her off Judd's lap. Apparently he desperately needed this catharsis. He had listened on several occasions when she had poured her heart out. It was time she returned the favor.

"The lake had been formed by a new dam and hadn't completely filled up yet. Those kids were stupid to be skiing there in the first place. This fool was even laughing his head off when the boat approached the stump sticking above the surface of the water.

"Hell, he was invincible. Nothing could touch him. Or so he thought," he said in a flat, empty voice. "He decided that he could swerve around the stump without any trouble at all." After a moment, he added, "He couldn't."

The resulting silence was broken only by distant thunder. It rumbled ominously. The sky flickered with lightning; the breeze picked up. But neither Stevie nor Judd noticed these changes in the weather.

"All his big plans were shot to hell," Judd continued. "One dumb move and the course of his life was changed forever. The seven-figure offer was revoked after the doctors told the team management that he'd never be pro material even if they did their best for his leg.

"He never got to play major-league baseball. After a year of reconstructive operations on his busted tibia, he went to work writing about the sports he could no longer play."

It began to rain. Fat, splattering drops fell onto the flowers that Stevie had so painstakingly cultivated. Rain splashed against the open windows. The curtains were driven into the room by the gusty wind. Lightning crackled and thunder crashed. The air turned noticeably cooler, a welcome relief from the humid heat.

Stevie was unaware of the storm, unaware of everything except Judd. She brushed back the strand of hair that had fallen over his forehead and smoothed out the frown between his eyebrows.

He gave her a twisted grin. "You won't want to read the book. I don't think it's going to have a happy ending."

"Why not?"

He slipped his finger into the neckline of her night-gown and slowly traced the edge of the material around the base of her neck. He did it without really thinking about it.

"For years after his accident, the protagonist was mad at the world, even madder at himself for screwing up his life. He went through the motions of living, but just like Rhett Butler, he didn't really give a damn. He worked hard at making everybody around him as miserable as he was himself. He got drunk often, slept with nameless women, picked fights."

"Fights?"

He shrugged, now toying with the buttons on her gown again by lightly plucking at them. "To prove to himself that the accident hadn't emasculated him. He wasn't a strutting jock anymore."

"Athletic prowess has never been the true measure of a man."

"Sell that theory to your average American male."

She lifted her shoulder in semiconcession, a move that caused his knuckles to make a dent in the inner slope of her breast. "How will the story end, Judd?"

"Ah, that's what's hanging me up. I'm up to the part where he finally settles into a well-paying job, which he goes through the motions of doing, expending as little effort as possible. He's got everybody but himself buffaloed into believing that what he's doing has merit. But what eventually becomes of this guy, who still resents like hell that he blew his one big chance in life?"

"I don't think you're giving yourself enough credit," Stevie remarked in a soft, sympathetic voice. "It takes a tremendous amount of talent to turn out a newspaper column every day. Being prolific is certainly no small thing when journalism is your occupation. Your columns haven't always pleased me, but they're never stale or… What's the matter?"

He was no longer touching her with subconscious, intimate familiarity. His eyes had turned as stormy as the night sky. "Have I said this story is about me?"

His sudden mood shift stunned her. "Well, no, not specifically," she stammered, "b-but I…assumed…"

"The character in my book is dissatisfied with his life. Do I look like a guy who's dissatisfied with his life?"

He stood up, practically dumping her onto the floor. She staggered backward in an attempt to regain her balance. When she did, she glared at him with contempt and fury. He had told her his sob story, but when it came time to accept her compassion, he had turned stupidly, defensively macho.

"What you look like is a joke of a journalist, who is finally getting around to hacking out the dreary novel that he's been claiming for years to have burning inside him to anybody dumb enough to listen to that drivel."

"You don't know anything about me, Miss Cute Buns," he said with a dangerous scowl.

"I know that you're too insensitive to write copy for sardine cans, much less a novel about human emotions and life's disillusionments. Speaking of which," she sneered, gesturing down at the table, "I think the subject matter of your book is self-indulgent and boring."

He took the steps necessary to close the distance between them. Through his clenched teeth he said, "Not if I detail the character's interactions with women."

"In that case, add disgusting to self-indulgent and boring and you've got my critique!"

On that outstanding exit line, she stamped from the room.

# Ten

It was still raining the following morning, but it wasn't the sound of thunder that awakened Stevie. It was the cramping in her lower abdomen. The twinges were like menstrual cramps, only more localized and more severe, particularly in her right side.

She got up and took two of her pain pills. Back in bed, she turned onto her side and drew her knees up close to her chest. Eventually the cadence of steady rainfall induced her back to sleep.

She must not have been sleeping very deeply, however. When she awakened again, Judd was speaking her name in gentle inquiry. She felt the mattress dip beneath his weight as he lay down behind her and placed a hand on her shoulder.

"Stevie, what's the matter?"

"Nothing." She lay unmoving, her eyes remaining closed.

"I could hear you moaning all the way in my bedroom. You woke me up."

"I apologize."

He swore beneath his breath and muttered something derogatory about the female psyche. "I don't care about missing out on some sleep," he hissed. "Are you in pain?"

"A little."

"Damn."

"Only a slight cramp. Don't worry about it. It'll go away."

"Where are your pills? I'll get them for you."

"I already took two."

"When?"

"I don't know. Not long ago."

"Why aren't they working?"

"They haven't had time."

"What can I do?"

"Nothing."

"Why are you keeping your eyes closed?"

"Because I'm sleepy." And because she knew, intuitively, that he had come to her bed as he slept in his—naked. "Go on back to bed. I'll be all right."

"Where do you hurt?"

Impatiently she snapped, "Where are my tumors?"

"What would help?"

"My heating pad might."

"Where is it?"

"I didn't bring it."

"Great."

He didn't say anything else, but he didn't go away, either. Stevie could feel him staring down at her. Abruptly, as though he suddenly made up his mind about something that had him in a quandary, he slid his arm around her waist, fumbling through bedding and cotton nightie before his hand found skin.

"Judd! What are—"

"Shh, shh. Lie still. I want to help."

"You can't."

"Maybe not, but I want to try."

"Why?"

"Because I was rough on you last night. I yelled at you and you didn't deserve to be yelled at."

"That doesn't matter. This isn't necessary."

"Look, this Good Samaritan gig is new to me, so give me a break and help me along, okay? Now, where do you hurt? Here?" He placed his warm hand over her lower body, applying just the right amount of pressure.

"Hmm." A soothing heat spread through her, melting away the pain, ironing out the cramps. It felt wonderful.

"Is that better?" He waited. "Stevie?"

She was already asleep.

When she woke up the third time, the weight of his arm was lying heavily in the hollow of her waist. His hand was still palming the area between her hipbones. The pain was gone.

The fingers of his other hand were ensnared in her hair where it mingled with his on the pillow they shared. If he was going to invade her bed, the least he could have done was bring his own pillow, she thought.

Her peevishness was a ruse she employed to convince herself that she didn't like feeling his solid presence along her back, touching from shoulders to toes, nor the warm, damp gusts of his breath against her nape.

She tried telling herself that his body was heavy and intrusive, when actually she relished the feel of it against hers. So much so that she reflexively snuggled closer to him.

Her eyes opened wide when she was alarmingly reminded that Judd's sleeping attire had been chosen for maximum comfort and left no doubt that she was in bed with an extremely virile man. Hoping that she wouldn't awaken him, she turned her head slightly.

He snuffled, stirred and opened his eyes. Their faces were very close. Stevie felt as though the bizarre occasion called for something. A thank-you. A tension-breaking laugh. A reprimand.

She neither said nor did anything, only lay there staring into a rugged, well-lived-in, beard-roughened face that was becoming distressingly dear to her.

When Judd finally moved, it was only to spread wide his fingers against her abdomen and to press it gently with the heel of his hand. Then, moving that hand to the curve of her waist, he slowly drew her onto her back.

His eyes went on a silent tour of her, touching everywhere: her hair, which he was lazily sifting through his fingers, her eyes, her mouth, her throat. He smiled with amusement as they roved down the prim bodice of her girlish nightgown to the satin bow that made it seductive. Gradually his gaze made its way back up to hers.

He moved again, this time to bracket her shoulders with his elbows. He used them to prop himself inches above her. He pressed one of his legs between hers, smooth flesh against rough. His thigh lay warmly and heavily in her cleft.

He took her face between his hands, sliding his fingers up through her hair and curving them around her head. His thumbs made light passes across her lips. They parted. The point of separation seemed to intrigue him, and he investigated it with the tip of his thumb.

Then he lowered his head and replaced his stroking

thumbs with a kiss as soft as the summer rain falling upon the leaves of the trees outside.

Reflexively Stevie's arms went around him. She splayed her hands over his broad back. Gaining confidence, she rubbed them up and down, eventually going as far as the dimples in the small of his back.

He released a low, primitive groan and pressed his tongue between her lips. His lips slanted across hers to achieve the best fit and ultimate satisfaction. His tongue probed deeply, masterfully, but unhurriedly. It was a tranquil, sleepy, rainy morning kiss.

It was delicious.

When it was over and they pulled apart, they gazed at each other with drowsy complacence. Strands of her hair had become enmeshed in his stubble. She reached up to pull them away, but he caught the tip of her finger between his teeth and nipped it, then bathed the ball of it with his soft, damp tongue.

She investigated his face with her hands, as one blind, ghosting over the rough, masculine features with curious fingertips. She tried in vain to smooth out the dense eyebrows, though she thought they were incredibly attractive just as they were.

He bent his head and kissed her bare shoulder. She slipped her arms beneath his again and gave him a hard, urgent hug, wanting to feel his weight pressing down on her again.

He granted her wish, readjusting his body against hers for an even more tantalizing match, then slightly rocking them together. His mouth tenderly ate at hers, giving it kiss after kiss—open, hot, wet and deep.

Slowly, taking it one small button at a time, he unfastened her nightgown. When he got to the satin bow, he raised his head and watched as his fingers pulled on one end of the ribbon until it came free. He moved the cotton aside.

Stevie gauged his reaction with trepidation, but there was nothing glowing in his hazel eyes except admiration and desire. His tanned fingers curved around her paler skin, cupping her breast. His expression grew as soft as the flesh he was gently supporting.

But Stevie didn't see that. By now her eyes were closed, and, between parted lips, her breath rushed in and out on shallow pants. Judd nuzzled the breast he held, rubbing it with his nose, his chin, his lips, lightly scratching it with his bearded cheeks. Stevie murmured with want and need, and responsively pressed her thigh against his, tilting her hips up and forward.

He kissed the very center of her breast, then took it between his lips and drew it into his mouth. After suckling her with tempered fervency, he kissed her raised nipple. He flicked it rapidly and lightly with the tip of his tongue.

Sensations exploded in her belly like holiday sparklers. She gave a glad, wordless cry. Judd pressed her femininity with his knee and made a grinding motion against it. She clutched his back, digging into the hard muscles.

He sent his hand beneath the sheet, beneath the nightgown, beneath the brief silk panties to caress softness and warmth and woman.

That's when they heard the knocking on the door downstairs, urgent knocking that couldn't be ignored.

The first words with which Judd greeted the new day were precise and profane.

* * *

He practically tore the front door off the hinges getting it open. A sodden delivery man, wearing a dripping yellow slicker, didn't look any happier to be there than Judd was to have him there.

"Took you long enough," the man complained.

"I was in bed."

"Hope you appreciate me coming all the way out here in this." He indicated the downpour that had made a quagmire of the clearing surrounding the house. Stevie's valiant little plants were lying vanquished in the mud like victims of a sea battle.

"Oh, yeah, I'm thrilled to see you," Judd mumbled sarcastically as he scrawled his signature along the dotted line of the receipt.

The delivery man handed him the plastic-wrapped overnight letter, hunkered deeper into his slicker and ran down the porch steps to his waiting van. Judd slammed the front door.

"Who was it?"

"A delivery for me."

"From whom?"

In his querulous mood, he hadn't even thought to check. When he read the return address, he cursed. "Mike Ramsey."

"What is it?"

"How the hell do I know? I haven't opened it yet."

He'd never been this frustrated in his life. There they'd been, in that cozy, rumpled bed, kissing like crazy, temperatures rising, things progressing nicely, and now *this*. He could gladly murder Ramsey for unwittingly interrupting.

He was none too pleased to see that Stevie had

quickly dressed. Her eyes looked enormous in her wan face, her expression a blend of apprehension and guilt.

Damn! He still had the taste of her mouth and the feel of her breast on his tongue. Even as enraged as he was over the interruption, all he could really think about was resuming where they'd left off.

But instinct told him that it wasn't going to happen. That's why he was so angry. Given a chance to think about it, to reconsider, to let her passions cool, she had backed out.

There was always an outside chance, however, that he was wrong, Judd thought optimistically.

He took a step toward her where she stood poised, as though for flight, on the bottom stair. He looked at her longingly and spoke her name in a hoarse, aroused voice. "Stevie?"

Wetting her lips nervously, she said, "I'll put on the coffee," and headed toward the kitchen at a pace that could fairly be classified as a run.

Judd waited to follow her until he'd exhausted his repertoire of obscenities. Having spent a majority of his adult life either in a locker room or newsroom, that file cabinet of his vocabulary was extensive.

Wearing only the shorts he'd pulled on before going downstairs to answer the door, he went into the kitchen. Flopping into a chair at the table, he ripped open the cardboard envelope while Stevie stood waiting for the coffee to finish perking.

Judd read the one-page, single-spaced, typed letter, then balled it up and stuffed it into the pocket of his shorts. "How long before that coffee is ready?"

"A few more minutes. What did your editor say?"

"Nothing of importance."

"Then why are you looking so surly?"

"Because I haven't had my coffee yet." He sounded testy even to his own ears. But it wasn't Stevie he was aggravated with. It was Ramsey, the situation, his aroused body that refused to relax. "There are other more…*pressing* reasons for my crankiness, but I don't think you really want to hear the details, do you?"

She gave a quick, negative shake of her head.

"I didn't think so," he said in an undertone.

"Is Mr. Ramsey begging now? Is he as low as a slug and groveling?"

"No."

"Then what does he have to say?"

"Not much."

*"What's in the letter?"*

Her outcry took him by surprise. Shifting his attention from his straining sex to her, he saw that she was drawn up as tight as a high-octave piano wire and obviously none too pleased with his reticence. "All right, you guessed. The letter was about you."

The instant he confirmed it, she dropped into the chair opposite his. "What did he say?"

"He informed me that you are missing," he said with a wry smile. "He told me that I was losing out on the hottest sports story so far this year. All any sports fan is talking about these days is Stevie Corbett's mysterious disappearance following her collapse at Lobo Blanco."

The light on the percolator blinked on, indicating that the coffee was ready. Stevie hadn't noticed it, so he got up. Returning to the table with two steaming mugs, he set one down in front of her and sipped at his own before continuing.

"Mike urged, *strongly* urged, that I stop pouting and

come back to work immediately. He says that with my network of sources, I should be able to track you down before anybody else gets warm." Smiling into his steaming mug, he added, "He seems to have conveniently forgotten that he fired me."

"What are they saying?"

"Who?"

"All the sportswriters. Surely there've been theories on my disappearance."

"Ah, let's see, Mike mentioned something about suicide and—"

*"Suicide?"*

"That's one rumor, yes, but since your body hasn't been found…" He shrugged. "Another hypothesis is that you're secretly hospitalized somewhere. And there's been mention of an exclusive and revolutionary cancer treatment center in the Bahamas. I've been instructed to forget my novel for the moment and find out which guess about the 'Corbett broad'—and that's a quote—is right."

"He knows about your novel?"

"I've mentioned it off and on."

She had hit the nail on the head during their shouting match the night before. For years he had been telling anybody who would listen about this terrific sports novel he was going to write someday. But someday had just never got around to happening.

Until now. It was here. After many false starts over the years, he was finally into the novel and loving every minute of it. It was gut-wrenching, head-splitting, nerve-racking, ego-deflating work, but the prospect of having to set it aside indefinitely was unappealing.

On the other hand, he had financial obligations—

like his expensive European car—that his checking account could cover for about another two weeks, and that was stretching it. He had to make a living to support his writing habit.

The solution to his problem was sitting across his grandma's oak table.

He was right on top of a hot sports story that he could sell to the highest bidder. With that nice, fat nest egg to fall back on, he could kiss Ramsey and the *Tribune* column goodbye, at least temporarily, and work full-time on the book he had to expunge from his system whether or not it was ever published.

"What are you going to do?"

Inadvertently Stevie had voiced the question he was wrestling with himself. She had the sense to look worried. She knew the importance of his decision and the impact it would have on her. She realized how valuable her story would be to the journalist who had an exclusive.

Judd ran his hand down his face. He felt terrible for a variety of reasons. His lower body was persistent in its reminders that it was as yet unappeased. A queasiness had seized his stomach, which he attributed to drinking his coffee too fast, although he knew better. It was the thought of another golden opportunity slipping through his fingers that made him ill.

He answered the only way he could, the only way that felt right. "I'm going back to work."

He saw her swallow hard, but watched with admiration as she lifted her chin a notch. "In Dallas?"

She had guts, alright. He wondered how he'd missed seeing that during all these years that he'd been poking fun at her in his column.

"No. In the dining room."

"You won't…won't tell anybody where I am?"

"It'll remain our little secret for as long as you want it that way."

Her relief was visible. She relaxed her rigid posture. Still, she didn't gush gratitude. She didn't genuflect. "Good," she said simply. "That will make my life easier, and I'm glad you're not forsaking your novel."

"Last night you said it sounded self-indulgent, boring and…what was the other word, disgusting?"

She had the grace to look chagrined. "You provoked me to speak unkindly."

"Speaking of provocative," Judd said, slowly leaving his chair and rounding the table, "this morning was—"

"Judd." She popped out of her chair as though her bottom had discovered a splinter in the smooth wood. "I wanted to explain about that."

He actually felt his face muscles forming his frown. "What's to explain?"

"Why it happened."

"I know why it happened. It's called lust, which according to Webster's is a noun meaning a desire to gratify the senses, bodily appetite, sexual desire, especially as seeking unrestrained gratification."

If the venomous look she shot him was any indication, she didn't think that was cute. "I was disoriented. Those pills are strong. I wasn't thinking clearly."

She was backing away from him, staying just beyond his reach. That angered him as much as her excuse for her passion, which he knew damned good and well had been as all-encompassing as his.

"Oh, I see," he said. "You couldn't desire me unless

you were under the influence of a controlled substance. Is that what you're saying?"

"Not exactly."

"Then what? Exactly."

"I don't want to make love with you," she declared curtly.

He barked a short laugh. "Like hell you don't."

That steamed her; he could tell. By now he knew the signs: a suffusion of color in her cheeks, a darkening of her eyes, which were the warm, soft color of expensive scotch but a hell of a lot more intoxicating, a determined lift of her chin.

"My life is in crisis," she said in a tight voice. "So is yours. Neither of us needs a romance right now with anybody, but especially not with each other. Maybe we should have taken our cue from Stockholm and—"

"I did. You were hot and ready for me then, too."

Stevie closed her hands into fists and took a deep breath. "We've only got a few days left before I promised to give my manager an answer. During that time, I think we should keep our friendship strictly platonic."

He drew close and sneered, "Tell that to your glands, baby."

She gasped with outrage, then whirled out of the room and up the stairs. He tore after her and got as far as the staircase before he stopped.

The Judd Mackie who hung out with the guys in bars after ball games and boxing matches was urging him not to be a nerd, to go after her. One kiss, one well-placed caress, and she'd be putty in his hands again, begging for it.

He deserved it, didn't he? Hell, he had given up two weeks' pay on her account, not to mention an outstanding story that would have earned him untold income. If his car got repossessed it would be *her* fault.

He had been hospitable, providing her safe refuge and fresh country air, meanwhile banishing himself from his own life and all the pleasures it afforded him, namely booze and broads.

She had cost him time, trouble and money. Was it asking too much for one roll in the hay?

But the Judd Mackie who knew that one roll in the hay with this particular woman would never be enough and who had promised that her secret was safe, forced him to turn and head for the dining room and the waiting typewriter.

Being honorable was new to him. He was bound to suffer a few growing pains, but figured that if he had any character at all, he could endure a few disappointments.

*Slightly more than a "disappointment,"* his wicked side mocked. It cruelly reminded him how much he wanted her sexually by flashing him a mental image of her breasts, flushed and dewy from his mouth's caress.

*Look,* he argued with his darker self, *I've never had to coerce any woman into bed with me and damned if I'm going to start with Stevie Corbett. Besides, I'm going to be so immersed in my book, I won't have time to think about sex.*

To which his tormentor cackled, *Tell that to your glands, baby.*

# *Eleven*

It rained steadily for two days, forty-eight interminable hours during which they had to tolerate the weather that kept them indoors, each other's fractious mood, the specter of their thwarted lovemaking—which each wanted to diminish in importance but neither could— and the desire that was as tenacious as the inclement weather.

During mealtimes they hardly spoke because when they did the conversations invariably resulted in arguments. To while away one long afternoon, Stevie drove into town and bought the foods necessary to prepare a special dinner, one that would showcase all her epicurean skills.

That turned out to be the evening Judd chose to write through dinner without taking a break. He asked her to bring him a tray in the dining room. After she had spent hours in the kitchen preparing the sumptuous meal, his simple request was tantamount to a declaration of war. She told him from the arched doorway that he could fix his own damn dinner tray and then go straight to hell.

They had another argument over the bathroom.

"Please don't leave damp towels on the floor," she said snippily.

"I wouldn't have to if you didn't hang every garment you own on the towel racks and curtain rod." He swatted at the damp lingerie dangling over the tub.

"Where am I supposed to hang them up to dry in weather like this?"

"Ever heard of a clothes dryer?"

"I can't dry my underwear in a clothes dryer."

Her incredulous comeback seemed to make no sense to him whatsoever. With a snarl and a curse, he stamped from the bathroom.

"It wouldn't hurt you to shave, you know," she called after him.

"What difference does it make to you?"

So it went until, finally, around noon of the third day, the rain stopped. An hour later the sun came out. Steam rose off the puddles in the yard, making the atmosphere as humid as a South Seas island.

Stevie ventured outside first to inspect her battered flower beds. The new plants lay in the mud, but she was confident that a few hours of sunshine would revive them.

"Are they on the critical list?"

Judd ambled out onto the porch. He was wearing his standard wardrobe—shorts. The only variation from day to day was the color of them. He no longer seemed to have any self-consciousness about his scarred leg. Most of the time he went without a shirt and shoes. Clasping his hands together, he turned them inside out and raised them high over his head in an expansive stretch.

"They'll make it, I think," Stevie said, averting her

eyes from the fine line of dark hair that arrowed into his waistband.

"I think I've grown bunions on my backside from sitting so long." He lowered his arms to absently rub that particular part of his splendid anatomy. "Want to play some tennis this afternoon?"

No suggestion had ever sounded so good. She desperately needed a hard, pounding match to work off her frustration. Maybe then she wouldn't feel as though her skin were shrinking around her, making everything inside her body feel tight and constricted.

"By all means," she told him. "Just say when."

"When. As soon as we get into the proper duds."

"And as soon as you shave."

He rubbed his bearded jaw. "You drive a hard bargain, lady." She stood her ground. Chuckling, he conceded. "Okay, okay, I'll shave."


"Fifteen, forty."

Bouncing the ball in preparation for her next serve, Stevie muttered, "I know the score."

"Sorry," Judd said, cupping his ear, "I didn't catch that."

Raising her voice, she repeated, "I said I know the score, thank you."

"You're welcome."

Gnashing her teeth, Stevie executed her toss and caught the descending ball at just the right angle, putting exactly the right amount of spin on it. Judd shouldn't have been able to return it.

He did. Easily. And because she hadn't expected him to, she was caught falling down on the job. She didn't make it to the corner of the court in time and missed the return by a mile.

"My game," he said cheerfully. "That makes it five to four, my serve. And we switch courts."

"I know the rules, Mackie."

She wrenched the top off the water thermos they'd brought along and tilted it to her lips. He had won the first set. She had barely taken the second in a tiebreaker. With this game, he could win the match. The possibility was untenable.

He was a smug, gloating winner who was enjoying rubbing her nose in her defeat. Oh, he was doing it sweetly, but she was suspicious of that guileless grin, which many times during the course of the match she'd wanted to slap off his recently shaven face.

She mopped her face with a towel and dried off the handle of her racquet before walking back onto the court.

"We're in no hurry," he said to her from the baseline, where he'd been practicing his toss. "If you need more rest time, feel free to take it."

Gritting her teeth, she said, "Just play."

"Okay."

He lobbed the ball like a rank amateur, so that his serve was high and had the hang time of a well-executed football punt. It bounced high. Stevie had to back up almost to the fence and that destroyed the timing of her forehand swing. Her return went straight into the net.

"Fifteen, love," Judd chortled.

Stevie threw down her racquet. "What the hell was that?"

"That was a missed shot."

She saw red. "I mean your serve, Mackie."

"What?" He spread his arms wide, all innocence. "You seemed a little tired today, off your game. I thought I'd make it easier for you."

"Don't do me any favors, alright?"

"All right." Then beneath his breath, but loud enough for her to hear, he muttered, "Geez, and I thought McEnroe was temperamental when his game went to crap."

Stevie tried to ignore him and her own mounting rage, knowing well that it was counterproductive and self-defeating, His serve came in low and hard on her backhand side. She returned it. They enjoyed a rally, but Stevie ended up with the point when her well-aimed overhead bounced directly in front of his feet.

"Fifteen all," she said with a sweet smile.

"Good shot."

"Thanks."

Thinking that she would try a similar shot on the next point, she moved to the net too soon. Judd sent a long backhand into the corner of the court and announced with satisfaction, "Thirty, fifteen."

She tied it up on his next serve. "Thirty all," she called out gaily.

Judd's smile wasn't quite as ingratiating as it had been, she noted with satisfaction. She watched his toss, saw the granite set of his jaw, saw his arm go back then arc forward. But just before he hit the ball, he said, "You forgot to wiggle."

The ball whizzed past her like a missile, bounced in the corner of the service court and landed against the fence with a solid *thwack*. Stevie rounded on her complacent opponent, who was inspecting the strings of his racquet.

"What was *that*?"

"That was an ace, something that doesn't get pulled on you very often."

She marched toward the net, a study in fury. "I'll tell you something else that doesn't get pulled on me. I've never played anybody who opened a conversation just as he was serving the ball. Nobody I know would resort to such a dirty, underhanded trick. Nobody but you, that is. What did you say, anyway? Something about a wiggle?"

"I said you forgot to wiggle."

She propped her hands on her hips. "And what, pray tell, does that mean?"

"Aw, come on, Stevie. We're alone here. We can be open with each other." He leaned across the net and gave her a knowledgeable wink. "I was referring to that little wiggle you give your backside every time you win a point."

Her mouth dropped open. "I have no idea—"

"Sure you do. You do it all the time. It's to make certain that everybody watching, whether from the stadium bleachers or on television, realizes that you've just done something swell."

It took an act of will to stop grinding her teeth. "I don't have to stand out here in this heat and listen to your insults." Reflexively she lifted her long braid off her chest and tossed it over her shoulder.

Judd aimed the handle of his racquet at her like an accusing finger. "That's another one."

"Another one what?"

"Another one of your cuteisms. The one with the braid is to show your degree of frustration either with yourself, your opponent or a line judge."

*"Cuteisms?"*

He flashed a proud grin. "I coined the word to encompass all the mannerisms you use to draw attention from your game to yourself. Since the way you look is irrelevant to the way you play, you're very clever to use such a tactic."

Stevie was too furious to speak. If she tried, she'd only succeed in sputtering incoherently. She turned her back to him and marched toward the parked car.

"Aren't we going to finish the match?"

"No!"

"You're quitting when it's match point?"

"Yes!"

"Why, because I'm about to beat you?" he taunted, falling into step behind her. "You couldn't stand being beaten by me, could you?"

"I'm having an off day. You said so yourself. It's the heat. I haven't practiced in days."

"Neither have I," he pointed out uncharitably. "And it's just as hot on my side of the court."

She slung her gear into the back seat of his car and got into the passenger side, slamming the door. He got behind the wheel and drove while she sat beside him, fuming in hostile silence.

The pressure had been steadily building. They had been working up to this fight for days. Erroneously Stevie had thought she would welcome a full-fledged blowout as a means of clearing the air. But she was far from having a good time. Probably because Judd definitely had the upper hand in this argument.

"There's nothing wrong with being a showman."

They were more than halfway home before he made that seemingly innocuous observation. It was enough to send Stevie's simmering temper skyrocketing.

"You don't get to be a top-seeded player by being cute, Mr. Mackie."

"Calm down. I'm not going to tell anybody that I beat you."

"You didn't!"

"Only because you refused to finish the match like the spoiled brat you are."

"You weren't playing tennis," she shouted. "The points you scored were scored by playing badly, not well. You were making a mockery of me and of the sport. Your game had nothing to do with talent, skill or finesse." Wanting to drive the next point home, she turned her head to look at him. "The same goes for your writing."

He brought the car to a jarring stop in front of the house. "What the hell is that supposed to mean?"

"You figure it out."

Leaving her things in the car, she got out and bounded up the porch steps. They hadn't bothered with locking the front door. She sailed through it and headed for the stairs. She had almost reached the top when Judd, taking the steps two at a time, caught up with her and grabbed hold of her braid.

"Ouch! Let go of me."

"Uh-uh. Not until you explain that last crack about my writing. What do you mean by saying that I lack talent and skill, etcetera?"

"I didn't say you lack them. There's just no evidence of them in your column."

"I graduated with a degree in journalism, remember?"

"What you print every day isn't journalism, it's gossip," she said, warming to her topic. "Anybody with an inferiority complex and an ax to grind could write what you do. So could anybody who wanted to avoid a real job by boozing it up every night and calling it research. Not to mention the womanizing."

"I haven't touched a drink since we got here. And as for womanizing…" He encircled her waist with his arm and yanked her hard against him. "I haven't done any of that since I left Dallas, either."

"Let me go."

"No way, baby. I've earned this kiss."

His mouth came down hard upon hers. She resisted by bowing her back, which only brought her up harder and higher against him. She tried to free her lips, but he captured her jaw in one hand and held her head steady while his tongue plumbed her mouth repeatedly.

Their breathing was harsh and loud in the otherwise silent house. The sounds of strenuous denial that Stevie uttered deep in her throat diminished to whimpers of desire. Her hands, which had been trying to push him away, began clutching handfuls of his damp tennis shirt. She angled her head, giving his lips better access to hers. Her tongue joined his in love play.

He raised his head suddenly and peered into her wide, dazed eyes. "Stevie?"

"What?"

Taking her hand, he slid it down his body and pressed it against the distended fly of his tennis shorts. "It wouldn't be fair of you to start something you don't intend to finish, would it?" She shook her head and reflexively squeezed the rigid proof of how much he wanted her. "Oh, God." Groaning, he gave her another searing kiss.

Pent-up frustration erupted in an explosion of sexual

desire. Their arms wrapped tightly around each other. Their kisses were carnal, ravenous.

Still clinging to each other, they stumbled into the nearest bedroom, his. Blindly he reached for the switch of the ceiling fan. It began to rotate over their heads and cast flickering shadows on the walls as they worked off shoes and bent to remove their socks. They bumped heads but barely noticed in their haste.

He whipped his T-shirt over his head. Stevie did the same. He reached for the front clasp of her bra and unfastened it, shoving the lace cups aside. He touched her briefly, feathering her nipples with his fingertips, making them instantly stiff.

Eyes trained on them, he unzipped his shorts and let them drop. Stevie shrugged off her bra and removed her shorts. Judd, with some difficulty and a near-comical grimace, removed his jock strap.

Stevie couldn't bring herself to glance down, though she wanted to. She hooked her thumbs into the elastic of her panties, but couldn't bring herself to take them off, either. She looked up at him with silent appeal.

"That's good enough for now," he whispered taking her hand and pulling her toward the bed.

He lay down on his back and pulled her on top of him. Cupping her head between his hands, he gave her a long, thorough kiss, sending his tongue deep into her mouth. His legs sawed restlessly against hers. One knee insinuated itself between her thighs and worked its way up until she was riding it.

With one hand, he began tugging her underpants down over her hips. Then he rolled her onto her back and removed them completely. His eyes swept her hungrily. His hands skimmed the surface of her body, touching her breasts, nipples, thighs, the cluster of curls covering her mound.

"Stevie," he mumbled thickly before levering himself above her and pressing his face into the cover of her shoulder.

"Judd?"

"Yes, sweetheart, right now."

"Maybe you should know—"

"I do know, baby. Believe me, I do."

"I'm a virgin."

# *Twelve*

His head popped up. Eyes that had been foggy with passion came into sharp focus as instantly as a high-tech camera.

"A *what*?"

Even after she repeated the word, he stared at her with patent disbelief. Slowly he eased himself up, rolled over to his side and sat on the edge of the bed, keeping his back to her.

"God, I wish I hadn't quit smoking."

He rested his face in his hands, digging into his eye sockets with the pads of his fingers. Eventually he peered at her over his shoulder. She had self-consciously pulled the bedspread over her.

"How did you wind up a virgin?" She gazed at him with puzzlement. "I'll rephrase. Why, *how*, are you still a virgin?"

"Maybe you should have finished what you started in Stockholm."

"With Presley Foster breathing down my neck? No thanks. Did he scare off all your would-be lovers?"

"In fairness to him, no. I did. Not overtly," she added

when he gave her a curious look. "I just never took the time to let anything develop. Potential boyfriends always took second place to tennis."

"Second place isn't a healthy or desirable spot for a man's ego."

"So I discovered." She moistened her lips nervously. "I wouldn't have told you if I'd known you were going to stop."

"I wouldn't have gone so far if you had told me sooner."

"Does it matter that much?"

He laughed hoarsely, humorlessly. "Yeah, it matters. A lot."

"Why? I don't think it would have mattered in Stockholm."

"Maybe, maybe not. But in Stockholm I was young and stupid. Now I'm old and stupid. At least when you're young and stupid you've got an excuse for being stupid."

Stevie closed her eyes briefly, then she stretched out her arm and laid her hand on his bare shoulder. "Please, Judd, come back."

Keeping his eyes averted, he stubbornly shook his head no. "I can't assume that responsibility, Stevie."

"It doesn't come with obligations."

"They're implied."

"Not to me."

"To me."

"Please."

"I said no."

A small, strangled sob escaped her.

Judd's head snapped around. He saw her tears, saw the pleading in her eyes. Apparently they touched him in a way her temper tantrums could not. The resolution keeping his lips compressed and uncompromising deserted him. His features softened.

He lay down beside her again and drew her against him. "Don't cry, Stevie. Don't." Typically a cynic where women's tears were concerned, he held her close and kissed her brow with commiseration.

She nuzzled his naked chest, rubbing her face against the pelt of crinkling hair. "Please, Judd, make love to me while I'm still whole. I want it to be you."

"Why?"

"Sentiment, maybe. Even though you doubt it, I know it would have happened in Stockholm if Presley hadn't stopped us." She touched his nipple with the tip of her tongue, licking it deftly, and pressed her palm against his hot, swollen flesh.

"Oh, baby," he moaned, threading his fingers up through her hair. "Stop."

"I don't want to stop."

"You've got to, or—"

"I want to be a complete woman once. Just once, Judd, please."

She dusted his chest with soft, airy kisses, swinging her head back and forth as she worked her way down. She kissed his stomach, then his belly, which was rapidly rising and falling. Her lips tracked the satiny stripe of hair that fanned out denser and coarser on his lower body. He was in a state of supreme agitation and had almost reached the point of no return when he closed his fingers around her head and raised it.

He rolled her to her back and leaned over her. "Okay," he rasped breathlessly, "if you're sure."

"Absolutely sure." He nodded grimly. Laughing, she

touched the corners of his mouth. "Your frown is death to my ego. You could look a little happier about it."

"I'm worried."

"I told you not to be. There are no strings attached."

"It isn't that."

"Then what?" Her eyes rounded and she gasped. "You *do* know how, don't you?" she asked teasingly.

"Yeah, I know how," he said, his intensity unchanged. "And hard and fast isn't the way to do it the first time. If you keep doing stuff like that…" He blew out a breath and shook his head as though to clear it. "I'm going to set the tempo. Got that?"

She nodded obediently, though she wasn't sure she could keep such a rash promise when her blood was surging through her veins with a mix of want and wonder. She wasn't sure Judd could stick with the plan, either. His breathing wasn't any steadier than hers and his face was ruddy with arousal.

"All right, kiss me," he instructed her huskily. "Forget everything you've ever heard about technique. Kiss me the way you think a 'bad girl' would and we'll both have a much better time."

Taking his advice as a challenge, Stevie linked her arms around his neck and drew his head down. His open mouth met hers, and it was a melding of dual passions. His tongue probed the soft, wet heat of her mouth, sliding in and out, mating with her tongue, which then returned the favor to him, apparently to his satisfaction, for he groaned with pleasure and drew it deeper into his mouth.

His hands rubbed her back, then gradually pulled the bedspread from between them until they were lying naked face-to-face again. She felt the warm, smooth tip of his shaft against her belly. His thighs pressed against hers. Her breasts lay lush and full against his hard chest; her nipples nestled in the dark, curly hair.

All the sensations were exquisite. The contact with his raw masculinity made her feel wholly female. She wondered how she had survived this long without being intimately acquainted with his body.

And she realized at that moment that she was falling madly in love with her enemy.

Asking him to make love to her had little or nothing to do with Stockholm or with sentiment, or any other excuse she could have conjured up. She wanted to be with Judd, be a part of him, entirely, without reservation or inhibition. It was as simple as that.

Though, actually, it wasn't simple at all. It was very complex. Too complex to muddle through while his mouth was inching down her throat.

He scooped her breast toward his descending mouth and sucked on the tip with strong, urgent tugging motions that touched off responsive chords in her womb. "Ah, Judd," she cried in ecstasy.

"You're sweet, Stevie. Very sweet." He moved to her other breast while his fingers caressed the nipple he'd just left wet and erect.

"Please," she gasped moments later as his tongue feathered one stiff crest. She thrust her hips forward, grinding them against his rigid manhood.

Moaning low, he smoothed one hand down her body and between her thighs. He caressed her gently, moving his fingers between the velvety folds. "Almost, but not quite," he told her, smiling gently into her face before lowering his head and kissing her stomach.

His hands stroked the insides of her thighs, urging

them to separate, though without any hint of threat, co-ercion or violation. He nipped her skin lightly with his teeth and bathed her navel with his tongue.

She cried his name sharply when he kissed the cluster of pale curls between her thighs. Then his tongue, soft and inquisitive and agile, entered her. He kissed her deeply, again and again, until her head was thrashing on the pillow and her body was quickening to the strokes of his tongue.

Rapturously she submitted to the spirals of sensation that were winding her being tighter and tighter. At the height of her release, she clutched handfuls of his hair and gasped his name.

A film of perspiration had broken out on her face when he raised himself above her. He sipped at it while he positioned himself between her thighs and lifted her hips against his.

Holding her there, he pressed into her by slow de-grees, letting her body gradually adjust to his hard length, so that by the time he was buried snugly inside her, the only difficulty either had experienced was in holding back the passion that demanded immediate fulfillment.

"You feel wonderful surrounding me," he whispered, softly kissing the lips she had bruised with her own teeth. He swallowed hard and squeezed his eyes shut for a moment, reveling in the ecstasy of being inside her. "You feel sensational."

She murmured his name in a breathy voice while her fingers ghosted lovingly over his face. She was unaware of the tears that glistened in her eyes, but he saw them.

"Are you okay?"

She nodded her head quickly. "Yes, yes, yes."

"Well, I'm not," he said, baring his teeth. "I'm about to die. But, God, it's a helluva way to go."

He began moving inside her, stroking her until they were both senseless and all that mattered was succumbing to the tumult of emotion that seized them. When they did, he pressed his forehead upon hers and chanted her name.

"Want me to—"

"No."

Judd chuckled. "You didn't let me finish."

"Whatever it is, I don't want you to do it because you'd have to move. And if you move, I'll have to," she said, yawning listlessly, "and I don't think I can."

Judd did move, but only to pull her into the circle of his arms and prop his chin on the top of her head. Stevie moved, too, curving her arm around his waist.

"Why did you taunt me on the tennis court this afternoon?" she asked.

"Because you were playing poorly, and the reason you were was that you didn't consider me a worthy opponent and, therefore, weren't putting forth any effort."

"I was playing poorly, yes, but not because I didn't consider you a worthy opponent."

"Then why?"

"My head wasn't in the game."

"Where was it?"

"Here."

"Here?" Judd angled his head back. "You mean here, like we are now?"

"Hmm."

"You just won't let me lie, will you?" he said around a resigned sigh. "In all honesty, that's the reason I was taunting you." Stevie lifted her head off his chest and looked up at him, her expression questioning. "Making love to you is all I've thought about since the other morning when we were interrupted."

"Me, too."

"All you had to do was ask, lady."

"I did."

He looked chagrined. "Oh, yeah, you did, didn't you? Well, you know what I mean."

Smiling, she returned her head to his chest and began idly plucking at the hairs tickling her nose. "I can't believe I'm lying here like this with you, naked and sated. I've often thought that if I ever got you alone, I'd kill you slowly."

He placed his lips close to her ear. "If you hadn't come when you did and given me the green light, you might have succeeded." She giggled and gave his buttock a hard pinch. "Imagine the headlines," he went on, undaunted, "'Famous Tennis Pro Screws Famous Sportswriter to Death.'"

"Will you behave? This is serious. I don't think you realize how badly your nasty articles have wounded me."

His soft laughter subsided. "Why didn't you just consider the source and blow them off?"

"Because almost everything you've written about me is true."

His hand ceased strumming her spine. He eased her off him, placed her on her back, and rolled to his side. Propped on one elbow and leaning over her, he asked, "What are you talking about?"

"Off-the-record?"

"In journalistic circles, when the interview*er* is in

bed with the interview*ee* in a state of undress and sexual repletion, it's generally understood that whatever is said is unprintable."

"Oh. Thank you for clarifying that."

"You're welcome. Now quit stalling and run that by me again. What do you mean, everything I've written about you is the truth?"

"A lot of it was. You've often said that I don't belong on a tennis court. In a way, you're right, Judd. From the very beginning my father discouraged me from playing because tennis was 'a rich kid's sport.' I played anyway, but what he had said stuck with me. It gave me a complex. I wasn't like the other players. I wasn't as... as *privileged*."

"That's nonsense."

"Maybe, but that sense of inferiority compelled me to prove myself. I had to work harder at it than anyone else, always playing catch-up. I was accepted into most clubs because of my ability on the court, not my pedigree.

"I always had to be better," she stressed, making an appeal for his understanding, "because acceptance depended on it. That's why, when I was financially able, I always dressed well and played up to the spectators. Don't you see, Judd? I was saying, 'Hey, look at me. I'm worthy of your attention.' I was desperate to win approval. And, yes, sometimes I even resorted to being cute just to ensure that I wouldn't be ignored.

"You saw through all my machinations," she told him in a voice husky with emotion. "You had me pegged from the very beginning. Your columns struck terror in me because they were so incisive. I feared that if my insecurities were visible to you, they must be to everyone else. I'm the classic sufferer of the impostor syndrome. You were my worst nightmare, the person who would expose me."

His eyes were fixed on her lower lip, but he wasn't contemplating its sexiness so much as he was arranging his own thoughts.

"If all that is true, Stevie, it was an accident. If I tapped into your insecurities, it was by chance and had nothing to do with incisiveness. Fact is, I took digs at you because I resented that a cute, young thing like you could do what you did so well and reach the pinnacle of your sport, when I'd had to fall back on writing about how others were doing what I wanted to do myself. Hacking out that dumb column is a far cry from a career in professional baseball."

"It is not dumb," she said, laying a sympathetic hand along his cheek. "I only said it showed no talent or finesse because I was angry. You've cultivated a faithful reading audience that wouldn't miss a single acerbic word. No writer can do that for any length of time unless there's substance behind his writing. Your readers aren't fools, you know."

"Thanks for the compliment." He finally surrendered to the temptation and kissed her lower lip. "But I know, deep down, that I haven't done a single worthwhile thing since I had that waterskiing accident."

His hazel eyes became dark and intent. "Not until I brought you here. Maybe I've redeemed myself for all the jealousy I've harbored against you."

"Jealousy?"

"Of you and every other pro who made it. I've been lashing out at all of you to some extent, but you were the easiest one to single out."

"Why?"

"Because you were atypical. You weren't muscle-bound and unattractive, which was my chauvinistic, narrow-minded opinion of what a professional woman athlete should look like.

"And," he added around a deep breath, "as long as I'm baring my soul, I might just as well go all the way. I was still miffed about Stockholm. I wanted to go to bed with you, didn't get to, so I was sulking like the little boy who didn't get his candy. Maliciously I disparaged the very thing I desired. Pretty juvenile, huh?"

"Pretty human."

"You're being generous."

"I'm in a generous mood." She smiled up at him and drew a line down his nose with her fingertip. "To prove just how generous, I'll forgive you every nasty word you've ever written about me on one condition."

"What?" he asked suspiciously.

She whisked a kiss across his lips. "Make love to me again."

"Stevie, we really shouldn't."

"Why not?"

He hesitated, which was a mistake. She took advantage of his indecision by sliding her hand down his middle and cupping the full heaviness of his manhood.

"We shouldn't because it might…uh—" he became hard beneath her rhythmic stroking "—might not be good for you," he finished lamely.

"I'll be the judge of that." Her lips nibbled at his chin, her teeth making scratching sounds against his stubble. Her hand became even more persuasive, her thumb lazily inquisitive. "Please, Judd," she breathed against his lips.

Moaning, he clasped her around the waist and pulled her on top of him. "Well, since you asked so nicely...."

# *Thirteen*

Insects gave up their lives against the windshield of Judd's stolen car. The gooey smudges they created made little difference to the thief who could barely see the markings on the interstate highway through her tears.

Stevie wiped her nose on her sleeve. After seventy-five miles she would have thought her supply of fresh tears would be exhausted, but it wasn't. Each time she thought of what she had left behind and the ordeal that she was facing, another hot, salty batch filled her red, swollen eyes.

She had left him and he'd been furious.

Even now, her heartache was overshadowed by the fear that Judd might somehow catch up with her. Glancing once over her shoulder as she had sped away from the farmhouse, she had glimpsed him, wearing only his underwear, running down the porch steps. His fist had been raised. He was cursing her and the rock that had gouged his bare heel.

It could have been a comic sight; it hadn't been. It had broken her heart, and it was still broken. She rather imagined that it would remain broken for a long time.

The skyline of Dallas was glittering and glitzy against the western horizon, deep indigo now in the waning dusk. In an hour she would be at her condominium, she calculated mentally. Allow an hour to make necessary phone calls and pack. Then…

She refused to think beyond that. The only way she would get through this alone, without jeopardizing her sanity, would be to take it one step at a time. First things first. Getting home was first.

As she took the exit in the concrete labyrinth that connected one expressway to another, she permitted herself to reflect on their afternoon of lovemaking.

Judd, speaking softly and sexily. Judd, his hands instructive and sensuous, guiding her hips down over him. Judd, hard and full and smooth, filling her. Judd, his lips hungry, yet tender, on her breasts. *Judd, Judd, Judd.*

She dashed tears out of her eyes as she switched lanes cautiously, unaccustomed to driving a sports car with an engine powerful enough to fly an airplane. He would never forgive her for "borrowing" it without his permission. He would never forgive her for leaving him stranded, either.

The farmhouse's old-fashioned bathtub had become a shrine in which they'd worshiped each other's bodies. Hands covered with soapy lather were the sexiest instruments ever employed to give carnal pleasure. Or was it that Judd just knew how to use them?

It had been a delight to discover that the undersides of her upper arms were particularly susceptible to open-mouthed kisses and that kisses to the backs of her knees left her weak.

Judd had a ticklish spot midway between his lowest rib and his right hipbone. He had a birthmark on his left shoulder blade, and he'd grown misty-eyed when she traced every inch of the ugly, jagged scars on his leg with her loving lips.

*This has always been an object of fantasy for me,* he had confessed, tugging lightly on her long, single braid.

*Really?*

*Really.*

*How?* He had only smiled mysteriously and demurred from telling her. *Then show me.*

Her seductive suggestion had turned his eyes smoky. When he acted out his fantasy with her full cooperation, their harmonious cries of fulfillment had echoed off the walls of the house.

That was the instant she knew unequivocally that she loved him, and her decision had dawned crystal clear. The solution to her dilemma had unexpectedly risen out of the murky depths of confusion and despair.

Life, in its simplest, most basic form was far more precious than any amenities it could afford, such as prizes and fame, respect and riches, the acceptance of either peers or strangers.

While Judd was still dressing, she had gone downstairs, ostensibly to prepare them a light supper. Instead she had grabbed her purse, taken his car keys, and left the house at a dead run, not so much because she feared his wrath over her deception and desertion, but because she feared that given time to think about it, she would change her mind.

She had got as far as the edge of the clearing before he ran out onto the porch, shouting after her, "What the hell? Stevie, come back. Where are you going?" Then, when he realized that she was escaping in their only means of transportation, he'd become furious.

"Damn you, what kind of stunt is this? Ouch! Hell!" Livid, he had cursed when he stepped on the stone. "When I catch up to you, I'll strangle you for this. Dammit," he had sworn, slamming one fist into his other palm.

Her condominium was dark. She was relieved to see that there was no one lurking about. Either the news hounds and merely curious had tired of their siege or had given up on Stevie Corbett altogether.

Her plants needed her immediate attention. She chided herself for forgetting to call the service that took care of them in her absence and vowed to do so at her earliest convenience, though God knew when that would be.

Her first telephone call went to her gynecologist, who was so glad to hear from her that he was nearly incoherent with relief.

"If I don't do it now, I might change my mind." She spoke so quickly that the words stumbled over each other. "I can be there in an hour. Can you make the arrangements that soon?"

He promised he could and would. The next call she made was to her manager.

"Stevie, thank God. I've been frantic."

"I needed time alone to think." She hadn't been alone, but Judd was too complicated to explain, even to herself. "I'm checking into the hospital tonight. The surgery is scheduled for tomorrow morning."

A significant pause ensued. "It's your decision, of course," he said.

"Yes, it is. My life is in the balance. That's more important than a career."

"Hey, it's only Wimbledon," he said with false cheer. "They have it every year. Next year it belongs to you."

They both knew better, but Stevie tried to inject enthusiasm into her voice when she said, "You'd better believe it."

He promised to notify everyone concerned and to issue a statement to the press, which had been having a field day speculating on her whereabouts.

"That's fine, but hold off until tomorrow after the surgery, okay? No matter what the outcome, we'd just as well tell them everything at once." He agreed before hanging up.

After the connection was broken, Stevie felt terribly alone. The silence in her house was depressing, so accustomed was she to hearing the pecking noise of Judd's typewriter in the background.

The framed photos on the walls, picturing her holding aloft trophies of victory, seemed to jeer at her. Memorabilia of her career mocked her from bookshelves and étagères. The prize from The French Open, so recently acquired, no longer seemed to belong to her.

"Too late to reconsider now," she reminded herself as she went into her bedroom and began packing a small suitcase. Then, like a prayer, she whispered, "Stevie, your life is in God's hands."

God had a lot of helpers.

At least there were innumerable people who got their hands on her before she ever made it to the operating room the following morning. By then she had been stripped of all dignity and privacy.

Leaving Judd's car locked in her garage—it wouldn't

do to have it stolen twice in one day—she was conveyed to the hospital by taxi.

In Admittance, she had to attach her signature to an endless number of insurance forms, as well as to a note to Jennifer. "My twelve-year-old daughter wants to grow up and be exactly like you," the star-struck receptionist told her.

From there she was taken to be X-rayed. Wearing nothing except a paper poncho, she was placed in a room as cold as a meat locker and instructed to wait, which she did for over an hour before an unapologetic technician came in to X-ray her lungs.

"There, that wasn't that bad, was it?" another technician asked as he slipped the syringe from her vein, from which he'd drawn what looked like a quart of blood. "You can relax now," he said, working her fingers out of the tight fist she'd formed. "Did I hurt you?"

"No," she replied gruffly. "I just don't like needles."

She was finally placed in a private room, but was granted little privacy. A stiff, no-nonsense nurse came swishing in with a sheaf of yet more forms to be signed. "They showed you the video tape downstairs?" she asked dispassionately. "Did you understand it?"

"Yes." The tape had explained all the things that could go wrong during abdominal surgery, each possibility more terrifying, irreversible and deadly than the last.

"Sign here, here and here."

The hospital chaplain came in next. "You're the celebrity in our midst," he said, flashing a glorious smile. After discussing the best remedy for tennis elbow, they bowed their heads over their clasped hands. He prayed for the skilled surgeon and her full, rapid recovery.

Stevie prayed for Judd's stone-bruised heel, forgiveness for stealing his car, protection from strangulation when he caught up with her and for a lawsuit against the hospital on her behalf if she should die on the operating table. She thought somebody should hold the institution accountable even if she'd signed forms absolving it of responsibility.

Her gynecologist came in next and explained the surgical procedure. "If the tumors are benign, and I have every reason to believe that they are, we'll remove them and you'll be as good as new."

"And if they're not?"

"Probably a complete hysterectomy, followed by treatment."

"What kind of treatment? Radiation?"

He patted her hand. "Let's get through the surgery first. Then if we have to discuss options, we will."

The anesthesiologist, who disturbingly reminded her of Count Dracula because of his steep widow's peak, came in and sat down on the edge of her bed. "First thing in the morning, you'll be given a sedative. We'll put in two IVs, one in your arm, the other on the back of your hand."

"I don't like needles," she said in a choked voice.

"I promise to send in my painless assistant. By the time you reach the operating room, you'll be drowsy. Sleep well tonight."

Sleep well? What a joke. She was cleansed from the inside out—a humiliating experience—and given a shot to make her sleepy. She refused anything to eat, even though it had been lunchtime that day since she'd had a bite.

Didn't any of these efficient ghouls realize that she

couldn't possibly go to sleep without the distant and reassuring sound of Judd's typewriter?

But he was miles away, stranded in the farmhouse. What if it caught fire and he couldn't get away? What if it began raining hard enough to cause a flash flood and he had no means of escaping high water? She tortured herself with hideous possibilities.

She must have slept, however, because when she was awakened by a smiling nurse, she was dreaming that Judd was chasing her with a foot-long hypodermic needle that was shaped like a tennis racquet, laughing maniacally and sneering that he'd teach her the consequences of stealing his car.

In a remarkably short time, she was prepped for surgery and, feeling like a pitifully abused pincushion, wheeled into the operating room. Where last night the hours had seemed to drag by, now everything accelerated to a rapid clip that panicked her. The surgeon squeezed her hand reassuringly and smiled from behind his mask.

"Everything is going to be fine, Stevie. Just relax now. Take deep breaths and start counting backward from ten."

Ten. *She wanted to halt things.* Nine. *She needed more time to think.* Eight. *She needed Judd.* Seven...

She weighed ten thousand pounds and these morons were ordering her to scoot across the bed. "That's it, roll to your other side, Miss Corbett. No, don't pull on your IVs. Just relax your arm. That's fine. Right there. Your operation is over."

"Is her catheter in?"

"Yes."

"Isn't her hair pretty?"

"Hmm. Ever seen her play?"

"Are you kidding? I can't afford the tickets."

"I meant on TV. Miss Corbett, did you hear me? Your operation is all over."

Clatter and clank of metal. Jarring motion. Light. So much light. Too bright. Telephones and activity and racket. Why didn't they just be still and quiet and let her sleep?

"Time to turn over again, Miss Corbett."

A groan. Her groan. No, don't make me move. A monster in green scrubs was insisting that she cough.

"Cough, Miss Corbett. Come on now. You've got to cough to clear your lungs." Let them stay clogged. "Miss Corbett. Cough."

She made a feeble attempt just so they'd leave her alone. Her reward was to have something very cold crammed between her thighs. "…to keep the swelling down." Someone jarred her bed again. Klutzes. They were all klutzes.

Her hand was tucked beneath the nurse's arm while she pumped the bulb of the blood pressure gauge. "That's good." The binding pressure around her arm was removed. "Miss Corbett, we've got to change your ice pack now."

"A drink?" Her mouth was sprouting cotton.

"You can have an ice chip."

A spoon, cold and hard, was crammed against her teeth, jarring her whole body. Precious ice. She sucked greedily.

"There, just that one. Turn over."

"I can't."

"Sure you can. Cough for me again."

"No."

"Cough." She did. "Good girl. And here's a fresh ice pack."

Thanks for nothing. My thighs are already numb.


"...can't come in here!"

"I'm in."

Stevie was aroused by the familiar voice, but opening her eyelids was nigh to impossible. Had they weighted them down with something, fifty-cent pieces like they did corpses in Western movies?

"Visitors are only allowed in Recovery every odd hour at ten till. That's the rule."

He told her what she could do with her rule and his suggestion wasn't very nice. "I'm going to see her whether you like it or not."

"I'm calling security."

"Stevie?"

"Judd?" she croaked.

"I'm here, baby."

A strong, warm hand clasped hers. She whispered, "Are you going to strangle me?"

"There he is, officer. He's not supposed to come in until ten till the hour."

"Later, baby."

A soft whisk of his lips across her forehead then he was gone.

It was probably just another bizarre dream.


"You're sure?"

"Positive."

"You took out everything even potentially dangerous?"

"Everything."

The doctor noticed that his patient's eyes were open and that she was solemnly regarding him and her disheveled visitor.

"You're doing fine, Stevie," he told her with his bedside smile firmly in place. "I know the recovery room is rough, but they'll be moving you to your room soon. Are you up to having a visitor?" She nodded. The doctor touched Judd on the shoulder. "Remember, only ten minutes. Don't get thrown out again."

Judd wasn't listening. His gaze was fixed on Stevie's face. He bent over her, careful not to dislodge any of the tubes. "I had to fight my way in here. I hope you appreciate it."

"How'd you find me?"

"I put Addison on your trail. I phoned him from a truck stop on the interstate. Ramsey wouldn't accept a collect call from me, the s.o.b., so I had to borrow change from the trucker I had hitched a ride with. He even felt so sorry for me that he bought me a cup of coffee, too. Turned out that he's based in Dallas and is an avid reader of my column. For his trouble, I promised him a season pass to the Mavericks' games."

She tried to follow the explanation, but it was far too complicated. "Addison?"

Smiling over her confusion, Judd said softly, "I'll tell you about it later. There's almost enough material there for another novel."

She tried to moisten her lips with her tongue, but her mouth was still too dry even though she had been allowed a few more ice chips. "Judd, what about my operation?"

He drew a more serious expression, leaned in closer, and when he spoke, it was in a raspy, confidential voice. "I might have known you were just showing off, pulling one of your cuteisms for the benefit of the crowd. Much ado about nothing."

"What was?"

"Your tumors. All those headlines and hoopla over a bunch of benign tumors." His tone was chastising, but there was a telltale moisture in his eyes.

"Benign?"

"Harmless little critters. Every last one of them."

She closed her eyes. Tears leaked from them. He brushed them away with the pad of his thumb. "They're sure?" she asked.

"If your gynecologist and the finest pathologist in Dallas know their stuff, it's a sure thing you're cured."

"Then they didn't have to do a hysterectomy?"

"If you discount your right ovary."

"They had to remove an ovary?"

He shrugged. "Inconsequential when you consider that everything else is intact and functioning. Oh, and while they were there, they took out your appendix. I told them I didn't think you'd mind."

"Judd," she whispered, tears of gladness bathing her cheeks.

"Hey, stop blubbering or that bitch of a nurse will have me kicked out again for disturbing the peace."

"You shouldn't have come."

"Those proverbial wild horses couldn't have kept me away."

Stevie sniffed back her tears. "I'm sorry I stole your car."

"What the hell? It really belongs to the bank more than it does to me anyway. Are you feeling okay?"

Laughing was out of the question, but she smiled. "I've got needles in my arm and hand, metal clamps holding my belly together, I can't even tee-tee on my own and I'm straddling an ice pack. They make me cough every so often, though I'm sure it rips out all my stitches. In short, I feel terrible."

"Not as terrible as I felt before I found out where you had gone. If you ever run out on me without an explanation again, I'll tan your hide."

She ignored the edict. "Did you write today?"

"Write?" he asked incredulously. "Stevie, I've been stalking the corridors of this hospital like a wild man waiting for you to come out of the anesthesia."

"You should've been home writing. Chapter seven needs work."

"Yeah, I know. It's dragging in—" He broke off. His eyebrows formed a fearsome V. "How in hell do you know what chapter seven needs?"

"I've been reading your novel."

"Since when?"

"Since you started it." She wanted to touch him badly, but couldn't find the wherewithal to raise her hand. "It's wonderful. Truly."

She felt the postoperative medication luring her back into oblivion. Before she succumbed, there was something she had to say. "Judd, I love you."

He took her hand and held it against his lips after pressing a fervent kiss on the backs of her fingers. "I figured that out when you decided to go for life instead of the Grand Slam. Want to know the real corker? I love you, too."

Smiling wryly, he realized that she'd drifted back to sleep. He regretted that she hadn't heard his first profession of love, but that was okay.

He would still be there when she woke up.

# *Epilogue*

❦

"Thank you."

"Thank *you*," the attractive young woman gushed. "I can't wait to read it. If it's half as good as your picture on the dust jacket, I'll be thoroughly entertained."

Judd glanced up at his wife, who was glaring at the gum-popping, high-strutting, miniskirted ingenue through slitted brown eyes. When they ventured back to her husband, he gave her a helpless shrug that was at odds with his smile, which defined masculine complacency.

"Mrs. Mackie, the line outside the door just keeps getting longer," the manager of the Manhattan bookstore said. "Mr. Mackie is going to be busy signing books for quite some time. Would you care to sit down?"

"I'm fine for now, but thank you."

He glanced at her shyly. "Would it be presumptuous of me to ask for your autograph, too."

"Not at all," she returned with a smile.

He produced a pad and pen. "I saw you play at the U.S. Open once."

"Did I win?"

"You lost in the quarter finals, but it was a close match."

Stevie only laughed.

"You're semiretired now, isn't that right?"

"I don't play competitive tennis anymore, but I'm busy organizing some instructional clinics."

"So I've heard. For underprivileged children, aren't they?"

After six months of recuperation following her surgery, her gynecologist had given her the go-ahead on any project she wanted to tackle.

Her brainstorm, which she had considered from every angle during her convalescence, had won Judd's hearty approval. He'd helped publicize the idea locally through his column in the *Tribune*. As a result, donations to support the project had poured in.

The original clinic in Dallas had received so many accolades that other cities had approached Stevie to organize similar programs for them. There were now Stevie Corbett Tennis Clinics nationwide, catering specifically to players who couldn't afford club memberships.

"The clinics are community supported and open to anyone who shows up wanting instruction," she said in response to the bookseller's question.

"Doesn't your husband mind sharing you with such a time-consuming undertaking?"

"Not at all. He understands my need to work. Besides, he's been busy himself."

"I understand that his daily column is now in syndication and that he's already at work on a second novel."

"That's right."

"What's it about?"

She gave the man a sweet smile. "I'm sworn to secrecy. You'll have to wait along with all his other fans."

There was a long line of them snaking out the door and down the sidewalk. Stevie watched as one elbowed his way through the crowd until he reached the table where Judd was autographing copies of his book. He introduced himself as a book editor for the *Times*.

"Can I have a minute, Mr. Mackie?"

"Nope," Judd said amicably, pointing down the line of people waiting to meet the author of the new bestseller. "But I can talk and sign at the same time. Ask away."

"Is the novel autobiographical?"

"Parts of it."

"Which parts?"

"In deference to my family and friends, I can't answer that question. I will admit that, as a young man, I wanted more than anything to play professional baseball. I was denied the chance. For years afterward, I harbored a lot of bitterness and carried a chip on my shoulder the size of Mount Everest." He closed the book he'd just signed, handed it to the customer and smiled a welcome to the next person in line. "Hi."

As he scrawled a brief message and his signature, he continued. "I was disenchanted with life, so I could relate to the protagonist in this book, who had also suffered a bitter disappointment."

"What changed your personal outlook?" the reporter asked.

Judd's gaze found Stevie's across the crowded bookstore. He saw her eyes shining back at him.

"I met somebody with real guts. She taught me through example that life is damn sure worth living even with all its drawbacks, and that sometimes we have to suffer a defeat in order to recognize a victory."

A sunny smile broke across Stevie's face. But it was immediately replaced by an expression of alarm. The alarm was telegraphed to Judd, who dropped his pen onto the table and left his position behind it.

He crossed the store in three strides and pressed his wife's hands between his. "Stevie, is something wrong?"

"Not at all, darling. Go back to work."

"Mr. Mackie," the bookstore manager said nervously, "people are waiting."

"I'll be right back," Judd told him, drawing Stevie down the narrow aisle toward the back of the store.

"But…but you can't leave now. Where are you going?" he sputtered. "What'll I tell the customers?"

"Tell them that I've been signing books for two hours and I have to take a leak. I'm sure they'll understand."

He left the bookseller, the reporter and those customers close enough to hear his statement gaping speechlessly as he pulled Stevie past the overloaded bookshelves into a rear storeroom that was even more cramped than the store proper.

"What's the matter?" he demanded the second the door closed behind them.

"Nothing."

"I saw your face, Stevie. You look like I do every time you playfully grab my—"

"Judd! People will hear you."

"I don't care. I want to know what brought on that expression that made you look like you'd just been goosed."

From the day they had returned to the east Texas

farmhouse following her surgery, he constantly wanted to be apprised of the state of her health. Only after she'd had a normal menstrual cycle did he begin to believe the doctor's positive prognosis. But he had never totally relaxed his vigilance where her health was concerned.

"I knew I shouldn't have listened when you begged to come along today," he said now, berating himself for letting her persuade him. "Let me put you in a cab back to the hotel."

"Forget it, Mackie. I love watching people adore you, because I adore you so much myself." She gave him a soft kiss. "Besides, I refuse to stay cooped up in that stuffy little room while you're out getting ogled by every woman you meet."

"Not *every* woman," he replied with the insufferable conceit she now found so endearing.

She linked her arms around his neck and moved in close. "You're incorrigible. Why do I love you so much?"

"How can you help yourself? What's not to love?" Slipping his hands to the small of her back he drew her even nearer and angled his parted lips over hers.

"Mackie, you've got people waiting."

"Let them wait."

He kissed her thoroughly, using his tongue to search the sweet recesses of her mouth. Their hunger for each other hadn't abated a single degree. Judd often joked that he was probably the only husband in history who'd had to wait twelve weeks after the wedding to consummate his marriage. Stevie would retort that he had only himself to blame since he'd insisted on bringing a minister to the farmhouse to marry them while she was convalescing and that, once he'd gotten her gynecologist's okay, he had certainly made up for all the lost time.

"Hmm, delicious," he said now, lifting his lips off hers at last, "I've been craving—" He broke off suddenly. His expression went completely blank.

Stevie began to laugh softly. "Now who looks like he's been goosed?"

"What the hell was that?"

"That," she said, taking his hand and moving it down to her swollen abdomen, "is our baby, moving for the first time."

Judd's adam's apple slid up and down his neck when he swallowed hard. "Oh, Geez," he groaned, "I knew I should have insisted that you stay in the room. I knew this would be too tiring. Standing up on this damn hard floor brought this on. Why aren't you sitting down?"

Happiness bubbled out of her in the form of soft laughter. "Will you calm down? It's normal. It's right on time. The doctor told me on my last visit to be watching for movement. There it is again. Feel it?" They waited expectantly, but nothing happened. "I guess he went back to sleep."

"Unfortunately," Judd said thickly, "touching you has brought me wide awake." He nudged her with his middle so she couldn't possibly mistake his meaning. "I'm a lucky cuss. Married to the sexiest prego broad on earth."

"Have I ever told you that you really have a romantic way with words?"

"No."

"Good."

It was a word game they often played. He was smiling at her wit as his hands skimmed past her thickened waistline and moved up to her breasts. Over the past few weeks they'd grown larger with her advancing pregnancy. "Tender?" he asked as he massaged them through her dress.

"Not as long as you're doing that."

He swept his thumbs across her nipples; they didn't disappoint him. "God, I love you. You came along when I needed you most." He swallowed hard again, this time with emotion. "Every time I think about your surgery and what could have been…" He let the unbearable thought go unspoken.

"But it wasn't, and we are blessed with each other." Again they kissed, putting behind it the love that brimmed in their hearts.

"Judd, it's happening again!" she said excitedly.

She guided his hand down to her tummy and they smiled radiantly at each other as the child of their creation moved within her.

"Does it hurt?" he whispered.

"No," she whispered back.

There was a knock on the door. "Mr. Mackie, the crowd is getting testy."

"What does it feel like?" Judd asked his wife, ignoring the panicked bookseller and keeping his voice low and stirring.

"It feels marvelous. It makes me feel alive and wonderful. Victorious. Almost as good as I feel every time you're inside me."

Judd laid his lips against hers and growled, "I've gotta go for now, Mrs. Mackie, but hold that thought."

\* \* \* \* \*

*Tomorrow's Promise*

# One

American Airlines flight number 124 from New Orleans to Washington, D.C., was in trouble. At least it seemed so to Keely Preston, whose cold, damp hands were clasped tightly in her lap as she stared anxiously out the window at the frequent blinding flashes of blue-white lightning.

The first-class cabin provided a more comfortable flight than the passengers in the coach cabin must be experiencing, but then Keely always flew first class for that reason alone.

"Miss Preston." Keely jumped and whipped her head around to face the airline hostess who was bending solicitously over the vacant seat on the aisle to address her confidentially. "Would you like something to drink?"

Keely pushed back a few strands of caramel-colored hair and tried to smile with tight, stiff lips. She wasn't sure she was successful. "No, thank you."

"It might help calm you. I've noticed that you're nervous about the storm. I assure you that everything is fine."

Keely looked down at her clenched hands and smiled in self-derision. "I'm sorry that it shows." She glanced back up at the attendant and smiled with more conviction. "I'm fine. Really."

The young woman smiled her professional smile and offered, "Ring me if you need anything. We should be out of the storm in the next several minutes and will land in Washington in about an hour."

"Thank you," Keely said and made the effort to relax, to sit back against the thick luxury of the first-class seat and block out the ferocity of the storm by closing her eyes.

The man across the aisle admired her display of courage, though he sensed she was terrified. As a matter of fact, he had admired everything about this woman since she had boarded the aircraft a few minutes after he had. She was in possession of many admirable qualities.

Her hair for instance. It was soft and casually styled. He despised trendy hairstyles copied from punk rock stars or women athletes. The lady across the aisle had hair that swept her shoulders each time she moved her head. It looked well-brushed and clean and he suspected it must smell like flowers.

He wouldn't be a man if he hadn't noticed her tidy, compact figure when she had passed him on his aisle seat to find hers one row in front of and across the aisle from his. She was wearing a green two-piece knit suit. The sweater tapered to a trim waist. The skirt clung to taut hips and widened gradually to flare just below her knees.

She had damn good legs too. He noticed that when she reached overhead to toss her trench coat in the compartment over her seat. That was when he had seen her in profile and noted that the front of her sweater conformed to a ripe, but not overfull, bosom.

To anyone's observant eye he had been engrossed in the stack of papers he had withdrawn from his briefcase soon after takeoff. Actually he had been covertly watching the woman. She had ordered filet mignon for dinner, but had taken exactly three dainty bites of it. One bite of broccoli. No bread. No dessert. She had drunk one-half glass of rosé wine and one cup of coffee slightly creamed.

He had read through several more of the official-looking documents after dinner, then stowed them again in his briefcase. He had been flipping through *Time*, but still continued to glimpse at the woman at regular intervals over the top of the magazine. Thus, he had seen and heard her exchange with the flight attendant. Now he gave up all pretense of reading and only watched her closely.

At that moment the airplane hit an air pocket and dropped suddenly. To a seasoned flier it was nothing to panic over. The woman across the aisle bolted upright and whirled her head around. Her eyes were wide with fright.

Before the man had thought about it, obeying a subconscious command he didn't stop to analyze, he was across the aisle and in the seat next to hers, holding her hands between the two of his.

"It's all right. Nothing to worry about. Just a little turbulence. No need to panic." Indeed, they seemed to be the only two in the first-class section who had even noted the sudden, and immediately corrected, loss of

altitude. The attendants were still in the galley, where
the unmistakable clatter of china could be heard. The
other passengers, few though they were on this late-
night flight, were either asleep or too preoccupied to
have noticed that the handsome young man had virtually leaped across the aisle to join the distressed woman.

The warm, strong, masculine hands that gripped hers
tightly were so well-groomed that Keely stared at them
for a moment before she lifted her surprised eyes to the
man's face. It was extremely close to hers but, oddly,
not uncomfortably so.

"I'm sorry," she heard herself say. What was she
apologizing for? "I'm fine. Truly. It's just…" The
hoarseness in her throat shocked her. Where were the
melodious tones that usually characterized her speaking voice? And why was she stammering like an idiot,
which surely this man must believe her to be. Who else
acted like such a complete ninny on an airplane but a
hysterical, neurotic female? And why didn't she feel
inclined to draw her hands away from his?

Instead she stared up into the blackest eyes framed
by the blackest brows and feathered by the thickest,
blackest lashes she had ever seen. There was a half-
inch-long scar on his cheekbone just under his left eye.
His nose was slender and finely chiseled. His mouth
was full and wide, the lips dangerously close to being
sensual. The jaw and chin were definitely stubborn and
male, but saved from austerity by a deep dimple in his
right cheek near the corner of that intriguing mouth.

"Well, what are friends for?" he asked, smiling that
heart-melting, confidence-inspiring smile that had become his trademark and anathema to his enemies.

*Hell, who are you kidding?* he asked himself. He didn't feel like a friend. The lightning that electrified the atmosphere outside the airplane was nothing compared to the bolt that had struck him right between the eyes and straight in the heart when he had first looked her fully in the face.

Green. Her eyes were green, wide, full of integrity, and sexy as hell. Her complexion wasn't peaches and cream. It wasn't that fair. More like peaches and… honey, sort of an apricot that would tan golden in the summer. It was tastefully enhanced with just the right touch of makeup.

The nose was perfect. The mouth…God, the *mouth*! Her lips were soft and glossed with a shiny coral.

She wore small gold loops in her ears. A slender gold chain gilded the base of her throat. She had no rings on the hands he still held. He celebrated that fact.

Her body was trembling slightly and for one insane moment he wished he knew what it was like to have her quivering beneath him in unleashed passion. The thought both thrilled and shamed him. It was obvious she wasn't soliciting for that kind of reaction from a man. The lust originated only in his mind, but it was undeniably there. Yet not base desire alone. He felt a compulsion to cover her. Not with dominance, but with protection. To shield her. To imbue her with his strength. It was a uniquely masculine emotion. And he had never felt it before with any female.

Some of the voracity of his thoughts must have shone in his eyes, for she was tugging gently on her hands. He released them reluctantly. "I'm Dax Devereaux," he said by way of introduction and to cover that self-consciousness that had suddenly sprung between them.

"Yes, you are," she said, then laughed softly, nervously, at her own words. "I mean, I recognize you now. I'm pleased to meet you, Congressman Devereaux. I'm Keely Preston."

His eyes narrowed as he stared at her, his head tilted in concentration. "Keely Preston. Keely Preston. Where have I heard that name? Should I know you?"

She smiled. "Only if you drive in New Orleans. I'm the traffic reporter on KDIX radio. I broadcast from the helicopter during rush hours."

He smacked his forehead with an open palm. "Of course. Keely Preston! Well, I'm humbled to meet such a celebrity."

She laughed again and he delighted in it. Her laughter had a low, musical sound. The lovely face wasn't tense any longer. "Hardly a celebrity," she demurred.

"But you are!" He leaned forward and whispered conspiratorially. "I know people who wouldn't dare drive to work each day without your guidance from above." He cocked his head and lowered black brows over his dark eyes. They stared at her in perplexity. "Forgive me for making such a crass observation, Keely, but if you fly every day why…?" He let the question trail off and she finished it for him.

"Why was I afraid a few minutes ago?" She turned her head to glance out the window again. They had flown through the worst of the storm, though streaks of lightning still lighted up the far horizon. "It's silly, I know. It's not the flying. As you say, I do that every day. I think it was the storm that upset me." It was a lame excuse and sounded so even to her own ears. She didn't want to guess how ridiculous it sounded to Dax Devereaux.

Why didn't she just explain to him? Why not tell him that Preston was her professional name, that she had another? Why not tell him why flying sometimes terrified her, that her job in the helicopter every day was part of her self-prescribed therapy to get over her own hang-ups?

Those things were difficult to reconcile to herself, much less verbalize. She knew from experience that it made men—single, attractive men—uncomfortable when she told them of her circumstances. They didn't quite know how to catalog her. To save herself and Dax Devereaux from such an embarrassing situation, she would stick to the vague answer she had given. He seemed momentarily satisfied with it.

To change the subject away from herself she asked him, "Are you going to be our next senator from Louisiana?"

He chuckled and ducked his head in an almost boyish mannerism. She saw a few strands of silver in his thick dark hair. Beautiful hair.

"Not if my opponents have anything to do about it. What do you think?" he asked her directly.

"I think you stand a very good chance," she answered unreservedly and honestly. "Your track record as a congressman is good."

Dax Devereaux had made a name for himself in her native state. He was known as the workman's politician. Often he could be found in jeans and a work shirt talking to fishermen, farmers, or blue-collar factory workers. His critics scoffed at his tactics and accused him of insincerity and flamboyancy. His supporters worshiped him. In any event, he kept the populace aware of his activities. No one in his congressional district was ignorant of their representative's identity.

"You don't think I'm an 'opportunist, constantly stirring up controversy for his own gain'?" he asked, quoting from a recent critical editorial.

She had read the editorial and smiled. "Well, you must admit that it doesn't hurt you to have a name like Devereaux when running for public office in the state of Louisiana."

He grinned back. "Can I help it if one of my great-great-grandfathers was an illustrious French Creole? I don't know if that's a help or a hindrance. Do you know how barbaric they behaved sometimes? Duels. They were a hot-blooded, short-tempered, snobbish bunch. One of my forefathers scandalized the family by marrying an 'American' girl after Jackson's defeat of the British. And a black sheep of the family even collaborated with the Yankees when the Union Army seized New Orleans during the Civil War."

She was laughing now. "Okay, okay. You're descended from a family of cutthroats and traitors." She looked at him speculatively. "I would think that you'd be a publicist's dream," she remarked candidly.

"Oh, yeah?" he asked and his eyes twinkled at her sudden embarrassment.

She floundered. "What I mean is your names both start with *d* and end with *x*. Surely a clever adman would do wonders with that during a campaign. And your youth and—and good looks. Sort of a John Kennedy type."

"Ah, but Mr. Kennedy had Mrs. Kennedy. I don't have an attractive wife as an asset." Keely knew that. Everyone did. His bachelorhood was a point his opponents played havoc with. Looking the way he did didn't help. Some considered a good-looking bachelor a threat and downright deadly when it came to effective politics.

She was staring into her lap. His knee was so close to hers she could feel the fabric of his pant leg against her shin. She didn't move away. Instead she raised her eyes to his and found him studying her closely. "I don't even have a good prospect for a wife," he said.

She swallowed. "Don't you?" The question was barely above a shaky explosion of breath.

"No."

That glorious sexual suppression. It was so exploited in movies, songs, and books. But it could be quite painful when one actually exercised it. The tumult that built in Keely's breast as she stared at Dax would not be squelched. For so many years it had been refused recognition, refused life. Now that it had a chance, it bloomed into enormous proportions, expanding her chest, filling her whole body, until her breathing was stifled. But before she died from that sweet suffocation, she was granted a reprieve.

The flight attendant stopped beside Dax's seat and said, "I see that the two of you have got acquainted. Can I bring you anything, Miss Preston? Congressman Devereaux?"

Dax hadn't taken his eyes off Keely and now he asked quietly, "Will you join me in a brandy?"

She tried to speak, couldn't, so only nodded mutely. He turned to the stewardess and said, "Two brandies." Keely took that time to restore herself. She ran her tongue over her lips, blinked several times, drew three deep breaths, and smoothed moist palms over her skirt. His leg was where it had been. If anything, closer. How tall was he? She hadn't had time to notice when he had suddenly appeared beside her, grasping her hands.

"Keely?"

She looked up at him. His face was serious. "If I run for the Senate, will you vote for me?" They laughed then and the tension was dispelled. They were served their brandies and she took a tentative sip. She didn't like it, but she didn't let him know that.

"Tell me about your work. It must be fun and exciting," he said companionably.

"It's much more glamorous from the outside than from within, I assure you. But I enjoy it."

"Do you ever get tired of being stormed for autographs by an adoring public?"

"Remember I'm on radio. People don't often recognize my face. But if I make a public appearance for the radio station, I enjoy a certain amount of VIP treatment."

"Maybe you should go into the more visible medium."

"Television? No, thank you!" she said with emphasis. "I'll leave the cameras to my friend Nicole."

"Nicole…? What's her name?"

"Nicole Castleman. She anchors the six-o'clock news on the television station that shares the building with my radio station."

"Yeah, I've seen her when I'm in New Orleans. Blond?"

"Yes. Men never forget Nicole," Keely said without rancor. "She and I have been best friends for years. She revels in her ardent popularity. When we're out together, she's the one who gets all the attention."

"I doubt that," Dax said succinctly. When Keely looked up at him, she saw that he meant it. She looked away quickly.

"I wouldn't trade jobs," she said.

"It must be demanding. Doesn't it interfere with your personal life? Your family?"

It was a veiled question and one that Keely chose to circumvent. She smiled up at him. "I manage to work around it." The subject was dropped.

The seat belt light came on and the hostess came by to pick up their glasses. The pilot announced their descent into National Airport. They listened, each without hearing, to the weather conditions in the capital. They didn't look at each other, but they didn't need to. The acute awareness was there.

His hand was settled on the armrest separating their chairs. It was strong, long, with tapering fingers, and sprinkled with dark hair. A beautiful hand. He wore a gold signet ring on the ring finger. An alligator band strapped a watch to his wrist. It had a round face with bold Roman numerals. All it did was give the time of day. There was no calendar, no alarm, no chime, no stopwatch, no flashing digits, no other gimmicks. Just two slender hands that indicated the time. She liked that.

Considering his profession, one would expect him to be dressed in conservative gray. But Dax Devereaux wore camel pants, a navy blue double-breasted blazer, a beige shirt, and a tastefully striped tie.

Was there anything wrong with him? One tiny flaw? So far Keely had seen none.

Dax too was staring ostensibly at his hand. In reality, he was calculating the distance between his dangling fingers and the smooth expanse of leg beneath them. She sat with her legs chastely crossed, but the position allowed him a tantalizing glimpse of silk-encased thigh. An edge of baby-blue lace peeked from under the hemline of her skirt. His heart thudded. A baby blue slip. Was it a half-slip or a whole one with satin straps?

He cursed the lecherous track his musings were taking. They were unfair to her. And they were making him light-headed. And uncomfortable. He shifted in his seat and turned to her abruptly. "How long will you be in Washington?"

"I—I'm not sure. It depends on...several things," she answered cryptically.

"Where will you be staying?"

Keely cringed on the inside. This was dangerous. He was getting too close. He was too attractive, too appealing. Now was the time to stop it before it got started. "I don't know. I thought I'd call a hotel from the airport."

He knew instantly by the averted green eyes and the wavering tone of voice that she was lying, but he forgave her gladly. She was only being cautious. It reconfirmed his earlier assessment. She wasn't hustling. He would find her.

"It's been a pleasure, Keely." He smiled and stuck out his hand in a friendly gesture. She accepted his hand in like manner and shook it, but she was marveling over how deep that dimple was.

"Thank you for coming to my rescue." Glistening lips parted to reveal bright, straight teeth and it was all Dax could do to tear his eyes away from her mouth.

"Goodbye," he said as he stood and backed into the aisle.

"Goodbye."

He returned to his seat to gather up his belongings and prepare for the landing, which was executed without a hitch several minutes later. Keely kept her head directed toward the front of the airplane or out the window, though she was conscious of him behind her.

When the 727 came to a standstill, she sat for a moment before getting up and reaching into the overhead rack for her coat. She studiously kept her eyes from Congressman Devereaux's vicinity, though she could tell out of the corner of her eye that he was shrugging into a topcoat. She decided not to put hers on yet. He might offer to help her. Then he'd have to touch her again and that was better avoided.

She picked up her purse and a small attaché and draped her coat over her arm before she stepped into the aisle.

He was waiting for her to pass ahead of him.

"Do you have luggage?" he asked.

"Yes. You?"

He shook his head. "I'm traveling light this trip," he said.

"Oh." There was nothing else to say. She stepped into the brightly lighted portable corridor that connected the aircraft with the terminal and walked along it at a brisk pace. This was ridiculous! Why didn't she just turn around and engage him in friendly inconsequential conversation? She knew he was right behind her. Why didn't he talk to her? They were both behaving like silly adolescents. But this was best. Discretion dictated putting as much space between them as possible. It was safer.

She walked into the airport. Just as she cleared the door, a rush of reporters holding cameras and microphones undulated toward it. Curiosity urged her to turn around.

Dax was immediately surrounded by the reporters and flashing cameras. He was smiling, fielding their rapid questions, bantering with them about the lousy Washington weather. While a more aggressive reporter was rattling off a question she couldn't hear, Dax looked up and caught her eye across the throng. His smile was almost apologetic. She mouthed a goodbye, then turned away and headed for the escalator.

When her one piece of luggage had been picked off the revolving carousel and checked against the stub stapled to her ticket, she hefted it off the ground and threaded her way through the airport and out onto the sidewalk. She easily hailed a passing cab and was standing aside as the driver placed her suitcase in the trunk, when another cab screeched to a halt in the next lane.

Dax shoved open the back door and cannoned out of the cab, skirted the rear end of the taxi, and jumped up on the curb in front of her. His breathing was labored. The night was cold. His breath fogged the air between them.

"Keely…" He looked disconcerted, impatient with

himself, anxious. "Keely, I don't want to say goodbye to you yet. Will you have a cup of coffee with me somewhere?"

"Dax—"

"I know. I'm a stranger. You're not the type to pick up a man on an airplane or anywhere else for that matter. I don't want the invitation to insult you. I just—"

He raked his hand through windblown hair. The collar of his coat was flipped up and framed the rigid planes of his jaw. The bottom of it flapped against his legs in the cold wind. The belt hung loose and untied from the loops. "Oh, hell," he cursed softly and shoved his hands into his coat pockets as he scanned the congested traffic. Then he looked at her again. "I just want to spend more time with you, get to know you better. It's not that late. Go for coffee with me? Please?"

How could anyone resist that dimple, that beguiling smile? Yet Keely Preston must. "I'm sorry, Dax. I can't."

Someone behind his illegally parked taxicab honked belligerently. Her taxi driver scowled at them impatiently. They were oblivious of it all.

"Are you meeting someone else?"

"No."

"Are you too tired?"

"No, it's…"

"What?"

"I just can't." She gnawed her bottom lip in vexation.

"That's no answer, Keely." He smiled gently and asked, "Do I repel you?"

"No!" The vehemence of her reply elated him and mortified her.

She looked away, darting her eyes unseeingly over

the traffic, the lights of the airport that shimmered through the soft mist that was falling. "That's why I can't go with you, Dax." She spoke so softly that he had to duck his head to hear her. "I'm married."

# *Two*

His head jerked back as if he had been kicked in the teeth, which is exactly how he felt. He stared at the top of her head, which was bowed as she looked at the damp concrete under her feet. "Married?" he croaked. It was unthinkable, abhorrent.

She looked at him then, straight in the eye and without expression. Her voice held no inflection as she answered, "Yes."

"But—"

"Goodbye, Dax." Keely stepped around him, yanked open the door of the taxi, and fell inside, saying "Capital Hilton" to the driver, who was glaring at her with open hostility for keeping him waiting so long.

The taxi lurched away from the curb and daringly forged its way into the flow of traffic. Keely didn't even notice. Her hands were covering her face and she was pressing the middle finger of each hand on the sharp throbbing pain in the center of her forehead.

The day had finally come. The day she had dreaded

for years. At 37,000 feet in the sky she had met a man. A man who made her situation that much more untenable.

Keely Preston Williams had been married for twelve years, but had been a wife for three weeks. She and Mark Williams were classic high school sweethearts. He was the star athlete in their small hometown in coastal Mississippi. She was a cheerleader. It was 1969. Drugs, hard liquor, and loose sexual mores hadn't yet made it to the high schools in the rural South. The community in which she and Mark grew up was still poignantly naive. Regional football, community-wide picnics, and church socials were still the mode.

After graduation Keely and Mark both enrolled in Mississippi State. Mark was an athlete, and as a result of a heavy class load and grueling football practices, his grades slipped until he failed out the first semester.

The Vietnam War was still a threat to any young man, and Mark fell victim to it. As soon as the draft board was notified of his grade average, his draft classification changed and he received his induction notice. Two weeks later he was on his way to boot camp.

It had been Keely's idea for them to marry as soon as they got word of his induction. She pressured him, cried, pleaded, threatened, until she wore him down. He finally consented against his better judgment and their parents were notified to meet them on a given day in their pastor's study. They were married.

They drove to New Orleans to spend the weekend, then returned home to live that fleeting two weeks with Mark's parents before the army bus carried him off. After three months at Fort Polk, Louisiana, he was sent to Fort Wolters, Texas. He had been selected to enter helicopter pilot training.

Forty weeks of pilot's training was crammed into twenty-five. After a six-month separation Mark was granted a one-week furlough with his bride before being shipped out.

The marriage had been consummated with the tender, restrained passion of the very young, but there was still something sweetly pure about their fervent embraces just before he left for the other side of the world and a hell he couldn't have imagined even in his most horrific dreams.

Keely continued going to school, busying herself with a job after classes in order to defeat expenses. At night she would write long, involved, newsy letters to Mark. She received his letters sporadically. Sometimes they came two or three at a time, sometimes weeks would go by without her once hearing from him. She pored over his letters, cherishing each word of love.

Then nothing. For weeks, a month, she heard nothing, nor did his anxious parents. Then she was visited by an officer dispatched from Fort Polk. Mark's helicopter had been seen going down, but his whereabouts and condition were unknown. He wasn't reported dead. His body hadn't been found among the wreckage. He wasn't reported taken prisoner of war. He had simply vanished.

And to this day that was all Keely Williams knew about her husband. He was one on a list of 2,600 men still classified as Missing In Action in Southeast Asia.

For the past several years Keely hadn't been idle, but actively strove to keep the MIAs on the public's mind.

She and other wives in similar circumstances had organized an action group called PROOF, taking its name from the initials of Positive Resolution Of Our Families. On most occasions Keely acted as their spokeswoman.

She leaned back on the smoky-smelling, dusty upholstery of the taxi and stared vacantly at the Washington scenery as it sped by. Twelve years. Was she any better off now than she had been when she had first learned of Mark's disappearance?

Drowning in a miasma of disillusionment and depression, she had finished school with a degree in journalism. She took her degree and moved to New Orleans. She landed a job on the *Times-Picayune* as a "gofer" with the grandiose title of copy editor. She stuck it out for several years, gradually working her way into the unenviable position of cub reporter. The events she was assigned to cover were so unimportant that her stories were buried in the middle of the newspaper.

Through the journalistic grapevine, she heard that a newswriter at a local radio station had abruptly left, due to an indiscretion with the switchboard operator on company time. On her lunch break Keely had gone to see the harried news director, charmed him into hiring her, and started her new job the next day. She liked the work. It was at least more kinetic than the dull stories she had been writing.

She met Nicole Castleman in the commissary when they reached for the same bottle of catsup at the same time. They became friends, and when someone conceived the innovative idea of putting a sexy-sounding woman in the traffic helicopter, Nicole suggested Keely.

Keely had listened to their proposal with a combination of terror and incredulity. She had never spoken into a microphone in her life. And to get in a helicopter every day! Mark! His helicopter had been seen going down under heavy fire. It had exploded, but no body was ever found. She couldn't.

But she had, seeing the job as her way of keeping Mark's memory fresh. Over the years it had begun to dim. Also the job forced her to meet her justified fear of aircraft head-on. Keely Preston Williams hated to admit fear of anything.

Her friendship with Nicole Castleman had cemented over the years. They were able to talk to each other with sometimes painful honesty. Last night Nicole had sat Indian fashion in the middle of Keely's bed while she packed. She had tried to talk Keely out of coming on this mission.

"Haven't you martyred yourself enough, Saint Keely? My God! Your dedication to lost causes is your only stupid trait," she had shouted even as she helped Keely select which clothes to bring.

"Nicole, we've been through this so many times in the years since I've known you that I can almost quote it verbatim. We should just record this conversation and then every time we feel the argument coming on play the tape and save ourselves the breath."

"Sarcasm doesn't become you, Keely, so cut the garbage about a tape recorder. You know I'm right. Every time you meet with those other wives, you come back depressed and stay that way for weeks." She leaned back, displaying her lush figure, which was enviable. It was only one of her assets. She had a veritable mane of blond hair and sea-blue eyes. Her smile was decep-

tively angelic. That cherub mouth was capable of un-
leashing a string of obscenities that could make the
brawniest seaman quail.

"It's something I have to do, Nicole. They have asked
me to be their spokeswoman because I'm the most qualified. I've told them I would. And I will. Besides, I believe in what I'm doing. Not for myself, but for the other
families. If Congress votes to have our men declared
dead, then their army pay, which is automatically channeled to us, will be severed. I can't stand by and see that
happen without doing something."

"Keely, I know that in the beginning, when PROOF
was organized, your motives were strong. But when
does this purgatory end? When the POWs were released
and Mark wasn't among them, you got physically ill. I
know. I was there. I saw you go through hell. Are you
going to put yourself through that again and again?"

"If I have to, yes. Until I know something about my
husband."

"And if you never know?"

"Then you'll have the supreme satisfaction of saying, 'I told you so.' Should I take this ecru blouse or the
gray one for that navy suit?"

"Gray and navy. Wonderful," Nicole had muttered in
total exasperation. "The ecru. It looks less widowish."

So now Keely was in Washington to face a congressional subcommittee on behalf of the wives and families of the MIAs to plead that the proposal to have those
unaccounted-for men declared legally dead be dropped.

When she faced that assembly of congressmen,
would her mind be on her plight? The plight of the
others? Mark? Or would it be on the man she had met

tonight? The one who had said almost shyly, "I just want to spend more time with you, get to know you better." And to whom she had had to say, "I'm married."

"Hilton," the cabby said tersely.

She realized then that they had been stopped for several seconds. "Thank you," she mumbled.

She paid the taxi fare, carried her one bag into the lobby, and checked into the room that had been reserved for her for weeks. Subconsciously she signed the register Keely Preston, then almost as an afterthought added Williams.

Her room was cold and sterile and impersonal, as hotel rooms in large cities are wont to be. What had their room been like where she and Mark had spent their short honeymoon? She couldn't remember. She could remember very little of their time together after they were married. When she did remember him, it was as a football hero, or as the president of their graduating class, or as her date at the Valentine Prom.

When they had lived that frantic two weeks with his parents, he had been nervous and embarrassed about having Keely sleeping in his room. That first night she had scooted across the narrow mattress to embrace and kiss him. He had shied away and reminded her in hushed tones that his parents were directly beyond the thin wall. The next night he had made some feeble excuse to his curious parents and hustled Keely out of the house. They had driven to the lake, parked, and climbed into the cramped back seat of his Chevy. For Keely, that night, and the others that followed it, had been less than earth-moving. But she had loved Mark and that was all that mattered.

Keely shivered in the cold room as she slipped out of her coat. She switched on the stereo system built into the bedside table, reset the thermostat, and began unpacking her suitcase, smoothing out the wrinkles of each garment before carefully hanging it up. She was almost done when the telephone next to the bed rang.

"Hello," she answered.

"Keely, this is Betty Allway. I was just checking to see that you had got here all right."

Betty was a decade older than Keely and had three children. Her husband had been missing for fourteen years, yet the woman refused to give up hope. She, like Keely, wouldn't take the legal action herself and have her husband declared dead. They had met several years ago and had served on PROOF committees together and corresponded often. As always Keely was inspired by Betty Allway's undaunted courage.

"Hello, Betty. How are you? The children?"

"We're all fine. You? Was your trip from New Orleans pleasant?"

A startlingly accurate vision of Dax Devereaux flashed through Keely's mind. Her heart did a somersault. "Yes. Uneventful." Liar, she accused herself.

"Are you nervous about tomorrow?"

"Oh, no more than I usually am when I have to face a group of grim congressmen carefully guarding the purse strings of the nation."

Betty laughed good-naturedly. "They couldn't be as intimidating as General Vanderslice. We've been through worse. And you know we all have confidence in you."

"I'll try not to let you down."

"If things don't work out like we want them to, it won't be because of you, Keely. What time should we meet in the morning?"

They made plans to meet in the coffee shop of the hotel and go from there to the conference room in the House of Representatives.

Keely hung up, trying to shrug off the despondency that had suddenly cloaked her, and began peeling off her travel-rumpled clothes. She was down to her underwear when the telephone rang again.

Betty must have forgotten a detail. "Hello," she said for the second time.

"You don't wear a wedding ring."

She gasped softly and clutched the half-slip she was holding in her hand against her body like a shield, as though Dax could see her through the telephone wires. She collapsed on the bed, her knees refusing to hold her.

"H-how did you know where to find me?"

"I put the CIA on your trail."

"The—"

"Easy, easy," he laughed. "Can't you take a joke? Actually my taxi followed you to the hotel."

She didn't say anything. He completely disarmed her. She was trembling, twirling the cord of her telephone in her fingers, staring at the striped bedspread, dreading the moment she would have to hang up, when she wouldn't be able to hear his soft breath in her ear.

"You haven't commented on my observation," he finally said to break the silence that neither considered uncomfortable.

"What? Oh, you mean about wearing a wedding ring? Yes, I do wear one, only not when I know my hands are going to perspire as they do when I fly. That's why I didn't have it on tonight."

"Oh." He drew in a deep, remorseful breath. "Well, you can't blame a guy for jumping to the wrong, albeit hopeful, conclusion then." When she didn't respond, he asked, "Can you?"

She laughed then, though there was really nothing funny about the situation. "No, I can't blame a guy for jumping to the wrong conclusion. I should have told you right away that I was married."

Another silence hung between them, this one slightly more tense than the last.

"You didn't eat your dinner on the plane. You must be hungry. Why not go out for a bite with me?"

"Dax!"

"Okay. I'm sorry. Perseverance runs in my blood."

Another silence.

"I can't go out with you, Dax. Please understand. You do, don't you?" It was suddenly vital to her that he did.

A soft expletive sizzled through the cables followed by a deep sigh. "Yes, unfortunately I do."

"Well…" she paused. What did one say at this point? It's been nice knowing you? See you around sometime? Good luck in your Senate race? What she said was "Good night." It wasn't quite as definite as goodbye.

"Good night."

She sighed regretfully as she replaced the receiver. She could almost hear Nicole screaming in her ear, "Have you lost your ever-lovin' mind?"

If they argued constantly about Keely's involvement in PROOF, it was nothing compared to their go-around about Keely's love life, or more to the point, the lack of one.

Nicole loved men. And they loved her. She went through them with the neglect that most women go through a box of Kleenex; she used and discarded them almost daily. But while she was with one, she loved him without limitation. Her men came in all shapes, sizes, and pedigrees. She adored them all.

How Keely could have stayed faithful to her husband for twelve years was beyond Nicole's comprehension. "My God, Keely. Twelve years of living with one man would be ghastly enough, but twelve years of living with a fond memory is absolutely asinine."

"He's not 'one man.' He's my husband," Keely said patiently.

"If this husband of yours comes home one day, which I hate to say I doubt, do you think you'll pick up where you left off? Come on, Keely. You're more intelligent than that. For godsakes. No telling what he'll have gone through. He won't be the same person you remember. You're not the rosy-cheeked cheerleader any longer either, my friend."

"Thanks," Keely cut in dryly.

"That's not a dig, it's a compliment. You're a woman, Keely. You need men—or if that's asking too much of your outdated morals—a man. I'll loan you one of mine."

Keely had laughed in spite of her pique. "No, thank you. I don't know any of yours that I'd have. Except for Charles, maybe." She slanted a shrewd glance at her friend.

"Him? He's not one of 'my men.'"

"No?"

"No!"

"He's in love with you, Nicole."

"Love! He's never even tried to take me to bed. All he wants to do is bug the hell out of me, which he does so well."

"He doesn't cater to your every whim, if that's what you mean."

"We're not discussing Charles and me," she said crisply. "We're discussing you and a man."

"Okay," Keely said dramatically. She planted her hands on her hips and faced Nicole. "Suppose I met *a man*. Do you think *a man* would be content for long to squire me around to movies and dinner without exacting some form of payment?"

"No. You're attractive, intelligent, and sexy as all get-out. He'd want to get you in the sack ASAP."

"Exactly my point. I couldn't do that, Nicole. I'm married to someone else. So, end of affair. End of friendship. I'm back to square one."

"Not necessarily. You *could* go to bed with him. You might even fall in this 'love' you put such stock in. You might even see your way to having Mark declared—"

"Don't say it, Nicole." The warning in Keely's voice silenced any argument.

Nicole hung her head in contrition and studied her well-manicured nails. Finally she looked up at Keely and smiled a repentant smile. "I'm sorry. I went too far." She came forward and embraced her friend warmly, kissed her on the cheek. "I only nag you because I love you."

"I know you do. And I love you. But we'll never

agree on this subject, so let's talk about something else. Okay?"

"Okay," Nicole conceded. Then she mumbled. "I still think a terrific roll in the hay with some mean stud would do you a world of good."

If Nicole knew that Keely had passed up an invitation to go for coffee with Dax Devereaux, one of the country's most eligible bachelors, she would no doubt strangle her.

*It's not to be, Nicole. Sorry,* she thought as she switched on the fluorescent light in the bathroom. A good hot shower was what she needed to ease the tension that contracted every muscle in her body. Then she would curl up in bed and study her notes for her speech tomorrow.

The shower, as it turned out, was lukewarm, but it sufficed, and she felt better when she stepped out and wrapped her washed hair in a towel and pulled on her thick terry-cloth robe. The blue hotel towel and her yellow terry-cloth robe clashed, but what difference did it make?

She was flipping on the lamp beside her already turned-down bed when there was a soft knock on her door. With the characteristic caution of a woman who lives alone, she walked carefully toward the door and checked to make sure the chain lock was in place. "Yes?" she queried softly.

"Room service."

She slumped against the door and pressed her forehead to the cold surface. Vainly she tried to calm the immediate acceleration of her heartbeat. She opened her mouth to speak, found that it had gone dry, and swallowed hard. "Are you insane?" she managed to rasp.

"I must be," Dax said. "This is one of the dumbest things I've done recently, but…" She could imagine his shrug. "May I come in?"

"No."

"Keely, your reputation, not to mention mine and my campaign, will be shot to hell if anyone comes down this hallway and sees me at your door. It would be just like Carl Bernstein and Bob Woodward to find me here. So please open the door before something disastrous like that happens. I have something for you."

Some intuitive niggling in the back of her brain told her that he wouldn't go away until he saw her. She unlatched the chain and drew open the door. Dax was standing on the threshold with a tray in his hands. He was dressed in a casual shirt and jeans. He wore a bellman's cap on his head.

She laughed as she sagged weakly against the jamb. "What are you doing here?"

"I live here," he said and brushed past her, setting the tray on a small round table.

"You *live* here?"

"Yeah. Upstairs on the top floor. It's not practical for a bachelor to own a house in D.C. Expensive as hell. So I keep a suite of rooms here."

"That's why it was so convenient to follow me. You were coming here anyway," she teased.

"It made it easier. I would have followed you anyway." He wasn't teasing.

She shifted uncomfortably and glanced at the tray,

which was draped with a white linen cloth. "What is that?"

"Room service," he said by way of a flippant explanation and took off the cap with a flourish. "I never lie."

Until then she had forgotten about the towel wrapped around her head, the homey terry-cloth robe, and her bare feet. Embarrassment climbed up her neck to blossom in her cheeks. She made to scurry past him. "I'll only be a minute."

"You look fine," he said, laughing and reaching out to grab her arm. If he hadn't touched her, it might never have happened. As it was, he did touch her.

It was the warmth of his fingers along the inside of her wrist that did more to halt her rush from the room than did the strength of his grasp. She skidded to a stop but didn't turn around to face him. His laughter subsided then died altogether.

It was with the merest tugging on her wrist that he turned her around to face him. Her eyes were wide with guilt and apprehension, his full of supplication. Gradually they inclined toward each other until his hand came up and cradled her cheek. Ebony eyes sought out and adored each feature of her face. His thumb stroked across her quivering mouth. Of their own volition her lids shuttered her tear-flooded eyes.

Dax hesitantly bent his head and brushed his lips across hers. White heat seared through him. Her breath escaped from slightly parted lips in a thin, anguished whisper. He stared down at her mouth, at the incredibly fragile eyelids fringed by long lashes, and succumbed to the temptation again. He touched her lips with his.

Instinctively she moved closer. Bodies brushed,

eased away, touched, fused. Then primeval hunger seized them. Caution was thrown to the wind, the barriers were broken down, and a flood of sexual tension that had been building since they first saw each other burst free of the dams of conscience and prohibition.

He clutched her to him as his mouth melded into hers. Strong arms, yet gentle, wrapped around her back and molded her against his body with such an exquisite fit that Keely was made dizzy by the sensations. Her hands found their way to his waist and settled lightly on his belt. Then around to his lower back. Then up to explore the smooth muscles under his soft shirt.

The towel became dislodged from her hair and fell to the floor. Her wet strands were ravaged by his fingers before they cupped her head and held it immobile while the exploration of her mouth deepened.

His mouth moved over hers, testing each angle, delighting in each nuance, savoring the taste. His tongue slid persuasively along her bottom lip before it dipped repeatedly into her mouth, taking and giving equally. The plunder increased in tempo and ferocity until it became too evocative, too fiercely passionate, too erotically symbolic, for them to ignore. They broke apart under the impact.

A tear trickled down Keely's cheek and she covered her mouth with a shaking hand. Dax held on to her shoulders lightly, searching her face, his dark eyes pleading for her understanding. She pulled herself free and flew across the room to the wide window. She leaned against the cold pane of glass, squeezing her eyes shut against her shame, sobbing in dry, heaving gulps.

Dax didn't follow her. Instead he dropped into a chair. His knees were spread wide, his elbows propped on them, his face buried in his hands.

After a while he rubbed his face hard. He looked at the woman still cowering at the window. "Keely, please don't cry. I'm sorry. I shouldn't have come here. I swore to myself that I wouldn't touch you, but..." he dwindled off lamely.

"It's not your fault," she said barely above a whisper. "I shouldn't have let you in." After a soul-searching moment she added, "I wanted to."

He was sitting in the chair, forlornly staring at the carpet between his shoes, when she turned around. "Dax, I haven't been fair to you. I want to tell you about me, my life. There are things you should know. Then you'll understand."

He looked up at her then bleakly. "You don't need to tell me anything, Keely. I know all about you. I'm one of the congressmen you'll be appealing to tomorrow."

# *Three*

Had he whipped a switchblade out of his pocket and threatened her life, she couldn't have been more stunned. Speechless, she stood there and stared at him. "That's impossible," she husked.

He shook his head. He made no other movement.

"But your name isn't on the list. I've had a list of the members of that subcommittee for weeks. Your name isn't on it." She was trying desperately to remain sensible, to set the world right again, to get things back on the proper footing.

"Congressman Haley from Colorado was voted last week to serve on the Ways and Means Committee. My constituents thought it would be a good idea for me to replace him on this one when the chair became vacant."

Keely still maintained her post in front of the window. Was it a bulwark she had erected in her mind? She had to leave its tenuous security sometime. Unconsciously she tightened the tie belt on her robe and pushed herself away from the window. She walked toward the bed, only to stop several feet from it. Her hands had nothing to do, so she crossed her arms defensively over her chest before facing him.

Anger championed her shame. "Well, Congressman Devereaux, you've certainly armed yourself with an arsenal of rebuttal, haven't you?" she asked scathingly. "My carefully planned speech about how we still hope that our men are alive will be worth only so much smoke, won't it?"

"Keely—"

"You should be proud of yourself. Tell me, do you go to this much trouble on every political issue you want voted your way?"

"Stop that!" he snapped. "I didn't know who you were until I got upstairs to my room. I had reams of paperwork to read over, to familiarize myself with, before tomorrow. Quite by accident I read that the spokeswoman for PROOF was one Mrs. Keely Williams. How many Keelys do you know? When I checked the desk downstairs and found out that a Keely *Preston* Williams was in Room seven fourteen, I put two and two together. I swear I didn't know about you until then."

"But when you found out, you didn't waste any time getting down here to see just how sincere we grass widows are, did you?" She covered her face with her hands, furious with the tears that wouldn't be stemmed.

"Dammit, my coming here, my kissing you, had nothing to do with tomorrow, or the outcome of the hearing, or anything else."

"Didn't it?" she flared.

"No!" he roared. He was standing now, facing her, hands on hips, as angry and distraught as she. When he saw the visible pain on her strained features, he emphasized more softly, earnestly, "No."

She turned away from him, hugging herself tightly, fearing if she didn't hold herself together physically, her spirit would shatter and fly apart. If she had felt torn between decisions before, divided by loyalties, the interference of Dax Devereaux in her life had compounded her quandary a hundredfold.

"You can't understand," she whispered.

He longed to go to her, take her in his arms, reassure her that everything would work out well, but he dared not. The dejection he read in her posture indicated the terrible confusion that gripped her. It was better to let her solve it in her own mind. "Maybe I *can* understand. Why don't you tell me?"

She faced him again with glaring accusation in the green eyes. Hastily he added, "Not as Congressman Devereaux. Explain it to me as Dax."

She sat on the edge of the bed, tense, her shoulders hunched in self-protection. He returned to the chair. Quietly, methodically, and with no dramatic gesture or inflection, she told him a capsulized rendition of her courtship and marriage to Mark Williams, his disappearance, and the resultant havoc it had wreaked on her life.

"I have neither the status of a widow nor of a divorcée. I'm married, yet without a husband or home or children. I live as a single woman, but am most definitely not."

She stopped talking, but she didn't look at him, only stared at her lap. After a length of time he asked quietly, "You never considered freeing yourself?"

Her head shot up. "You mean have Mark declared dead, don't you?" she asked incisively. Involuntarily he flinched under the harsh quality of her question. "No. In spite of stringent advice against it, I've remained faithful to my husband and the belief that he's still alive. On the outside chance that he does come home someday, I want to be here for him. There would be no one else. Since he was reported missing, his father has died. His mother is in a nursing home. She is no longer able to take care of herself. The grief…" She sighed and rubbed her forehead with her fingertips. "Mark's paycheck goes to support her. I don't keep any of it for myself." Now she looked at him. "Dax, it's her and the wives with children who desperately need that money. If that bill is passed to have our men—"

She broke off abruptly and raised her chin defiantly. "But then, you'll hear my formal speech tomorrow, won't you?"

He stood up then, looking as tired and despondent as she. "Yes. I'll hear it tomorrow."

Without another word he walked to the door and opened it. On the threshold he turned to face her. "Don't forget to eat something." He indicated the long-forgotten tray with a quick jerk of his chin. "Good night, Keely," he said softly. Then he was gone.

Keely stood in the middle of the suddenly empty room and stared at the closed door. A hopelessness that she hadn't acknowledged in a long while smothered her like a shroud. She felt desolate and lonely. So lonely.

And in spite of it all, she longed to feel again the strength of Dax's arms and the urgent pressure of his mouth.

* * *

Her critical appraisal of the image in the mirror determined that she looked as good as she could. Maybe she shouldn't have listened to Nicole and brought the gray blouse instead. It had a simple rolled collar that tied in a chaste bow. The one she had brought had tulle-lined lace inserts on the collar and across her collarbone. Well, she sighed, it was too late now. Maybe that touch of femininity relieved the severity of the navy suit with its straight skirt and blazer.

Navy suede pumps, a matching purse, and her cashmere coat the same color as her caramel-colored hair completed her ensemble. She tucked her trim leather attaché under her arm and took the elevator down to the lobby to meet Betty Allway for breakfast.

"You look gorgeous as always," Betty remarked with a spark of envy tempered by honest admiration. "How do you stay so slender living in New Orleans, the eating capital of the world? I'd weigh four hundred pounds in a month."

Betty's good humor was infectious and Keely found herself chatting about her work and asking Betty about her children. The older woman supplied her with an animated tale about each one of them.

"The baby was only four months old when Bill was reported missing. He's never seen him. Now that 'baby' is a strapping basketball player on the high school team." A touch of sadness came into her usually optimistic eyes and Keely reached over to cover the work-worn hand with her own.

"It never gets easier to accept, does it?" Keely mused

aloud. "We learn to live with it. But I don't think we ever truly accept it."

"I know I can't and won't. Until I've got a positive confirmation of Bill's death, I'll go on believing that he is alive." She took a sip of coffee. "By the way, we may have a fly in the ointment. Congressman Parker, the chairman of the subcommittee, called me this morning."

Keely thought she knew what might be coming, but she said a cool "Oh?" before taking a small bite of her English muffin.

"One of the congressmen I thought we could count on for support has been chosen to serve on a standing committee. He's been replaced by a Daxton Devereaux from Louisiana. Do you know him?"

Keely edged away from a direct answer and said, "Everyone in Louisiana has heard of Dax Devereaux." Cautiously she asked, "Do you think he'll be an opponent?"

Betty stared concernedly into her coffee cup while an unobtrusive waiter filled it for her. "I don't know. From what I understand, he's politically ambitious. He's a likely candidate for the Senate in the next election."

"That doesn't really mean anything. He may see taking our side as a point in his favor."

"What about his economic policy?"

"I'm not in his congressional district, so I don't really know," Keely answered truthfully.

"I've heard that he advocates tax cuts. He's a fanatic for trimming down government spending. That definitely worries me."

Keely tried to interject a bright nonchalance into her voice when she said, "Well, the jury is still out. There are ten other men on that subcommittee. Let's not concede defeat yet."

"Never!" said Betty heartily and then laughed without humor. Her steady gray eyes met Keely's over the cluttered table. "I know it's not fair, Keely, but we do depend on you so much to do our talking for us."

That was the last thing Keely wanted to hear this morning. She felt like Judas. "I know you do," she said. "I'll do my best." What would Betty think of her if she knew she had been kissing Dax Devereaux last night with an abandon that even now made her blush in remembrance?

"We'd better go," Betty said briskly. "Let's not give them the satisfaction of our being late. The others will meet us there."

They settled the bill and went outside. The rain was gone, but a cold, biting wind was sweeping through the capital. They hailed a cab, and the driver fought morning rush-hour traffic to deposit them in front of the House of Representatives.

Keely had never dreaded anything more than she did facing Dax. Her night had been a restless one. She had dreamed of Mark and that always upset her. It had been a regular occurrence when he had first left for Vietnam. Even after he was reported missing, he had played key roles in her dreams.

Over the years, however, the dreams had become less frequent and dimmer, more nebulous. When he invaded her subconscious mind, he was still a youth, a nineteen-year-old boy. Now, if he were alive, he was a mature man. What did he look like? She had no idea, and that haunted her. The man to whom she was linked by name and holy vow she might not even recognize if they accidentally met on the street.

"Keely?" Betty's tentative nudging roused her from her reverie, and she asked, "Are we here already? I was rehearsing my speech in my head." When had she started lying so blatantly and with such constancy? Since she had met Dax. Since she had talked to him, laughed with him, touched him, kissed him. Since she had admitted only to herself that, for the first time in years, she wanted to experience the physical loving of a man.

There were three other women who met them in the corridors of the Congress. They, too, were actively campaigning to prevent the MIAs from being classified as dead. Keely knew them all and greeted them warmly.

A page ushered them into the chamber where the subcommittee hearing was to be held. Keely was seated at a table with a microphone mounted on it. Betty was beside her. The others took seats behind them.

Keely took her notes out of the attaché, stacked them neatly, arranged her purse on the table, anything to keep her eyes from scanning the room, though she didn't think Dax was there yet. Pages, aides, reporters, and the other committee members moved around the room, greeting each other, shaking hands, talking, reading newspapers or briefs. Keely took off her coat and a page rushed to help her. She was thanking him graciously over her shoulder when she saw Dax walk into the paneled room.

Their eyes met and locked. Each was powerless to control the intense attraction, so they graciously surrendered to it and allowed themselves the luxury of looking at each other. For a moment they were held captive by the other's presence in the room, oblivious of everyone else. Keely saw mirrored in his face the same yearning she felt. It held on tenaciously. All through the restless night when she had awakened from her dreams, it hadn't been the security of Mark's arms she longed for, but Dax's. The whispered words of comfort she imagined hadn't come from her husband's lips, but from a mouth juxtaposed most alluringly to a deep dimple. It had been Dax's eyes, dark and fathomless, that had warmed her chilled soul.

Their binding gaze wasn't broken until another congressman moved in front of Dax and took his hand in a hearty, backslapping handshake. Keely faced the front of the room again, tugged the hem of her skirt down over her crossed knees, and read—or pretended to read—the papers she held in her damp hands. How could she possibly live through this?

A few minutes later the hearing was called to order. Congressman Parker of Michigan, the chairman, made his opening remarks and introduced each member of the subcommittee to the representatives of PROOF. When he introduced Dax Devereaux, Betty's elbow touched Keely's right ribs gently. She wasn't sure what that covert gesture was supposed to convey and she didn't turn her head to look at Betty and find out. Dax was obviously the youngest member of the subcommittee. He was unequivocally the most handsome. But was he friend or foe? There were eleven congressmen serving on the committee, the majority party having the advantage of one. Dax was of the majority.

Congressman Parker adjusted the half-glasses on his

nose and peered over the silver rims at Keely. "Now, Mrs. Williams, I think you have prepared a statement on behalf of PROOF. We should like to hear it at this time."

"Thank you, Congressman Parker." She addressed the members of the committee, the press, and then in her well-modulated, softly Southern voice, presented the case for PROOF. She neither read her copious notes nor quoted anything by rote. Instead she spoke conversationally, with conviction, but on a personal level, as though she were addressing each committee member on a one-to-one basis.

In conclusion she said, "It is our most sincere hope that you, as esteemed and knowledgeable representatives of the American people, will table this proposed bill. That you will keep those classified as Missing In Action alive until we are all satisfied to the contrary."

No one moved for a moment, impressed by her informative collection of facts and her unemotional, but puissant, presentation of them. Then under the cover of the restless shifting of people who had sat still and quiet for a long time, she heard Betty's "Bravo." Her acclaim was echoed by the women sitting behind them.

"Thank you, Mrs. Williams." Congressman Parker looked down either side of the table, which was set up panel-fashion to face the women, and queried, "Gentlemen? Does anyone have points for discussion?"

For the next hour and a half Keely and her group fielded questions and asked many of their own. Points were scored and lost on each side, but most of the committee members seemed in sympathy with the lobbyists if not in agreement with them.

Keely tried to keep her eyes off Dax, but it was almost impossible. He didn't contribute anything to the heated discussion, but sat back, his fingers tented over the bridge of his nose, and listened closely. She wished she knew what he was thinking.

Only one of the congressmen was openly hostile, Congressman Walsh from Iowa. His questions bordered on belligerence, and he made what he considered to be valid observations with an attitude of condescension.

"Mrs. Williams," he addressed Keely directly in a bored, half-amused voice. "Forgive me for pointing out that your appearance doesn't exactly denote poverty. Most of you who are married to or mothers of the MIAs have made new lives for yourselves. Don't you feel the least bit guilty about bleeding the federal government of moneys that may best be appropriated elsewhere?"

Keely bit back a nasty retort that would tell the congressman in no uncertain terms what she thought of him and his heritage. Instead she said levelly, "I don't think any of us should feel guilty about accepting pay for a job done, do you, Congressman? Our husbands or sons are considered to be still in the service of their country. They should be paid just like any other soldier."

"Mrs.—"

"Please, may I finish?" she asked coolly, and he grudgingly assented. "There is more involved here than money. If our MIAs are declared dead, then whatever measures the government and the army are taking to provide us with information will desist immediately. We must not let that happen as long as there is the slimmest chance that these hundreds of men are still alive, possibly being held prisoner or surviving by whatever means they can."

The sanctimonious, pompous man leaned back in his chair and crossed his stout arms over his protruding belly. "Do you actually, in all honesty, believe that your husband, or any of these men, is still alive?" Before she could answer, he turned his shiny balding head toward Dax. "Congressman Devereaux, we haven't heard from you. You served in Vietnam, did you not?"

Keely's surprised eyes riveted on Dax and she was disconcerted to find him staring straight at her. "Yes," she heard him answer. She had no idea he was a veteran of the war.

"In what capacity?" the older man persisted.

Each eye in the room was now trained on Dax. "I was a Marine captain."

"For how long were you in Vietnam?"

"Three years."

"A Marine captain sees quite a lot of action, I would imagine," the man drawled unctuously. "Basing your answer on what you experienced there, would you say it's even conceivably possible that these missing men are still alive?"

Dax sat forward and rested his folded hands on the table in front of him. He studied them for a long moment before he answered the loaded question. "The war in Vietnam broke all the rules of warfare. I wouldn't say that it was conceivably possible that small children could be bribed to walk into a group of GIs and pull the pin on a hand grenade, but I saw it happen. Nor is it conceivably possible that commanding officers could be shot by their own men who were strung out on drugs, but I saw that happen too. During one skirmish I sustained a minor flesh wound. An old Vietnamese civilian gave me a drink of water and bandaged my wound before the medic could get to me. The next morning his head was mounted on a pike not ten feet from where I was sleeping." He fixed hard, cold eyes on the flustered congressman and said with a brittle voice, "In a war of such atrocious impossibilities, anything is conceivably possible. That's the only way I know to answer your question."

There was not a breath in the room. Tears blurred Keely's vision as she watched Congressman Parker call the meeting adjourned for lunch.

There was a flurry of people gathering up their coats and briefcases, laughing and chattering in a vain attempt to alleviate the dark mood Dax Devereaux's words had cast over the room.

The women of PROOF congratulated Keely as a group and then singly for her eloquent expression of their petition and hugged her in turn. She pulled on her coat and neatly replaced the papers in her attaché case. It was an extreme effort not to look at Dax, who was being besieged by constituents and reporters.

"Keely, thank you," Betty said and hugged the younger woman to her. "You were wonderful. I don't know if we'll succeed or not, but at least we gave it our best shot."

"We're not done yet. I don't think Congressman Walsh is finished. If anything, I think D—Congressman Devereaux's elocution angered him and made him even more resentful to us."

Betty looked at the retreating bulk of the man as he imperiously shoved his way past eager reporters.

"That big blowhard," Betty scoffed. "He's only trying to get his name on the six-o'clock news. I'm afraid that if they compare him to Dax Devereaux, he'll come out looking like a fool—which I personally think he is." Her eyes surveyed the room and latched on to Dax as he was being interviewed by a network television reporter. "Have you ever seen a man as gorgeous as that one?" she whispered to Keely.

"Who?" Keely asked with feigned ignorance even as her heart started thumping in her breast. "Oh, you mean Congressman Devereaux? I guess he is rather charismatic. But you're not the first woman in the country to notice, you know."

"My guess is that he'll go far, at least with the women voters." Betty giggled girlishly. "Who could resist that dimple? And what he had to say—"

"Excuse me, Mrs. Allway, Mrs. Williams."

They turned to face a serious, middle-aged man in a brown tweed suit that could have stood a good pressing. His sparse salt-and-pepper hair was sticking out around his head as though he had just come in from a gale wind. He looked at them through wire-framed glasses that were popular a decade ago. "Yes?" Keely replied.

"I'm Al Van Dorf of the Associated Press."

"Hello, Mr. Van Dorf," Betty answered for both of them.

"It seems that the two of you more or less represent PROOF, at least you've always been more vocal than some of the others. I was wondering if you'd join me for lunch. I'd appreciate an interview with you."

"Keely?" Betty deferred to her. Keely took an instant liking to the reporter. He didn't seem the aggressive, boisterous type. She liked the fact that he seemed nervous about asking them to lunch.

"I think that would be all right."

"Thank you," Van Dorf said. "Both of you." He included Betty in his self-effacing smile. He handed Keely a piece of paper. "Here's the name of the restaurant. The reservations have been made. I'll meet you there in say—" he consulted a wristwatch "—half an hour. That should allow us time to get there."

"Fine. We'll be there," Betty said.

"Ladies." He shifted his tape recorder from one hand to the other and gave them an old-fashioned half-bow before scampering off, just as a television reporter approached the women for a statement. Betty backed away, leaving Keely to face the lights and cameras alone.

By the time they edged their way out into the corridor, said goodbye to the other women of PROOF, answered the questions of the competitive reporters, and wended their way through the miles of hallway to the outside of the Congress, they barely had time to flag a cab and get to their luncheon appointment.

In the taxi Keely brushed her hair and applied fresh lipstick while Betty powdered her nose. They were only a few minutes late when the taxi pulled up in front of a quiet-looking restaurant on an avenue not far from Embassy Row. They hurried inside and were greeted by a maître d' who was escorting them to a table before they could even identify themselves.

Keely almost stumbled on the well-worn carpet under her pumps when she saw Dax sitting along the wall on the banquette. Van Dorf, Congressman Parker, and Congressman Walsh stood as the two women approached the table. Betty seemed as alarmed as Keely as they were greeted by the small assembly.

"Mrs. Allway, Mrs. Williams, I'm glad you could make it," Van Dorf was saying in a much more assured voice than he had used on them in the congressional chamber. What had happened to his shuffling timidity? "You know these men, of course, but let me reintroduce you. Congressman Walsh from Iowa, Congressman Parker from Michigan, and Congressman Devereaux from Louisiana."

The ladies extended their hands to be shaken by each of the men. Dax shook Betty's hand and said, "A pleasure, Mrs. Allway." As his firm fingers closed around hers, Keely dared to raise her eyes to his. They were warm and gave off a hungry look that she hoped fervently no one else could discern. That's why she was so shocked when he said, "Mrs. Williams, how nice to see you again."

# *Four*

Keely covered her gasp of surprise by saying, "Hello, Congressman." His fingers pressed hers quickly before releasing them.

"You know each other?" Congressman Parker voiced the question all the others were silently asking.

Keely knew that Betty Allway's eyes had gone wide with disbelief and that her mouth had formed a moue of perplexity, but she dared not look at her friend.

"Yes," Dax answered easily. "We were on the same flight last night and introduced ourselves then. Mrs. Williams." He moved aside, allowing Keely to slide onto the banquette between him and Parker. Taking his cue from Dax, Congressman Walsh, oozing charm, held Betty's chair for her and she sat between him and Al Van Dorf.

Keely admired the aplomb with which Dax had handled the awkward situation, though she thought him dangerously honest. What would the other congressmen think? Would it disturb them to know she and Dax had met beforehand? Apparently not. Parker was already studying the menu through his half-glasses. Walsh was boisterously hailing a constituent sitting at another table. Only Betty seemed somewhat shaken. Keely noticed that her hand was trembling as she took a sip out of her water glass.

Dax, seemingly unaffected, helped Keely off with her coat while chattily asking Van Dorf about a recent banking scandal the reporter had uncovered. The hand that smoothed down her back as he adjusted the coat along the banquette belied his indifference to her.

The waiter took their drink orders and Van Dorf asked, "Does anyone mind if I smoke?" Without waiting for a response, he lighted up a short unfiltered cigarette. He talked around it as he set his tape recorder in the middle of the table. "I thought it would be beneficial if we had a casual, off-the-cuff meeting away from the hearing chambers. The issue at hand involves money, politics, foreign policy, the military, and human emotions. I think you can all see why I consider it to be an important news story. Will you indulge me and speak candidly?"

"Everyone knows how I feel about this," Walsh huffed.

"We can always count on you, Congressman, to be vocal about your position on any topic," Van Dorf said. The stodgy representative from Iowa missed the subtle insult. Van Dorf's eyes, which had looked at Keely and Betty with such humility only an hour ago, now shone with rapacious incisiveness behind his glasses. Had the man undergone a personality change? Keely was coming to realize that she had been hoodwinked, as had many of Van Dorf's former victims.

She picked up the stiff linen napkin folded over her place setting and laid it in her lap. Dax was doing the same. Keely's eyes glazed in shock when Dax clasped her hand under the table and gave it a hard, quick squeeze. When he brought his hands back to the table-top, his innocent expression gave away nothing. Keely hoped her rapid, shallow breathing could be accounted for by the off-color joke Congressman Walsh had just told.

When the waiter came back to take their lunch orders, Keely said, "Caesar salad, please."

When Dax had asked for a steak sandwich, he turned to her with a mock scowl. "That's not much lunch for a growing girl."

She laughed softly. "That's why I don't eat much lunch. I don't want to grow."

"You don't eat enough anytime."

"I ate—" She was about to tell him that she had eaten a half of one of the four sandwiches he had left in her room last night when, out of the corner of her eye, she caught sight of Van Dorf across the table. He had the look of a fox. It was a silly notion, but she could almost imagine that his ears had grown sharp and pointed as he strained to hear their conversation without appearing to do so. "I guess my appetite isn't very active," she finished.

Since Betty was conversing with Walsh and Parker, it looked quite normal for them to be talking together, but Dax sensed, as she did, Van Dorf's interest. He turned toward the reporter and asked, "Al, are you still playing racquetball when you're not chasing down a hot lead?"

Dax had an uncanny knack for tapping into someone's vulnerability. Van Dorf automatically launched into a detailed account of his latest bout, of which he was the victor. Keely wondered what the reporter would think if he knew that the shin of her crossed leg was being safely protected by Dax's calf beneath the table.

During the meal the chatter was limited to generalities. No one broached the subject that weighed so heavily on all their minds. But when their after-lunch coffee had been served, Van Dorf changed the tape in his recorder and lighted another pungent cigarette. "Do you think your husband is still alive, Mrs. Allway?" he asked brusquely.

Betty, taken completely off guard, sputtered around the sip of hot coffee she had just taken. "I—I couldn't…. Why…"

Keely quickly came to her rescue. "That isn't the point of the hearing, Mr. Van Dorf. Whether Bill Allway or my husband or any of the MIAs is alive isn't the issue here. Our immediate goal is to see that channels to confirm or deny their deaths are kept open. And at the same time to allow their families to collect money rightfully due them."

"Do you agree with that, Mrs. Allway?" Van Dorf asked.

"Yes," Betty replied, her equanimity restored.

"I'm curious to hear what the army has to say this afternoon," Parker said. "Do you have any idea what their stand will be, Mrs. Williams?"

"The last time we had a meeting with military personnel, they were supportive. I hope their attitude hasn't changed."

Walsh leaned back in his chair and said expansively, "Now, little lady, you—"

"Please don't address me as a 'little lady,' Congressman Walsh. I find it offensive," Keely said firmly.

Walsh looked momentarily nonplussed, then he grinned patronizingly. "I assure you I didn't mean—"

"Of course you did," Keely said. "Your opinion of us is all too apparent. You consider us to be a group of hysterical women wasting your valuable time. I wonder what your attitude would be if we were a group of men making an appeal. Would that give us more credibility? I assure you that there are numerous men in our organization, Congressman. Fathers, sons, brothers. They are just as concerned and resolved as we, but they find it harder to address such an emotional issue publicly. For that reason you'll find more women actively engaged in our efforts."

There was a silence around the table. Finally Congressman Parker said quietly, "I'd hate to think that anyone serving on this or any other committee would be blinded by prejudice of any kind." He glanced balefully at Walsh.

"Well, I certainly meant no offense and I wouldn't want to be accused of being chauvinistic. I apologize, Mrs. Williams," he blustered.

Keely's tone didn't soften, but she said, "Apology accepted. I'm sorry I broke your train of thought. What point were you about to make?"

And so it went. For the next half hour ideas were exchanged and discussed. All the while Van Dorf looked on with almost lascivious curiosity, his eyes darting around the table like a ricocheting bullet. His recorder didn't stop. When he was presented with the check, he scrawled his name across it and stood abruptly. "I guess it's time we all made our way back. Thank you for consenting to this luncheon. The maître d' will hail cabs for us," he said as they all stood.

"I think I'll walk a few blocks," Parker said. "Mrs. Allway, may I help you with your coat?" He matched action to words as he escorted Betty toward the door.

"Devereaux, do you want to share a cab with me?" Walsh asked.

"Thank you, but I need to stop by my office. I'll take my own."

"Then if you don't mind, I'll grab the first one."

"Not at all," Dax answered as the other congressman lumbered off.

Van Dorf, after pocketing his cartridge tapes, rushed toward a cigarette vending machine. Keely and Dax were granted a few moments of relative privacy.

"Remind me never to get your dander up," he whispered near her ear while holding her coat as she slid her arms in. "You've got sharp claws."

"That ignorant, bigoted buffoon," she said. "He's laughable. Imagine him holding a congressional seat. It's frightening."

"You were superb." His hand rested against her waist. Only to the casual observer would it appear that he was escorting her in a detached gentlemanly manner. To one more observant his touch would look like a caress.

"Why did you tell them we had met before?" she asked over her shoulder.

"For your information, Van Dorf is ruthless. He's

after the next Watergate story. Be careful of him, Keely. He's a wolf in sheep's clothing."

"I likened him to a cunning fox rather than a wolf. He led Betty and me to believe that we were his only guests for lunch. He failed to mention that you congressmen would be here. He made a self-effacing, pleading invitation, while all along he was baiting a trap."

"That creep. I'd like to cram that tape recorder of his down his throat. Or somewhere even more appropriate."

Keely couldn't stop the laugh that threatened. She turned to face him. "Remind me never to get your dander up," she taunted. He smiled, deepening the dimple. "Your fiery Creole heritage is showing."

"Is it? I'm sorry."

"Don't be. It's rather attractive."

"Do you think so?"

She looked around nervously. Betty and Congressman Parker were standing by the door watching for the promised taxis. Van Dorf was cursing the vending machine that had taken his change but hadn't come forth with the cigarettes. Walsh had left.

"Why did you tell them that we had met last night?"

"That was your original question, wasn't it? You see, when I'm around you, I have a hell of a time keeping my mind off— Never mind. To answer your question, if Van Dorf or anyone like him had seen us talking together last night and then we pretended never to have met today, that would pique someone's curiosity. Telling the truth is always the best policy."

"And if someone had seen you either coming into or going out of my room last night, what then?"

His eyes twinkled with devilish humor. "Then telling a lie is always the best policy."

She laughed. "You're a politician, all right."

He wasn't offended. Indeed, he laughed. His smile softened measurably when he asked, "How are you? Did you get any rest last night?"

She wished he wouldn't look at her with such concern. His eyes touched on each feature of her face and they grew warm under his interest. Why wouldn't her heart slow down? It beat so strenuously that it stirred the lace across her chest, a fact that Dax's wandering eyes took note of. "I didn't sleep too well, no."

"I take full responsibility for that."

"You shouldn't."

"But I do," he stressed. "I shouldn't have upset you. And don't deny that I did. When you first told me at the airport that you were married, I should have left you alone. That would have been best."

"Would it?"

"Wouldn't it?"

Pulled together by some invisible, inexplicable force, they felt themselves moving closer. Dax could feel the blood rushing to his extremities. His fingertips throbbed with it, with the need to touch her. The scar under his eye twitched. Too vividly his lips recalled the feel of her mouth beneath them. His eyes bored into hers.

Reflexively she licked her lips and he followed the sensuous course of her tongue with his eyes. "Yes," she said breathlessly. "It probably would have been best."

"I've forgotten the question again."

"Keely?"

"*What?*" She spun around guiltily when Betty called

to her from the door. "Is the cab here?" she asked on a gulping breath.

Betty eyed her flushed cheeks and agitated breast suspiciously. "Yes."

They said their goodbyes to Dax and their thank-yous to Van Dorf who was demanding his lost money from the management. Congressman Parker went out with them.

When they were situated in the back seat of the drafty taxi, Keely ineffectually fumbled with the clasp of her purse. "You don't have to tell me, but I confess I'm curious," Betty said.

"About what?" Keely strove for nonchalance, but knew she wasn't fooling anyone. Especially herself.

"Come on, Keely. This morning when I asked you about Dax Devereaux, I presented you with a golden opportunity to tell me about your meeting him last night. You didn't."

"I didn't think it was important."

Betty reached out and took Keely's damp hand in her own. She held it until Keely raised her eyes and looked at the older woman. "Women are characteristically more perceptive than men. Hopefully no one else at that table noticed the undercurrents running between you and the handsome congressman every time you looked at each other, but I did. I'm not being nosy. Your personal life is none of my business, Keely. I don't presume to censure you. I'm only cautioning you to be careful. Don't do something that will open you up for criticism, something that could jeopardize your reputation and integrity, not to mention PROOF."

Keely shook her head emphatically. "I would never do anything that stupid, Betty. You must know that."

"I know you *think* you wouldn't. I may seem old and dried up to you, Keely, but I'm a woman who hasn't had her man for over fourteen years. A man with Dax Devereaux's charm could tempt a saint to fall from grace."

Keely turned her head away, her eyes staring sightlessly at the Washington Monument that pointed toward heaven like an accusing finger. "I know what you mean."

The afternoon session of the hearing was taken up by the dull, routine, monotoned recitations of an army general. He read one affidavit after another from various branches of the military. The names and ranks were impressive, but the documents shed no new light on the issue. The general straddled the proverbial fence whenever an exasperated Congressman Parker tried to pin him down to a definitive statement. He had been coached to keep his comments generic and his opinions qualified. When the gavel banged on the block, dismissing the session for the day, everyone greeted it with a collective, bored sigh of relief.

Keely lost sight of Dax as he left the chambers. She and the other members of PROOF arranged to meet at Le Lion d'Or and treat themselves to a lavish dinner.

"We deserve it after two hours of General Adams," Betty said.

They went to their separate rooms when they arrived at the Capital Hilton. Keely wasn't looking forward to the evening as she should. Even a hot shower, careful grooming, and dressing in her coral print crepe de chine dress didn't generate any enthusiasm for the hours ahead. By an act of will, when she met Betty in the lobby, she pushed her despondency aside.

The meal was sumptuous, the atmosphere serene, the service without flaw. By tacit agreement the women who joined Betty and Keely didn't talk about the hearing or speculate on its outcome. They discussed fashions, the latest Hollywood scandal, their children, hairstyles, movies, books, and diets. They laughed, knowing what Congressman Walsh's comment would be if he saw them at the expensive restaurant.

Keely contributed to the conversations, ate and drank her fair share but by the time she waved good-night at her floor of the hotel and got off the elevator, she was exhausted and ready to fall into bed.

All evening her mind had strayed to thoughts of Dax. She saw him as he had been on the airplane, solicitously clasping her hands, reassuring her. He came to her mind looking as he had last night wearing the bellman's cap and holding the tray on his shoulder, laughing and teasing. Then her mind homed in on what she most wanted to forget—his eyes, his mouth, passionate and hot and hungry, his hands.

She slammed the door behind her when she reached her room, slung her coat over a chair, and tossed her purse and room key onto the dresser. "What in the hell am I doing?" she angrily asked her image in the mirror. "You're only torturing yourself, Keely."

Her limbs felt like lead appendages as she undressed. She flopped down onto the bed when she was at last washed, creamed, and brushed. Reaching for the alarm, she cursed under her breath when the telephone rang.

"Hello." Would it be Dax?

"Hi! Whatcha doin'?"

"Nicole! Hi." She ignored a pang of disappointment and put it down as indigestion.

"You sound tired," Nicole said.

"Do I? It's no wonder. I…uh…I didn't sleep well last night and today was hell. That congressional chamber seems to have walls that close in the longer you're there. What's happening at home? Everything all right?"

"Fine. Charles roped me into having dinner with two sponsors tonight. You should have seen their wives. Charter members of the Blue Hair and Mink Club of Suburban America. D-o-w-d-y! And Charles was his typical pain-in-the-posterior self."

Charles Hepburn was one of the television station's most successful salesmen. He sold more commercial time to more local clients than all the other salesmen together. His quiet, efficient manner attracted potential sponsors even before they enjoyed his thorough personal handling of their accounts.

"Nicole, you're not fooling me. You adore him."

She sighed theatrically. "I guess he's okay. If there's absolutely no one else around and absolutely nothing else to do."

Keely laughed in spite of her dour mood. Nicole had the gift of cheering up even the most dismal of days, for she never let herself get depressed.

"Hey, the newspapers here are full of Dax Devereaux being on that subcommittee. I didn't know that, did you?"

"Not until I got here, no."

"Well?"

"Well what?"

"Oh, hell, Keely. Are you going to make me drag it out of you? Have you met him?'

"Yes."

"And?"

"And what?"

Nicole's expletive made Keely cringe. "You're going to melt the cables if you don't stop talking like that over the telephone."

"Don't be coy with me," Nicole said crossly. "What do you think of Devereaux?"

"I don't know much about him. I've barely met him, Nicole."

"Oh, for sweet Pete's sake! You know he's the most gorgeous hunk of male flesh that's been available in a long time. If you've laid eyes on him at all you know that. And it's more than eyes I'd like to lay on him."

"Nicole!" Keely cried. "When did you meet him?"

"I haven't—not really. He was at a party last summer, and while I didn't actually *meet* him, I certainly knew he was there. He squires that Robins broad around. You know, the one who married that nice old man who conveniently croaked about six months after the nuptials and left her all that glorious money, the house in the Garden District, the cotton plantation in Mississippi, and the fleet of ships."

Keely's throat constricted. Dax and Madeline Robins? Had she known that? She was surprised to realize how much it hurt to visualize Dax with the flamboyant and merry widow who was touted for her beauty.

"Are you still there?" Nicole demanded when Keely failed to respond.

"Y-yes. I'm just tired, Nicole. Thank you for calling, but I really need to get to sleep."

"Kid, are you all right? You sound funny. Is everything there okay?" Nicole had dropped her cheerful bantering and Keely knew the concern in her friend's voice was genuine.

"Yes," she sighed. "It's just, well, you know, Nicole. I don't want to upset you by talking about PROOF."

"Oh, that. Well, that's why you're there, isn't it? And you know how I feel about it, so I won't belabor my point."

"Thanks."

"It wouldn't hurt if you had a wild fling while you were there though. Go to a triple-X-rated movie and sit next to a real pervert. Or have a hot and heavy affair with a visiting despot from some wonderfully decadent country."

"Goodbye," Keely called in a high singsong voice.

Nicole laughed. "Party pooper. Bye."

Without another word Nicole hung up. Keely was smiling when she replaced the receiver. She never remembered laying her head on the pillow and closing her eyes.

When the telephone rang again, she didn't realize at first that several hours had passed. Groping in the dark for the instrument, she finally found it, but missed her ear twice before fitting the receiver to it. "Hello."

"Good morning."

Her eyes sprang open. What a delightful way to be awakened—with a man's voice. This man's voice.

"Is it morning?" she asked. Her words were muffled by the pillow.

"Did I wake you up?"

"No." She yawned. "I had to get up to answer the phone."

"Very funny."

"No, it wasn't. It's too early for humor. What time is it?"

"Seven."

She rolled over and confirmed the time by the digital clock on the bedside table. "Oh, my God," she groaned. "I've overslept."

"What's the harm? The hearing's not till ten. You've got plenty of time."

"I know. It's just that I'm used to getting up early for my job. I feel self-indulgent when I sleep late."

"What time do you usually get up?"

"Five."

"Ugh! Why?"

"Because we're in the helicopter by six-thirty. Rush-hour traffic, remember?"

"I only called because I didn't get to say goodbye yesterday afternoon. I had mounds of paperwork to do in my office, and I knew I couldn't see you alone anyway."

"I went to dinner with the other ladies last night." Whom had he had dinner with? "I was exhausted when I came in. I was history once I got into bed."

"You needed the rest. You'll have another long day today."

"Yes."

There ensued a silence rife with so many things left

unsaid. Unspoken words hung between them, dancing along the line that connected them, begging to be uttered. "Well, I guess I'll see you later, then." Dax said at last. It wasn't at all what he wanted to say.

"Yes." Was that the best her brain could do? She was repeating herself like a parrot.

"Goodbye." A low sigh.

"Goodbye." A low sigh echoed.

"Keely?"

"Yes."

"While you're sitting behind that table all prim and proper today, know that at least one man in the room is wishing he could be holding you."

The line went dead in her hand.

# Five

For another day and a half the hearing droned on. PROOF found an ally in a POW who had returned home when the prisoners were released. In a poignant speech he related how he and the other prisoners of war never gave up hope and faith in their country. Even when they were subjected to the vilest indignities, he told his rapt audience, he and the men imprisoned with him never even considered that they would be abandoned and forgotten.

Keely and the other PROOF delegates celebrated this small victory, but their jubilation was short-lived. A representative of the Treasury Department testified to the amount of money it cost the taxpayers to pay the salaries of these men yet unaccounted for and possibly long since dead. Congressman Walsh and a few of the others nodded sagely as they listened to the financial report. Keely wished Walsh's fat stomach would suddenly start paining him in proportion to its size.

Through the hours of close confinement in the committee room she adroitly avoided any encounter with

Dax, intentional or otherwise. He too had apparently decided that contact with her would be disadvantageous, for he didn't make any overtures toward her.

They appeared to be strangers, unaware of each other, but beneath the surface the awareness was a choking reality. Keely often felt Dax's eyes on her. Remembering their early-morning telephone conversation, she blushed to the roots of her hair, whether she met his eyes or not. Glancing at him was an urge she didn't resist often enough.

His mannerisms were becoming endearingly familiar. His tasteful neckties rarely remained knotted for longer than an hour. Impatient, restless fingers would tug on the knot until it loosened. The collar button of his shirt would be freed from its hole. The strong, tanned column of his throat would expand with his now unrestricted breathing.

He sat leaning back with his elbow propped on the padded maroon leather arm of his chair. His chin rested on his thumb, three fingers covered his upper lip and mouth, and his index finger lay along his cheek pointing unerringly to the faint scar just below his eye.

He listened carefully; he watched intently; he jotted down notes with a rapid scrawl.

He looked at Keely.

Once, his steady gaze was so compelling that she courageously, albeit unwisely, met it. Her heart skidded to a jarring halt. Her breath was trapped in squeezing lungs. Perspiration lubricated her palms. Her stomach knew the fluttering of a million wings. His eyes let her know that his thoughts were no more on what the speaker was saying than were hers.

The finger lying along his cheek lifted in a silent hello. The motion was so subtle that no one would even see it unless the salutation was meant for him. Keely saw it and acknowledged it with a brief lowering of her eyelids. The message said more than merely hello. It said: *I wish I could talk to you. I wish we weren't in this particular place at this particular point in time, doing what we're doing. I wish...* So many things that were impossible.

At noon of the third day, when Congressman Parker adjourned them for lunch, he recommended that they take the rest of the afternoon and the next day off.

"We've had three full days of discussion, I think we all need time to digest what we've heard, assess our opinions, do our own research, and clear out the cobwebs, so to speak, before a final discussion." When the motion was unanimously agreed to, he banged the gavel and the committee hearing was adjourned.

"What a break," Betty said gratefully. "I need a day to do my hair and nails. I'm running out of money too and need to find a bank. What about you, Keely? Want to get in some shopping this afternoon?"

Keely smiled, but shook her head. "I don't think so, Betty, but I'm sure some of the others will go with you. If you don't mind, I'm going to beg off. I think I'll go to my room and collapse with a good book or a good nap."

Betty laughed and patted the younger woman's arm. "Then I'll say goodbye. See you later for dinner?"

Keely considered for a moment then said, "Sure. Call me when you get back to the hotel."

Betty turned and walked away, but not before glancing worriedly behind Keely. Before Keely could wonder why, she felt the light tap on her shoulder. Dax was there, smiling too widely, too brightly, too openly, to denote intimacy. "Mrs. Williams," he spoke quickly. "I haven't had a chance to talk to you since we met at lunch the other day. I hope you aren't finding the hearing too tedious."

"Not at all, Congressman. I more or less expected things to move slowly. It will be to our advantage, I think, for all of you to weigh the issue carefully."

He nodded in deep concentration as though she were expounding on something of great importance. He moved closer, folded his arms over his chest, and studied the toes of his polished loafers. His voice was so low she could barely hear him when he said, "How are you really?"

"Fine."

"I have to go to a damn cocktail party tonight at the French Embassy. I was told to bring a date if I wished. You wouldn't consider..."

The invitation was left dangling, but she supplied the rest of it. "No, Dax," she murmured. "You know that wouldn't be wise."

His grim expression perfectly suited the topic they should have been discussing—the MIAs. "Yeah, I know," he muttered. "Well, let's hope things work out for the best for everyone, Mrs. Williams," he said more loudly and stuck out his hand for her to shake. Their eyes locked when their hands clasped and, for a heartbeat, the rest of the world fell away. All too soon it came back.

"Hey, Congressman," Al Van Dorf said from behind them. "I wondered if I might get a statement from you about that armaments proliferation bill being talked up in committee."

"Sure, Al. Enjoy the time off, Mrs. Williams," Dax said politely.

"Thank you. I will. Mr. Van Dorf." She nodded her goodbyes and left the two men. Leaden legs carried her out of the chambers. It took several minutes for her to hail a cab on Pennsylvania Avenue. She didn't mind. She almost wished she had agreed to go shopping with Betty. The afternoon hours yawned before her. Anything was better than sitting morosely in a lonely hotel room, yearning for things that couldn't be.

As it turned out, she remembered very little of that dismal afternoon. She returned to her room and immediately fell asleep, not waking until Betty knocked on her door several hours later. They decided to stay at the hotel and eat at Trader Vic's because of the inclement weather.

When they were done with their meal and crossing the lobby toward the elevator, Betty said, "I bought a new suit today. Why don't you come up and I'll model it for you. There's an old Robert Taylor-Barbara Stanwyck movie on television tonight. Of course, you probably don't remember them."

Keely laughed. "I certainly do! You won't mind the company?" She hated the thought of returning to her room. After her nap she knew she wouldn't be ready to go to sleep for hours.

"No, I'd love it. Let's really misbehave and order up a bottle of wine," Betty said with adolescent enthusiasm.

Several hours later Keely was feeling mellow after

drinking a few too many glasses of wine and watching the sentimental, romantic black-and-white movie. She and Betty had giggled like schoolgirls over the wine and cried over the tender love story. She left Betty yawning sleepily and weaved her way down the deserted hallway.

The elevator doors swished open. Keely was instantly sobered when she saw Dax leaning against the back wall. His previous gloomy slouching posture was replaced by one of rigid attention, as though an order had been snapped by a drill sergeant intolerant of laziness. He uncrossed his ankles and dropped the overcoat that had been draped over his shoulder and held by one finger. His face broke into a wide grin. "Going up?"

"No, down."

"Come along for the ride," he invited. When he saw her hesitate and glance around apprehensively, he said, "No one can blame us for meeting accidentally in a public elevator when we're staying in the same hotel. Besides that, what could possibly happen in an elevator?" He was teasing, but Keely's eyes dropped involuntarily, but significantly, to the lushly carpeted floor of the cubicle. "Forget I said that," he growled. "Get in."

She stepped through the sliding doors and they closed behind her, sealing them in, separating them from the rest of the world, creating their own universe.

She cleared her throat self-consciously. "How was the party?"

"Loud. Smoky. Crowded."

"Sounds fun."

He hadn't given a damn about the party, could barely remember it though he had left it only minutes ago. He had had a terrible time. He had eaten the rich can-

apés, all the while wondering what Keely's favorite
foods were, wishing they could be sharing a peanut
butter sandwich and popcorn in front of a fireplace, on
a couch, in a bed…

He had drunk perhaps a tad too much of the limitless
liquor, wondering if she liked chilled white wine. While
listening to the shrill voice of the buxom, overjew-
eled wife of a foreign diplomat, he was seeing Keely's
mouth, shimmering with spilled wine. He imagined his
tongue lifting golden droplets from the petal-soft lips.

The other men at the fete had ogled a senator's secretary whose well-known figure had been touted and
tasted by every male on Capitol Hill. Tonight the generous body had been encased in a tight red dress. Pen-
dulous breasts and broad hips had swayed invitingly.
Only a week ago Dax's comments on the woman's anatomy would have been as clever and imaginative as anyone's. Tonight she had seemed obscene and stupid. His
thoughts had centered around a much daintier figure.
Softly feminine, yet neat. Curvaceous, yet compact.
Touchable, yet…untouchable.

"You're home," she said softly. The elevator had as-
cended to the top floor and the doors had slid open.
Across the hallway was his suite of rooms, void of
warmth. The only source of heat in which he found
comfort this night was standing with him in the elevator, looking at him with bemusement.

"Where were you just now?" he asked.

"In Betty's room. We watched an old movie and de-
molished a bottle of wine."

"Red or white?"

She closed her eyes as if savoring the vintage.

"Golden," she whispered. Her eyes flew wide when his anguished groan filled the small cubicle like the roar of an angry, thwarted tiger. His finger pressed the button for the seventh floor and it lighted up as the doors closed. "What—"

"I'll ride with you to your floor," Dax said by way of explanation.

"You shouldn't."

"You don't have to remind me."

She looked away, hurt by his sharp tone. "I'm sorry," he said contritely. "I'm not angry at you. I'm mad at—"

"I know," she interjected quickly. The less said, the better.

The elevator stopped on her floor and the door opened, but before she could step out, he pressed another button. She didn't notice which one and it didn't matter. The doors closed again. "Dax—"

"I'm picking you up tomorrow morning in front of the hotel. Ten o'clock. Dress casual."

"I can't," she objected, shaking her head.

"Can't dress casual?" he teased. For the first time she saw the familiar smile, the one that deepened the dimple and lightened his dark eyes from ebony to chocolate.

She gave him a withering look. "I can't meet you."

"Sure you can."

The elevator stopped, the doors opened, and Keely and Dax were both surprised to see a middle-aged couple standing on the other side. They had almost forgotten that they weren't the only two people in the world. "Good evening," Dax said genially. "Where to?"

"Three," the man said.

Dax pushed the specified button for the man and

leaned negligently back against the wall as though he were only a casual passenger in the elevator. "Are you from out of town?" he asked.

"New Mexico. Las Cruses," the man answered. The woman was staring at Dax's discarded coat still lying on the floor. She raised myopic, suspicious eyes to Keely, who smiled sickly. The woman grasped her husband's arm as though seeking protection from these immoral, large-city types.

"Ah, there's a fine university in Las Cruses," Dax said.

"New Mexico State," the man said proudly.

"Right!" Dax snapped his fingers. Keely could have throttled him. He was enjoying himself.

The elevator stopped at the third floor and the man ushered out his disapproving wife. "Have an enjoyable stay," Dax said with a smile that should have graced a Chamber of Commerce brochure. The doors closed again. "Now, as I was saying…"

"No, *I* was saying that I can't go anywhere with you, Dax."

"We're taking the day off. Having an outing. We've both been cooped up in that stuffy room for too many days and it's beginning to play on my nerves. And if I may say so, you're looking a little peaked yourself."

In fact, the opposite was true. Her cheeks were flushed from recent embarrassment and wine consumption. Her eyes were large and shiny remnants of her uninterrupted sleep that afternoon and tearful enjoyment of the movie. Her hair was beguilingly mussed. She had never looked more beautiful, more alluring, sexier.

His eyes riveted on her lips, which had parted with the intention to argue, but any arguments died unspoken. Even without the benefit of artificial gloss, her mouth shone with its own dewy softness and he longed to drink of it.

"Why can't two friends spend a few hours in each other's company?" They weren't friends and never would be and they both knew it. But his gravelly words took up time and space necessary to keep him from crushing her against him as he ravaged that kissable mouth.

They didn't speak again, only looked at each other, saying more silently than verbal communication would allow them. This time when the doors opened on her floor, he pressed the Door Open button.

"Ten o'clock tomorrow."

"Someone—anyone—might see us. Van Dorf..." Her objections meant nothing. There was no doubt in either's mind that she was going to meet him.

"No one will notice. I borrowed a friend's car. It's a silver Datsun. I'll circle the block until you come out on the K Street side. Don't look furtive or guilty. Just open the car door and get in."

"Dax—"

"Good night." He placed his index finger on her breastbone and pushed her gently across the threshold of the elevator. He wasn't trying to get rid of her; he was removing the temptation to commit a criminal offense. He released the button on the panel and the doors closed between them.

For long moments Keely stared at the doors, not seeing them, not seeing anything. Dazedly turning toward her room, she was already in a quandary about what to wear the next day.

Her final choice was a pair of gray flannel slacks, a black turtleneck sweater, and a herringbone blazer that matched both. Black suede boots would keep her feet warm, as the weather was cold and rainy, not yet conceding that spring was imminent. She had no idea where Dax was taking them, so she wanted to be prepared for any eventuality. At five minutes to ten she picked up her overcoat and left her room.

Her heart was thudding with guilty anticipation as she crossed the crowded lobby with what she hoped looked like nonchalance. No sooner had she reached the broad doors than she saw a low, sleek silver Datsun slow to a crawl beside the curb. Pushing the door against the strong wind, she whisked through it, ducked her head to be sure it was Dax behind the wheel of the car, and opened the door. They both laughed when she plopped into the deep leather seat and sped away.

"Good morning," he said, taking advantage of a red traffic light to turn his head and look at her.

"Good morning."

"You're right on time."

"Punctuality is one of my virtues. How many times did you go around the block?"

"Three. Impatience is one of my virtues." They laughed again with the sheer pleasure of being alone together. He resented the light for turning green and forcing him to pay attention to his driving.

"Where are we going?" Keely asked, not caring.

"Mount Vernon."

"Mount Vernon!" She looked through the tinted car windows at the drizzle and low-hanging, ominously threatening clouds. "Today? Who would go to Mount Vernon on a day like today?"

He stopped at another traffic light before answering her. Swiveling to face her, he tweaked her nose. "No one. That's why we're going there."

She acknowledged his astuteness with a slight bow. "You're not a senatorial candidate for nothing, Mr. Devereaux. You're positively brilliant."

"Sometimes I'm so smart it's frightening," he boasted and got an elbow in his ribs for punishment.

She didn't bother him while he threaded his way through the traffic on Constitution Avenue toward the Lincoln Memorial. She folded her coat behind the bucket seats, placed her shoulder bag beneath her legs, and tuned in a stereo radio station agreeable to them both.

They crossed the Potomac River on the Arlington Memorial Bridge and took the Memorial Highway along the river toward George Washington's homestead. The woods that lined the road were still-naked reminders of winter.

"This will look lovely in a few weeks when the dogwoods and redbuds start blooming," Keely mused.

"Yeah. I love it at home when all the flowers bloom. We have azaleas on all four sides of the house, and it's a magnificent sight when they're in full bloom. We hire a man whose sole responsibility is to take care of the flowering shrubs."

"We?"

"Well, that's not quite accurate. I still consider the main house my parents' home. Several years ago they moved to a smaller house on the other side of our property. Ostensibly the move was to keep my father from having to climb stairs, but I think it was to make me feel lonely rattling around in that large house all by myself and to provide an incentive for me to find a wife and start having grandbabies."

"Why haven't you?"

"I haven't found anyone important enough to me to share my life with." His eyes wavered from the scenic highway to look across the narrow space of the car at her. "When I do find her, I'll fight like hell to get her into that house with me."

Her throat closed as tightly as the fists she clenched in her lap. She looked away from the compelling force of his eyes. "What's it like? Your house. Is it antebellum?"

He faced the road again. "No. The Devereauxs did have an ancestral home, but it was razed by the Union Army during the war. It took us until 1912 to recover our losses from the war and Reconstruction and build another. I love it, but I'm not going to tell you much about it. I want you to see it for yourself sometime."

"Is it in Baton Rouge?"

"Twenty miles from there."

"How much land do you have?"

He shrugged self-consciously. "Enough to farm profitably and raise a few horses."

"Are you dodging my questions? You're not giving me straight answers, Mr. Devereaux, a talent you've no doubt perfected from dealing with reporters."

He laughed. "You've found me out."

She didn't press the issue and he didn't volunteer any more information. Obviously he was embarrassed by his family's wealth. It had been the topic of many unflattering editorials.

The remainder of the fifteen-mile trip was passed in companionable silence. When the car pulled into the parking facility, it joined few others. Where usually there were dozens of tour buses, today only one was parked in the lot provided them.

"See? What'd I tell you?" Dax asked. "We'll have the place virtually to ourselves. I doubt if George and Martha ever had it so good." He chucked her under the chin before lifting his overcoat from behind his seat and getting out.

He opened her door and held her coat while she slipped into the arms. His hands settled only slightly and briefly on her shoulders before he clasped her elbow and steered her toward the gate.

The lady in colonial costume behind the grilled window said, "You certainly didn't pick a very nice day to visit us, but I hope you'll brave the rain and see all the outbuildings too. Tours start every twenty minutes or so. We don't keep to a rigid schedule except during the summer when we're crowded. There's a group waiting to go up to the house now. You can join it. A guide will be along shortly."

"Thank you." Dax flashed his famous smile. "I wanted to come on a summer day, but this is the only day my sister could come."

Keely gazed up at him in stupefaction. She felt her lower jaw drop to hang open stupidly. When they walked away, Dax's gait was jaunty. "You're crazy!" Keely admonished under her breath.

Dax didn't look at her. He was busy fishing his collapsible umbrella out of his deep coat pocket. He pushed the button and it mushroomed open with a loud pop. "Do you really think people are going to believe I'm your sister?" she demanded, stopping on the gravel path leading up to the house.

He looked down at her as he held the umbrella over them as protection against the light rain. He studied her objectively. "No, I guess they won't. We'd better practice the act. Here, hold this." He thrust the handle of the umbrella into her surprised hand.

"Sis!" he exclaimed, grasping her by the shoulders. "Look at what a beautiful woman you've grown into." He lowered his head and kissed her soundly on the mouth. "Let me see you."

Stunned by his playacting, Keely stood docilely while he unabashedly opened her coat, then moved aside the lapels of her jacket to rake is eyes appreciatively over her sweatered chest. "Never would I have guessed when you were all arms and legs and flat chested that you'd round out so nicely."

Vexed, Keely opened her mouth, but she didn't have a chance to rebuke him before he rushed on. "You look gorgeous in any color. Do you know that?" His banter took on a different tone. Her cheek was grazed with gentle fingertips. "You're wonderful in black. I like you in that green you were wearing on the airplane." His voice lowered and became husky. "And you're delicious in yellow terry cloth. Is there any color in the rainbow that dulls your eyes, or makes your complexion sallow, or fails to make your hair come to life?"

His thumb mesmerizingly traced the curve of her jaw. She saw herself mirrored in the dark depths of his eyes and was shocked at the wistful expression she saw on her face. He shouldn't stand so close, but she didn't want to destroy this moment by pointing that out.

His fingers really shouldn't touch her lips. It was far too intimate a gesture and destroyed the brother/sister act. But even as her mind objected, her lips obeyed his urging and parted slightly.

His head was lowering dangerously close when a party of four came hurrying along the path behind them. Dax backed away from her. "Come along, sis," he muttered, taking the umbrella and ushering her toward the small group of tourists waiting at the base of the rise on which the stately house sat.

After only a short wait a guide came down the path and led the soggy, but undaunted, group up the hill to the house. The guide's spiel was rehearsed, but thankfully, she made the recitation colorful and conversational. Like the others in the group, Keely and Dax listened. They climbed the stairs, they peered into roped off rooms, they noted what should be made note of, and they wouldn't remember any of it later.

When the official tour was over, they were again invited to view the outbuildings and grounds. Most of the others trailed off toward the tack room and kitchen. Keely and Dax headed toward a small building that housed personal effects of the Washingtons.

"Did you ever think," Keely said, "that if you ever

become president, two hundred years later people will be traipsing around your house looking at your razor?"

"I use a disposable razor, but remind me to always keep my false teeth polished." They laughed and quite spontaneously he hugged her.

They walked to the tomb where the Washingtons were interred. Dax said quietly, "Did you know it was rumored that Washington was in love with another man's wife?"

"He was?" Keely asked on an uneven breath.

"Yes. So they say."

"How tragic."

"Maybe not," Dax countered. "The love he had for that woman may have been something very special."

"Yes, maybe." Why did she feel like crying?

"It certainly doesn't take anything away from what he did for his country. I can't see that it matters much."

"Not now," Keely said thickly. "But then, when it was happening, it might have mattered a great deal to those who were involved."

His sigh stirred her hair that had somehow come to rest against his lean cheek. "I guess you're right."

They left the grave site and made their way back to the main compound. Trying to shrug off the pensive mood, Dax suggested they eat a snack before starting back. "I understand the restaurant here isn't too bad. And we certainly don't need a reservation," he said as he opened the door leading into the virtually deserted dining room.

Maple tables and chairs were arranged in neat rows across the hardwood floors. Each window was flanked by starched white ruffled curtains. Brass candlesticks with tall narrow chimneys adorned each table and cast a soft glow on the provincially papered walls.

Only three of the colonial tables were already occupied. Fires were glowing in the fireplaces and Dax led Keely to a table near one of them and close to a window that overlooked the manicured grounds. A waitress rushed to take their orders for clam chowder. When they had done justice to the soup, Dax signaled her and she scurried over again.

"We'd like dessert too. What have you got?"

"Homemade pies are our speciality. Cherry, apple, and pecan."

"Terrific. We'll have two pieces of cherry."

"No, I want pecan," Keely interposed.

Dax looked comically thunderstruck. "You can't come to George Washington's house and not have cherry pie. It's anti-American."

She laughed, but said to the waitress, "Pecan, please."

"Okay," Dax said grudgingly. "And we want two scoops of vanilla ice cream on each."

"No, I want whipped cream on mine."

He turned and glared at her. "Who's doing this, you or me?"

She and the waitress laughed at his villainous scowl. "You didn't ask me what I wanted and I want whipped cream."

Dax shook his head in frustration then asked with exaggerated courtesy, "Coffee?"

"Tea," she replied primly.

The waitress, pen poised over her tablet, was shaking with laughter. "Cream?" she asked.

"No."

"Yes," Keely answered at the same time.

Dax looked up at the waitress and said in a loud stage whisper, "She thinks she's a liberated woman."

The waitress leaned down and said to him, "I like to see marriages where each partner is considered an individual." Then she walked away with her skirts swaying saucily behind her.

Keely stared down at her left hand, which lay on the tabletop. It was a natural enough mistake. There was the simple gold band encircling her third finger. Out of her peripheral vision she saw Dax's hand move closer until it covered hers.

"She thinks you're married to me," he said softly. "As long as she thinks that and she doesn't recognize either of us, I suppose it's all right if we hold hands." His long fingers laced with hers and squeezed tightly.

"I suppose so," Keely said, returning the pressure.

They stared at the fire that popped and hissed cheerily. They stared at the rain that fell monotonously and heavily and ran in wide rivulets down the panes of glass. It blurred the scenery, softened the sharp angles of the world, dimmed the harsh light of reality, and made it easy for them to pretend for a while that things weren't as they were. And because they couldn't help themselves, they stared at each other.

The warm ambience of the restaurant surrounded them like a cocoon. The clatter of china and silverware in the kitchen couldn't override the silent messages each transmitted. The movements of the other patrons or waitresses didn't distract their eyes from the other's face.

"I just noticed for the first time that your ears are pierced," Dax commented. "Did it hurt?"

"Like hell."

His grin was wide, but he didn't laugh aloud. "You'd never make a politician, Miss Preston. You're far too straightforward."

Miss Preston. Not Mrs. Williams. Here with him now, she was Miss Preston. "How did you get that scar under your eye?"

"Is it unsightly? I'll have plastic surgery."

"Don't you dare! It's—" She was about to say beautiful, but amended it for fear he would take umbrage at such a feminine adjective. His dark brows arched in silent query at her pause. "It makes you appear very rakish," she said.

"I'm a regular swashbuckler. As a matter of fact, there was a seedier Devereaux involved with the Laffites."

She squinted her eyes and tilted her head. "Yes, I can see you as a pirate."

"Maybe I should have *my* ears pierced. No, just one of them, I think. That's much more…rakish."

They were laughing when the waitress set down the tray between them.

"Do you want something else?" Dax asked when they were finished.

"Are you serious? I can barely breathe," Keely said.

"Do you want to race to the car and burn off a few of those calories?"

"I'll be lucky to waddle," she confessed as he held her coat for her. They settled the bill and regretfully left the warmth of the restaurant for the cold outside.

They splattered through puddles as they dashed for the car. The rain was coming down more earnestly than it had all day.

The cold motor took some coaxing to get started, but then it roared to life, and Dax carefully steered it out onto the highway.

"It's really coming down," Keely remarked worriedly when they had driven a few miles through sheets of rain. Even with the rapid, insistent cadence of the windshield wipers, the road was obliterated by a virtual wall of water.

"It's crazy trying to drive in this. I think there's…" His voice trailed off as he searched the side of the road through the foggy windows. "There it is," he exclaimed and pumped the brakes until the car slowed enough for him to turn into the innocuous side road.

"I'm going to stop here until this lets up."

# Six

The lane was rutted and the sports car bumped along it for several yards before Dax braked it to a stop. He parked under the semiprotective branches of an oak and cut the motor. The ensuing silence was deafening. The radio's music ceased abruptly. The windshield wipers stopped their drumming. The motor's throb no longer vibrated. Only the rain persisted.

Dax reached across the seat and touched her shoulder. "Are you warm enough? Do you need your coat?" They had taken off their outer coats and folded them behind the seats again before leaving Mount Vernon.

"No, I think the heater had time to warm up the car enough for now."

"If you get cold, tell me. I can either get your coat or let the motor idle for a few minutes." His hand slid down her arm and took her hand. He massaged it. "Your hand is freezing."

"I know. I can't ever get them warm."

"Put them in your pockets."

"It doesn't help."

"Then put them in my pockets." He was only half teasing.

"Then what would you do to keep yours warm?" It was a challenge she couldn't resist issuing.

His eyes twinkled through the gloomy atmosphere. "I'd think of something," he answered in a low rumble. His fingers aligned with hers and he pressed each one in turn. He studied the contrast of his hair-sprinkled hand with the smooth frailty of hers. Then he raised her hand to his mouth and lightly brushed his lips across the fingertips.

"If I had to accidentally meet the wife of an MIA on an airplane, why did she have to look like you? Be you?" His mouth was moving against her palm now, talking into it, kissing it.

"You shouldn't say—"

"Shh. If I can't do anything else, at least let me talk, Keely." His hot tongue darted quickly into the center of her hand and her breath caught in her throat. "But then if you hadn't looked like you, I doubt if I would have gone barreling across the aisle of that airplane like some misplaced Sir Galahad to rescue you, would I?"

She couldn't answer. His tongue was sliding between her fingers at their base, slowly, leisurely. It was too sexy a gesture to allow, but too blissful to stop. He covered his mouth with her hand and lifted his eyes to hers.

The air in the small enclosure was redolent with ungratified passion. Their breath created a moist veil on the inside of the cold car windows. Each sound was amplified in the silence. When Dax leaned closer to her, the rustle of his clothing sounded like leaves in an autumn breeze. Each sight was magnified. He could almost count the dark lashes on her lower eyelid. The corner of her mouth quivered slightly with each breath. It was a beautiful mouth, and he had claimed it as his the first time he saw it.

Keely never remembered feeling quite this helpless—knew indeed that she had never felt this way in her life. She was floating weightlessly, yet a heavy pressure made her lower body ache with longing. She felt imbued with a strength she had never before experienced, but her muscles seemed to have liquefied. Her whole body tingled with life, yet she knew this panting desire closely resembled dying.

She didn't know she had reached for him until she saw her hand smoothing back a damp, errant strand of dark hair from his forehead. She watched as her thumb stroked across the faint scar beneath his eye.

Only her name, spoken with the reverence of a prayer, hovered between them before his lips caressed hers. Had she closed her eyes she might never have known that he touched her, so light was the touch of his mouth on hers. But she had been watching and now saw him draw back. Disappointment swamped her. She wanted to know the heat and urgency of his mouth. He had told her impatience was one of his virtues. She was desperate for a display of that impatience now.

But Dax wasn't about to rush this moment or take advantage of her mood. He took her hands and slipped them under his sweater, pressing them against the hair-roughened skin. "Warm them on me." He dropped the sweater back into place and held her face cupped between his palms. Cautiously she moved her fingers against the skin that was as hot as a furnace. He watched her expression. Her eyes closed as she became braver and moved her hands in ever widening circles. Lips, soft and pliant, parted as she emitted a sigh. His mouth was suddenly there, resting on hers, drawing in the breath she expulsed so sweetly.

His tongue slipped past her lips and traced the row of teeth. A gentle nudge was all it took for her to lift that barrier. The tip of his tongue found hers and explored it with erotic leisure. Then he searched each crevice of her mouth, wantonly investigating, sensuously seeking out the places that, when found, caused her to strain against him.

His tongue withdrew, but hers followed. Tentatively, maidenly, she parted his lips and they opened for her. He was surprised at her inexperience, the youthful awkwardness, the timidity with which she kissed him. He accepted the timorous flutterings of her tongue until they became well-planned strokes. When it slid along the roof of his mouth, he groaned and crushed her against him.

Breaking apart to draw breath, he rasped against her ear. "Don't ever be afraid of me, Keely. There is no need to be." He had taken her shyness as fearful caution.

"I know, I know. It's not that. It's…I'm afraid I'm not good at—I was so young and it's been so long—"

"You're sweeter because of that. If only you knew how much sweeter. And you'll learn. We'll learn together."

He hooked a finger in the high collar of her sweater and lowered it to avail himself of the skin underneath. Nibbling lips wandered along her neck to her ear. He teased her earlobe with his tongue and caught at the gold sphere adorning it with his teeth. They laughed softly. Her laughter turned into gasps of ecstasy when he probed the inside of her ear with his tongue. She shuddered.

"Are you cold?" he asked.

She shook her head, just barely, not enough to dislodge his mouth. "No."

"Tell me."

"I will." Cold? She would never be cold around him. His mouth was relentless. She never thought a man could be so sensitive to what a woman wanted... needed. Dax seemed to glean and anticipate her every carnal wish. He wasn't greedy and fumbling. Every move was slow, practised, and choreographed to bring her pleasure.

The increasing palpitations in her throat frightened her. She feared she might not be able to breathe much longer. Her hands moved restlessly under his sweater around to his back, seeking a handhold before she slid off the edge of the world.

He kissed her again, deeper, with a hunger tempered by caring. His hands eased from her cheeks down to her neck and encircled it. His thumb charted her collarbone. When he lowered his hands to embrace her, they ghosted over her breasts.

*God help me,* Dax requested silently. *Don't let me touch her. If I do, I'll never be able to let her go.*

He felt her imperceptible reaction. Her soft, rapid breaths struck his mouth like puffs of cotton. He felt the muscles of her thighs contract as they lay against his. His hands lingered indecisively, waiting. Catching her bottom lip between his teeth, he worried it gently. Meeting his fervor equally, she murmured something incoherently and raised herself to just beneath his hands.

Emboldened by her response, his good, honorable intentions dissolved and his hands closed over her. Their sighs of pleasure echoed each other. By slow degrees Keely relaxed and offered herself up for his further exploration. She leaned back into the car seat and locked her hands behind his back, pulling him closer.

He kneaded her gently, caressed her. He learned her by the sensitive employment of his hands. He closed his eyes and visualized what he was touching—the texture, the color. It was agony not to see, but heaven to imagine. He had felt the bra immediately, but knew it couldn't be much. For as he cupped her and lifted her with his palms, his thumbs fanned her nipples, which were aroused and impertinently demanding his attention.

"So lovely," he murmured as he pressed his face into her round softness and breathed deeply of her fragrance, which had permeated the knit of her sweater. With nose and mouth he nuzzled her while his fingers continued their tender torment. "You feel so good," he whispered just before his lips closed around one distended nipple. His tongue dampened her sweater.

"Oh, Dax!" She shoved against his shoulders with the heels of her hands. He bumped his head on the ceiling of the car as he jerked upright.

"Did I hurt you?" he asked, alarmed.

No, no. It wasn't pain she was feeling. Mark had touched her there, but had never done anything as intimate as Dax just had. Never had she felt a spear of pleasure piercing her so deeply that it went straight to her womb and opened up a floodgate of desire that overflowed until she wasn't able to contain it. It had thrilled her, frightened her, terrified her.

He could read the fear on her face and blamed himself for putting it there. Guiltily, wearily, he shook his head. "I'm sorry, Keely. I only wanted to touch you, to kiss you."

Sadly she stared out the windshield as he slipped the car into gear. The rear wheels spun, trying to gain traction on the mushy turf. Finally the car lurched forward and Dax maneuvered it back onto the highway.

The rain had lessened significantly to a dreary mist. The windshield wipers clicked back and forth, making the only sound in the car. When the radio had come back on with the motor, Dax had switched off the silver knob. He cursed the slow bumper-to-bumper rush-hour traffic as they approached the city.

The brakes screeched when he pulled the car to a halt outside the hotel. He was a long time looking at her and when he did, he was struck to see tears glistening in her eyes. Her mouth was working with emotion.

"Keely—"

"It was a beautiful day. Forgive me, Dax, for— It wasn't your touching me that I was frightened of, but of my not wanting you to ever stop."

Before he could reply, she was gone and running toward the doors of the hotel.

She lay huddled under the covers, clad only in her underwear. She wasn't sure how much time had elapsed since she had let herself into the cold, lonely room, stripped off her clothes, which still lay where she had dropped them, and crawled into the false sanctuary of the bed. Convinced that she needed rest, she tried to sleep, but it eluded her.

Her mind wouldn't let her escape from this maelstrom of indecision and guilt—guilt over betraying Mark, if not in deed, then certainly in thought, guilt over leading Dax on so shamelessly. He would despise her after today. She couldn't blame him.

Her heart jumped in her chest when she heard the light tapping on her door. She had put out the Do Not Disturb sign when she came in and had taken the telephone off the hook. But whoever was on the other side of the door wasn't taking her at her word.

She threw back the covers and padded to the door, putting her eye to the fish-eye peephole and seeing a man dressed in a hotel uniform. "Yes?"

"Mrs. Williams?"

"Yes," she repeated, this time in affirmation.

"Are you all right? I'm Mr. Bartelli, an assistant manager here at the hotel. A Mrs. Allway has been trying to reach you and hasn't been able to get through. She was worried and requested that I come check on you. Are you well?"

"Yes, Mr. Bar—Bartelli. I only wanted to rest undisturbed. I took the telephone off the hook. Please tell Mrs. Allway that I'm fine and that I'll see her in the morning." She could have offered to call her friend herself, but she didn't want to speak to anyone.

"Very well. You're sure we can't do anything?"

"No, I'm fine, thank you."

"Good night. I apologize for disturbing you."

"Good night." She watched in the distorted glass his minuscule figure disappear down the hall.

Since she was already up, she decided to take a shower before going back to bed. It worked well to soothe and relax her. Almost too well. Feeling languid and warm as she stepped out of the shower, she caught her reflection in the mirror. Her skin was rosy from the hot water. Her breasts tingled from the shower's invigorating spray. Watching herself in the mirror, she raised her hand and lightly touched the pink crown. It pouted in instant recollection of Dax's touch, his lips. Unbearable heat spread like an ink stain over her skin.

Ashamed and embarrassed by her own physical need, she got back into bed and pulled the covers tightly around her. Never had the bed seemed so empty and unwelcoming. Yielding to an immature temptation, she laid the extra pillow against her, snuggling to it, rubbing her hands along it, wishing that it were warm vibrant skin covered with springy hair, wishing that it would speak to her the words of a lover. But there was no surcease to be found either physically or spiritually.

The pain in her heart conquered her control and she gave way to tears.

In the morning she felt somewhat better, or at least determined. She had been playing with fire and she had no one to blame but herself for getting burned. Time and again she had told Nicole it wasn't worth the time and effort to become involved with a man, because it could only end in disaster. She hadn't heeded her own words where Dax Devereaux was concerned. It was only a shame she couldn't gloat to her friend in New

Orleans that she had been right. Nicole, nor anyone, would ever know about Dax. What was there to tell? It was over before it was begun.

Her cinnamon-colored crepe dress didn't quite match her military posture, but she convinced herself it did. She peeled her hair back into a sleek bun on the nape of her neck and disdained any jewelry. She didn't want to look or feel feminine and vulnerable.

Earlier she had called Betty Allway and they agreed to meet and ride to Capitol Hill together as they had done that first day. When they arrived, Keely entered the subcommittee chamber with a straight back and raised chin, looking neither left nor right. She took her chair and then buried her nose in notes that blurred before her eyes.

Only when Congressman Parker called the hearing to order did she raise her eyes. Purposefully she didn't look in Dax's direction, yet she knew he was there. She could see him out of the far corner of her eye. He was wearing a gray jacket, a light blue shirt, a maroon tie. She refused to allow her eyes to waver from Congressman Parker's face.

"We are going to hear this morning one more time from the army. Colonel Hamilton is going to read an affidavit documenting strides the various military branches have taken toward finding the MIAs. Colonel Hamilton, you have the floor."

For two hours the colonel took advantage of his platform and read every word of the affidavit in a nasal monotone. Had Keely not been strung so tightly by nerves, she would probably have gone to sleep. Several times Congressman Walsh's snore rose above Colonel Hamilton's steady drone.

Keely studied her cuticles, the wood grain in the table, the spiderweb in the chandelier. She didn't look at Dax. Betty shifted uncomfortably beside her and once leaned forward to say, "I'm glad he's such a bore. This might really damage our case if he were the least bit interesting and anyone were listening." Keely only smiled. What would her friend think if she knew what a traitor she was?

A few minutes before noon Colonel Hamilton finally wrapped up his remarks. Congressman Parker banged the gavel to get everyone's attention again and looked down at Keely. "Mrs. Williams, before we adjourn, would you like to say anything more?"

Keely hadn't expected this unscheduled courtesy and nervously moistened her lips with the tip of her tongue. She sat up straighter in her chair and surprised herself by speaking in a level voice. "Only that we have said all that should be necessary. Speaking for all of us, I can't believe that you, as representatives of the American people, would even consider introducing a bill that would declare any citizen of our country dead, when proof of that death is nonexistent.

"True, it may save tax dollars, but what is a man's life worth? Can something that intrinsic be appraised? Personally, I feel that at least some of these men may yet be accounted for, found to be alive, but if they aren't, don't their families deserve to be honored, repaid for the suffering they have endured? If Congress declares these men dead, and severs their pay, then America has just cast off one of her children in the cruelest of manners."

Congressman Parker smiled at her with secret approval while her constituents applauded. He glared down either side of the panel tables as if daring anyone to dispute her. When no one did, he picked up the gavel and banged it loudly on the block. "We are adjourned until two-thirty when we will reconvene to announce our decision. Members of the subcommittee will please take a brief lunch and meet back here at one forty-five for discussion." The gavel crashed again and they were dismissed.

Keely was surrounded by photographers and reporters. She answered what questions she could, avoided others, and methodically threaded her way toward the door. When she was free of the room, she broke through the throng with an apology and dashed for the ladies' restroom. Betty was close behind her.

"You were wonderful, Keely. Thank you." The older woman hugged her tight, but when she pulled back, she was struck by Keely's shattered features. "Are you okay? You're as pale as a ghost."

"No, I'm fine. Really." One wouldn't have believed it by the deep breaths she was pulling in. "It was so crowded in there and all the people and flashing lights on those cameras. I don't want to be the focus of attention."

"Then you shouldn't look so tragically, beautifully, heroic." When Keely's lips didn't show even the faintest smile, Betty said quickly, "Why don't I go out ahead of you and fend them off. I'll wait for you at the top of the stairs. Take your time." At the door of the lounge she paused and turned around. "Keely, I think we've won."

For the first time Keely smiled back. "I do too."

"See you in a minute."

Keely collapsed onto a stained, threadbare chair and covered her pale face with her shaking hands. It was over, or almost so. Everyone was lauding her, and she didn't deserve it. *I don't, I don't,* she averred as she breathed deeply. Forcing herself to move, she went to the sink, washed her hands, smoothed her hair, and applied fresh lipstick, which made her paleness even more noticeable.

Picking up her coat and purse, she opened the door and stepped into the empty hallway. She was looking the other way, and when she turned around, she pulled up short and gasped when Dax loomed largely in front of her.

"Easy, easy, this is only another of our chance meetings," he said under his breath and behind a camouflaging smile.

She glanced over his shoulder and saw Betty's silhouette at the end of the long corridor. "What are you doing here?"

"I work here," he quipped. She tried to brush past him, but he caught her arm and said, "I'm sorry. I don't mean to be cute, but dammit, I want to talk to you." He released her arm and when she didn't move away, he rushed on in a quiet undertone. "I tried all night to call you, but your phone was off the hook. I called down to the main desk—anonymously, I might add—and asked the hotel management to check on you. I was informed by Mr. Bartelli that he already had. You were fine, but only wished to be left alone."

"That's right, I did...do."

"Then you're out of luck."

"Dax—"

"Shh. Here comes Radar Ears Van Dorf. Are you on the eight-fifty flight to New Orleans?"

"Yes."

"We'll talk then." He raised his voice. "So, speaking off the cuff, I'd say that the committee will table the bill, Mrs. Williams. Well, hello, Al. Why aren't you eating lunch like all the other nice press boys?"

"Because I'm not nice," he said, smiling that obscenely cunning smile. "Mrs. Williams, you were as eloquent as always. Do you mean everything you say?"

Taken off guard by his blunt question, she replied heatedly, "Of course I do!"

"Okay, okay. I was just asking. By the way, I tried to reach you for comment all day yesterday. You were out. The doorman at the Hilton said you'd left that morning in a silver sports car."

She resisted the urge to glance worriedly at Dax. Instead she answered calmly. "That's right. I went sightseeing with a friend."

"It wasn't exactly an ideal day for sightseeing, was it?"

"No, it wasn't."

"But you went anyway. Hmm. Wouldn't want to tell me who that 'friend' was, would you?"

"No, Mr. Van Dorf, I wouldn't. It's none of your business."

Van Dorf stroked his chin as he looked at her. She met his incisive stare unflinchingly and only hoped he couldn't see her heart as it hammered against her ribs. He turned his foxlike face toward Dax. "You weren't available either, Congressman. Funny, isn't it, that you two are either together, like now, or nowhere to be found?"

"I'd say it was a downright shame that I wasn't available for an interview with you yesterday, Al. You know I never pass up an opportunity for free publicity." Dax's smile was so genuine, that Keely almost believed it herself. How far could anything Dax said be trusted?

"If you gentlemen will excuse me, Mrs. Allway is waiting for me." Without another word she moved past them and by a sheer force of will kept herself from running down the hall in cowardly retreat.

It was no surprise later that afternoon when Congressman Parker announced to the anxious members of PROOF that, for the time being, the bill that would have declared the MIAs dead was to be tabled. He thanked everyone involved for their time and adjourned the hearing one last time.

An undignified period of celebration ensued. PROOF members weepily hugged Keely and Betty. Sympathetic members of the press came over to offer their congratulations. The committee members who had obviously argued in their favor came by personally to congratulate Keely on their victory.

Across the room she felt the magnetic pull of Dax's eyes and met them. Al Van Dorf's speculation had been a warning and Dax wasn't about to jeopardize either of their reputations by publicly talking to her again. His eyes were warm with gladness over her triumph. But they bespoke more than that. They held a pride for her, the woman she was, and her knees went weak under his silent praise.

He ducked his head slightly before turning away, as though to say, "I'll see you later." But he wouldn't. After a hasty lunch she hadn't tasted, didn't even remember, she had gone back to the hotel, packed her bags, and sent them on to the airport via the hotel's limousine service to be checked in with the airline.

Then she had called and changed her reservation to an earlier flight. She and Dax had done nothing that either should be ashamed of—yet. They shouldn't press their luck. This time she had escaped unscathed, and it had made her more resolute than ever not to become involved with a man until she knew what had happened to Mark. "I'm still married," she had repeated to herself like a catechism. And now she said the words again as she watched Dax's retreating back, fighting the urge to run to him and beg to be held and supported by his strength.

Betty was disappointed to learn that she was leaving. "I thought maybe all of us could go out and celebrate tonight. I know none of the others are leaving until tomorrow."

"I'm sorry, Betty, but I need to get back. The radio station wasn't too thrilled with me for taking time off." That wasn't true. Her employers were proud of her stand on the topic of MIAs and never chastised her for taking time off to further PROOF's cause. Another lie. Ever since she met Dax… "I've already called them and told them I'd be there tomorrow. Have a glass of champagne for me."

"We will." Betty laughed. "Several, I'm sure. Take care of yourself, Keely. You can't know how much you mean to us. No one could be a better spokesperson than you. Thank you again."

Keely hailed a cab outside the Congress and it took her straight to National Airport. She went through all the mechanics of boarding a domestic flight without conscious thought. Her mind was on what Dax would do and how he'd feel when she wasn't on his flight. Would he be worried? Angry? Both? Would he demand to know which flight a Mrs. Keely Williams had taken? Or would he ask for Keely Preston? He would ask for neither. He couldn't afford to.

What had he wanted to talk about? He hadn't seemed angry like he had been the evening before when he had let her out at the hotel. What would he have said to her tonight? It didn't matter. Nothing could change their circumstances.

She tightened her seat belt before the airplane taxied and took off. She declined dinner and pushed her seat back into a reclining position, feigning sleep to prevent constant attention from the stewardesses.

The flight was routine. There were no thunderstorms. Nor was there anyone to hold her hand.

# Seven

"Why won't you come with us?"

"I've told you, Nicole. I don't want to."

"That's no reason."

"It's the best reason."

"I'm sick of the Sulky Sue role."

"Then leave me alone," Keely shouted and, planting both hands on the edge of her desk, shoved her chair back. Pushing out of it, she went to the grimy second-story window and looked down on Chartres Street. It was a drizzly day in the French Quarter, perfectly matching her mood. She had been avoiding Nicole for the past few days, but her friend had finally trapped her in her office at the radio station.

Actually her "office" was little more than a closet at the end of a long, murky hallway at the back of the building. Into the room had been crammed two ugly olive-green steel desks. Keely shared the office with the midnight-to-six disc jockey, whom she had never even met. She knew him only by the picture of him and a leggy blonde that was signed: *It was fun, Cindy.* The photograph was stationed on his littered desk in what could be presumed was a place of honor.

Keely sighed and closed her eyes. She wished when she opened them that the rain would have washed away some of the dirt on the window. But it wouldn't. Nor would the dull ache around her heart have disappeared. None of that was Nicole's fault, however, and she regretted having snapped at her friend. Nicole's nagging was a product of concern. Keely turned to face her now, though she remained standing at the window.

"I'm sorry," she said. "I'm in a foul mood and I shouldn't take it out on you."

Nicole hitched her shapely hip over the corner of the disc jockey's desk, upsetting the picture of Cindy. "You certainly shouldn't. To look at you one would think I was your last friend, so you'd better treat me nice." She crossed her arms over her generous breasts and eyed her friend speculatively. "I'm dying of curiosity, you know. When are you going to break down and tell me?"

"Tell you what?" Keely asked innocently and found a thread on her cuff that required her undivided attention.

"Tell me why you've been dragging around here like a damn zombie since you got back from Washington last week. Tell me why you look like hell, and why you won't confide in your best friend about something that's obviously upset you."

"Is that a new pair of earrings?"

"Don't you dare try to get me off the subject, Keely Preston," Nicole warned. "I want to know what happened to you up there that made you even worse off than you were before. And God knows that was bad enough. So lay it on me. I'm not leaving this room and neither are you until you tell me."

"Who set you up as judge of how bad off I am?" Keely asked crossly.

"I did, since you apparently need a keeper to prevent you from closing a shell around yourself like a damn clam or something. What gives, Keely?"

Keely took the few steps back to her desk and flopped down in the creaking chair. She leaned her head on the cracked imitation leather and closed her eyes against the perpetual headache she couldn't seem to shake. "You know what gives, Nicole. You yourself said I'm this way every time I do something for PROOF."

"Yes, but you scored a great victory this time. You should be happy instead of miserable. And don't deny that you're miserable, because I know better. You make Hamlet look like a comedian."

Keely smiled, but the attempt didn't quite make it to a full-fledged laugh. "I *am* happy about what we accomplished. I'm just tired."

"Try again."

"I don't want to be around people just now, that's all." *I met a man, a wonderful man. He kissed me, touched me, like no other man ever has. I think I've fallen in love. What am I going to do about it?* What would Nicole's reaction be if Keely said aloud what she was thinking?

"That won't do, Keely. You need to be with people. Come on and go to this reception with us tonight. We won't stay long, I promise. When you say it's time to leave, it'll be time to leave."

"I don't want to."

"But you *need* to, dammit!" Nicole said in exasperation. "Dress up. Have a drink or two. Dance. Live, Keely." She jumped off the desk and dug her fists into her hips. "If you don't come with us, I'll have to endure Charles all by myself. You wouldn't wish that on me, would you?"

Keely did laugh then. "Why don't you give that guy a break? I know you're crazy about him and just won't admit it. All right, all right." She put up her hands to ward off Nicole's objections. "You wouldn't be with Charles by yourself. You said you had a spare man."

"We do. And frankly, he's as dull as Charles. If I can stand it, you can. The point is you'll be in a public place instead of holed up at home and you'll be in the company of other human beings instead of by yourself. Come on."

"Where is it and what is it?" Keely asked in resignation.

"It's at the Marriott. Formal. Something for the Arts League. Charles is going to represent the television station since it's airing public-service announcements for the League. We'll pick you up at eight."

"I don't know, Nicole," Keely demurred.

"Eight o'clock," Nicole said firmly. "And for God's sake, do something with your hair. I hate it all slicked back like that. You look like Jane Eyre."

"You're certainly literary this morning. First Hamlet, now Jane Eyre. Have you read either one?"

Nicole laughed good-naturedly as she sashayed toward the door. "Heavens, no. I only read porn. Keeps me in practice." She winked wickedly before the door closed behind her. Then Keely heard her call from half-way down the hall, "Eight o'clock."

Eight o'clock. Would she feel up to facing the world by then? She doubted it. She hadn't felt like facing it so far. Erroneously she had thought that once she got away from Washington and back to work, memories of Dax would soon fade and she would forget all that had happened. It wasn't to be. The longer she was away from him, the larger he loomed in her mind. Every minute of the day she wondered what he was doing, whom he was with, what he was wearing, what he was feeling, if he thought of her.

It was wrong. It was insane to perpetuate an impossible dream, but she couldn't help herself. She stared often at the telephone, willing it to ring. In some secret corner of her mind she had thought—wished—that he would call. After all, she wasn't on his flight as she should have been. Hadn't he been the least bit concerned about what had happened to her? Of course, if he had been in New Orleans the past few days, he would have heard her on the radio and known she was at least alive.

Apparently his disinterest indicated what he felt about their interlude in Washington. It had been just that, an interlude. A disappointing one for him, she was sure, since she hadn't "come across." Dax Devereaux didn't have to fool with a woman like her, since many were far too willing to accommodate him.

Nicole was right. She was at a dead-end street and she must turned around and go in a different direction or keep running into the wall. Tonight she would make an effort to return to the world of the living. Checking her watch, she noted that she was due at a sponsor's meeting and she hadn't even read through the agenda.

Taking a compact out of her purse, she grimly admitted that Nicole was right. She did look like hell. Her complexion was sallow, her eyes lackluster, her hair a disgrace. She hadn't done her nails since her return from Washington.

"Okay, Keely, you've mourned long enough," she said to her reflection before snapping the compact shut. Before reading the copy for her commercial about the virtues of a steel-belted radial tire, she telephoned a beauty salon and made an appointment for the works.

Not bad, she thought critically as she looked at the results of her two hours in the salon and another hour spent at home on personal grooming. She had had a half inch taken off the bottom of her hair, getting rid of the cursed split ends. It had been arranged in a casual top knot, soft but sophisticated, with tendrils grazing her cheeks and nape.

She had put an oatmeal mask on her face, and now her complexion was glowing radiantly. She had applied her makeup tastefully and well, and if that sad look in her eyes wasn't completely gone, it was somewhat screened.

When the doorbell rang, she picked up her evening purse, swung her black satin cape over her shoulders, and went to meet her "date."

As Nicole had said, he wasn't very exciting, but he politely introduced himself as Roger Patterson as he escorted her down her brick sidewalk to the car waiting at the curb. He was the liaison between the Arts League and the media. Keely thought he had chosen his profession unwisely, for he was a self-effacing type that one would forget five minutes after meeting him.

He held the door of Charles's Mercedes open, and she settled in the back seat. "You look sensational," Nicole enthused.

"How do you know?" Keely asked cryptically. "You haven't even seen me yet."

"You had only one way to go. Unless you had died."

"You *do* look lovely, Keely," Charles Hepburn spoke to her via the rearview mirror.

"Hello, Charles. How are you?"

"I'm well, thank you."

"Did you meet Randy?" Nicole asked, turning around to them from her position beside Charles in the front seat.

"Roger," he corrected quietly.

"Oh, I'm sorry."

"Yes, we met," Keely said quickly and gave her date an easy smile.

Keely's house was actually a duplex carved out of an old house in the Garden District. The area was known for its lovely homes, some of them previously neglected, now being restored and converted from enormous one-family dwellings to apartments and condos.

Charles drove them up St. Charles Avenue to Canal and then toward the Mississippi River to the Marriott. He left his car with the valet service. They entered the hotel by the side door and traversed the sprawling lobby crowded with tuxedoed men and formally attired women. "I think the receptionist is up on the third floor in one of the ballrooms," Roger said unnecessarily since there were signs to that effect posted throughout the lobby on brass easels.

"Oh, I love affairs like this. But then I love affairs of any kind," Nicole said naughtily. She was actively taking note of who was there and what they were wearing and whom they were with.

They were walking toward the escalator past the open bar when Nicole exclaimed, "Madeline Robins is wearing her famous diamonds, I see. They really look tacky with that dress. Who is she— Oh, it's Dax Devereaux. Look, Keely. You met him, didn't you?"

Keely's heart had dropped to the floor and she had stumbled over it. Roger put a tentative hand under her elbow when her footsteps faltered. She looked in the direction of Nicole's gaze and her breath lodged in her throat when she saw the shining black hair, delicately sprinkled with silver at the temples, and knew that it could only belong to one man.

Even as she spotted him, Dax leaned back to laugh at some amusing remark the stunning woman next to him had said, and his black eyes lighted on Keely. His reaction at seeing her was as volatile as hers at seeing him. His grin fell, and the flash of white teeth disappeared. He looked as if he had been struck a physical blow and couldn't quite believe it.

"Are you going to speak to him, Keely?" Nicole asked expectantly.

"N-no." Keely stuttered, looking away from him hastily. "He's with a group. Perhaps I'll see him later. I barely know him, after all. He probably doesn't even remember meeting me."

Nicole's look frankly said, *Liar.* But she didn't pursue the matter as they rode up the escalator. Under the pretense of straightening her cape, Keely glanced over her shoulder down onto the lobby below and her eyes locked with Dax's as he watched her progress up the conveyor.

She forced herself to turn away and join the others' chatter as they rode up to the third floor. At the coat check she allowed Roger to slide the cape from her shoulders and disappear with it into the throng of men who were doing likewise.

Charles gasped when he took Nicole's fox coat from around her. "Your eyes are buggin' out, Charles," she teased. Indeed, she wore an eye-popping dress. It was black georgette. The long sleeves were slit from cuff to shoulder, and the neckline was slit from neck to waist. It intimated more than it revealed, but the effect was startling. As always she looked gorgeous.

Though she didn't realize it, Keely looked just as stunning. Her black taffeta tulip skirt, called that for its rounded hem that became a slit to just above her knees, provided an enticing view of her legs. The cerise blouse was moderately plunging and fitted her bosom and waist like a second skin, but the ruffled collar that stood against the back of her neck and the soft peplum at the top of her hips kept it from feeling sexy. Her black satin sandals were by Jourdan and had a thin line of rhinestones around her ankles in lieu of a strap.

"Listen to that heavenly music," Nicole said, undulating in rhythm to the orchestra's dance music. "Come on, Charles, and dance with me."

He glanced worriedly at her breasts swaying unrestrained under the sheer fabric and said, "All right, but if you get carried away and come out of that dress, I'm taking you home."

"And then what?" she asked invitingly as she dragged him onto the dance floor.

Keely laughed. She liked Charles Hepburn and knew that he was in love with Nicole. He was older, at least forty-five, but his receding hairline inspired confidence. His body was perfectly maintained by daily workouts in a downtown gym. His small frame was wiry and bespoke a strength that would have done a much younger man proud. He was mild mannered and courteous to a fault. Keely sometimes thought Nicole would treat him better if he'd lash back at her just once, but his patience imitated Job's.

No matter how many times Nicole vehemently denied it, Keely thought she cared more for Charles than she was willing to admit. Perhaps his serious, mature nature frightened her seemingly carefree friend. As Keely watched them dancing, she was convinced more than ever that whatever their feelings for each other were, they ran deep. Nicole was brushing herself against Charles and smiling in a way he couldn't resist. His hand stroked her back. Keely wished they would stop fooling themselves and each other and admit their mutual affection.

"Would you like to dance?" Roger interrupted her reverie hesitantly. She had almost forgotten him.

"I don't think so right now. Maybe later. I would like something to drink." She wasn't much of a drinker, but seeing Dax, especially with Madeline Robins, had upset her more than she wanted to give credence to.

"Yes, of course." Roger seemed relieved to be of some use to someone. "What would you like?"

"Something cool. A vodka collins?"

"Vodka collins. I'll be right back." He wove his way through the crowd and was soon swallowed up by it. Feeling self-conscious at being left alone, Keely located a table with four vacant chairs and claimed it for them. She signaled to Nicole and Charles as the dance finished and they left the floor.

Settled with drinks, they passed the first hour of the reception in easy companionship. People they knew stopped by frequently to chat. Ones they didn't know came by to meet and be met. She knew Nicole was a celebrity, but it never ceased to amaze her that people thought of her in that light too. Often when she was introduced and the person put her face with the familiar voice on the radio, they became tongue-tied and effusive.

Society's stars were out. A few of the New Orleans Saints were there; several celebrities who were performing in town had been invited to attend the fund-raising function. It was a glamorous crowd, exciting. The food on the buffet tables was sumptuous. The dance music couldn't have been surpassed.

And Keely was ready to leave within a few minutes of her arrival.

Miserably she had noticed that the table Dax and Madeline shared with three other couples wasn't far from where she was sitting. She was forced to watch his attention on the other woman. He got her drinks. She ate off his plate and he playfully slapped her hands away. She kissed his cheek. He helped her find a lost earring. They danced. They whispered. He kissed her lightly on the mouth.

Keely excused herself and found the ladies' lounge, staying in there an inordinate amount of time. When she came back, Nicole and Charles had disappeared and she saw Roger on the other side of the huge room chatting with the symphony conductor. She took a sip of her watery drink to give her hands something to do.

"Do you get your jollies by standing up men in airports?"

The slippery glass, beaded with condensation, nearly fell through her fingers. She set it down on the tablecloth and turned her head to see Dax leaning over her with both hands braced on the back of her chair.

"No. I wasn't in a very jolly mood that day."

"I was. Until I got to the airport, on the airplane, waiting for you, and not knowing what in the hell had happened to you."

She lowered her eyes from his accusing ones. "I'm sorry."

"Then dance with me."

"Where's Madeline?" she asked cattily.

"Do you care?"

"Don't you?"

He only shrugged and took her hand to pull her to her feet. Since she had been seen dancing with Roger and Charles and several others, it wouldn't look all that strange for her to dance with the congressman, would it?

His touch burned her skin and she couldn't have stopped herself from being drawn into his arms under the penalty of death. The song was a slow, love ballad. The strains of the music surrounded them. The lights were appropriately dimmed. His hand was on her back, pressing, caressing without even moving. His mouth was against her hair.

"Do you know what I'd like to be doing?"

She shook her head.

"Nibbling your rhinestones."

It took her a moment to realize what rhinestones he was referring to. The only ones she had were the ones around her ankles. She laughed breathlessly. "Shame on you."

"Those are without a doubt the sexiest shoes I've ever seen. I might develop a real shoe and foot fetish and became a dyed-in-the-wool pervert."

She looked up at him in mock dismay. "What! And ruin your political career?"

"Or enhance it." He laughed and pressed her head back against his shoulder. "Sexual fantasies are 'in' now, you know. Lately I've become an expert at them. Want to hear some?"

"No. I'd be too embarrassed."

He tilted his head to look down at her. "You probably would be," he whispered. "You play a very active role in them."

"Dax, you shouldn't talk to me this way."

"All right, I'm sorry," he said, then belied his contrition by expanding his chest and flattening her breasts against him. He executed a flawless turn, giving him an excuse to splay his hand on her back and bring her closer. "Is it okay to tell you how beautiful you look tonight?"

She lowered her eyes, only to raise them again. She couldn't keep from looking at him. It was a constant internal war. For every time she looked at him, it necessitated raising her head from his shoulder. "Yes, and thank you. You look very distinguished in your tuxedo too. It suits you."

"Who's the man?" he asked abruptly, adroitly dancing them to the darkest corner of the floor.

"What?"

"The man you're with. Is he someone I ought to start hating?"

She colored with pleasure at his jealousy. "No. I only met him tonight. I really came with Nicole and Charles."

"Good." He smiled and she returned it. His arm tightened around her, but no one would have noticed unless they saw the melting expression in each of their eyes.

She pitied every other woman in the room for not knowing what it was like to be held in Dax's arms. The hard pressure of his thighs sent an exquisite thrill up her own as they rubbed together. In the hand held by his she felt the hypnotizing massage of his thumb in her palm. His breath was hot and fragrant on her face and she barely restrained herself from gulping in great amounts of it to fill her own lungs.

He too was thrilling at the opportunity of holding her. Her breasts gentled against him. The tops of them swelled between the ruffles of her blouse and he was made dizzy by the sight and the sweet smell that rose from that velvet cleft. He longed to press his mouth there, to feel the texture of her skin against his lips, against his tongue. He ached. And the ache was made more profound by the way she naturally curved up against his middle, fitting him so well it made their dancing evocative of another act.

All too soon the song ended. His wistful smile matched hers as he escorted her back to her table. She pulled up short when she saw the Robins woman standing beside it talking animatedly to Nicole.

Dax propelled Keely forward until they reached the group. "There you are, darling. I wondered when you were going to remember who you came with." Madeline was smiling, but her eyes slithered menacingly over Keely.

"Madeline, this is Keely Williams. Or Preston, if you prefer her professional name. She is actively involved with the MIA issue. We met recently in Washington." Dax said all of this unemotionally, as though he didn't feel the mounting tension around the table. "Keely, this is Madeline Robins."

"Mrs. Robins," Keely said coolly.

"How nice to meet you," Madeline said with a voice well-trained to conceal unspoken epithets. "It's such a pity about your husband. Nicole was just now telling me how bravely you face life without knowing whether you're a wife or a widow."

There was no way to respond to that, so Keely didn't even try. Nicole broke in. "Keely, we haven't met the congressman."

"Oh," she said, tearing her eyes away from Madeline who had possessively linked her arm through Dax's. In the shiny metallic green dress Madeline wore, Keely thought her long limbs resembled drooping seaweed as she tenaciously clung to Dax. "I'm sorry. Congressman Devereaux, this is my friend Nicole Castleman, Charles Hepburn, and Roger…uh…"

"Patterson," the man supplied and stuck out his hand.

"Congressman, I've been wanting to meet you for a long time. I'm an admirer of yours."

"Thank you, Roger. Call me Dax."

*God bless Nicole,* Keely silently offered up as her friend took over. She flirted harmlessly with Dax, saying how long she had wanted to meet him, but always missed him. He said he felt like he knew her from having seen her so often on television. He chatted with Charles, asking about rates politicians had to pay for television-commercial airtime.

"Call me later in the week," Charles said. "We'll set up an appointment and I'll discuss it with you. Generally speaking, the more commercials you buy, the cheaper the rate per commercial. If your commercials run during the news shows, they are more expensive, but you reach the greatest number of people."

"I'm lost." Dax laughed helplessly. "I'll need your expert opinion, so I'll take you up on your offer to discuss it."

"I'll look forward to it. It will soon be time for you to start planning a media campaign," Charles added. "It can be expensive. I hope you're prepared for it."

"I'm helping him be prepared for it," Madeline said, snuggling closer to Dax. "I've already got a campaign fund started. I'm going to see to it personally that Dax is elected to the Senate."

A look of annoyance momentarily tightened Dax's mouth, but then he smiled genially. "I need all the help I can get."

They chatted inanely about the reception and estimated how much cash it was raising for the various arts. The weather was discussed at length. Then an awkward silence ensued. They had said all that could be said in a group of strangers.

"It was nice to meet you, Mrs. Williams," Madeline said by way of dismissal.

"Thank you," Keely replied, and only courtesy forced her say, "It was nice meeting you too."

Dax shook hands with Charles and Roger, kissed Nicole on the cheek with an old-world flourish, and did the same for Keely. His mouth touched the skin of her face only fleetingly, yet her body sang with sensations when he raised his head and for a moment his eyes met hers. "I enjoyed our dance, Mrs. Williams. It was a pleasure to see you in a less austere atmosphere. Congratulations again on your victory in Washington."

"Did you support us, Congressman Devereaux?" she asked goadingly. The others might just as well have not been there. Dax filled her field of vision. His voice was the only sound she heard. The depth of his dark eyes was her firmament.

"Do you even have to ask?" The dimple beside his mouth deepened with his smile. Regretfully he straightened and took Madeline's arm. "Good night, everyone."

Roger held Keely's chair for her. As she sat down, making a production of smoothing her skirt, she heard Madeline purr, "I think everyone who should see us here has seen us. I'm more than ready to leave whenever you are, darling."

Keely's throat squeezed shut and even the hasty swallow of the fresh drink Roger had had waiting for her didn't help relieve the tightness. Charles made some mildly humorous remark, but when she looked up with a stiff smile plastered on her face, she saw that Nicole wasn't laughing either. Instead she was staring at Keely. Her blue eyes lifted to the retreating couple, then dropped back to Keely. Her eyelashes fluttered guilelessly and her mouth curved angelically. Keely didn't trust that innocent expression for a moment and was immediately suspicious of the gleam in her friend's eyes.

They availed themselves of the dessert buffet then decided they had had enough of the gala.

While the men were getting the wraps, Nicole sidled up to Keely and said, "Devereaux's some hunk, isn't he?"

Keely answered levelly. "Yes, I suppose he could be called a 'hunk.'"

"You told me when I called you in Washington that you'd barely met him."

"I had."

"You could have fooled me by the way he danced with you. You two seemed real chummy out there."

"He was only being polite."

"Uh-huh. And I'm a three-toed aardvark, but let's skip that for now. What do you think of Madeline Robins?"

"She's all right, I guess."

Nicole leaned forward and whispered, "And you're a liar, Keely Preston. She's on the make and you know it and you don't like her any better than any other woman does." She pursed her pretty mouth and said, "I wonder how involved the congressman is with her."

"Is there any doubt?" Keely asked bitterly. Where was Dax taking her now that, as Madeline had pointed out, everyone who needed to see them had seen them?

To her mansion? His house in Baton Rouge? A room in this very hotel?

"Oh, I'll grant she has the hots for him," Nicole said. "But somehow I get the notion he's not quite as ardent as she is."

"I wouldn't know about either's love life and I care less."

Nicole only smiled blandly as Charles draped her coat around her shoulders. As they left the hotel Keely was grateful they didn't see the other couple. She tried to act unaffected, but wished more than ever that she hadn't come tonight. She should have gone with her first instinct and stayed at home, letting her desire for Dax Devereaux die a slow, graceful death. Now the wounds had been reopened just when they were about to heal. Now she had that recovery process to go through again. Only this time there was an additional irritant in the wound. Madeline Robins. And how many others?

She shook Roger's hand graciously at her door and thanked him for the evening. "I hope you enjoyed yourself," he said, and Keely doubted that he had had any better a time than she had. Charles honked a goodbye when they pulled away from the curb.

Inside her own house she let go her rigid control and slumped against the door. Tiredly, dispiritedly, she crossed to the sofa table and switched on the small brass lamp. Dropping her cape and purse on the love-seat-sized sofa, she leaned down and unfastened the tiny buckles that held the rhinestone bands around her ankles. Dax's words came back to her and she blushed. She told herself it was only the blood running to her head from her bending position, but his suggestion induced all kinds of sexual visions. She kicked the sandals from her feet, reducing her height by several inches without the high heels.

She undid the covered buttons down the front of her blouse as she was crossing to the staircase. The doorbell pealed loudly.

*Did I leave something in the car?* was her first thought.

Hastily rebuttoning her blouse, she opened the door a crack, peering out.

"Hi," he said.

"Hi," she answered.

# *Eight*

Instinctively her hand went to the wall switch to turn off the porch lights.

His voice, tinged with humor, came to her out of the sudden darkness. "Do you think we're under surveillance?"

"I don't know. Could we be?"

She felt, rather than saw, his careless shrug. "I'm willing to take my chances."

She moved aside and let him through the door. He took three steps into the room and looked around it with appreciative eyes. Keely was proud of her house. The building had been in sad disrepair ten years ago when someone had bought it and divided the rambling structure into two separate condominiums. It had been completely restored and modernized then, but when she bought her half three years ago, she had decorated it to suit her.

The exterior of the house typified early New Orleans with its used redbrick, white shutters, and black iron grillwork on the windows and around the narrow balcony on the upper floor. Keely had furnished it with a tasteful combination of old and new. Fruitwood antiques she had picked up in attics and out-of-the-way shops were mingled with pieces upholstered in contemporary fabrics. Stark white woodwork accented the sand-colored walls. Muted shades of rose, blue and green were used as accent colors in throw pillows, framed graphics, and the padded fabric that covered one wall in the dining room. The effect was beautiful.

"I like your house," Dax said without turning around. "It looks like you."

"A hundred and seven years old?"

He turned to face her then and the twinkle in his eyes was mischievous. "It's amazing how you relics are holding up." He shook off his overcoat and came back to the door to hang it on a brass hall tree. He pivoted slowly until they were standing face-to-face.

It might have been hours, years, small eternities, or it might have been only seconds that they looked at each other. For however long, it was enough to convey all the longing, need, and frustration that each had suffered since last they were together.

The facades of decorum were torn down and all that was left standing was the naked desire that each had for the other. There were no observers, there were no rules, there were no conventions that had to be satisfied. For the moment it was only them, and they put away conscience, yielded to the attraction that continued to haunt them, and lived only for the present.

He extended his arms slowly and closed them around her. Her arms lifted to his shoulders. Their bodies gravitated toward each other, until they touched from breast to knee in one unbroken line.

He lowered his head and nuzzled her hair, her ear, her neck. His lips made a pass across her jaw, up to her cheekbone, over her brow, and down her nose until they came to rest at the corner of her mouth.

"I couldn't stay away from you. I tried. I couldn't."

His mouth closed over hers and it blossomed open. He drew on her as though she were the energy supply necessary for his life force. She gloried in her ability to sustain him and hoped his appetite for her would never be satisfied.

His tongue played havoc with her senses, first plunging deep, then teasing with rapid, elusive dartings. The sensual lingual stroking went on and on, robbing her of breath, yet bringing her to life. Every cell in her body was awakened to his touch, his smell, his taste, and the low sounds that emanated from his throat. Her breasts were imbued with desire, much as a mother's would be with milk. They ached to be relieved of this tingling fullness. Conversely, her womb contracted against a vague emptiness that longed to be filled.

His arms relaxed, but only enough to cradle her face between his hands and look down into her swimming eyes. "Why did you do that to me, Keely? Why did you leave without a word of goodbye? Do you know how frantic I was at that airport? How was I to know you hadn't been abducted or something? Horror scenes out of the worst nightmares came to my mind. Why did you do it?"

"Dax," she groaned. "I thought it was best if we

didn't see each other alone again. Things were…are… getting out of hand."

"I'm sorry about what happened after we left Mount Vernon. Keely, I'd never do anything to hurt or insult you. My God! I wanted to apologize to you. I tried, but you took your phone off the hook and then the next day there wasn't an opportunity."

For torturous moments his fingers lightly explored the features of her face, gliding over them, comparing textures. "Despite what my adversaries say, I *do* have some moral fiber. I know you're another man's wife. If you were my wife, I'd kill any man who touched you." Now he pulled her close in a smothering embrace. "But God forgive me, I want you."

"Ask for my forgiveness too, Dax."

He didn't need a second invitation. His tongue delved past her lips and swept her mouth like a searing torch. His body melted along her in a heart-stopping juxta-position.

She knew she was slipping from a world held to-gether by gravity into one of random bliss. His mouth drew her beyond the boundaries of conscience and re-gret and she never wanted to return. Without anchor, aimlessly, she floated in a sea of passion. In her thirty years she had never known the seductive power of a man's touch. Desire rioted through her veins, seek-ing an outlet, electrifying her nerve endings until they hummed.

"You're beautiful," he said against her mouth. "While we were dancing, I wanted to do this." His head came down to kiss the valley between her breasts just above the edge of her bra. His head oscillated with agonizing slowness, stroking her not only with his mouth, but with nose and chin as well. His hand closed over one breast and treated it to a lazy massage. The top curve of the other was kissed by parted lips and a languid tongue. He kissed again. And again. Lower. And lower still until...

"Keely, Keely." Her name was an agonized cry ripped from a hoarse throat. He rested his forehead on hers. "We can't do this any longer, Keely."

"I know."

"I can't bear it."

"Neither can I."

"I have to go."

"I understand."

"Are you getting up at five tomorrow?" he asked, taking his overcoat from the hall tree and pulling it on.

"Yes." She tried to smile, but her lips quivered uncontrollably.

He checked the tailored wristwatch. "You won't get much sleep. It's late."

She couldn't have cared less. "Are you driving back tonight? To Baton Rouge?"

He shook his head. "No. I have business here tomorrow. When I'm in New Orleans, I stay at the Bienville House. Do you know it?"

"In the Quarter on Decatur?" He nodded. "I know it, but I've never been inside."

"It's clean and quiet."

"I suppose it is." They were saying nothing they wanted to say, only biding time until they would have to part.

"Who lives in the other side of the house?"

"An older couple. He's a philosophy professor at Tulane. They share the house with a Great Dane that's taller than I am." Another attempted smile. Another failure.

"You were lucky to get the side that—" His amiable mood finally played out and the temper erupted with volcanic impetus. He cursed viciously as he slammed his fist into his opposite palm. "*Dammit!* What in the hell am I standing here babbling for? I don't give a damn who lives in the other side of your house. I'm only talking to keep my hands off you. I don't even know what I'm saying. I'm only thinking of how I want to be making love to you, naked and freely, and not like two grappling adolescents.

"I want to see you naked, Keely. And I want to lie down beside you naked. I want us to maybe hurt each other a little, and soothe each other a lot. I want to kiss your breasts and stomach and watch your face while I'm doing it. I want to know what your thighs feel like.

"If any of this disgusts you, I'm sorry, but it's what I feel, what I've felt since I first saw you on that damn airplane." His voice had risen to a level she had never heard before. At his sides his fists clenched and un-clenched as though he were trying to grip the reins of his temper and haul it in, but couldn't.

"It's not just something I feel in my loins. I could satisfy that anywhere. But it's something I feel in my brain and in my heart too. I deluded myself into think-ing I could be your buddy, your pal. But I can't, Keely. I can't be with you and not touch you. Do you under-stand? These clandestine meetings compromise us both and, speaking for myself, will soon lead to insanity. It will be best for both of us if we don't see each other again. Goodbye."

Without another word he flung open the door and closed it behind him with finality. Keely stood motionless, though tremors of anguish were tearing through her body.

*He's right. He's right. We've known all along that nothing could come of this. It's better this way. It is. It is.*

Then why was her face bathed with tears?

"Here we are at eight fifty-six and I'm going to let Olivia Newton-John take you into the second shift this morning. One more word from you, Keely. How do things look from up there?"

Keely spoke into the small microphone that curved around her cheek from the headpiece she wore. "It's looking good, Ron," she said to the rush-hour DJ. "The police are still working that six-car pileup on the Pontchartrain Expressway at the Broad Street exit. All but one lane are still closed. Anyone going that direction may want to consider an alternate route. All in all it's been a rather calm morning."

"Thank you, darlin'. How about coffee later?"

"No, thank you, Ron. I'm all tied up today."

He groaned heartbrokenly. "Folks, our angel in the sky has a heart of stone."

Keely switched off her mic as the DJ said his farewells to their audience and switched on the promised recording. Every day they carried on that ridiculous repartee over the airwaves and their listeners seemed to eat it up. She often received fan mail that asked her not to be so hard on poor old Ron who was obviously in love with her. Little did the writers of such mail know that he was married, had three children, and lived in relative peace under his real name in Metairie.

She sighed as Joe Collins, the veteran helicopter pilot, banked the aircraft and changed their direction. As usual, her knuckles whitened a bit as the ground tilted. Her husband had disappeared after a helicopter crash. She never forgot that.

"You all right this morning, angel?" Joe teased, though his eyes were concerned as he looked at his passenger.

"Yes." Keely smiled wryly. "I didn't get much sleep last night." That was true. After Dax left her, she had passed the hours in dreary contemplation until it was time for her to shower and dress for work.

"You're sure that's all?" Joe asked her as he set the chopper down on the Superdome parking lot where he picked her up every morning and afternoon.

"Yes. I've just got a bad case of the doldrums. Nothing to worry about."

"I'm not convinced, but I won't pressure you into talking. See you this afternoon."

"Sure." She stepped out of the chopper, grabbed her things, and slammed the door shut. She ran under the rotating blades until she had cleared them and then turned to wave as Joe lifted off.

Keely trudged to her car and unlocked the door. She had thought seriously about calling in sick this morning, but decided she would be better off going to work as though nothing had happened last night. It was better to stay busy than to mope around her empty house, thinking about her empty life.

She drove through what lingered of rush-hour traffic into the French Quarter, which always had traffic jams. At that time of day the narrow streets, not suited for modern traffic, were crammed with delivery trucks making stops to the many restaurants and shops in the Vieux Carré. She finally pulled into the parking lot on the roof of one of the old buildings and walked the block to the studios of KDIX.

Yesterday's rain had stopped and a watery sun was trying to shine, an attempt that Keely found offensive. She wanted nothing to brighten this day. She was in a black despair and she wanted the world to know it.

For a long time she stared out the window of her office, reliving those moments when Dax had held her, kissed her. She had vivid recall of everything he had ever said to her. She believed everything he had ever said. That's why she didn't doubt that he wouldn't see her again. They couldn't be "friends" and nothing else. The chemistry between them was too electric. Every time they were together they betrayed not only Mark, but their own principles. She didn't need him in her life, complicating what was already an untenable situation. And he certainly didn't need her in his. His adversaries would have a field day should he have any relationship with the wife of an MIA, especially one as visible and vocal as she.

Determined not to dwell on Dax, she went to her desk and mechanically reduced the pile of unanswered mail, returned telephone calls, and spoke at length with the producer of the morning show. Since she had to work a split shift and report on the afternoon traffic as well, she usually took off at noon and didn't have any obligations until three-thirty when she met Joe again at the Superdome.

It was almost time for her to leave when the door to her office burst open and Nicole rushed in. "Thank God you're here," she said, out of breath. "You just saved my life."

Keely couldn't help but laugh at her friend's obvious relief. Her beringed hand was splayed across her heaving chest in a gesture of thankfulness.

"Tell me quick what I did," Keely said.

"You're going to be the live interview on the noon news."

"Guess again."

"Keely, don't go cute on me. I'm not kidding. Our scheduled guest just called and he's sick and can't come. Unless you want our viewers to see fifteen minutes of my vacation slides, you're going to take his place. I'll interview you about the MIAs and what happened in Washington last week. It's current and newsworthy. So what's the problem?"

She didn't feel like living much less like going on television—that was the problem. "Nicole, any other day I would, but I don't feel well today. I look worse."

"Bullfeathers. You look gorgeous as always."

"I have circles under my eyes!" Keely exclaimed.

"So do I," Nicole shouted back. "Makeup works wonders. Besides, you wouldn't let a few dark circles under your eyes stand between me and ruin, would you?"

"Nicole, I know if you thought real hard, you could call in a favor on someone. How about the mayor? He's always good for last-ditch efforts."

"He's boring as hell too. You've got a good story

here, Keely. Get yourself together. We go on in ten minutes," she said, checking her watch. "God, I haven't even looked over the script. Come on." She went to Keely's desk and, grabbing her by the arm, hauled her to her feet.

"I've got the cramps," Keely whined.

"Take an aspirin."

"This dress is—"

"Beautiful."

They had reached the door. "Oh, hell, why not?" Keely asked herself under her breath.

"That's the spirit," Nicole said as she pulled Keely down the hall. At the door of the ladies' room she stopped. "Do whatever you need to do and then come on down. The interview will be after the weather segment, about twelve-twelve, but get there quick so you can be wired for sound. And if I start asking stupid questions, interrupt with a lengthy explanation. I haven't boned up on this." She shoved Keely through the restroom door.

Peering into the wavy mirror over the water-stained sink, she tried her best to bring some semblance of cheerfulness to her face. She added blusher to her cheeks, darkened her lipstick, and brushed her hair. The jade silk shirtwaist dress would show up well on camera. At least she wasn't wearing a stripe or check that would "crawl."

Checking her wristwatch, she noted that it was straight up noon. She left the restroom and walked down the concrete staircase to the wide thick doors of the studio. The red On Air sign was lighted, but she opened the door wide enough for her to squeeze through. The studio was darkened except for the circle of light around the news desk where Nicole and her co-anchor, a young man, were reading the news.

She let her eyes grow accustomed to the darkness before gingerly stepping over the cables that stretched across the studio floor. When a commercial came up on the monitor, the floor director detached his head-piece from one of the cameras and came up to her, taking her arm.

"Hello, gorgeous," he said freshly. "Allow me to escort you to the interview set if you please. Will you have an affair with me?"

"Only when your wife gives you permission, Randy," she laughed. "How are things?"

"Chaotic as usual. Thanks for helping out today. Some wouldn't want to share the set with Devereaux."

"Dev—" The name died on her lips as she stepped up onto the set under Randy's guiding hand and saw that Dax was already seated on the small sofa and wired for sound.

"I think you two know each other," Randy said as he gently pushed Keely down beside Dax and handed her a microphone. "Don't let that snag your silk," he warned.

"Randy, we're thirty seconds out of the break," one of the cameramen called.

"We'll be coming to you out of the next break," he said before skirting back to his camera and replacing his headphone.

"Why didn't you tell me?" Keely asked out of the corner of her mouth.

"I didn't know," he replied under his breath, making an overt show of straightening his necktie.

Her head whipped around. "Didn't know?"

"Not until this morning. Nicole called me early, full of apologies. Said to be here at noon. Here I am."

Keely adjusted her weight away from his warm presence so close beside her on the small sofa. Tugging on the hem of her skirt, she mumbled, "She duped us both. The same act was played on me. I didn't know you were going to be here. She said I was saving the show because their interview guest wasn't able to come. I'm sorry."

"I'm not."

She looked at him again, but before she could speak, the studio lights glared on, illuminating the set. "Hello, sexy!" The director's voice boomed at them from the glass booth suspended above the studio floor. Keely realized that they had gone into another commercial break. The cameramen were deftly wheeling the three cumbersome cameras toward them and focusing on her and Dax. "Oops, sorry, Congressman. I was talking to our own Keely there."

"Hello, Dave," Keely said, shading her eyes against the bright lights and waving to the man behind the control board in the booth. Unexpectedly her voice reverberated through the studio.

"Give me a level please," they heard Dave say. Then to Keely he said over the speaker, "Try again, this time for a mic check."

"Hello, Dave. This is Keely Preston with a mic check. One, two, three."

"Sounds grrrrreat, honey throat. Congressman Devereaux, will you be so kind?"

"Hello, Dave. How is the new baby?"

"Well, I'll be damned! That's right. Last time you

were here my wife was in the hospital. Thanks for re-membering. Both are doing well."

"Good," Dax said.

The disembodied voice then said in exasperation, "Nicole, will you please get your sweet tush on the set? We're into the last sixty seconds."

Keely had noticed that Nicole had jumped from the news set and raced over to the studio mirror to check her perfect hair. Quickly now she crossed the cavern-ous room and plopped down on the chair opposite the sofa, clipping a microphone to her collar. "Goodness," she said breathlessly. "This has been some day. Hello, again, Congressman Devereaux." She studiously ig-nored Keely, and Keely knew just how flustered her friend was. Since when did Nicole say "goodness"?

"Call me Dax, please," he said.

Nicole smiled. "I will, but not during the interview."

"Coming to you on camera two, Nicole," Randy in-structed quietly, replacing Dave's booming directions. "Fifteen seconds."

"Ready, you two?" Nicole asked. Without waiting for an answer, she faced her camera, licked her lips, and smiled. When the red lights on the front of the camera flashed on, she said, "Today on the interview portion of our show we have with us our own Keely Preston and Congressman Dax Devereaux."

For the next seven minutes Keely and Dax fielded Nicole's questions and brought up points she failed to mention. The interview went smoothly. Keely and Dax seemed interested in each other only through the issue they were discussing.

Once when he was speaking with his controlled, convincing voice, Keely turned her head to look at him. He used his hands to make a point and it occurred to her how familiar the gesture was. Each point he made was concise, clear, explicit. He never minced words when someone's welfare was concerned. Some might label him a zealot. Keely admired him as a man of strong convictions.

"Thank you both," Nicole said when she closed out the interview and the news show concluded. She stood up, taking off her microphone. "I can't tell you how I appreciate your dropping everything and doing this for me."

"I'm glad I could do it," Keely said, barely containing her fury, while fumbling to free herself of the microphone. She knew exactly what Nicole had had in mind by inviting both of them on the show. Keely had denied having any undue interest in Dax when Nicole had grilled her about him last night. She should have known Nicole wasn't a fool, and if she was attuned to anything, it was to the relationship between men and women. "Excuse me now. I have work to do." Without another word to either of them, Keely brushed past Dax and left the studio.

She was trembling as she climbed the stairs to the second floor and navigated the labyrinth of corridors to her own secluded office. She sank into her chair and covered her face with both hands, breathing deeply. This time fate had had help, but it had brought Dax and her together again. She had reconciled the fact that Dax would hold no place in her life.

Last night, in frustration and anger, he had come to that conclusion and, showing more discipline than she ever could have, had said that he wasn't going to see her again. Now, only a few hours later, they had been together, sitting in close proximity on the same sofa, breathing the same air, and it had been painful to be that close and pretend indifference.

One thing was certain, she wasn't going to sit in this gloomy office nursing her wounds. The faster she was away from this building, the better.

She was taking her coat from the hook on the wall when the door quietly opened and Dax slipped inside, shutting the door behind him.

They looked at each other for long, silent moments, Keely's hands frozen in the process of lifting her coat down. He kept his back to the door, as if keeping opposing forces at bay.

"Where are you going?" he asked at last.

She put her coat on. A defense mechanism? Yes. She felt exposed, vulnerable. Irrationally and irritatingly her heart was pumping in her chest. "Out. I take several hours off in the middle of the day."

"Oh," he answered, but made no move to get out of her way. *God, she's beautiful,* he thought. Last night he had meant every word he had said. It was lunacy for them to continue these secret meetings. He despised lying and sneaking. In this context it added an element of seediness to the feeling he had for Keely, and for that reason alone he wanted no part of a secret rendezvous.

There was no way he could turn off his desire for her, so he would eliminate the temptation. A clean break. Surgical severance. Cold turkey. Unconvinced but determined, he had walked into that television studio.

Seeing her had obliterated even the smallest shred of resolve.

Dignified, he had sat and answered Nicole's questions logically and concisely, and all the time he had been making love to this woman in his mind. He hadn't been immune to her nearness. Her body radiated a heat that beckoned to his. He was aware of each move she made, no matter how slight. Watching the gentle rise and fall of her chest, he logged each breath she took.

"I came to tell you that I didn't know you were going to be on that program today. I was as surprised to see you as you were me."

"I didn't think you had anything to do with it. The whole thing smells of Nicole. She arranged it."

"Why? I mean, beside the fact that she thought we'd make an interesting interview."

"I don't think she'd have thought we'd be nearly so interesting if she hadn't seen us dancing together last night." Keely looked away from him. "She…uh…she started asking me leading questions afterward." Knowing now her leaving would be a futile attempt to put this all behind her, she slipped out of her coat and rehung it on the hook in the wall. She dropped her purse on top of her desk and sat down in the squeaky chair.

"What kind of questions?" he asked, coming to the side of her desk and hitching a hip over the corner.

"Questions about you. How well I got to know you in Washington."

"What did you say?"

"That I'd barely met you."

"And what did she say?"

Keely looked up at him and replied solemnly, "She

said that she couldn't believe that by the way we were dancing together."

He leaned forward and captured one of her hands. His thumb smoothed over each long, oval, manicured nail. "What else did she ask?" When he lifted his eyes, it was only as far as her mouth. As if sensing his appraisal, her tongue darted out. It was such a dainty pink thing to wield such power. Seeing it made him tremble inside.

"She wanted to know if I considered you a hunk." A smile tugged at the corner of her mouth.

A smooth black eyebrow arched over an amused eye. "A *hunk*? Now, that is interesting. And I can't wait to hear what you said." He leaned closer to her, over her.

She had to tilt her head back to look him in the face. "I said I suppose you could be called a hunk."

He cocked his head sideways and asked teasingly, "You said that about me?"

His smile was infectious and she responded, saying coyly, "In a moment of weakness."

They laughed together softly. His index finger came up to investigate the tilting corner of her mouth. It stroked leisurely along her bottom lip until it found the opposite corner just as intriguing. His hand left her mouth only to curl his fingers around her neck beneath her collar and draw her up toward his descending lips. His other hand lightly brushed past her breast when it slipped under her arm to press against her spine and arch her up to him.

The clicking of the doorknob was like a gunshot in the room and they sprang apart. Keely bolted out of her chair, but Dax stood in front of her, facing the door, as though to protect her. They sagged in relief when they saw Nicole standing just within the door. She closed it behind her quickly.

"For godsakes. You two are a case. Don't you know that if you're taking *that* kind of lunch hour you should lock the office door?" Hands on hips, she admonished them like an aggravated parent.

Keely pushed Dax aside and rounded the desk. "Nicole, I could easily strangle you for the stunt you pulled today. Why did you do it?"

Completely unaffected by her friend's anger, she hopped onto the DJ's desk, upsetting poor Cindy again. "Don't pretend to be angry about seeing each other again. It was obvious to me last night that you two are dying to jump on each other's bones, so I appointed myself matchmaker, that's all," she admitted happily. "It worked, judging from what I saw when I came in. I'm only disappointed that I didn't find you in a more compromising position."

"Nicole!" Keely exclaimed, her cheeks flaming with hot color. "Dax…I mean…we…"

Dax came up behind her and placed a reassuring arm around her shoulders. "Nicole," he said calmly, "apparently you noticed that Keely and I became attracted to each other while we were both in Washington. It was accidental. Neither of us planned it, but it happened. Each of us sees the futility in our developing a relationship. She's married." He looked down at Keely sadly. "And I'm running for the Senate. Having an…affair with a married woman wouldn't make for good politics, even if Keely would consent, which she would never do. Last night after the gala we decided that we shouldn't see each other anymore, privately or publicly if it could be avoided. That's why we were both rather disconcerted to see each other today."

"Last night?" Nicole asked sharply, coming off the desk. "After the party? Where?"

Dax glanced at Keely and when she nodded, he added, "At her house."

Nicole slumped back against the desk. "Jimineeeee. Did anyone see you there?'

"Why?" Keely asked, not liking the way Nicole was gnawing her lower lip.

"Well, I'm not the only one who noticed the... warmth...with which you two danced. That's why I came up here. This is the first edition of the evening paper. I thought you ought to see it."

For the first time they noticed the folded newspaper she held in her hand. She extended it toward Keely. With a sinking feeling in the pit of her stomach, Keely unfolded the front page of the society section. There, in a picture no one could miss, were Dax and she dancing, holding each other tightly. His face was bent low over hers, which was raised to his like a flower to sunlight. Their smiles were intimate, more telling than the way he held her. Under the picture the caption read: "Congressman Devereaux and Keely Preston, wife of an MIA. Their turn around the dance floor turned heads."

"Damn," Dax cursed under his breath and flung the newspaper to the floor. "Damn."

Keely folded her arms across her middle and turned away, going to the window and staring out.

Nicole cleared her throat. "You'd better get your stories straight," she warned. "Someone's bound to pick up on this. Dax, did anyone see you at Keely's house?"

"I don't think so. I parked at a restaurant on St. Charles and walked over."

Keely turned around and stared at him. "You did? I didn't know that."

"You didn't? How did you think I got there?"

They took the steps necessary to bring them together. She shrugged. "I didn't think about it. You were just there." She picked at a piece of lint on his jacket lapel. "You shouldn't have done that. It's a dangerous neighborhood after dark. You could have been mugged."

"I'm a hunk, remember?"

"No, I mean it," she said earnestly. "Weren't you cold?"

He smoothed back a strand of her hair. "When I left? Are you kidding?" The private joke was chuckled over.

"Yoo-hoo. Remember me?" Nicole said and they turned toward her with glazed eyes as though they truly had forgotten her presence in the room. "Personally I hope you tell the world to mind its own bloody business. I would love nothing better than for you to start—or continue—a hot and heavy affair. But if valor comes before lust, which I sadly suspect it does in this case, you'd better be prepared for the repercussions this picture is bound to generate. Incidentally, there's an accompanying story you failed to read that hints strongly there may have been more going on in Washington than that subcommittee hearing. By the guilty looks on your faces, I think their suppositions aren't too far off base."

She went to the door. "Please remember that I'm not the enemy. I'm a friend. And I'm sorry about doing what I did today. Had I seen the paper first, I probably would have come up with something less public to bring you two together." She squinted her eyes. "On the other hand, that could be your excuse for last night. You had been invited to come on today's show to talk about the MIA issue and you were only rehashing what had happened in Washington. It isn't much, but it may be all you have."

With that she was gone. Dax and Keely stared at the door even long after it had closed. Finally they turned to each other. He sighed and rubbed the back of his neck. "I guess the decision has been made for us."

"I guess so. I'm sorry, Dax. I wouldn't have jeopardized your Senate race for anything in the world."

"I know. I knew exactly what I was doing when I asked you for that dance. I deceived myself into thinking that I could hold you platonically." He gestured at the paper lying at his feet. "A picture's worth a thousand words."

"We'll just have to make sure that we don't give them any more fuel. You said last night that we shouldn't— couldn't—see each other again, no matter how innocently. What happened today should reinforce that decision." She looked up at him. "I'm still married, Dax. Whatever else is a contributing factor, that one remains the same, and it's the one that makes all the others so vitally important. I'm married."

He went to the door, but turned to her before opening it. "You'll be okay, won't you? What if you're cornered and asked to comment on the picture?"

"I'll plead stupidity. I met you in Washington. We went to lunch with a group of congressmen, a noted journalist, and another member of PROOF. I respect the stand you took for our cause. I fully endorse you for the Senate. Beyond that, nothing."

He nodded his head bleakly. He looked like a man going to the gallows, delaying his departure for as long as he could. "If you ever need me for anything...."

Her eyes answered for her.

Then he was gone and the pain was unbearable. Blindly she groped her way back to her desk and lay her head down on her arms. The shrill ring of the telephone was a rude interruption to her gentle weeping.

"Yes," she grated into the receiver.

"Ms. Preston, this is Grady Sears at the *Times-Picayune*."

She gripped the receiver harder and mustered all her poise. "Yes?"

# Nine

That was only the first in a series of similar calls. The persistent reporters were vastly disappointed by Keely Preston Williams's calm responses to their barrage of insinuating questions. When asked if she and Congressman Devereaux were romantically involved, she laughed lightly.

"I'm sure the congressman wouldn't be at all flattered to have his name romantically linked with an old married lady's."

"Your husband has been missing for over twelve years, Mrs. Williams. And you're not exactly old. The congressman's romantic encounters are legion."

*Are they? How many have there been? Am I just one among many?* "I don't know anything about Congressman Devereaux's love life past or present."

"How do you account for the intimacy with which you two were dancing?" This asked with a leer. "Pictures don't lie, Mrs. Williams."

"No, but they can be misinterpreted. The congressman and I were celebrating a mutual victory in Washington. He supported PROOF's cause. If he uses as much finesse during his campaign as he did on the dance floor, he'll be certain to win the election."

This last was said through a tight throat and stiff smile. She sounded like an idiotic, simpering female, but that was better than sounding like a guilty correspondent in a tangled love affair.

All the interviews followed the same pattern. Since she and Dax didn't provide another opportunity to fan the flames of scandal, it was dying a rapid death. Just when she thought she had dodged even the most incisive reporters, she learned she had yet to dread the worst of them.

It was four days after she and Dax appeared on the news program. Joe was returning her to her car at the Superdome after a hard day. Three never-say-die reporters had called her for further comment.

"Looks like you have company," Joe shouted over the loud clapping of the rotary blades as he set the chopper down.

Keely had already seen the car parked beside hers and now she saw the man opening the door and sliding from behind the wheel. It was Al Van Dorf.

"Looks like I do," she said grimly. Thanking Joe for returning her safely, she waved him off, and rather than run from under the blades as she usually did, she walked with a measured tread toward her car. Van Dorf had positioned himself between her and it.

He watched the helicopter lift off and bank sharply in the direction of the hangar, where Joe kept it when it wasn't being chartered.

"Never ceases to amaze me how things fly," he said, still looking at the diminishing helicopter.

"Hello, Mr. Van Dorf. What brings you to New Orleans? Did you run out of things to write about in Washington?" *Easy, Keely,* she cautioned herself. It wouldn't be in her best interest to antagonize him. She softened her sarcastic words with a gracious smile and could tell by the probing look he turned on her that he didn't know if her question had been intentionally snide or not.

"Let's just say that there are more interesting things to write about down here right now." The feral eyes gleamed at her from behind the outdated eyeglasses. His smile was slow in coming and insolent when it finally materialized. "Like you and Congressman Deveraux for instance."

Her look of total bewilderment was worthy of an Oscar. "I—I don't understand. Congressman Devereaux and *I?*"

"Why don't we go somewhere and have a drink and talk about it." He moved to take her arm. She eluded him gracefully but left him with the distinct message that she didn't want to be touched.

"No, thank you, Mr. Van Dorf. I'm on my way home."

"Well, then, I guess we'll just have to talk here." He reached into his breast pocket and pulled out a folded page of newspaper. Keely knew immediately what it was. He studied the picture of them dancing with an objective tilt of his frazzled head. "You take a nice picture, Mrs. Williams."

"Thank you." She could fence with him as long as he could with her.

"Would you say the congressman takes a good photograph? He's a handsome devil."

"Yes, he is. Very handsome." Her ready reply surprised him. He seemed almost angry that she wasn't showing any nervousness. Taking advantage of his guard being down, she asked, "What did you wish to speak to me about, Mr. Van Dorf?"

He eyed her shrewdly. This lady was no easy case. If she was going to play rough, then so was he. "Is Devereaux as good at lovemaking as he is at debate?"

If the question was geared to shock her, it was successful. For a moment she was too stunned to speak. When she did, she found it difficult to form words with her rubbery lips. "Your inference is unforgivable, Mr. Van Dorf, and I don't choose to honor it with a denial."

"Aren't you and Devereaux lovers?"

"No."

"Then how do you explain this picture?"

"How do you explain it?" she fired back. Shock had been replaced by anger and she barely contained her impulse to strike against that knowing smirk that twisted his mouth into an ugly grimace. "People dance together all the time. Do you imply that the President is having an affair with every woman he dances with at a White House reception?"

"Yes, people dance together all the time, but rarely with such sublime grins on their faces."

"Congressman Devereaux is a charming man. I find him intelligent, charismatic, enthusiastic. I admire him for the stand he took on the MIA issue. I respect the courage with which he faces his critics. Admiration and respect. That's all I feel for him." *Liar,* her mind accused, making her even more determined to put Van Dorf off the track. "How you detect something illicit from one dance is beyond me. Do you consider that good journalism?"

"It's not just one dance, Mrs. Williams," he replied coolly. "It's all those covert looks and smiles in Washington. It's a rainy day that neither of you can or will account for. It's a gut feeling I have."

She laughed mirthlessly. "If your 'gut feeling' is your only source of information, you'd better find others more reliable. I have never been Congressman Devereaux's lover." That was the truth. "I will never be." That remained to be seen. "Nor do I want to be." That was a lie. "Now, I've granted you all the time I intend to. I would think you'd have better things to write about than 'covert looks and smiles,' all of which are only figments of your exploitative imagination."

With that, she pushed past him and went to her car, unlocked the door with shaking hands and got in. She was pulling her coattail free of the door when he asked her, "What does the congressman think of you?"

"Ask him."

He smiled that lazy, smug grin. "Oh, I intend to. You can bet on it."

She slammed the door, started the engine, and, controlling an urge to race out of the parking lot, drove away at a reasonable and, what she hoped was, an unperturbed speed.

Later that night, as she got into bed, she was still quaking with anxiety. What could she have said that she hadn't? What had she said that she shouldn't have? Did Van Dorf believe her? Probably not, but he would have nothing else on which to build a story. If he did print a story hinting at a relationship between them, he'd look like a fool. He had no proof, no definitive facts. His material would be purely conjecture. And when it came to the bottom line, they were innocent.

Of course he might stumble upon the fact that Dax had been at her home after the Arts League benefit. It would take some strong convincing on their part to persuade him that nothing had happened, especially since he was prepared to believe the worst. But in fact, nothing *had* happened. They had absolutely nothing to feel guilty about.

Everyone believed her to be Dax's lover. Could no one imagine that Dax could have a platonic relationship with a woman?

For the past two days Dax's sexual exploits and his long list of "companions" had been counted and recounted. Vehemently she had denied being the next name on that list, but that's what she was automatically suspected of being. Had she submitted to Dax's lovemaking, would that be all she was to him? Another notch in his belt? No, no. Yet…

She had read an interview with Dax in last evening's paper. When asked about the now infamous photograph with Keely Preston, he had answered glibly, "I wish they had printed the picture of me with the representative of the Longshoremen's Union. It was a much better picture of me, though that burly longshoreman wasn't near as pretty as Mrs. Williams."

He had laughed it off, made light of it. Of course under the circumstances that's all he could have done.

But maybe that's how he really felt. Maybe he wasn't suffering as much as he had told her he was.

Tears blurred her vision as she stared across her bedroom at the bookcase. The photograph taken of her and Mark on their wedding day was in its place on the third shelf. The bride had bangs and two long skeins of hair hanging over either shoulder to her breasts. Her pure wool dress was hemmed at least six inches above her knee and looked ridiculous with the white patent leather boots that hugged her calves. A traditional wedding dress had been out of the question. There hadn't been time to select one. But had she really got married looking like *that*?

Her burning eyes slid to the young man in the picture. Mark. *Where are you? What happened to you? Do you live? My sweetheart Mark. For you were a sweetheart. Kind, generous, tender, fun, all of those things. The perfect first love.*

In the picture his hair was cut in early Beatles fashion with long bangs sweeping his eyebrows. That was only days before the army had sheared off his hair at boot camp. His pants and the sleeves of his jacket were too short and tight for his athletic frame. His shoes looked tiny in contrast to the then fashionable bell-bottom cut of his trousers.

Both of them were wearing silly smiles, quite pleased with themselves for having done such a grown-up thing as getting married.

She sat up to look at the photograph more closely. The girl in the picture seemed someone else. She had no relevance to the woman Keely Preston Williams was now. She was as foreign to Keely as a stranger. This Keely couldn't relate to that girl child.

Nor, if Mark were still alive, was he that same young man. She couldn't attach a face, a voice, a smile, a personality, to the man Mark would be if he should come back. The boy in the picture was gone, vanished. And, just as surely, the girl no longer existed either.

Keely lay back down and stared at her ceiling. She tried to remember what it felt like to be kissed and caressed by Mark, but all she could focus on were Dax's kisses and caresses. She didn't recall ever losing all sense of time and space when Mark kissed her. Perhaps her heart had accelerated and her palms had grown moist with anticipation, but she didn't remember that weighty warmth invading her limbs or that liquid, melting sensation that was debilitating and life-giving at the same time.

Closing her eyes, she beckoned to an imaginary lover. When he came, he didn't have the young, blond good looks of her husband, but dark hair and eyes, inherited from French Creole ancestors. His movements weren't fumbling and apologetic, but practiced and patient.

No clumsy hands roamed her body, but ones sure of their talent to arouse. They didn't grope for erogenous places, but went to them unerringly, touched them reverently. Greediness and haste were anathema.

His kiss was deep, engaging every part of his mouth and hers in a sensuous ballet. Teeth, lips, and tongue were erotic instruments that tantalized, stroked, sipped, and probed.

A dimpled mouth murmured something against her

breast before raining light kisses on the soft flesh. A tongue swept the nipple silkily as though coaxing it to relax, but the pouting tip became harder.

The persuasive hands stroked downward, touched, found. She welcomed her ghost-lover. He accepted the invitation, whispered accolades in her ear, praising her femininity even as he claimed it.

Together they moved, giving and receiving equally. That aching void that was so much a part of her was filled. She became one with this lover who breathed love words in her ear as his body spoke a poetic language all its own.

Writhing in unfulfilled longing, Keely arched her hips upward, begging her imaginary lover for release. It came over her like a warm blanket, smothering her momentarily until she was clutching at air to fill starved lungs.

Ever so slowly she coasted down. Her eyes fluttered open and she dazedly wondered what had happened to her. Realization brought with it an inundation of shame. For when she had beseeched her lover for surcease, it hadn't been her husband's name she called out, but that of Dax Devereaux.

Her pillow absorbed the scalding tears of bitter remorse.

"Wanna take some sandwiches to Jackson Square for lunch?"

As with most of Nicole's telephone conversations, this one was without preamble. "I don't—"

"Have you got anything better to do?" Nicole demanded with a touch of asperity.

"No," Keely admitted.

"I'll see you at the front door in half an hour. I'll bring the sandwiches."

Since that day she had played the trick on Keely of getting her and Dax on the news show, Nicole had given her wide berth. They had spoken occasionally on the telephone and met in the hallways at the studio, but there hadn't been the usual camaraderie between them, and Keely missed it.

At the appointed time she went downstairs and met Nicole at the front door. They exited the building on Chartres and walked the few blocks east toward the historic square. This was one of Keely's favorite places. With Saint Louis Cathedral, the Presbytere, and the Cabildo on one side and the Pontalba Building on the adjacent side, she sometimes envied missing all the memorable events that had occurred here or near this landmark. She satisfied herself with strolling among the sidewalk artists who lined the walkways around the square with their wares.

Today the sun was shining and a pigeon was happily sitting atop Andrew Jackson's head as they entered the square from the north gate in front of the cathedral. Early spring flowers were just now hinting at the promise of blooms. Selecting a deserted bench, Nicole dug into the paper sack and extended a wrapped sandwich to Keely.

"The suspense is killing me," she said, biting into an egg salad on wheat bread. "Am I or am I not?"

"Am you or am you not what?"

"Forgiven." Nicole said the word softly and looked at Keely with such contrition that Keely couldn't help but laugh. Laying her sandwich in her lap, she put her arms around her friend and hugged her tight. "You are and I'm sorry too. I've missed you."

Nicole pulled away and blinked back rebellious tears. "Well, thank God that's over. I thought I'd have to wear sackcloth and ashes the rest of my life. And I look ghastly in gray."

Her retort didn't fool Keely. She had been emotionally moved and had obviously missed their shared confidences as much as Keely had. "What you did was hitting below the belt, but at the time that was the least of my worries," Keely said, shaking her head. It had been two weeks since she had seen Dax. Wasn't time supposed to heal all wounds? She had disproved that fallacy. The longer she went without seeing him, the more she craved the sight of him.

"Do you want to tell me about it? That is, what I can't piece together."

Keely slid a look in Nicole's direction. "And what have you pieced together?"

Nicole wrapped the remainder of her sandwich back in the cellophane and opened a canned soft drink. Offering another one to Keely, she said, "I think you must have met somewhere in Washington, been instantaneously attracted to each other, known from the beginning that things could get sticky considering your stations in life, and your consciences and libidos have been battling it out ever since."

Keely looked absently at the statue of Andrew Jackson, where more pigeons had now lighted. "That about sums it up."

"Keely, why are you martyring yourself? If you want

to have an affair with him, have one. So he's a congressman, he's still a man. And who really gives a flying fig
in this day and age who sleeps with whom? Be selfish.
Think about yourself for a change."

"I have to think of him too."

"Why? He's a big boy. He went into this with his
eyes open. Knowing you, I hardly think you enticed
him beyond the point of no return, did you? Wasn't he
the aggressor?"

"Well, yes, but…I told him right off that I was married, but I didn't refuse to see him either. It was so…
he was…"

Nicole mumbled an expletive under her breath.
"Have you slept with him?" At Keely's shocked look
she hurriedly justified herself. "Well, hell, I don't see
any reason to beat around the bush about it. Have you?"

"No," Keely said, barely above a whisper.

"Then no wonder you're miserable. Why for godsakes are you feeling so ashamed? It's not a permanent
condition. Sleep with him and get him out of your system. It's not as if you're in love—" She broke off with a
sharp intake of breath. Putting her hand under Keely's
chin, she yanked her friend's face toward her and saw
the tears beading in anguished green eyes.

"My God," she whispered. "You *are* in love with
him. With Dax Devereaux. Jimineee, Keely. When you
do something, you do it up big, don't you? I encouraged
you to have a nice, uncomplicated affair and you choose
a congressman hoping to be a senator and then you go
and fall in love with him to boot."

Keely was stung by Nicole's chastising tone. "I
wouldn't want to have an affair with him if I didn't love

him. I'm not like you. I can't separate sex from love. With me they're one and the same. I can't treat going to bed with a man as casually as you do."

The moment the words left her mouth, she wished to recall them. She covered Nicole's suddenly limp and lifeless hand with her own and pressed hard. "I'm sorry," she rasped. "I wouldn't have said that had I not been so upset. You know I don't censure you. What you do, how you feel about things, is your business."

Nicole snorted a short laugh. "Hell, if anyone knows my reputation, it's me." She stared into space for a moment and then turned her head with its glorious riot of hair toward Keely. "Didn't it ever occur to you that I might rather be like you?"

"*Me?*" Keely asked, genuinely incredulous.

"Does that surprise you? I don't know why it should. Maybe you don't realize how unique you are. You stand for something. You were given values, standards to live by. They weren't preached at you. You learned them by example.

"I'd love to be ladylike the way you are. My language is deplorable and I know it. My behavior is outrageous and I know it. I would like to have refinement, speak softly and with gentility. I'd like to have the respect people have for you." She uttered that hard laugh again. "Fat chance of that."

Keely hesitated before asking quietly, "Why—why do you…go…with so many men?"

"You mean sleep with so many, don't you?" Her question was tinged with bitterness, but it was aimed at herself, not at Keely. "I guess I'm only living up to what was always expected of me. My mother deserted my father and me when I was too young to remember it. But he never let me forget it. Every day of my life he reminded me how like her I was—a born slut, no good, doomed to a life of sin and immorality. He took out all his anger at my mother on me."

She traced the nap of her twill skirt with her finger, remembering the painful past. "I've analyzed myself, you see. I'm looking for someone to love me, hoping to find in each man I'm with the father-affection I never had. From the day I needed a training bra my father called me a tramp. He was right. I am a tramp. A high-classed one, but a tramp just the same."

"Don't say that about yourself, Nicole. You're not! You have a great capacity to love, you've just never channeled it in the right direction. I think you're afraid to love someone, afraid that they'll reject you the way your father did."

"We were talking about you, remember?"

"Now we're talking about you. Behind this tough I-don't-give-a-damn facade you show the world, there's an insecure, lonely woman begging to be loved for herself and not for the flamboyant image she projects. And a sensitive man is bound to see that woman." She looked at Nicole's averted face and said, "Charles Hepburn perhaps."

Nicole laughed in earnest now. "Talk about rejection! I've tried every trick in the book to get that man in my bed, and he's turned me down flat. It's not that *I* want *him,* it's that he *doesn't* want me. It's become a matter of pride with me. A challenge." She covered her heart with her hand and said theatrically, "He holds great stock in commitment."

"Good for him."

"Well, he can forget it if he thinks I'd give up every other man for *him*." They were quiet. Nicole moved a pebble along the concrete with the toe of her shoe. "No matter what I've said to you in the past, I do respect you and your ideals."

Keely smiled. "And I covet your courage. Sometimes I think morality is little more than fear of reprisal."

Nicole moistened her angelic mouth and asked hesitantly, "What does Dax feel for you, Keely?"

"I don't know. He's said things that made me think that…but then…" She trailed off without finishing.

"Will you give me credit for knowing a little more about men than you do?" Nicole asked. When Keely looked at her and nodded, she said, "I think he's got it as bad as you do. Wait a minute and let me finish," she said, stepping on Keely's attempt to interrupt. "Don't get mad or anything, okay? I made a play for him myself."

Keely felt her jaw drop in disbelief and Nicole rushed on. "Now, I said not to get mad at me. Hell, it was worth a try, wasn't it? At the time I only guessed that you two may have something simmering on the back burner. It was after the interview when you went stalking out of the studio like an offended saint. I put all my 'come on' powers into play, but the man was totally unresponsive. Zilch. No go. He didn't even play along, pretending to be interested, but rudely kept turning his head looking at the door you'd gone through."

"That hardly proves anything."

"No, but when I saw you together, he was…I don't know…attentive, protective. Knowing his reputation with females, most of which is exaggerated conjecture, I'm sure, I didn't expect him to be so…" She searched for a word and came up with "Absorbed."

"Whatever else he is, he is not on the make. I'll admit I've turned down few offers, and in all modesty, few of mine have been turned down. It's not something I'm particularly proud of. What I am proud to tell you is that your man didn't even see these." She cupped her breasts, lifting them and then letting them fall. "He didn't see this hair or these eyes, all of which have been known to drive men crazy. He saw only you, Keely." She stopped speaking to judge the effect her words were having on Keely.

"Take that for whatever it's worth. If I were to gamble on it, I'd bet that you and the congressman haven't had the last chapter written yet."

Keely shook her head in denial. "No. I appreciate everything you've told me, but it was over before it ever got started."

"Strictly off the cuff," Nicole said haltingly. "If you had your choice tonight, who would you rather be with? Dax or Mark?"

Keely jerked upright as though she'd been slapped. "That's not fair! There's no way I can answer that."

Nicole looked at her sadly and said in a sympathetic undertone, "You just have."

# *Ten*

Keely and Nicole were weak with laughter as they pushed open the heavy studio doors on their way out. They were clutching each other, leaning into each other, giggling like sorority girls. It had been two weeks since their picnic lunch in Jackson Square. The confidences shared that day had added a new dimension to their friendship. Today Nicole had talked Keely into having dinner with her between the evening newscasts.

"Can you believe it? I mean *really,* can you believe it?" Nicole gasped, dabbing at the tears in her eyes. "When I said…when I said…when…" They collapsed into another fit of giggles as they made unsteady progress down the hallway.

"You must share the joke." They turned together to see Charles Hepburn walking toward them. Dax Devereaux was with him.

The laughter seemed to be sucked from Keely's body by a giant vacuum. Her mouth was still open in a wide smile, but no sound came out. She couldn't draw a breath. Seeing Dax had robbed her of even involuntary functions.

"Oh, Charles," Nicole said, going to him and wrapping her arms around his neck. She was still laughing helplessly. "Did you see the newscast?"

"No, Dax and I were just concluding our meeting. What happened?"

"It was a disaster. You'll probably lose all the sponsors you've so carefully stroked. But it was so funny!"

Her laughter was infectious. Dax was smiling. Charles looked at Nicole as if she were a delightful and precocious child and said, "Well, tell us."

"Okay," she said, straightening and clearing her throat. "I was introducing this news story about CPR. They're holding free teaching sessions in the public schools this week." She inhaled deeply to suppress the giggles that were already making her voice ripple. "Anyway, the last thing I said was, 'Pay close attention. The next thing you see might very well save your life or the life of someone you love.' They rolled the tape, but instead of the news story about CPR it was a laxative commercial!"

The men joined the laughter. Nicole fell against Charles like a rag doll. He caught her to him, hugging her while they laughed. "I had just said it was going to save their lives and here was a box of laxative on the scr-screen. You fin-finish, Keely. I can't."

Keely cast a fleeting look at Dax then spoke to everyone in general. "Well, they dumped out of the commercial and came back to Nicole. She was laughing so hard she could barely speak. When she finally did, instead of going back to her script, she handed the whole thing off to the weatherman."

They all laughed again and for a moment she was distracted by Dax's deep dimple and flashing teeth. "The poor man wasn't expecting it. He didn't even have his coat on. Luckily his mic was clipped on. Anyway, like a real trouper, he started jabbering about highs and lows and pressure systems and only then realized that a cigarette was dangling from his mouth."

"That's when it really got funny," Nicole chimed in. "I guess he thought no one would notice if he just let the cigarette casually fall out of his mouth to the floor. But he'd forgotten all those papers and things he uses. The cigarette fell right into a big pile of them around his feet and started smoldering. So here he was stamping on the floor, trying to put out the cigarette and waving that pointer of his. It looked like a magic wand that had a will of its own." She was doing a comical imitation of the stomping foot and waving stick and they all laughed again until they were gasping for air.

When he was somewhat restored, Charles said, "You'll probably all be fired in the morning. I may recommend it myself."

"Are you kidding? Management wouldn't dare fire us. It was the most spontaneous, entertaining newscast they've ever had. We probably won points with the viewers."

While she and Charles bantered the issue, Dax and Keely were thirstily drinking up the sight of each other. She was thinking that the lines around his eyes looked more finely etched, as though he hadn't been getting enough rest. He was thinking that her eyes looked enormous and green in her pale face.

She was thinking that the sprinkling of silver hair at his temples was more obvious. He was thinking that her hair looked lovely as it framed her face. He knew it smelled like flowers.

She was thinking that the dimple beside his mouth was more beguiling than ever. He was thinking that her mouth had never looked more kissable, parted as it was with her quick, light breathing.

She was thinking that his necktie was always perfectly knotted. He was thinking how enticingly the slender gold chain lay against her throat.

She was thinking that he'd never looked taller or stronger. He was thinking that she'd never looked more delicate or feminine.

She was recalling her vivid fantasy and blushing prettily. He was conjuring up fantasies even as he stood there, his blood flowing with unerred direction to the center of his body.

"What do you say, Dax."

Dax and Keely jumped slightly, caught unaware by Charles's question. "What? I'm sorry," Dax said. "I missed the question."

"I asked if you minded if I invite Nicole and Keely to dinner with us."

Dax looked back at Keely, his eyes shining. "No, of course I don't mind. I rather like the idea. Not that I don't find your company interesting, Charles." He looked back at the man and smiled.

Charles laughed good-naturedly. "I take no offense. Frankly, I'd rather have the ladies along to decorate our table too. We'd planned on going to Arnaud's. Does that suit you?" he asked them politely.

"Yes," Nicole enthused, glaring at Keely with a look threatening that she'd better not protest. For good measure she said, "You and Dax could probably talk about radio advertising. I'm sure you know more about that than Charles does."

"I'd be glad to help any way I can," Keely said meekly. The discussion was rhetorical and they all knew it. Nicole had only provided them with an excuse should they be seen together.

The die was cast. Keely had had nothing to do with this accidental meeting. Dax seemed amenable to the suggestion that she and Nicole accompany them to dinner. Of course, what else could he do? Worriedly she glanced up at him, an apology in her eyes. But his eyes were shining down on her with a warmth that told her he didn't mind the situation in the least.

Without speaking, he took her lightweight raincoat out of her hands and held it for her. She turned her back and slid her arms into the sleeves, keeping her distance. She thought if he touched her, she would crumble. But miraculously she didn't. He leaned forward until she felt his chest against her back. His head came down level with hers and he turned to speak into her ear. "Is this all right with you?"

His voice was a caress, low and vibrating, like the music of a cello. She tilted her head to one side and turned slightly to look at him. So close. His clean, brisk, citrusy cologne was intoxicating. The tip of her nose almost touched his chin, shadowed this late in the day by a hint of beard. Short sideburns tapered beautifully into the hair that grazed the top of his ear. It looked so soft. Her fingers ached to touch it.

"Yes, it's fine with me." Her whisper was husky and intimate and said more than the words she had uttered.

"We'll have to walk a block to where my car is parked. I hope you don't mind, Dax," Charles said as he draped an arm around Nicole's shoulders and led her toward an exit.

"Not at all," Dax said.

Once on the narrow, uneven sidewalk, Dax placed his hand under Keely's elbow. Any gentleman would have done the same. It was only a courtesy. But would anyone else make such a mundane gesture feel like erotic foreplay?

He wrapped his fingers around the bend of her arm. His thumb wedged itself into the crevice of the elbow joint. Sliding back and forth, it stroked sensuously. Then he rolled his thumb over the two round bones, moving her skin, reminding her of other caresses in other places.

In the back seat of Charles's Mercedes they sat calf to calf, knee to knee. Touching nowhere else, they stared at the contact spot, feeling the heat that rose from it. With each movement of the car, the hosiery covering her knee slid along the flannel covering of his.

Nicole and Charles kept up a lively conversation. Keely and Dax responded in desultory tones, as though to say, "Don't bother us, we're busy thinking of each other."

Charles found a parking space on Dauphine so they only had to walk a block down Bienville to the restaurant. The maître d' knew his stuff, for he called each of them by name and deferentially escorted them to

Charles's reserved table in one of the more intimate corners of the restaurant.

Usually Keely reveled in the European ambience of Arnaud's. She liked the crisp, understated, elegant decor, the hushed, accented voices of the waiters. Even the dishes and cutlery wouldn't dare clatter loudly in this restaurant and destroy the atmosphere.

Tonight she was aware of nothing but the man sitting adjacent to her. Under the pretense of sharing a menu, they looked at each other. It was an opportunity for his shoulder to press hers, for his thumb to caress her index finger. When Charles asked for their choices, they were flustered and embarrassingly unprepared to tell him. Quickly they ordered the trout meunière, and, being relieved of that duty, happily went back to staring at each other. Charles took it upon himself to complete their order for them, guessing correctly that they wouldn't care what they ate.

"Dax and I spent most of the afternoon together," he said after the waiter left their predinner drinks on the table.

"Did you?" Nicole asked. "Did you buy some television time?"

Dax placed his forearms on the table and leaned forward slightly. "Charles has got a stupid client, I'm afraid. The more he tried to explain my options, the more confused I became. And it's so expensive, not even counting the—the production costs." His inflection rose on the last words, making them a question.

"Yes," Charles said. "Before we can run a commercial for you, you have to have a commercial." He smiled genially. "I'll happily recommend some production houses for you."

"I've been thinking. I should hire professionals to take care of all this for me. They could better coordinate all the media ads. What do you think?" Obviously Dax respected Charles's business acumen.

"I think you'd be greatly relieved of a lot of tedious responsibility so you could better concentrate on other things."

The waiter had brought a linen napkin-lined basket of French rolls. The hard golden crusts kept their white centers soft and doughy. Dax broke off a piece of one, buttered it liberally and handed it to Keely. The pillows of his fingertips touched hers at the moment their eyes held and locked. Only the barest movement of flesh on flesh electrified them. The magnetic field that surrounded them was only broken when an obsequious waiter served them crocks of onion soup.

The restaurant wasn't crowded on this weeknight, but nevertheless they were wary of curious eyes and made the supreme effort of appearing no more than dinner companions. Throughout the meal the conversation was light and amusing, peppered as it was with Nicole's naughty statements, which she said only to aggravate Charles and try to shake his stoicism.

"Would anyone care for dessert?" Charles, acting as host, offered.

"I'm too full right now," Nicole said.

"I'd like some coffee," Keely said and Dax concurred. When it came, he automatically added cream to hers and stirred it for her. The natural intimacy of the gesture wasn't wasted on Charles and Nicole, but the knowing look they slanted at each other went un-noticed by the other two diners.

In the foyer of the restaurant as they were shrugging into their coats, Nicole said, "I like to walk a while and then go for dessert. And you know what I like best? Beignets at Café du Monde."

"You want to walk all the way to Café du Monde?" Charles asked.

"Sure, Grandpa. Aren't you up to it?"

"I'd probably make it there, but I doubt if I could make it back. Besides, you don't have time. You have to go back to work, remember?"

"We can take a cab from there back to here. And there is a network movie on tonight that runs late, so the news will be late too."

Charles looked at Keely and Dax who were stand-ing close together, not caring what the plans were, so long as they didn't have to leave each other right away.

"Dax? Keely? Are you game?"

"I don't have any plans," Dax said.

"Neither do I," Keely said.

It was settled. They were thrilled. They could have an evening together and as long as they were protected under the auspices of business, they could always jus-tify being seen together.

"Let's go down Bourbon Street," Nicole said and Charles groaned. "Come on, you old fuddy-duddy," Ni-cole taunted.

"Nicole," he said patiently, "Bourbon Street is noisy, dirty, crowded, immoral, and decadent."

"I know. I adore decadence," she said, her blue eyes dancing. She grabbed Charles by the arm and virtually dragged him the half-block to the intersection of Bourbon and Bienville.

They mingled with the throng, which was nothing to what it would be in a few weeks during Mardi Gras. The sounds and smells of Bourbon Street, New Orleans, were uniquely its own. The spicy aroma of seafood gumbo mingled with those of beer and the musty dankness that was inherent to the French Quarter. Live jazz blared out into the streets from the many nightclubs and blended discordantly with Cotton Eyed Joe being played by a country-western band. Barkers in front of the topless bars swung open the doors teasingly while touting the physical attributes of the dancers within. One could usually catch a glimpse of bare skin illuminated by flashing colored lights.

On the front of one such entertainment hall was a sign that read: "World-Famous Sex Acts Performed." "I wonder what makes them world famous?" Charles asked pedantically.

"Well if you have to ask, it's for sure you've never seen them performed," Nicole quipped. He sighed tiredly and, placing an arm around her shoulders, steered her away as though she were a recalcitrant child.

They meandered farther down the legendary street until the neighborhood became less commercial and more serene. They turned onto St. Peter Street, which would eventually lead them to Jackson Square, and the café.

The street was deserted and dark. Walking by twos, Charles and Nicole led the way, going past closed shop fronts, art galleries, and grillwork gates that protected alleys leading into private inner courtyards.

Dax raised his arm from the middle of Keely's back and settled it along her shoulders, pulling her closer. "How have you been?"

"Fine. You?"

"Fine."

"You look tired. Have you been working?"

"Yeah. I've been in Washington for the past three weeks. The congressional calendar is full. We're trying to get in all our business before the closing of the session."

"Oh."

"I had dinner at the White House with the President and the First Lady."

"Truly?"

"Yes." He grinned boyishly. "Business, of course, but it was nice to be invited."

They walked in silence then Dax said, "I read what you said in the newspapers."

"I read what you said too."

"Don't believe everything you read."

She turned to look at him. "No?"

"No," he said, shaking his head.

"Like what for instance?"

"Like for instance that I think of you as an admirably courageous woman who is fighting for a great cause and that I have no romantic inclinations toward you."

Her heart was pounding in her temples. "I shouldn't believe that?"

"The first part, yes, the second part, no. If you only knew how romantically inclined toward you I was, you'd be afraid to walk down this dark street with me. You'd know why I haven't eaten or slept properly in the last month. You'd know why I count at least ten new gray hairs every morning. I hope it's true that they say that gray hair inspires confidence."

They had reached Jackson Square now. The gates around the park itself were locked for the night, but they walked in front of the Pontalba Building, ostensibly looking in the shop windows on the street level, but seeing nothing.

"Did you have a tough time with the reporters?"

"Not really," she answered. "For a few days, that's all."

"I'm sorry, Keely. I'm accustomed to it, but I know you're not. I wish you could have been spared that."

"I survived. Van Dorf was—"

"Van Dorf! He came to see you?"

"Yes. He was at my car one day when Joe deposited me at the Superdome."

"That jerk," Dax growled. "One of these days…. He didn't hurt you, did he?"

She laughed softly and smoothed the lapel of his raincoat in a comforting gesture. "No. He only implied some rather nasty things."

"What kind of things?"

She averted her eyes away from the probing strength of his. "He only said…you know…asked me things about you."

"What did he ask?" he persisted.

Flushing, she tried to look away, but he wouldn't allow it. He captured her chin in his hand and forced her head back until she had to look at him. "What did he ask?"

She licked her lips. "He asked me if you were good in bed."

"He what!" His hands went to her shoulders and gripped hard. "He asked you that? So help me, Keely, if he prints one libelous word about you—"

"But he didn't and he won't. He may be ruthless, but he's not stupid. He knows he has nothing to write."

"What did you tell him?"

"The truth. I don't know."

He tried to contain the smile that suddenly threatened, but failed, and finally gave in to it. "Take a guess."

She leaned away from him and looked sharply into his mischievous eyes. "What?"

"Take a guess as to how I am in bed."

"No!"

"Come on. Be a sport. Take a guess. I'll give you a hint."

"I don't want a hint."

Ignoring her, he leaned down, settled his lips against her ear, and whispered, "I'm not world famous yet, but I'm working on it."

He lifted his head slowly, studying her reaction, while she puzzled through what he had said. Then remembering the earlier conversation between Charles and Nicole in front of the nightclub, she burst out laughing. He caught her behind the head and pressed her face into his shirtfront as she laughed. His fingers interlaced behind her head and his thumb slipped under her hair to massage behind her ears. Eventually her laughter subsided and she raised her head. She watched his mouth as he spoke.

"I want to kiss you so bad I hurt. But this is a bit too well lighted and public, don't you think?"

Dumbly she nodded. Reluctantly he released her and they went to join the other couple at the street corner who were waiting for the light to change. They crossed Decatur and went past the Washington Artillery Park to the Café du Monde. Over a hundred years old, the café was still one of the most popular spots in the city. Serving only beignets, the fried doughnuts covered with powdered sugar, and coffee, it never lacked for customers during its twenty-four serving hours each day.

They chose a table on the covered porch even though the evening was cool and misty this close to the river. The chairs were chrome and green vinyl, the tables gray Formica, but it was for the hot coffee and doughnuts that one came to Café du Monde. That and to watch the constant flow of traffic—pedestrian, horse drawn, and motor—that circumnavigated Jackson Square.

They ordered two helpings of doughnuts, three black coffees, and one café au lait for Keely. In a matter of minutes the hot fragrant sugar-coated doughnuts were served with steaming mugs of strong chicory coffee.

They fell onto the doughnuts ravenously. Each bite unsettled the fine sugar on the doughnuts until a soft white cloud seemed to drift over the table and cost them all valuable eating time while they laughed. Faces, hands, and clothes were also dusted with the confectioners' sugar, but it was a messy hazard they gladly suffered.

Keely and Nicole each got a plate of leftover sugar to blot up with moistened fingers. Nicole was licking hers clean, her motions deliberately provocative, when she said, "Let's go up on the levee." Her eyes half closed as she eyed Charles seductively.

"You have to go to work."

"I have time." Without waiting for permission or assent, she left her chair and went toward the tunnel that connected through to the boardwalk built along the levee, affectionately named the Moonwalk. Lampposts with appropriately dim lights had been strategically placed along the walk, shedding enough light to keep one from stepping off into the Mississippi River, but not too much to destroy the romantic atmosphere.

The others followed Nicole's lead, and by the time they came out of the tunnel, she had already selected a bench for her and Charles. By tacit agreement when he sat down beside her, Keely and Dax walked farther on. They became absorbed by the shadows and swallowed by the mist that was lightly falling as they claimed their own bench. Lights on either bank of the river made wavy reflections on the surface of the water. What wasn't so pretty in the daytime looked magical by night.

Dax curved an arm around her shoulders and pulled her under its protection. She lay her head against the hard biceps. Her eyes were closed. She could feel his breath on her face, drawing nearer. Gently he blew against her eyelids, her mouth. It opened slightly to take in the air he expelled. Then his lips touched hers.

Now, after having been denied so long, they extended the torture, heightened the anticipation, perpetuated the excitement. He kissed her with closed lips once, twice, a third time. The light brushings couldn't really qualify as kisses, but more as caresses of mouth against mouth.

Cupping her palms over the hair above his ears that she had longed to touch before, she closed her hands around his head. His tongue played temptingly along the line where her lips came together, flicking and stroking until her own came out to meet it. Her tongue became a wild thing, forever imprisoned but now freed to do what it would. It outlined his lips, delved into the dimple, tormented the corners of his mouth until it opened under her probing. She swept the honeyed cave, taking up his nectar and leaving hers. Her tongue slipped behind his teeth and glided over the roof of his mouth. With deep anguished moans they fell apart.

They stared at each other without speaking. Their eyes wandered freely, giddy with the privacy they'd been granted and taking liberties otherwise prohibited. Hair, eyes, ears, noses, mouths, were perused at leisure until they could bear it no longer and came together again with hungry passion.

Their mouths fused, dispelling the doubts that had clouded their minds. Did she mean all those frivolous things she had said about admiration and respect? Has he truly left a trail of brokenhearted mistresses? How much does she pine for her husband? Does he love Madeline? Does she miss me? Does he miss me?

At long last he released her lips only to bury his mouth in her mist-dampened hair. "God, Keely, these past weeks have been hell. I've thought of nothing but you."

"I've been miserable, confused. I thought maybe you meant everything you told those reporters."

"No. You know better. Open your coat, please. I want

to… There… All of that was just words, something to say. I never meant any of it."

"I thought so, but you weren't here…" They kissed.

"I wanted to call, but I thought up all sorts of nightmares about wiretaps and…don't bother with the buttons. I just want to feel your hands on me…yes…oh, sweet…" They kissed again. "…wiretaps and all, you know…you taste so good, Keely."

"Are you worried about things like that?" she asked on a soft groan as he captured her earlobe with his teeth.

"More for your sake than mine…. This is so soft…"

"Dax…" She sighed. "What did we do to make such a stir? Yes, touch me…."

"You feel so right…. So many people saw us dancing. I wasn't aware of the audience we were drawing. I wasn't aware of anything except holding you and wanting you…. Oh, yes, sweetheart…there." He pressed his hand over hers, trapping it against his shirtfront.

"I want you, Keely. I want to make love to you, to be inside you. I want you so bad I taste you with every pore."

# *Eleven*

Her fingers furrowed through his hair, holding his head tightly against her breasts. She groped for something to say. There were no words of comfort she could share with him, because she was as bereft as he. Did he know she ached for him as badly as he did for her?

Charles spared her having to offer any trite platitudes. She saw him strolling toward them, stopping at a discreet distance to stare out at the river. Keely nudged Dax, softly saying his name, and he sat erect, following the direction of her gaze. Charles cleared his throat loudly. "Excuse me, but Nicole must get back to the studio. Of course, if you wish to stay—"

"No," Dax said gruffly, finding it necessary to clear his own throat. "We'll go too." He stood and offered his hand to Keely. She hastily buttoned her coat, picked up her belongings, and joined him to follow Charles's hollow footsteps down the boardwalk.

Nicole was languishing on the bench, looking smug and satisfied. Keely shot an inquiring look in Charles's direction, but his bland expression gave away nothing. Still waters ran deep, Keely thought with a smile.

They retraced their way back to the front of Jackson Square. "Since your cars are parked in the KDIX parking lot, I thought we'd all walk Nicole back to work and then I'll get a cab to my car from there," Charles explained with the thoroughness of a scoutmaster.

"That's fine," Dax said. He placed a firm arm around Keely's waist as they walked along the fog-shrouded sidewalks. "To hell with my image. It seems to get worse the harder I try to improve it." He set their pace, slowing in order that Nicole and Charles would be well enough ahead of them to give them privacy.

"What did Madeline think of the publicity linking your name to mine?" Keely asked.

"I don't know. I didn't ask."

"You don't care then about her opinion?" she asked shyly.

"Not where you're concerned. She's got a lot of money, she's nice to look at, and on occasion, she can be fun. But she's also got a vicious streak. She's possessive and grasping and ambitious and jealous."

"Have you and she...?" Keely couldn't bring herself to ask the question and sucked her chin against her chest, staring at the wet concrete under her shoes.

They had almost gone a block before he answered. "I don't think it would be fair to Madeline or any other woman for me to answer a question like that."

"I'm sorry, Dax. I had no right to ask that." She gnashed her teeth, wishing she hadn't even hinted at the question.

"You have every right, so don't apologize. I'm glad

you asked. It means a lot to me that you care about such things. Most people don't these days." They had reached their destination and paused at the corner of the building. He closed his arms around her and spoke gently. "I promise you, Keely, that since I met you, I haven't been with anyone else."

Joy bubbled inside her, and as she clung to him, she squeezed her eyes shut in ecstatic relief. The idea of him being with someone else had plagued her. Now her heart sang, albeit unfairly, to know he hadn't slaked the passions she'd induced on someone else's body. Feeling guilty over her selfishness, she pulled away to look up at him as she said, "You didn't have to tell me that."

"But you're damned glad I did, aren't you?"

Was she so transparent? Did he already know her that well? "Yes," she said honestly.

His finger traced her hairline as he murmured, "It wouldn't be fair to take another woman to bed, Keely, when I'd be wishing it was you lying with me."

"Dax—"

"I came back here to see if the two of you were making out all right—no pun intended—but you seem to be doing fine," Nicole teased. "Charles has magnanimously consented to see me home properly, so he'll be staying through the newscast. You're welcome to stay too."

"I need to get home," Keely said. "I have to be up at five, remember?"

"And I'll see Keely to her car," Dax said. He went to Charles and shook his hand. "Thank you for an enlightening day and a wonderful dinner. I enjoyed it all.

As soon as I've firmed up someone to handle the media campaign for me, they'll be in touch with you."

"KDIX will appreciate your business. Good luck, Dax."

"Thank you. Good night, Nicole."

"Good night, everyone," she called back airily as she sailed through the employee entrance that led to the studio. She was dragging Charles behind her like a queen with a conquered foe.

Dax looked after them pensively. "They're in love with each other, aren't they?"

"Yes. Charles knows about it. I'm not sure Nicole does yet."

"What a pair! Who would ever guess they'd choose each other?"

Keely smiled, but it was a sad expression. "I'm not sure such choices are ours to make."

Dax caught her meaning all too well. "No, I guess they're not," he said huskily. "Some things just happen, don't they?"

The parking lot was eerily dark and deserted as they walked up the ramp to where their cars were parked. Besides her compact, the only other car on the lot was a chocolate-brown Lincoln.

"Is that yours?" she asked.

"Yes."

Done with conversation, he slipped his hands inside her coat, settled them on her waist, and pulled her to him as he backed her against the car. Her feet were trapped between his. Touching from ankle to chest, he leaned forward and took her lips under his.

She lost all perspective of the environment under

the demands of his mouth. The muffled sound of traffic below, the mist that cloaked them like an ethereal veil, the hard surface pressing into her spine, all vanished with his touch. His mouth and the sensuous way it possessed hers were her only sources of reference.

When at last he lifted his mouth from hers, it was only far enough for him to speak. "Keely, would you even consider coming to my house for the weekend?" He paused for her to respond, but shock had rendered her mute. He pressed his advantage and rushed on. "I don't want you to misconstrue my invitation. There are no strings attached. I'd just like for you to come to my house and meet my parents."

It was such a dear, desperate, appealing invitation that Keely's heart was breaking that she must refuse it. Even though his intentions were honorable, Dax knew as well as she did that staying in the same house together overnight would be torturous and dangerous.

But not wanting to turn him down outright, she waltzed around a refusal. "Do you think that's wise?"

"It's positively crazy." His finger traced the delicate bones of her jaw. "I thought coming to your room at the Hilton was the dumbest thing I'd ever done. Inviting you to spend the weekend at my house outdoes that. Nevertheless, I'm asking."

"I'd like to meet your parents, but what would you tell them about me?" Suddenly she wondered how many women Dax had taken to his house for a weekend and it pained her to estimate.

"I'd tell them that you are a lady I hold in high regard. My father will exercise all his Southern gentlemanly charm on you and my mother will deluge you with recipes and antidotes for every catastrophe."

She laughed and toyed with the brass button on his jacket as she asked casually, "Does anyone live with you? A housekeeper or anyone?" Her voice was high-pitched and wobbly.

He lifted her chin with his finger and looked long and deep into her eyes. "She goes home after dinner."

"Oh."

He didn't release his hold. Rather he kept her head tilted back as he said, "Keely, I wouldn't expect you to change your mind about anything on the short drive from here to there. Nor do I want you to compromise any standard you've set for yourself or for me. If it'll make you feel any better, I'll supply you with nails and a hammer and you can seal yourself into your appointed bedroom as soon as the sun goes down." He smiled, but she felt that he meant it. "I just want us to have some time alone. To talk and walk. We can work in the garden, or ride horses, or go fishing, or neck, or take a boat out, or rearrange the furniture, or—"

"Wait! Back up."

"Well, the furniture in the library needs rearranging. I've been think—"

"No, before that."

"I have a small lake on the property and we could—"

"Before that."

"Let's see." He squinted his eyes, feigning concentration. "Oh, you mean the part about necking?" His lips curled into the devilish grin she adored and he said, "I just threw that in to see if you were paying attention." She laughed and he added, "But it's a hell of a good idea."

He laid his forehead on hers while he swayed them back and forth as they hugged. "Will you come?" he asked softly.

Maintaining their position, she answered soberly, "I can't, Dax. You know that. I'd love to, but I can't."

He was silent for a while, absorbing what she had said, swallowing his disappointment. "I promise to be on my best behavior."

"But I may not be on mine. Rather than relaxing, I think we'd both be tense and uptight, and that wouldn't be any fun."

"I won't let that happen. I promise to be relaxed."

"The risk we'd run of having someone find out I was there would be too high. We'd both be ruined should that happen."

"It's always a possibility, but I'd take every precaution to see it was kept a secret." He pushed his fingers through her hair until they rested on her scalp. "Please come, Keely." When he felt the negative shake of her head, he urged hastily, "At least say you'll think about it. I'll wait until the end of the week for your answer. Just say you'll consider it."

Her answer would probably be the same at the end of the week, but this was a small concession she could make. "All right," she said, lifting her eyes to his. "I promise to think about it."

She thought about it. All day. All night. All week.

By Wednesday she was in an abominable mood. It seemed that asinine drivers chose that day to have an orgy of fender-benders that tied up traffic on major arteries and kept her and Joe frantically trying to keep up with them and inform commuters of the hazards they posed.

"Keely, what the hell is going on today?" the afternoon DJ asked her after he had started a Willie Nelson record.

"I'm doing the best I can, Clark," she snapped back into her microphone. "We've had five accidents reported in the last twenty minutes."

"Well, it sounds like you're rambling all over town," he grumbled.

"We are! I'm getting airsick flying around up here in circles. I don't orchestrate these accidents you know."

"Okay, okay. Sorry. Just be more concise, please. You've taken up far too much of my airtime."

Keely switched off her communicating device and Joe laughed when he heard her mumble, "Conceited ass."

At one minute to five on Thursday morning her telephone rang.

"Hello."

"Well?"

"I don't know yet."

He hung up.

At seven-thirty that evening her telephone rang again. She was contemplating her answer over an omelet. "Hello."

"Well?"

"Give me until midnight."

During the long evening hours she pondered the dilemma. Dax had promised that he wouldn't consider her going home with him a reversal of her convictions. She trusted him. He would never force or coerce her into his bed. It was herself that she didn't trust.

During the past week she had guiltily dragged out pictures of Mark, written letters to his mother, looked through her high school yearbook and scrapbooks, trying to convince herself that she still loved him. Yet she couldn't conceive of him as anything except a two-dimensional image on a piece of paper. He wasn't flesh and blood, and light and heat, and sound and smell.

How long was she going to cling to this fond memory? It was more than remotely possible that Mark had been dead for years. Was she going to waste her life, her youth, her love, on stubbornness that she had convinced herself was honor?

She freely admitted to herself that she loved Dax. This was no adolescent infatuation, but the love of a woman for a man. It carried with it no idealistic illusions, but all the pain and heartache that went hand in glove with true loving. She and Dax weren't children, innocent of the injustices that could be handed down. Hopefully, they would have the fortitude to face them.

Her decision was made then. She would spend the weekend with Dax. She wouldn't be aggressive, nor resistant, but would respond with love to whatever circumstances presented themselves. They would both know when and if the time was right.

With that glowing thought she attacked her closet with a vengeance, looking for just the right clothing to take with her. Horseback riding, fishing, walking, all the things he'd said they'd do ran through her mind as she made her selections and set them beside her opened suitcase. Two days? In half an hour she had already picked enough clothes to last at least two weeks.

The telephone rang at ten minutes to twelve. He's early! her heart sang. He couldn't wait to hear her answer any more than she could wait to give it.

Picking up the receiver, she shouted, "Yes, yes, yes. I'll come."

There was a silence on the phone, then a woman's voice said, "I'm sorry. Is this Keely Williams?"

The voice rang familiar. "Yes," she answered cautiously.

"Keely, this is Betty Allway."

"Betty!" she exclaimed, intensely embarrassed at the way she had answered the phone and wondering guiltily how she was going to explain herself. But why should she? All that guilt was behind her now.

Before she could say anything, Betty was speaking again, and this time Keely heard the tension in her usually friendly voice. "Keely, I've got some news."

Slowly, like the balloons that were leaking their helium, Keely gradually sank down on the edge of her bed. Her eyes went straight to the picture of Mark on the bookcase. "Yes?"

"Twenty-six men have come out of a jungle in Cambodia. They made their way to a Red Cross refugee camp. The Red Cross notified our military, which received permission to go in and pick them up. They're being taken to Germany first for immediate first aid and observation. As a matter of fact, they're already there. The day after tomorrow they're being flown to Paris. We've been invited to go and meet them."

The silence was long and palpable. Betty didn't interfere with Keely's roiling thoughts. She let the younger woman digest the news and all that it portended.

When Keely spoke, it was with a hoarse croak. "Is— is Mark—"

"The army hasn't released any names yet. I'm not even sure that they've identified all of them. As you can imagine, some of the men are delirious with malnutrition or disease. All I know is that they number twenty-six."

"When were you called?"

"About an hour ago. General Vanderslice called me from the Pentagon. They're pulling together an official delegation from the United States to go over there. The State Department, the Congress, the military, you and I and PROOF, and a selected group of media representatives will be invited to go on a government-chartered plane. For the time being, until we ascertain the condition both mentally and physically of these men, they'll be kept more or less isolated."

"I see." Keely looked down at her hand and was surprised to see that it was shaking violently, as though she had a palsy. Perspiration was inching down her sides and the backs of her knees. A loud roaring in her ears handicapped her hearing.

"Will there be any problem with your going, Keely? I don't know how long we'll be gone. I would say at least three or four days."

"N-no. Of course I'm going." She knew she was about to weep and she crammed a fist against her tight thin lips. "Betty, do you think—"

"I don't know," Betty answered intuitively. "I've asked myself if Bill is one of them a thousand times already, but there's no way to know. I hated to even tell my children for fear they'd get their hopes up too high. Fourteen years is a long time to wait for this day. Now that it's here, I dread knowing. I only have to convince myself that I'll be happy for whoever is on that list of men."

"Yes. I will too, of course," Keely said disjointedly. She ran her hand over her eyes abstractedly. Every muscle in her body had contracted when Betty had told her the news and now that she was forcing herself to relax, she found it painful. "When do we leave? Where?"

"The plane leaves from Andrews Air Force Base at six o'clock tomorrow evening."

"Tomorrow?" Keely asked weakly. So soon. Not enough time to prepare oneself mentally.

"Yes. We'll be met at National and escorted to Andrews. Pandemonium will reign, I'm sure, so be ready for it."

"I'll see you there then. I don't know when I'll be arriving. I'll call the airlines right now."

"There are only twenty-six of them, Keely."

Twenty-six out of over two thousand. They were both thinking how slim were the chances that either of their husbands would be in that group. "I know, Betty. I'll try to remember that."

The older woman sighed. "I'll see you tomorrow." She hung up.

Why were they not rejoicing? Because they were afraid to. Yet. Keely's eyes stared vacantly at the clothes strewed across her bed and when it came back to her why they were there, she folded her arms over her stomach, gripping it as though in agony, and rocked back

and forth. Her keening wail could have issued out of
the jaws of hell.

When the telephone rang a few minutes later, at
straight up midnight, she didn't answer it.

# Twelve

The space between her shoulder blades burned with fatigue. Keely hunched her shoulders, drawing them up under her ears as far as they would go, held them there for several seconds, then let them drop again. She closed her eyes and rolled her head around on her neck, stretching it.

The room was crowded, stuffy, and overheated. A pall of cigarette smoke hovered overhead, clouding the chandeliers that dripped crystal. The long reception room in the American Embassy in Paris today looked like anything but a formal parlor. Coatless men, unshaven and grim, leaned against the walls, arranging themselves in small groups to converse in hushed tones. At intervals the groups shifted as though programmed on a timer.

Reporters checked and rechecked their recorders. Photographers fiddled with cylinders of film and flashing devices. Television news teams monitored their batteries carefully, making sure they would have power when they needed it.

Only the military men in their crisp uniforms didn't seem wilted and disgruntled. Instead they briskly entered and left the room periodically on official duties not apparent to anyone else. Keely had guessed that their business wasn't really necessary but contrived to give the impression that everything wasn't as stagnant as it seemed.

She and Betty sat side by side on a small sofa. For hours they had been in this room awaiting word, any kind of word, on the men who were now, as rumor had it, in another part of the embassy. But rumors had come and gone. Some had proved to be correct, most had not. Keely doubted the veracity of anything she heard.

For fifteen hours, since the motorcade had rolled through the streets of Paris from Charles de Gaulle Airport to the embassy and disgorged the official delegation, they had been sitting in this room.

Everything that could be said both privately and publicly had been said. All they could do now was wait. Reading was out of the question, as words held no meaning to them now. The view from the windows facing Avenue Gabriel had lost its fascination. Talking was an exhausting exercise. Thinking was impossible. So they sat silently, staring vacantly, praying unconsciously. Waiting.

The flight over the Atlantic had been grueling. Keely was interviewed by numerous reporters, all jealous and greedy of her time. Congressman Parker, who had been asked to be part of the delegation because of his chairmanship of the recent subcommittee hearings, had finally come to her rescue, asking the reporters to let her rest for a while. In a fatherly gesture he had patted her on the shoulder and urged her to try to sleep.

But sleep was made impossible by the presence of two other passengers on the airplane. One was Congressman Devereaux. The other was Al Van Dorf.

A television reporter had been asking her an involved question when Keely saw Dax come through the door of the aircraft. Her tongue stumbled over an answer to the question, but she didn't hear the next one over the pounding in her ears. She had had to ask the reporter to repeat it.

Dax's eyes met hers only briefly, but they communicated an encyclopedic amount of information. They told her that he was as bewildered by this situation as she. They told her that he was torn between hope that Mark was one of the few men who had made it out of Cambodia alive and distress to know what his sudden reappearance would mean to them now. His eyes wished her happiness, but selfishly admitted wanting to share that happiness. They told her he didn't want to be here but had to be here. He couldn't stand by somewhere else awaiting word and not know immediately if the name Mark Williams appeared on that all-important list. The strongest message his eyes bespoke was that he wanted to hold her.

All of that was conveyed in one puissant glance. She hadn't dared to look at him during the remainder of the flight nor since they had been ushered into this reception room and erroneously told that a spokesman for the army would be with them shortly.

Even had she been inclined to look at or talk to Dax against all common sense to the contrary, the eaglesharp eyes of Al Van Dorf prevented her. He watched her like a scientist watches a cell under a microscope. Keely knew that each move she made, each word she spoke, were being carefully chronicled in his notebook. She had come to loathe the sight of that green looseleaf tablet and the busy pencil. For all his covert surveillance, he had approached her but once.

His strolling gait had brought him to the small sofa on which she and Betty sat. He stood in front of her, forcing her to look up at him like a petitioner. "Mrs. Williams, are you optimistic that your husband is among these twenty-six men?" He fired the question at her without preliminary small talk.

"I'm trying not to be too optimistic," she replied.

"Do you hope he is?"

She jerked her head up and glared at the reporter with stormy green eyes. "Either you are incredibly stupid, Mr. Van Dorf, or the question is unworthy of you. Either way, I refuse to answer it." She could feel Betty's surprised eyes on her, but she continued to stare down Van Dorf. At last she won, and he dropped his eyes to his hateful notebook and made a notation that she knew was intended to frighten her.

Betty cleared her throat diplomatically. "Mr. Van Dorf, I'm afraid that both Mrs. Williams and I are rather too wrapped up in our own thoughts to be very cordial about answering questions just now. If you'll excuse us, please," she said.

Van Dorf bowed to her slightly but said, "I have one last question for Mrs. Williams." Turning back to her, he asked, "Did you know that Congressman Devereaux was coming along on this trip?"

"No. Not until I saw him board the airplane." That was an honest answer.

Van Dorf grinned that foxlike grin and asked suggestively, "Why do you suppose he did?"

Keely knew the question was asked in hopes of dismantling her composure. She looked up at him placidly and answered, "You should ask Congressman Parker that. He himself told me he had invited Congressman Devereaux to come."

"Seems strange," Van Dorf mused aloud, "that out of all the congressmen in Washington, he would choose Devereaux."

"Not at all," Betty said. She was on Keely's team even though she wasn't sure what game they were playing. "Congressman Devereaux served on that subcommittee, as you well know, Mr. Van Dorf. He supported our cause and was against that bill. He's a veteran of the Vietnam War. Why you're surprised that he should be here, I can't fathom. Now, please, neither I nor Keely feel like talking."

Van Dorf didn't take hints too well, but he ambled off after staring down Keely once more with deadly eyes behind the deceptively meek eyeglasses.

"Thank you," she said to Betty when he was out of earshot.

"What is it with him and you? Why does he keep asking you about Devereaux?"

"I don't know."

"Are you sure?"

She looked quickly at Betty, but then away guiltily. She was spared having to answer when one of the Marines stationed at the embassy marched up to Betty.

"Mrs. Allway?"

"Yes?"

"Will you come with me please at the request of General Vanderslice?"

Betty looked quizzically at Keely, who shrugged her shoulders, then stood up to be escorted by the uniformed man through the ornately carved doors.

Another hour went by, in which Keely sat alone. At any given time she knew what Dax was doing, though her eyes never singled him out. He ran a weary hand around his neck. He shook off his suit coat and draped it over the back of a chair. He unbuttoned his vest. He looked at her. He coughed three times, crossed to the table where ice and canned soft drinks were available. He poured a Coke into a plastic cup, took one swallow, and then abandoned it on the table. He looked at her. He locked his fingers high over his head, stretching expansively. He conversed in undertones with Congressman Parker. Together they looked toward the door through which Betty had passed with the Marine, then started talking again. He looked at her.

The door behind the podium was flung open by two Marines who barely had time to clear it and snap to attention before General Vanderslice bustled through. Not one of his silver hairs was out of place. His uniform jacket buttoned over his solid torso with a meticulous fit. His eyes darted over the room, assessing the situation even as he strode toward the mounted microphone. His carriage was a textbook of perfect military bearing.

Everyone in the large room ceased speaking as though a switch had been turned off. All eyes riveted onto the commanding presence of the general, who placed a sheaf of papers on the lectern.

"Ladies and gentlemen, your patience is commendable. I know how anxious you have been. I realize the limitations of comfort this room affords. I know you've had no rest since the long flight. I apologize for the delay, which seems inherent to an occasion of this importance." His speech was as precise and clipped as his body language.

He cleared his throat and glanced at the papers under the microphone. Keely looked down at her clenched hands, her heart slamming against her ribs. Her glands refused to secrete any saliva, and her tongue, when she tried to swallow, only stuck to the roof of her mouth.

"I want to introduce a man to you. Often in my military career, I have paid homage to men others considered to be heroes. Through whatever motivation, these men exhibited inconceivable courage and valor."

He paused and drew a deep breath. "William Daniel Allway was a major when he was sent to Vietnam sixteen years ago. This morning he has been promoted to the rank of lieutenant colonel."

Keely clamped her fingers over her mouth to cover her cry of joy. Bill Allway! Betty's husband. Tears ran unchecked down her cheeks, but she wasn't even aware of them as she looked toward the doors behind the podium to see a tall, bony man in an ill-fitting army uniform leaning against Betty's supportive arms.

General Vanderslice turned toward the couple and said kindly, "Colonel Allway, will you and Mrs. Allway come forward, please."

The cacophonous racket that roared through the

room was only a small element of the pandemonium that broke loose. Cameras popped like fireworks. The applause and cheering was deafening. Many, caught up in the enthusiasm of the moment and forgetting decorum, jumped onto chairs, whooping and hollering, giving Bill Allway a true hero's welcome.

Keely jumped to her feet, applauding tearfully for the safe return of her friend's husband. One thing was undeniably certain: Mark Williams was not among these few men. Had he been, she would have been called away for a private reunion with him as Betty had been.

When the celebration finally began to recede to a dull roar, Bill Allway approached the microphone. He was thin to the point of emaciation. What hair he had left was white. His cheeks were sunken, his nose pinched, his eyes ringed with dark circles. But he was radiant as he clutched his wife to him tightly.

General Vanderslice tried to be heard over the ruckus. "As most of you know, Mrs. Allway has faced her husband's long absence with the same indomitable spirit that he has shown. I know, because I've had more than one run-in with her." Laughter rumbled through the room. "I can't tell you what pleasure I felt to know that Bill Allway was one of these returning men and that Mrs. Allway, because of her involvement in PROOF, was also here. Colonel Allway, as top-ranking officer and leader of the returning MIAs, has requested the privilege of introducing them to you. Colonel Allway."

Bill and Betty unabashedly clung to each other as he assumed General Vanderslice's position behind the lectern. He looked down at her and kissed her lightly on the mouth. Again the crowd went wild.

Betty looked beautiful. Love exuded from her as her eyes stayed glued on her husband. He finally brought his shadowed eyes back to the crowd and addressed the suddenly hushed room.

"It's…it's…so good to see American faces again." His voice cracked and he ducked his head self-consciously. He shouldn't have worried about the tears that flooded his eyes. Many eyes in the crowd were moist with emotion.

"You are all curious, I know, to learn how we made it out, where we've been, and how we got there. You'll be briefed thoroughly, I promise." He smiled, and the stretching skeletal expression was heart-wrenching. "It will take days and even weeks to fill you in on the details that, in my instance, encompass fourteen years. As you must understand, the armed services will have to analyze the information we've brought out with us before it becomes public knowledge."

General Vanderslice interceded momentarily. "There will be a press conference immediately after we identify the men with Colonel Allway." He stepped back and Bill Allway had the floor again.

"The names will be read alphabetically along with the soldier's hometown and the date he was reported missing."

Television cameras from all over the world were aimed at both Bill Allway and the doorway through which each soldier would pass.

"Lieutenant Christopher David Cass, Phoenix, Arizona, June 17, 1969. Lieutenant George Robert Dickins, Gainesville, Florida, April 23, 1970."

Each man was applauded and cheered. Keely, like

everyone else in the room, was bursting with happiness for each of the depleted soldiers who passed shyly through the door. They had survived years of deprivation, disease, starvation, torture, and battle, and yet they seemed afraid of the lights, the people, the cameras, the attention. They all sported new haircuts. Their uniforms were new, if loosely fitting. And their faces bore the ravages of their experiences like identifying badges.

When he had read through the list and twenty men stood solemnly at the front of the room, Bill Allway said, "There are five men unable to be introduced here. Two of them are critically ill, so we are withholding their names for a few hours until they can be examined and their conditions more accurately appraised."

He drew Betty closer to him and continued. "I'm not a chaplain, but if Chaplain Weems will indulge me, I'd like to offer a prayer."

Even the most steadfast atheist couldn't argue with an appeal like that. Every head in the room was bowed, save for the photographers holding the video cameras in focus. A hush fell over the room. Bill's voice was as scratchy as sandpaper, but had he been a renowned orator, he couldn't have commanded such keen attention.

"Father, it is with exultant hearts that we come to You in thankfulness for life, for deliverance, for freedom. We pray for the countless men still struggling for survival. They remain nameless and faceless, yet You know them. Make them aware of You. Those of us who have been in hell know that Your presence can be felt even there. We, who against all odds, are alive today, pray that our lives will be lived honorably and to Your glory. Amen."

If previously there were any dry eyes left in the room, there were no longer. A subdued General Vanderslice approached the microphone while Bill Allway assisted his wife off the platform. "We ask your indulgence. It has been suggested that the press conference take place two hours from now in this room. That will allow you to take a much needed break and give these men time to collect their thoughts. I'm sure you can all understand a certain confusion and bewilderment on their part." He consulted a silver wristwatch and said, "The press conference will begin at three o'clock. Thank you all."

The door closed behind the returned soldiers as they filed through it. Bright lights were switched off. Cameras were replaced in their metal boxes. Cigarettes were lighted. Coats were retrieved. The lighthearted, jubilant, and triumphant mood prevailed as members of the press corps, dignitaries, and advisers gravitated toward the wide double doors.

Keely, no longer a focus of attention, dropped back onto the couch and stared absently at the carpet. Only when another pair of shoes, black loafers, came into her field of vision, was she cognizant of her surroundings. She raised her eyes slowly up the long legs, past the belt buckle with the congressional seal stamped into the gold, past the necktie long since loosened for comfort, to the face she loved.

The rich dark eyes begged her forgiveness, forgiveness for feeling a twinge of relief that Mark Williams hadn't walked through the door. Her eyes told him that she understood his relief. Her lips couldn't quite produce a smile.

"I'm sorry. Do you believe me?" he asked for her ears alone.

"Yes."

He shoved his hands in his pockets and stared over her head at the picture on the wall of Washington crossing the Delaware. "What will you do now?"

She dropped her head and noticed a coffee stain on her skirt. She must truly look a mess. When had she last showered, slept, changed her makeup, eaten? She couldn't remember.

"I don't know," she said, shaking her head. "Right now I can't think past a bath and a few hours' sleep."

"It was an unfair question."

She looked up at him again. "No, it wasn't."

Most everyone else had left, but they weren't aware of it. He knew by the look on her face that she was suffering and he cursed his inability to comfort her. *I want to hold you, Keely.* "Are you going to the hotel before the news conference?"

*Dax, I need you.* "Yes. I guess so."

He moved aside as she stood up and gathered her belongings. *You look so helpless.* "Have you got everything?"

*I feel so helpless. I need your strength.* "Yes. I was told our luggage would already be at the hotel."

"Good." *Do you want me to hold you?*

*Yes.* "Yes."

"Do you know which hotel they've designated you? They had to divide us up from what I understand. Tourist season." *I wish you were in my room.*

"They told me I'd be at the Crillon." *I wish I were staying with you. I'm afraid when you aren't with me.*

*Thank God. I can keep an eye on you.* "Me too."

*Thank God. You won't be far away.* "Good."

They had reached the front of the building now where members of the delegation were being loaded into waiting limousines. Actually it would have almost been easier to walk, since the hotels were so close, but since the courtesy was being offered, no one was refusing it.

"We have room for one more for the Crillon," said one of the embassy attachés. "Mrs. Williams?"

She turned and looked beseechingly toward Dax. She didn't want to leave him. "You'd better go on and take full advantage of the time allotted," he said kindly, thinking he'd die if he couldn't touch her soon.

"I'll wait. I don't— Thank you again, Congressman Devereaux, for your concern. I'll never give up hope."

He knew by her sudden switch in tone and dialogue that Van Dorf was more than likely lurking near them. A quick glance over his shoulder confirmed it. "I'm holding up the others. Goodbye." She shook hands with Dax perfunctorily and then went down the steps to be whisked away in the limousine.

Dax stood there, bereft, looking after the black limousine. "She seems upset," Van Dorf commented at his side.

Dax shot him a deprecating look. "Wouldn't you be, Van Dorf? She had a glimmer of hope that her husband might yet be alive, and not only was he not among the men who have come back, but she still doesn't know his status or hers."

"Surprising," Van Dorf said offhandedly.

Against his better judgment, Dax took the bait. "What is?"

"Her seeming concern over her husband."

Dax could feel his blood rising. "Why is it surprising?"

Van Dorf laughed scoffingly and it was a nasty sound. "Oh, come off it, Congressman. You're a man of the world. She's a hot little broad. How long do you think a sexy looker like her can live without a man? One month? Two?" He laughed again. "Surely not twelve years."

The French temper that flowed with every beat of Dax Devereaux's heart had never been so provoked. His hands formed iron fists at his sides and it was all he could do to keep them there and away from Van Dorf's throat.

"In your case, Van Dorf, ignorance isn't bliss, but a pity. You obviously don't recognize honor and decency in anyone else because you've never found them in yourself."

Dax stalked away, still marveling over the fact that he had kept himself from murdering the man. Van Dorf watched his angry departure, smiling with evil relish.

Keely bathed, washed her hair, and cleaned her face before collapsing across the bed. She awoke an hour later when her tiny travel alarm went off. She sat up, groggy and befuddled. The short nap might possibly have done more harm than good.

Dragging herself off the bed, she considered skipping the press conference, but immediately decided against that. She had to go. Her absence would appear graceless and would no doubt be noted in news accounts. Especially those written by Van Dorf. She hadn't even spoken to Betty yet and she wanted to meet Bill.

Her dress was a straight sack that she belted with a gold link belt. The green color was springlike, but the long cuffed sleeves would keep her warm. She brushed her hair and didn't even bother with electric curlers. Its natural wave was enough for now, encouraged as it was by the early Parisian spring humidity.

Arriving back at the embassy, she noted that the reception room had been swept, cleared of debris, and aired. A long table with a row of microphones had been set up instead of the single lectern that had been used that morning.

She took a seat in the last row of chairs and graciously accepted numerous condolences, assuring the sympathizers that she was grateful for the safe return of the men who had made it. Officially she said, "I think this only reinforces that our government's efforts to secure information about the MIAs not be abandoned. There is still a very real possibility that many more men are in Vietnam and Cambodia struggling to get out alive. I hope that what we hear from the survivors today will shed some new light on the problem."

She saw Dax come in and take a position next to Congressman Parker along the wall in front of the windows. He nodded imperceptibly and she drew strength from even that small gesture.

As promised, General Vanderslice began the proceedings on time. The returnees took seats behind the table, Bill Allway in the middle, Betty seated in an extra chair directly behind him.

The barrage of questions began and for the next two

hours the men were quizzed in a dozen languages. It was learned that ten of the men had escaped a prisoner of war camp together and over a period of a year and a half picked up the other sixteen men. During the months they had been together, three of their original number had died. Their names were read and duly recorded. The stories they related were incredible. What they had lived through was incomprehensible and the more their audience heard the more appalled it became.

Before dismissing the conference, General Vanderslice announced that the men had consented to an interview session the following morning. Everyone stood and applauded the soldiers as they left the room.

Keely waited for the throng to thin out before she stood to leave. Just as she was pulling on her light raincoat, Congressman Parker came up to her. Dax was with him. "Mrs. Williams, would you care to join Congressman Devereaux and me for dinner?" he asked politely.

Should she? The senior congressman didn't know he would be acting as a chaperon, but his presence would serve as her and Dax's protection from speculation and suspicion.

She was about to give him her affirmative answer when a Marine came up to them and saluted smartly. "Excuse me, Mrs. Williams, but Mrs. Allway sent for you. She needs to talk to you about the men still in the hospital."

Keely's heart lurched. Could this be happening now? Was this another shot in the dark? Or did Betty know…?

"I—I'll come right now," she stammered to the Marine. Turning back to Dax and Congressman Parker, she said, "I'm sorry, but—"

"No need to apologize, Mrs. Williams. This may yet be news of your husband," Parker said.

She avoided Dax's eyes as she followed the Marine's lead out the room and down a gloomy hallway into a deserted office. She was impressed first by the quiet. All day her ears had been adjusting to a din, now the silence caressed her ears gently and she welcomed it. Her escort left her alone.

A door opened on the other side of the empty office and Betty and her husband stepped through it. For a moment they looked at each other over the expanse of desks and carpet, then Keely rushed to the couple and threw her arms around Betty.

"I'm so thrilled for you, Betty. My joy couldn't be any greater."

"Keely, Keely," Betty said in her ear. "I'm sorry. I shouldn't be so happy."

"Of course you should!" Keely pulled away to look at the older woman's concerned face. "You should be ecstatic. And I know from watching you today that you are." She turned to the gaunt man standing beside Betty. "Hello, Bill," she said. "I've heard so much about you. Welcome back." She extended her hand for him to shake but, at the last moment, impulsively hurled herself at him and hugged him tight. Her embrace didn't offend him. She felt his thin arms enfold her.

"Betty has told me about you and how you've campaigned for the MIAs. I only wish your husband were with us."

Keely then remembered why she had been summoned. She searched their faces but saw no suppressed good news behind their compassionate expressions.

"The men in the hospital…?" She left the question open-ended.

Betty shook her head sadly and took Keely's hands between hers. "I'm sorry, Keely, but no, Mark isn't one of them. That's why I called you in here so Bill and I could talk to you alone. I didn't know how much hope you were holding out, and I wanted to spare you any false optimism."

"Keely." She turned blind eyes toward Bill Allway when he spoke her name in that gravelly voice. "After Betty told me about Mark, we immediately questioned the others if they knew anything about a helicopter pilot by that name. We gave them the date his chopper went down, any detail we knew that might be helpful. No one could provide us with any information. Of course the soldiers still hospitalized haven't been interrogated."

Keely turned her back on them and walked to the window, staring out over the Paris skyline that was being lighted now in the dusk. "Thank you both for your consideration. In view of the fact that you haven't seen each other in fifteen years, I'm humbled that the few hours you've been together you've spent much of it thinking about me and Mark. Thank you," she repeated.

"Keely—"

Not able to bear any more sympathy, she whirled around and interrupted Betty before she could say any more. "I'm fine, really. You two need time alone. Go on. I'll be fine. Indeed—" she tried valiantly for indifference "—Congressman Parker has invited me to dinner." She peeled her lips back into what she hoped was a smile. In the waning light of the office the Allways must have been fooled.

"If you're sure…" Betty hedged.

"I'm sure. Now go."

"We'll see you tomorrow," Bill said.

"Of course. Good night."

They left through the door from which they had entered and she was alone. More alone than she had ever been in her life.

She felt like she was on some kind of emotional pogo stick, being catapulted up into an emotional upheaval only to be hurled again to the bottom. She hated this conflict of emotions she felt. She wanted to be delirious with happiness for the Allways, and she was. But she couldn't help but be jealous that Betty's sentence was over.

Or was it? What would the Allways' marriage be like now? Could they pick up where they left off after fourteen years of separation? Having seen them together, Keely thought their chances were extremely good.

But what of her and Mark? How would she have felt today if she had been called out to meet a man, a man she didn't know, a man she was bonded to by marriage vows and legality, but no longer felt an affinity for? At the first sight of him would all the feelings of love she could no longer conjure come rushing back? Would she have flung herself into his arms? Or would she have been frightened to think that this stranger was her husband—this stranger she didn't recognize because all traces of youth and exuberance had been cut away by war as cleanly as by a surgeon's scalpel? Betty had had the advantage of years, of knowing her husband as a man before he went to war, of learning the

ins and outs of his personality. She and Mark had had
no such luxury.

The walls of the office were suddenly claustropho-
bic, and she left, avoiding the crowd at the end of the
hallway and exiting through another door. Getting her
bearings, she walked toward the Champs-Elysées. The
avenue was jammed with honking, belligerent traffic
that characterized the city's perpetual rush hour. Pedes-
trians crowded the sidewalks. As Keely walked, skirting the moving mass, she found it offensive that to so
many people this had been just another workday. Some
had no more to worry about than what they were going
to eat for dinner or if they should stop at the dry clean-
ers tonight or wait until tomorrow.

The Place de la Concorde was thronged with laughing tourists and Parisians impatient with laughing
tourists. As she was jostled through the crowd, she wondered idly how many times the horses of Coysevox at
the entrance of the Tuileries Gardens had been pho-
tographed. Little of the world-famous square with its
obelisk in the center attracted her attention for more
than a moment at a time. Her thoughts were elsewhere.

Pont de la Concorde took her across the Seine onto
the Left Bank. One of the bateau-mouche dinner ex-
cursions glided beneath the bridge as she crossed it.
She didn't even see the beautifully lighted boat. She
just walked.

On the Boulevard Saint-Germain, she stopped at an
intersection to wait for a break in the traffic. Much to
her distress the man standing next to her was finding
her fascinating and wasn't taking her ignorance of the
French he was pouring in her ear as discouragement.

He moved closer, almost knocking her off the low curb. She regained her footing and shot him an annoyed look, which he took as a challenge and smiled.

With foolhardy bravery she ran in front of a tour bus to cross the street. Upon reaching the other side, she was grateful that she had escaped both a sudden death and the amorous attention of the Frenchman. A few blocks farther on she felt the pent-up weariness finally manifesting itself. She sat down on a sidewalk bench and stared sightlessly, dejectedly, in front of her. She only wanted to be left alone, to be invisible, to evaporate. She was tired of coping.

The ingratiating voice intruded again, this time as her ardent pursuer sat down close beside her on the bench. She was glad her knowledge of the language was limited. His tone was lewdly suggestive. She shook her head forcefully and tried to scoot away, but to no avail.

Then another French voice, this one growling and threatening, came from behind her and her aggressor jumped to his feet, made a placating gesture with his hands, and fled down the sidewalk as though the hounds of hell were after him.

She looked up to see Dax standing behind her. He didn't speak, but came around the end of the bench and sat down beside her. The understanding smile, the black liquid eyes that related so much, the security that he represented, were her undoing.

When she fell toward him, his arms were opened to receive her and to cradle her head against his chest.

# *Thirteen*

Holding her still and tight, he didn't disturb her bout of weeping. The slim shoulders under his arms shuddered with the sobs that seized her. He bent his head over the soft brown hair and inhaled the fragrance as he would have inhaled her sorrow if he could.

He wasted no energy worrying about the curious picture they must make. All his thoughts, his being, were absorbed by this woman. She was so very precious to him. He had admired her strength of character, her beauty, her achievements, the career she had made for herself. Now this new fragility awakened in him yet another emotion. His passions surged to the surface and he became fiercely possessive and protective. He might very well have killed anyone who attempted to hurt her.

Long after the tears were spent and only dry sobs shook her, he held her. Whatever would be said and done would be initiated by her. The violet sky deepened to a darker indigo and then gradually faded to black, and still they sat, wrapped around each other.

When she raised her head, she looked away, wiping

her mascara-streaked cheeks and smoothing back her hair. He didn't admonish her grooming efforts and tell her she looked beautiful. He thought she was beautiful, despite her dishevelment, but he knew she wouldn't want to hear it. She would be self-conscious now, shy of him, and ashamed of her loss of control. He would give her free rein. She would chart the course, set the pace.

"Will you walk with me?" she asked.

He stood and gave her his hand. She accepted it, but dropped it when she had taken but a few steps. He didn't try to regain it, though he wanted to surround it with his hand in a symbolic gesture of the protectiveness he felt. They walked slowly, not talking, looking through a shop window when something struck her fancy. Only slight smiles, soft sighs, poignant glances, were used to communicate.

He had no idea how long or how far they walked. It didn't matter. He was faintly surprised when she paused and faced him. "Are you hungry?"

He smiled. "A little. Are you?"

"Yes."

"Then I'll be glad to buy you dinner."

"Where?"

"You choose."

"All right."

The first restaurant they came to was passed over because it was crowded and noisy. The next one's bill of fare featured only cold sandwiches and she admitted to being hungrier than that.

The third one they came to was perfect. It was typically French with checked tablecloths, dim candles, and one lone daisy in a bud vase on each table. The sidewalk dining area had been closed for the night, but the low-ceilinged interior suggested an aura of welcome intimacy.

As soon as the garçon had showed them to a table, Keely said, "May I be excused for a moment?"

"Of course." Dax didn't sit down until she had disappeared through a narrow shadowed opening leading to the back of the restaurant. When she came back to the table he saw that her face had been cleaned, her hair had been brushed, and she had applied fresh lipstick. He didn't touch her when he held her chair.

She munched on a piece of hard crusty bread. "I didn't know you spoke French."

He smiled humbly. "Only one of my many accomplishments."

"What did you say to him?"

"The waiter?"

"No, the man who followed me."

He was momentarily distracted by the tongue that glided across her lips to pick up vagrant bread crumbs. He found it hard to remember what she had asked him. "Uh…oh, that. Well, it isn't found in any dictionary," he grinned. "Do you know what you want to eat?" he asked, opening the well-worn menu.

"I'll let you order. I'm fond of coq au vin."

"Then you're in luck because it's right here," he said, pointing to the menu. "Coq au vin. Salad?" She nodded. "Soup?"

"I don't think so."

The waiter stepped forward. If the tuxedo he wore was shiny and his cuffs a bit frayed, they didn't notice as Dax gave him the order. As a matter of fact, neither of them could ever recall what he looked like. They were only looking at each other.

"Did you want a drink?" Dax asked.

"No. Coffee after dinner."

"Okay." He leaned his elbows on the table and cupped his chin in his fists.

She looked through the curtained windows at the steady stream of traffic on the boulevard. "How did you know where to find me?"

He wished she would look at him. Her voice sounded remote and her despondency was killing him. "I met Betty and Bill Allway in the hall. They told me what they had discussed with you. I thought you might need…someone. When I went into the office where they said you'd be, you were already gone. I ran like mad to catch sight of you. Your long legs sure can cover ground."

The attempt at humor worked and she laughed as she finally turned her head to look back at him. "Anyway," he continued, encouraged. "I only followed you to see that you were all right. When I saw that guy getting fresh, I closed in."

"You were just in time."

"Sure you weren't just being coy with him? I may have ruined a good thing." The first interjection of humor had worked, so he pressed for two times in a row.

This one was successful too. She laughed again and he could see a discernible difference in her posture as she began to relax.

By the time their salads arrived, they were chatting easily, though about nothing pertaining to what had brought them to Paris, to this small café, in the first place.

"He'll be offended if we don't drink any wine with dinner. This is Paris, you know," Dax leaned forward across the table and whispered conspiratorially.

"Watch it, you're getting salad dressing on your tie."

He looked down quickly. "Oops. Sorry." He picked up the drop of vinegar and oil from his tie and licked it off the end of his finger. "What about the wine?"

Keely glanced at the waiter who was hovering nearby in an expectant attitude and she suspected that he could understand their English perfectly. "Well," she demurred, "if you think he'll be offended if we don't…"

Dax took his cue and signaled the waiter over. He was at the side of their table before Dax had completely lifted his hand. The order was given and accepted in French. Keely sat and watched, bemused.

The waiter went briskly toward the rear of the restaurant and was back in an uncannily brief space of time. He carried a chilled carafe of white wine on a tray.

"This is the house wine, guaranteed to be excellent. Or so he says," Dax said to her. He went through the wine-tasting ritual, comically swishing it around in his mouth like mouthwash and rolling his eyes. The waiter tried to look aghast, but found the performance so entertaining that he looked down at Keely and smiled as though the two of them were patronizing a willful eccentric.

Dax swallowed loudly. "Wonderful, beautiful!" he exclaimed and gestured that the waiter was to fill their glasses. He did and left the carafe on the table.

"Oh, Dax! I just remembered Congressman Parker. What did you tell him?"

"That I had jet lag. I made your excuses too."

"Thank you."

The food was delicious. The chicken was cooked to perfection, as were the small white potatoes, green beans, and baby carrots. No sooner had he taken away their empty plates than the waiter brought out parfait glasses of chocolate mousse with a mound of whipped cream and chocolate shavings on top. They delved into those and when she could only eat half of the rich dessert, Dax finished it for her, complaining that she had eaten off all the whipped cream.

The carafe of wine was empty and they sat, mellow and satisfied, over cups of coffee. The dishes were taken away by a deferential subordinate of their waiter. When only the sputtering candle and the drooping daisy in the center of the table were left between them, Keely knew the time had come for them to talk.

"Dax," she opened slowly, "I know that you'd never ask, but you must want to know what I'm feeling."

"You're right on both accounts. I'd never ask. And it's up to you whether you tell me or not. My only job is to be here if you need me."

She raised swimming eyes to his and her mouth trembled deliciously and dangerously. "I *do* need you."

"You've got me." He wanted to reach across the table and take her hands between his, but his motion to do so was arrested when he saw her fold her hands together at the table's edge.

"I don't know if any of this will make sense. I haven't categorized my thoughts, so I may ramble."

"I won't mind."

She drew a heavy, shuddering breath. "I think that I must not be a very nice person. Today I was sickened with disappointment. But the heartache I felt because Mark wasn't among those soldiers wasn't for him. It was for *me*."

She slumped against the back of her ladder-back chair and toyed with the tablecloth at the edge of the table, pleating it between her fingers to fit the rim. "All I could think of when I realized that he wasn't one of the twenty-six men, was that my travail wasn't over. Not only was he not among the living, but I still don't know if he's among the dead either. I've progressed nowhere, but only remained stationary."

She lifted her eyes briefly as though to check to see if he were listening. She needn't have worried. He was hanging on to her every word.

"And then when those pitiful specimens of men faced that room of us so bravely, so…warily, I saw myself for just how selfish I am. Or am I?

"All afternoon we listened to those men recounting their experiences. Time and again they stressed that they had lived as they had to, doing whatever was necessary for survival. I suppose that would encompass every aspect of living, wouldn't it?"

She didn't expect an answer, so he gave none. She darted him a fleeting look and licked her lips before she continued. "What I mean is that those MIAs said they knew of American servicemen who didn't necessarily want to come home. What if Mark has a life there he doesn't want to leave? He may have a wo-woman and children. He may have lived with her for years. She, not I, would be his real wife.

"I had to face an undeniable truth about myself today, especially after I saw Bill and Betty together. It's not really Mark that I miss. He may very well be dead. But if not officially, he's been dead to me for many years. What I miss is the status of being married. Had it not been for Mark, whom I loved very much at the time, I might have chosen to live singly for years. Or had his death been reported, I might have chosen to marry again. But as it turned out I didn't ever have a choice.

"I've grown accustomed to the fact that I may be a widow. What I can't reconcile is that I still don't *know.* Fate has robbed me of having a choice in the direction my life will take." She looked at him then, pleading with her eyes for his understanding. "But I *do* have a life, Dax. And I don't want to waste it."

For long moments they didn't speak. The waiter, ever watchful, didn't approach the table. Something in the way the man looked at the woman, the way she stared into his eyes, the way they seemed oblivious of their surroundings, kept him at his discreet distance.

When at last the heavy silence was broken, it was Dax who broke it. "You're wrong, Keely. You make a great deal of sense. And you are positively entitled to a few selfish thoughts. You have one uncommon virtue that you don't credit yourself with."

She raised her head and met his glowing gaze across the table. "What?"

"You're totally honest, with yourself and now with me. Very few of us are willing to admit to shortcomings, or even to recognize them. Yet you've confessed to a questionable selfishness when a truly selfish person wouldn't even see themselves as such."

"Are you just saying that to make me feel better, to absolve me of guilt?"

"No."

"Are you sure?"

"Yes. I'm trying to be honest too."

She sighed and he thought he detected relief in that sigh. She tried to smile. "I *did* ramble, though."

He caught her effort to relieve the portentousness of the moment. "A bit," he said, smiling.

"I still have ambiguous feelings about…everything."

"You most probably always will, Keely."

"Yes." A melancholy tone crept into her voice and she stared out the window for a moment, lost in thought. Then she looked at him again. "Thank you for being… for being you."

"I didn't do anything."

"You listened."

"That's not much."

"It's a lot."

Covering his self-consciousness over praise he didn't feel he merited, he said, "Shall we leave or would you like something else?"

"No, thank you."

They stood and Dax left a roll of French francs in the center of the table. He saluted their waiter before he followed Keely through the door.

"What now?" he asked, taking her arm companionably. "Sightseeing, a nightclub, or home to bed?"

It took him a moment to realize that she was resisting his guiding hand and he glanced back to where she stood rooted to the sidewalk while Parisians hurried past her.

His eyes locked with hers and held. He took two steps back until he was standing inches from her, searching her eyes for what he wanted so desperately to see. "Keely?"

Her eyes didn't waver. If anything they widened, deepened, darkened, until he was drowning in their green depths. "I want you," she whispered. "I need all of you." He couldn't hear her, but he read the words on her lips.

She saw him swallow, saw the Adam's apple bob in his throat before coming to rest again. He hadn't misinterpreted her meaning. His hands came up to rest on her shoulders. He came half a step closer until she could feel the fabric of his clothing rustling against hers.

"You know—" He tried to get the words out, but they stuck in his dry throat. He had to make a second effort. "You know that I want that more than anything else in the world, and I will hate myself later if I change your mind. But, Keely, you're extremely vulnerable right now. Your emotions are running high. We've shared an intimate dinner with candlelight and wine and this is Paris, the most romantic city in the world. I'd never want you to look back on this night and think that I had taken advantage of you and your state of mind."

His grip became tighter, his voice more urgent, breathless almost. "Are you sure, Keely? Because if we go to a room together and get even the least bit comfortable, there'll be no stopping me this time. I want you to know that. *Are you sure?*"

Romance was still very much alive in Paris. There was even a smattering of applause by passersby when she came up on her tiptoes, placed her hands on his cheeks, and kissed him gently on the mouth.

The room they checked into was in a small family-owned hotel on one of the side streets off the Boulevard Saint-Germain. It was only four stories tall, and the second story was given over to several sitting rooms and a kitchen available for guests' use with certain stipulations that were painstakingly explained to an impatient Dax and Keely.

They were led up wooden stairs to the third floor. Each floor was only two rooms deep divided by a central hallway, and there were only eight rooms on each floor. The wainscoting was oak. The wallpaper was outmoded. The runners down each hall were tasteful Oriental imitations. All was spotlessly clean.

Dax conversed fluently with their hostess, a short, plump, rosy-cheeked woman with luxuriant white hair piled carelessly on top of her head. He translated their conversation, telling Keely they were lucky that an occupant had left earlier that day. They had been given the corner room that had two windows. She smiled at him as they followed their hostess's quick, surprisingly light footsteps down the hall.

Indeed the room did have two windows perpendicular to each other in the corner of the room. They were shown how to open the exterior shutters once the windows were raised. The bathroom was proudly opened and they were treated to a demonstration of how the faucets worked, how the commode flushed, how the shower nozzle in the narrow tub was to be handled, and how to use the bidet. Her cheeks flaming, Keely refused to meet Dax's amused eyes.

After being assured that they didn't need any more towels, an extra blanket, nor wine or coffee, their hostess departed. She graciously, but firmly, refused Dax's offer of a tip and closed the door behind her after wishing them a good-night.

Alone now, they were suddenly stricken with bashfulness and nerves. Their eyes didn't know where to look. They didn't know what to say. Their hands seemed idle and useless.

Keely finally slipped off her coat and draped it over the old-fashioned Boston rocker in one corner of the room. The cushions on it matched the patchwork-print pillows decorating the bed, which was covered with an ecru chenille spread. The fringed border grazed the polished wood floor.

Keely moved out of his way as Dax took off his lightweight overcoat and laid it across the opposite arm of the rocking chair. There was a chest of drawers with a framed oval mirror hanging over it. Keely went to it and stared unseeingly at her reflection before making a show of fluffing her hair. Dax was at the window fiddling with the latch.

At the same moment they turned to each other wordlessly. As if programmed to move with synchronized motions, they walked toward each other, meeting in the center of the room. His hand was raised to caress her cheek. They jumped apart when a timid knock was magnified in their ears to sound like a battering ram against the door.

Dax lunged toward it and pulled it open. Apologizing profusely, their hostess handed him a bouquet of fresh flowers in a china bowl. She had arranged the flowers that morning, but had failed to bring them up. Dax took the bouquet, thanked her, and closed the door again.

He stood awkwardly, holding the flowers as though at a loss as to what to do with them. He looked at Keely.

"They're pretty," she said. "Why don't you put them on the chest of drawers?"

"Yeah." He sounded grateful for the idea and rushed to place the flowers on the chest as though their container were burning his hands. He inspected the flowers. They could have been a rare masterpiece. "They look good there."

"Yes, they do."

He turned to look at her again. "Uh…would you like to use— You can have the bathroom first."

She looked toward the door to the bathroom. "I'm not sure I need—I mean, why don't you go first."

He smiled tensely, briefly, so that it was really just a nervous jerking motion of his mouth. "Okay. I'll be right out."

The door closed behind him and immediately Keely heard the faucets running full blast and wondered what he could possibly be doing that would require so much water.

She gazed around her in perplexity. What should she do? Undress? Get in the bed? Should she take off everything or just partially undress? God, she couldn't believe her stupidity. She was thirty years old and she didn't know how one went about going to bed with a man.

She decided to split the difference and only take off

a few garments. That would indicate interest, but not aggression. With that in mind, she stepped out of her shoes and unbuckled her belt. What to do with them? The closet? Yes.

She went to the narrow door and opened it. She placed her shoes neatly on the floor and hung her belt in a hook behind the door. Now what? Panty hose were the least sexy garment she could imagine. Better to dispose of them now than have to worry about them later.

The water in the bathroom was suddenly turned off. She panicked, fearful that he would come through the door and catch her ungracefully peeling off her panty hose. She virtually ripped them from her legs and balled them up. The doorknob on the bathroom door rattled noisily. She threw the panty hose into the closet and slammed the door shut just as Dax opened the bathroom door.

He looked at her curiously. "All done," he said. "It's yours."

"Thank you." She grabbed up her purse and brushed past him toward the sanctuary of the bathroom. There was no sign of all the water he had splashed. He must have dried the basin with the damp towel that hung from the shower curtain rod that encircled the tub.

Needlessly she washed her hands. Needlessly she brushed her hair. She dabbed perfume from a tiny purse vial behind her ears and on her neck. She wished she hadn't cried earlier. Her eyes still showed evidence of her weeping, but there was no help for that. Taking a deep breath, she left the bathroom, switching off the light behind her.

Dax had turned off the overhead light and left on

only a soft lamp beside the bed. The bed! It was turned down. The linens were snowy white in the softly glowing light.

Dax was shirtless and his feet were bare. Since the clothes he had taken off weren't visible, she wondered if he had seen the discarded panty hose when he put his clothes in the closet.

She dumped her purse in the rocker on top of her coat. When she turned around, he was standing close.

He took her breath away. Broad shoulders sloped down to the wide muscles in his chest. His ribs were leanly covered with taut skin and tapered down to a flat stomach and narrow waist. It was all forested with dark springy hair that grew in a fascinating pattern.

Was it her imagination, or was his hand trembling when he reached up to smooth it down from the crown of her head, past her ear, to rest on her shoulder? Still keeping space between their bodies, he leaned down to kiss her sweetly on the mouth. The kiss was excruciatingly tender as his lips pressed upon hers, held, then moved. Lips parted, tongues touched, mouths opened, passions ignited.

"Keely," he grated against her lips. His hands roamed up and down her back. "I've waited so long for this and now I can't believe it's happening."

"It's happening." He moved closer and she felt the angles and planes of his body adjusting to fit hers. "Dax," she said anxiously, "I'm nervous."

His self-derisive laugh was a soft puff of air against her ear. "I am too."

"You are?"

"Yes." His fingers tangled in her hair and forced her

head back. "But I want you, Keely. I want you." His mouth claimed hers again in a consuming kiss. His breath in her ear had caused cold chills to race along her spine. Instinctively she moved toward him for warmth, and all the loneliness she had felt that day, had felt in her lifetime, was incinerated by his heat. His arms closed around her. His mouth sipped at hers and she knew what it was to be cherished. Her fear and anxiety vanished. This was Dax. She wanted this as badly as he. This wasn't a performance. This was a sharing experience. When the time came, she would know what to do.

He stepped back from her and, staring directly into her eyes, brought his hands to the back zipper of her dress. His eager fingers finally released the tiny hook from its eye, then he drew the zipper down with agonizing slowness. His eyes never left hers and the only movement apparent was the leaping flames of desire.

When the zipper tab was at last at the end of its track, he pulled aside the two back panels of her dress, slipped them over her shoulders and down her arms until they were freed. Rather than simply drop the dress to the floor, he stooped down, and she placed her hand on his bare shoulder for support as she daintily stepped out of it. He straightened and almost reverently folded the dress over a low footstool in front of the rocker.

His eyes showed supreme discipline when he faced her again and looked, not at her body, but into her eyes. His hands closed around her throat gently while his thumbs stroked along her moist lips. They parted slightly and his fingers detailed the row of perfect white teeth. He felt the soft purring vibration in her throat when his thumbs glided down her slender neck to her collarbone. Tracing it with sensitive fingers, he marveled at its delicacy.

Then all ten fingertips combed down her chest so slowly that she closed her eyes, begging him silently to hurry, but all the while reveling in the time he was taking.

His fingertips brushed across the top curves of her breasts. Skin on skin was such a delicious sensation. But it wasn't enough. They both ached for more. His hands closed over her and she leaned into his palms. Only then did he lower his eyes from her face to watch what his hands were about.

He unclasped the front fastener of her peach-colored bra and the veil fell away. His eyes riveted on the desire-swollen breasts as he removed the brassiere and tossed it away.

Keely had expected him to touch her again, so she was mildly surprised when his hands caught her wrists and brought them around his neck, overlapping them and securing them behind his head. Then his hands stroked down the undersides of her arms, over the valleys of her underarms, the sides of her breasts, and around to her back as he pulled her against him. "Keely, you feel so good," he ground out with an insufficient breath.

She buried her face in the curve of his shoulder and languidly moved her torso against his. The crinkly hair teased her skin and set all her nerve ends laughing in sheer joy at the differences in their bodies.

He kissed her then and she could tell by the hot insistence of his mouth that he was suffering from and thrilling to the same driving desire that had her whole body sensitized to a high level. His mouth explored hers thoroughly then trailed down her neck and chest to her breasts.

"Let me taste you, Keely."

"Yes, Dax, yes."

He bent over her and she fell across his arm for support. Her head went back and her back arched as his open mouth first skimmed her breasts randomly, then closed around one nipple, drawing on it gently.

She had never known such erotic possession. Out of all the men in the world, was it Dax alone who knew how to use his lips and tongue, his whole mouth, to bring pleasure beyond description? It seemed that there was a cord that wound through her from the tip of her breast to the secret part of her body. When Dax's tongue touched her nipple, she felt that touch deep inside her womb. Her femininity became full and warm with an ache that demanded to be assuaged.

Her fingers slid upward from his neck where he had placed them to weave through his thick raven hair. She felt her arms lower even as his head moved down to kiss the underside of her breasts and continue downward to count her ribs with nibbling lips.

Dropping to his knees, his hands smoothed over the satiny half-slip that was the same peach color as her bra. He placed his mouth against her stomach. His breath was hot and moist as it filtered through the fabric.

Then the elastic waistband was lowered over belly and hips until her slip dropped around her ankles in a frothy, lacy heap. His hands spanned her naked waist, his thumbs pressing into her navel. Then as his hands slid around to her back, his mouth replaced his thumbs and gave that shallow indentation ardent attention. He kissed it as he would have her mouth.

His palms were warm as they slipped beneath the scant swath of cloth that was her panties. His hands molded to the curve of her hips. Then the panties went the way of the half-slip over her hips and thighs and past her calves to the floor. What was revealed was revered with eyes and hands and mouth that looked and touched and kissed. With his tongue he branded the skin of her stomach, hips, and thighs until she couldn't bear any more and, with a desperate cry, felt her knees buckle and thump against the wall of his chest.

He was ready. Standing quickly, he pulled her against him and caught her under the knees and back and lifted her to carry her to the bed. She was laid down with a care usually reserved for breakable objects.

He was away from her only long enough to rid himself of his clothes. The zipper of his pants rasped softly in the room. The snap clacked loudly. Then in one swift motion pants and underwear were gone and he was splendidly naked and looking down at her hungrily. Had he not been Dax, the starved, glazed look in his eyes would have frightened her. Instead she felt an answering hunger deep in the pit of her stomach.

"Keely, beautiful Keely," he said as he gradually lowered himself over her and gathered her to him. She absorbed his weight, adjusting her body beneath his and awakening them anew to the precision with which they fitted.

He pressed into her and a sharp, near virginal cry alarmed him. "Oh, God, Keely!" he cried in anguish and cupped her head, holding it protectively against his shoulder. "Darling, did I hurt you?"

"No, no," she sobbed. "Please, Dax. It's wonderful… please, Dax…" she begged.

The magic was spun. Her arms came from around his back to intertwine with his. Tightly laced fingers lay on either side of her head on the pillow. Thighs stroked thighs. Stomachs kneaded each other in a rhythmic cadence. Hair-roughened chest pressed smooth breasts. Mouths fused. Spirits sang. Essences were exchanged.

Shaken and weak, they lay perfectly still, his head beside hers on the pillow. Long moments passed while they savored the interlocking intimacy of their damp bodies. His voice seemed to come from far away, though she could feel his lips moving on her ear. "This is what my life has been for, Keely. This moment. This is why I was born. To be here with you like this. Do you understand?"

She could only nod. She did understand because she felt the same way, only she was too swept away by the miracle of it to say so.

# *Fourteen*

"How long have I been asleep?" he asked when he opened his eyes. She was watching him. Waking up had never been this nice.

"A half hour or so. I don't know. It doesn't matter." Her fingers wandered over his cheekbones, down the aristocratically shaped nose, across the lean cheek, to the silver hairs at his temple.

He shifted his weight, rolling over to face her and splaying his hand on her back to draw her closer. "How could I have slept?"

"I think you were worn out," she said mischievously, draping her arm over his shoulder.

He swatted her bottom playfully. "And you weren't?"

"Oh, yes, I was," she laughed. "But I couldn't have slept." An inquisitive finger slid along his lips and she wondered how they could be so firm and yet feel so soft against her body.

He captured her hand and murmured against the palm, "Why is that?"

"Because that's never happened to me before," she said quietly, watching his reaction. "Never like that."

His eyes across the pillow sparkled with a happy pride he was trying hard to keep at bay. "No?"

She shook her head. "No." Comparisons weren't fair to Mark. She had told Dax all he needed to know.

"I'm glad. I'd be less than honest to say I wasn't."

Her emotions were too strained to say more. She groped for a more neutral subject. "Is this where you were wounded in the war?" she asked, tracing the puckered white scar beneath his shoulder blade with her finger.

"Yes. Luckily it was a piece of shrapnel that had lost most of its momentum before it got to me." She kissed the spot. "It's ugly because it took several days to get to the medics. By that time it was badly infected. They had to gouge out about a pound of flesh. It left quite a hole."

"Please don't tell me." She kissed his chin. "And the one under your eye?"

"My cousin and I got in a fight when I was about thirteen." He saw her disappointment and laughed. "Sorry, nothing more dramatic than that."

"How dare he pick on you." The seductive tone of her voice caught his attention and he watched in wonder and surprise as she knelt over him. Her hair fell softly around her face. The planes and valleys of her body were cast in sharp relief by the soft glow of the lamp. Light and shadow highlighted gentle mounds and tapering curves. Almost shyly she bent down and kissed his mouth.

His hand came up to clasp the back of her head and hold her over him. But he let her be the aggressor. Her tongue probed his mouth timidly until she breached the barrier of his teeth. Then she explored at leisure.

Her tongue made repeated dipping forays into his mouth. He was reminded of a child licking an ice-cream cone, who after each lick, returns his tongue to his mouth to savor the taste.

Pulling up only slightly, she kissed the scar under his eye then the dimple beside his mouth. Her lips settled on his neck and in one long, sensuous, fluid motion slid down to his chest. His fingers became twisted in her hair as he clenched his fist convulsively. His other hand settled in the curve under her hip and with only the slightest suggestive tug she raised one thigh over his.

"Keely, that's wonderful," he said as her lips sucked at his skin. His words were barely audible.

It gave her a heady, gratifying feeling to know she could bring him this much pleasure. She kissed her way down his stomach, delighting in his uneven breathing and murmured phrases.

Her mouth followed the tapering design of hair that became silky around his navel. When she examined that crevice with her tongue, his knee trapped her thigh against his. Her lingual exploration continued, and she found a thicker, rougher thatch. Dax's short ragged breathing stopped altogether. His fingers entangled in her hair, pulling it painfully. The muscle beneath her cheek contracted spasmodically.

She hesitated but a moment before kissing him again.

"Oh, God…sweet…" He lifted her, shifting them until she lay beneath him.

He pressed her back against the mattress with his kiss. It was a deep, drugging kiss that involved not only their mouths but their bodies as well. When his tongue pressed deeper into the hollow of her mouth, it was symbolic of another possession, another void he filled.

He raised his head and looked down at her. "The most beautiful sight I've ever seen was your face in that instant you knew what it was to be a woman fulfilled. Shine for me again, Keely."

The words he whispered heightened her love because she knew that her fulfillment contributed to his. His hands, as they stroked down her sides and over her hips and thighs, were like the touch of a velvet glove. His mouth on her breasts was alternately rapacious then soothing and brought her closer to what he wanted to see.

As her tumult built, so did his. What he wanted to witness was almost denied him. For at the last moment they did that little bit of dying together.

At dawn they left. Their hostess, who apparently ran the hotel single-handedly, was distressed over their hasty departure. Repeatedly Dax assured her that the room had been more than satisfactory, but that other matters prevented them from staying any longer. She looked sad standing at the concierge's desk as they left her hotel.

Paris was barely awake. The streets looked washed clean from the nocturnal rain. Merchants and vendors were rolling down their awnings and preparing for a day of business. The aroma of fresh coffee and croissants filled the air.

They stopped at a sidewalk café not yet open and asked the proprietor for a take-out order. He grumbled, but being a true Parisian at heart and having a penchant for lovers, he relented and filled a sack with croissants and gave them plastic cups of steaming coffee. They munched as they strolled without undue haste.

They didn't speak of why they had to go back to the Crillon, they simply knew that they must. Instead they whispered and laughed in intimate exchanges that brought blooming roses to Keely's cheeks and gave Dax's grin a satyric quality.

"You love me so well," he said.

"Do I?"

"You love me well. Perfectly."

Her eyes dropped to the half-eaten croissant. "I couldn't stand it if you thought I was forward or crude—"

"God, no." He collected the refuse of their breakfast and shoved it into a trash receptacle. He came back to her, reaching out to smooth her cheek. "You are totally female, Keely, and I love all the physical parts of you that make you female. I also like your daintiness and delicacy, your ladylike demeanor and prim mannerisms.

"I also adore that you shed them like clothing before you come to bed with me. But never in a million years could you be crude. Don't even think such a thing."

"Dax," she said softly, tears shimmering in her eyes.

"I can't stand this any longer," Dax muttered impatiently and hailed a taxi.

"What?"

"I want to kiss you right now."

"No one's looking," she challenged.

"They will be if I kiss you the way I want to," he warned.

He hustled her into the back seat of the cab and gave the driver their destination. "I told him to take the long way," he said to Keely before he fell on her with the desperation of a dying man seeking sustenance.

He kissed her aggressively, hungrily, powerfully, as though he wanted to stamp his seal of ownership on her. She knew that in an endearing way he was convincing himself that even if they weren't securely locked in their small room, she still belonged to him.

When she managed to pull her mouth free, she pushed against his chest. "Dax, the driver."

"Let him get his own girl," he growled.

She laughed, struggling against him and only exciting him more. Before she knew what he was about, his hands were inside her coat. "Dax! Do you realize what you're doing?"

"Uh-huh." He smoothed his hands over her unfettered breasts beneath the soft dress. He had talked her out of wearing the bra this morning. His touch set off a chain reaction of sensations throughout her body and she strained against him.

The ardency of his kisses and the persuasiveness of his hands depleted her consciousness. They could have been driving for hours or merely minutes when she finally realized that the cab driver was calling something in French over his shoulder. "Dax," she murmured and firmly pushed him away. "He's saying something to you."

He sighed, sitting up and straightening his clothes. "The Crillon is in the next block."

Dax paid the driver and hauled her out of the back seat by pulling on her hand. She fell against him, laughing, and his arms enclosed her briefly before they turned toward the hotel.

Keely froze.

Walking toward them were the Allways. Their arms were linked around each other's waists. They were smiling happily, but their smiles turned to expressions of shocked dismay when they saw Keely and Dax in an embrace resembling their own.

The four stared at each other in stunned silence. It must have been the Allways' idea to have a quiet, private breakfast away from the throng of reporters and prying eyes. The interview session was to begin at ten o'clock. They were hoping for a couple of hours alone before an exhausting day.

Seeing them had been more than a mild shock to Keely. It had been an assault. A piercing spasm of guilt struck her in the heart, and following the millions of capillaries that radiated into every part of her body, the guilt pervaded her, seeped into her, until she was saturated with it.

She had betrayed these friends. They had remained faithful to each other, to their wedding vows, and to their conviction that their partner was surviving, if for no other reason than to see the other again.

She had betrayed her husband by sleeping with another man. Her sexual unfaithfulness was only a particle of her adultery. She had given all of herself to Dax, freely and wildly. She had retained nothing, held none of herself in reserve for Mark lest he return one day. Everything had been given to Dax and there was nothing left to give to anyone else.

She had betrayed herself by thinking she could put

away every moral conviction she held dear in the name of love. Her loving Dax couldn't justify her betrayal of Mark. Love based on betrayal and deceit could never be blessed. She knew that and, until last night, had stood by that principle. But now in the light of day and in view of two who had withstood untold adversity to finally be brought together, she saw that she had been deluding herself. Love was never free. The price must always be paid.

"We were just going out for breakfast," Bill Allway said calmly, breaking an awkward silence that Keely wasn't even aware of.

"Would you like to join us...?" Betty asked graciously, but her voice trailed away to nothingness before she even completed the invitation. There was no condemnation in her eyes, but Keely felt like a scarlet letter had been branded on her chest. The evidence couldn't be more incriminating. She and Dax had got out of a taxi just minutes after dawn with their clothes rumpled and their faces flushed. What other conclusion could be drawn except the correct one? She thought that if she didn't die from guilt she would surely die of shame.

"No, thank you." Keely answered Betty's invitation for both of them.

Dax stood by silently and stared at her.

"Well, then, we'll be getting on our way," Bill said. "Betty?" He took his wife's arm and all but dragged her away. She was staring at Keely and Dax as though she still couldn't believe what her eyes had seen.

"Look at me," Dax hissed when the Allways were out of earshot.

"No," she said and turned away from him.

Her arm was practically wrenched from the socket as he whipped her around to face him. "Look at me," he commanded.

She jerked her head up and stared at him mutinously and his heart twisted when he saw the hard, closed, determined expression on her face. "I know what you're thinking, Keely." His voice was tight with suppressed tension.

"You couldn't possibly imagine what I'm thinking."

"Yes, I can. You're awash with guilt over what happened last night." His hands came up to grip her shoulders. "Seeing Betty and Bill set your conscience working overtime again. They are a lovely, happy couple, Keely. I couldn't be happier for them. But what happened to them doesn't have anything to do with you and Mark."

"It has everything to do with it," she argued stubbornly. "Betty was faithful. I wasn't."

"Faithful to whom? To a man you can barely remember? To a man you'll probably never hear of again?" He despised the cruelty of his words but he couldn't afford to be kind.

"Up until yesterday, Betty didn't know her husband was alive. Now he's back with her. Something could happen just that fast and Mark would be home expecting his wife to be waiting for him."

Dax looked around him impatiently as though he couldn't stand to hear what she was saying. Frustration screamed from every cell of his body. Finally his roaming, directionless eyes returned to her. "That is a very slim, remote possibility. What happened between us is a sure thing." He softened his voice to match the warming depth in his eyes. "I love you, Keely. I love you."

Her hand flew to her mouth and mashed her flattened lips to her teeth. She squeezed her eyes shut and shook her head. "No," she wailed softly. "Don't say it now. Not now."

"I'll say it until I know you hear me. I love you."

She fought his restraining hands with newfound strength and gained her release. "No! It's wrong, Dax. It always has been. Don't you see? I'm still not free to love you. It will never be right for me to love until I know that Mark is dead."

She stumbled backward, fearful that he might come after her and take her in his arms and she would be doomed again. "It isn't possible. Leave me…leave me alone. Please."

She turned and fled, nearly knocking down a man standing in the door of the hotel. It was only after she had reached her room and collapsed on the bed in a torrent of tears that she sat bolt upright and took a heaving, shuddering breath of fearful realization.

That man had been Al Van Dorf.

Dax raced down the concourse, his heart pounding with each footfall. He barely noticed his exertion. With the least bit of encouragement he felt he could fly.

To think that only this morning he was in the depths of despair when he watched with an empty heart as Keely ran away from him. He had all but flattened Van Dorf when he made some snide remark about whether they were coming or going.

He had pushed past the man and stormed to his room,

ready to do combat with anyone brave enough to test his temper. He never remembered feeling that helpless and angry in his life.

For hours he had paced his room and with each hour his frustration mounted. Looking at the situation from an objective point of view, he could see that there was no right side nor wrong side. No easy answer or simple solution was going to jump out at them. Their problem couldn't be solved by careful deductive reasoning. It could only be resolved by making a judgment call, by weighing one strong emotion against another equally strong. It was a decision involving Keely's conscience. God! He was afraid what her decision would be.

Congressman Parker had called his room and he had all but yanked the telephone out of the wall in his haste to answer it, thinking that maybe Keely had had a change of heart. "Yes," he barked.

"I surrender," Congressman Parker laughed.

Abashment and disappointment did battle, and disappointment won. "I'm sorry. What can I do for you, Congressman?"

"I'm glad you offered your services, because I *do* have a favor to ask. I'm expected to attend those interview sessions today, sort of be on hand should any question pertaining to legalities or congressional options arise. I'm also expected to go to the hospital and visit those soldiers as a representative of the administration. I doubt if the President would object if I asked one of his pet congressmen to fill in for me there. Would you mind?"

Dax ran a hand through his hair. He might as well. He wasn't up to another day in a crowded room filled with photojournalists and reporters. If he stayed here, he'd only think about Keely and that wasn't getting him anywhere either. "Certainly. Give me time to clean up. What info do I need before I go?"

"We lost one of those boys, Dax. Last night. He just couldn't pull through."

"Damn!"

"Yeah. I'll send a folder down to your room with stats about each one of them. When you're ready to go, ask the desk to send a car. Take your time. There's no hurry. Oh, except for the plane leaving tonight."

"What plane?"

"Some had requested that they be sent right home and the President has agreed. So those who feel up to it are returning tonight as well as anyone on the original delegation who wants to go on home."

"What time does the plane leave?"

"Nine o'clock. From de Gaulle. I'll jot down all the particulars in one of the folders."

"Thank you."

"Thank you, Dax. Say hello to those soldiers for me."

So he had gone to the hospital as a substitute emissary. God, what if he hadn't gone? What if the corporal named Gene Cox had been asleep? What if he had been the unfortunate one to die during the night?

He shivered even as sweat rolled down his torso. His coat flapped against his legs and he hefted his bag into a sturdier grip. His feet thudded on the carpeted concourse. He could see the gate. It was still crowded. Good, the plane hadn't taken off yet. Thank God the government hadn't made an exception and done something on time.

He ignored the curious stares directed at him. He ignored Congressman Parker's signal for Dax to join him. His eager gaze swept the waiting room until it found the woman sitting all alone on the far side of the room looking out at the black night where only the blue runway lights relieved the stygian darkness. He could see her reflection in the glass, her desolate expression.

He dropped his bag where he stood and elbowed his way toward her. She saw his image in the glass as he loomed up behind her. His heart was rent in two at her immediate and visible distress.

"I've got to talk to you," he said urgently.

"No," she said, not turning around. "It's all been said."

He knelt down beside her chair and spoke softly. "If you want the whole world to hear this, witness this, then fine. But I believe I've got something to tell you that you'd rather hear in private. So what's it going to be?"

She turned to look at him then. He met her rebellious gaze levelly. He saw her belligerence waver, then fade. "Very well," she said and stood up, waiting for his lead.

He indicated with his head that she was to follow him. Obediently she did so. Most of the other waiting passengers were too tired or apathetic to notice their departure. When they reached the wide central aisle of the airport, Dax looked around until he saw a deserted alcove that housed pay telephones. He took her elbow and steered her toward it.

She turned to him as soon as they had reached the alcove that offered them only a modicum of privacy. "What do you want?"

He could forgive the cold haughtiness with which

she faced him. He could forgive it because he knew that within a matter of moments her feelings would be quite different. Best to get the worst of it out of the way and proceed from there.

"Keely," he began gently, "Mark is dead. He's been dead since the day his chopper went down almost twelve years ago."

There were no manifestations of the emotional tumult she must surely be experiencing. There were no tears, no audible gasps, no hysterics, no gladness, no sorrow, nothing but a stoic mask and impenetrable green eyes that gave away nothing.

"Did you hear me, Keely?" he asked at last.

She nodded before she spoke. "Y-yes." She swallowed and cleared her throat. "How did you…how do you know?"

He told her then about his going to the hospital in lieu of Congressman Parker. "After my official duties were over, the four MIAs and I began talking as one vet to another. Just out of curiosity's sake, I asked each of them the circumstances behind his disappearance. One of them, an army corporal named Gene Cox, mentioned the date of a helicopter crash. Keely, it was the same day Mark's chopper went down.

"I asked Cox what had happened and he said the helicopter had been hit and was already burning when it crashed. He and the pilot were able to get out before it exploded. They crawled into the jungle, which he said was 'creeping' with Viet Cong. Both of the pilot's legs were broken and he must have had internal injuries. He died within an hour of the crash. Cox covered him with some thick foliage, hoping that the Cong wouldn't find the body and— Well, wouldn't find it.

"Then Cox was captured and taken prisoner the next day." He took her hands in his and squeezed them tightly. "Keely, the helicopter pilot's name was Mark Williams. He was a tall blond guy who spoke with a Southern accent."

He had expected her to possibly slump against the wall or perhaps to lean into him for support as she tried to assimilate what he had told her. He had planned to hold her close, not as a lover but as a friend, until she was ready to talk about what this meant to them. He had expected tears perhaps over the wasted life of a young man, maybe even a little bitterness over the war to which he had been sacrificed.

In all his imaginings he hadn't anticipated the reaction he got.

She jerked her hands free of his as though flinging off something hideous. The only sound she made was a laugh, harsh and without mirth, but rife with contempt. "How could you, Dax?" she asked, loathing dripping off every word. "Whose conscience are you trying to salve—mine or yours?"

He stared at her in mute astonishment. "Wh—"

She laughed that horrible laugh again. "I've no doubt that this soldier Cox told you his story. But I find it a shade too coincidental that the pilot's name was Williams and that he spoke with a Southern accent. Did you think I was so gullible that I'd believe that?"

His jaw, which had been hanging slack in puzzlement, was now hardening as he tried to get control of his quickly slipping temper. In deference to the situation he managed to contain it. "I'm telling you the truth, dammit." He pushed the words through his teeth. "Why would I lie about something this important?"

"Because I told you this morning that I couldn't belong to you, that we couldn't have a life together until I knew about Mark's fate. I think you conveniently worked his name into the story this soldier told you. That would make a neat, tidy little package, wouldn't it?" She shook back her hair with an angry toss of her head. "You have a reputation for getting what you want, Congressman Devereaux, by fair means or foul. I think you've just lived up to that reputation."

His proud ancestors could tolerate just about anything except a slur on their family name. So could Dax. But any intimation that his integrity wasn't sound was the one thing he would never forgive.

He straightened to his full height and looked down at her with violence smoldering in his eyes. "All right, Keely. Believe what you will. Sacrifice your life too. Hoard your love like a damn miser. I think you actually thrive on your self-imposed martyrdom. It sets you apart, doesn't it, from the rest of us animals? But be forewarned, the human race finds saints immeasurably tedious."

She whirled away from him and crossed the concourse to the boarding area. Though his heart was being chiseled away piece by piece, his pride wouldn't allow him to call her back. How could she believe him capable of something so despicable after last night? Last night... He covered his face with his hands, trying to wipe out the memories of shared joy, ecstasy. It was impossible that she could think—

"Your woman run out on you?"

Al Van Dorf's drawling voice thrust Dax abruptly back into the present. He dropped his hands and jerked his head around to see the smirking grin he detested. Van Dorf was leaning negligently against the wall just inside the alcove. His mocking arrogance was the last straw for Dax's tenuous composure.

He lunged at the reporter and his Marine-trained instincts took over. Before the man realized what had happened to him, he had been uprooted, yanked farther into the shadows, and pinned against the wall. Both hands had been clamped behind him by an iron fist. His eyeglasses had been knocked askew. Dax's knee was rammed up into his crotch, causing him to squeal a high, pitiable screech. A hard forearm was pressed like a crowbar across his throat.

"You've opened your wise mouth once too often, Van Dorf."

"I saw—"

"You saw *nothing*. You heard *nothing*. *Nothing* you can prove, anyway. If you ever make one of your sly innuendos to me again, I'm going to sue you for so much money that even if I lose, your reputation as a credible journalist will be so shot to hell that no news service or two-bit rag will touch you with a ten-foot pole. Not only that, but I'll beat the bloody hell out of you. Do I make myself clear, Van Dorf?"

For emphasis, he pushed his knee higher and the man whimpered, confirming what Dax had always suspected—he was a coward. "I asked you a question, Van Dorf. Do I make myself clear?"

The man bobbed his head up and down as far as

Dax's stranglehold would allow. The devil eyes that glared at him threatened that the congressman might yet change his mind and go ahead and kill him. It was with vast relief that he felt Dax's hands gradually relax.

"What I said goes double for Mrs. Williams. If I read one word of insinuating copy with your byline on it, I'll kill you."

Then, in a gesture of disdain, he turned his back on Van Dorf, who was still struggling for air. He strode back to the boarding gate, picked up his bag where he had left it, and went to stand in formidable solitude against the wall, waiting for the long overdue airplane back to the United States.

# Fifteen

The moon was on the right side of the aircraft. Keely was staring out a window on the left side, so only a diffuse silver glow alleviated the black night. The stars seemed far away. The clouds below the aircraft were a thick, seemingly impenetrable blanket.

"Are you sleeping?" The question roused her from her stupor and she turned her head to see Betty Allway leaning across the aisle seat. Since the reporter who had been sitting beside Keely originally had taken her rude silence as a hint that she didn't want to talk and moved to another seat, she had been sitting alone.

"No," she answered the older woman's question.

"Do you mind if I sit beside you for a while?"

Keely shook her head and picked up her raincoat, which had been lying in the seat to discourage anyone else from sitting there. "What's Bill doing? Sleeping?"

"Yes," Betty said. "He gets frustrated because he tires so easily. I'll have to keep an eye on him so he doesn't do too much when he first gets home. I'm sure his inclination, and the army's, will be to try to make up for the past fourteen years in a few weeks. I'm going to fight them both to see that that doesn't happen."

Keely responded with a warm smile. "You're entitled to a little possessiveness, I think."

They sat in awkward silence for a moment. Keely couldn't forget Betty's surprised expression when she had seen her and Dax getting out of the taxi that morning at dawn. It was a wonder the woman would speak to her at all. After all the heartache they had suffered together, she hated to lose the friendship of a woman she had long admired.

"Keely," Betty said hesitantly. "I don't want to butt in where I'm not wanted or needed, but you do look like you might need someone to talk to. Is that the case?"

Keely's head fell back onto the seat cushion and she closed her eyes for a moment before responding. "I guess I'm just feeling the letdown. The past three days have seemed like a lifetime and I'm exhausted. I never did carry fatigue well." She tried to smile, but it turned out to be a travesty of that expression.

"No, Keely. It's more than that. And I think it has a lot to do with Dax Devereaux." She leaned over the vacant seat between them and took Keely's hand between her own. "Are you in love with him?"

She was tempted to lie, to answer vehemently in the negative. But what good would it do? Betty had seen them together on so many occasions she was bound to have put the pieces together to form a complete picture. She had heard Van Dorf's leading, provocative questions. The woman could think no less of her than she already did. She rolled her head toward the other woman, though she didn't raise it off the cushion. Meeting

Betty's eyes openly, she said, "Yes, I'm in love with him."

"Ah," she said thoughtfully. "I thought so. May I overstep the bounds of curiosity and ask since when?"

"Since the night I arrived in Washington for the subcommittee hearing. We met that night on the airplane. I didn't know then that he was on the committee and he didn't know that Keely Preston and Mrs. Mark Williams were one and the same."

"I see."

"I don't think you do. I—we—never intended it to happen. We both fought it. Particularly me. But—"

"You don't have to justify love, Keely." She continued to hold Keely's hand, stroking it absently as she said, "Does he know how you feel about him?"

"I don't know. I'm sure he must, but I…we had an argument of sorts. He did something—" She rubbed her forehead with her free hand. "Never mind. A relationship between us is impossible for so many reasons."

"Mainly being?" Betty asked leadingly.

Keely looked at her in surprise. "Mainly because I'm still married and I don't know if my husband is alive or dead. Your situation has changed, Betty, but mine hasn't, remember?" She instantly hated the sarcastic tone she had used. "I'm sorry," she said contritely. "Please, Betty, I'm sorry. I don't know what I'm saying."

"Don't apologize, Keely. I think I can understand the emotional conflict you're suffering. Perhaps you've suffered long enough. Maybe you should consider having Mark declared dead and marry your congressman." Had the woman said she was going to jump out of the airplane, Keely couldn't have been more stunned.

After all the years they had campaigned on behalf of the MIAs, after their avowals that they would never give up hope on their men being accounted for eventually, she couldn't believe her ears had heard Betty right. "You can't mean that."

"Yes, I do," Betty said firmly.

"But—"

"Let me confess something to you, Keely. For these past years I've taken advantage of you. No, let me finish," she said when Keely was about to object. "You did our cause a world of good. You were a perfect representative for us. You are bright, beautiful and successful. You added a credibility to us that I played to the hilt. Somehow, with you as our spokesperson, we didn't seem so much like a group of hysterical females.

"Ever since our last trip to Washington, I've felt ashamed of myself for encouraging you, albeit subtly and without malice, to waste your youth and vibrance and love on Mark's memory. I even remember cautioning you about jeopardizing your reputation with a man like Dax."

"I never did anything I didn't want to do, Betty. I felt, and do still feel, as strongly as I ever did."

"But now you've got another cause, one equally important, to rally behind. If you love this man, and I think you do or you wouldn't be wallowing in so much guilt, you should be with him, Keely. If his behavior is any indication, I think your feelings for him are reciprocated. He needs you. He is alive and he's here in the present and in the flesh. Mark is not and may never be."

Keely faced her friend angrily. "How can you say that? Less than a week ago you had no idea that Bill was ever coming home. Now he's here. You waited all those years, you were—were faithful." To her chagrin tears were rolling down her cheeks.

"Yes. And I had three children to consider. I'd also had ten beautiful years with Bill, which weren't as easy to forget as a few weeks. We had a life together. You and Mark didn't. I can't tell you what to do, Keely. I can only say that if you want to be with Dax, you should be. Don't sacrifice your happiness and his forever."

Keely was shaking her head, unaware of the tears that continued to flow. "It's too late, Betty. I don't agree with what you've said about deserting the cause I've fought for so long. I can't just drop PROOF. Others are still depending on me. Especially now that these MIAs have returned, we have new hope, perhaps channels of investigation we didn't know existed will open up. But all of that aside, Dax and I were doomed before we were begun. If ever there was a spark of love between us, it's gone now."

She looked at Betty and the older woman thought she had never seen such naked sadness and disillusionment on a face so young. "I'll get over this depression once I get home to New Orleans and back to work."

She didn't know how wrong that prediction would prove to be. She was so exhausted by all that had happened in Paris and by the ceaseless interviews she had granted during her brief layover in Washington, that when she arrived home she took her telephone off the hook and barricaded herself in her apartment, sleeping around the clock for almost twenty-four hours.

When she finally woke up, she realized that Mardi

Gras week was in full swing. Finding a parking space was unheard of. Waiting for a table in a restaurant took hours. To walk down a sidewalk one had to detour around the bleachers set up along the parade routes and dodge revelers, who were generally inebriated and noisy. In her current state of mind the merrymaking was repugnant.

She called her producer, begging for several days vacation she had accumulated. After receiving his grumbling consent, she packed her car and drove to Mississippi to visit with her parents.

They were sensitive to her dark mood and trod lightly around her. She ate well, slept as well as dreams would allow, and took long, solitary walks along the Gulf shore. A short visit to the nursing home where Mrs. Williams stayed almost negated what strength she had built up, and she came away from the institution feeling that nothing would ever be right in the world again.

When she returned to work, everyone treated her with effusive, deferential kindness. She felt like a mental patient who had just been released. She despised the patronizing tones everyone used when talking to her and the pitying looks and the false jocularity.

Nicole, who couldn't bear depression of any kind, steered clear of Keely, except for a few commiserating telephone calls. She didn't bring up the subject of Dax Devereaux. Once she mentioned that she had read of his rapidly growing popularity because of his activities concerning the returned MIAs. Keely made no comment, so Nicole took the hint and dropped the subject. Just by looking at her, anyone could tell that Keely's self-possession was eggshell thin. Nicole, like everyone else, didn't want to be the one responsible for cracking it.

After three weeks of avoidance Nicole invited herself over for dinner. "Can you believe it? I've got a Saturday night without a date. I'm coming for dinner. Make that spaghetti casserole with all the gloriously fattening cheese in it."

Keely laughed. "If there's anything I hate it's a shy guest. What else would you like?"

"That layered chocolate thing with the cream cheese and pecans."

"Anything else?" Keely inquired dryly.

"Loaves of French bread."

"Anything else?"

"No," Nicole said flippantly. "I'll bring the wine."

She did. At seven o'clock that evening Keely, jean and sweatshirt clad, answered the door to Nicole, equally sloppy, carrying a jug of red wine under each arm.

"This is going to be a blast. I'm going to eat myself into oblivion. When one doesn't have a date for Saturday night, there's only one consolation—blow your diet. Besides I heaved my guts up yesterday and couldn't hold anything down all day. I deserve a feast."

"Nothing serious or catching, I hope," Keely said, leading Nicole into the kitchen.

"I don't think so. Just one of those twenty-four-hour bugs."

"Well, just in case, don't breathe on my plate."

"Just get it ready and—" She broke off when the doorbell rang. "Damn! Who can that be? I look like hell and didn't want anyone to see me."

"I don't know who it could be," Keely said. "I didn't invite anyone else."

"Well, I'll get rid of them, whoever it is. I don't intend to share any of that delicious-smelling food."

Nicole flounced through the door and Keely was distracted by the boiling spaghetti. She didn't turn around until she heard Nicole call her name in an uncharacteristically subdued voice. "Keely, there's a man, a soldier, to see you." Her blue eyes reflected her bewilderment.

"A soldier?" she asked on a high note and dropped her wooden spoon onto the countertop.

Nicole nodded.

Keely went past her, drying her hands on a dish towel as she walked into her living room. The soldier was standing nervously, twisting his cap in his hands. He was pale and thin and had the sallow complexion of one who had been recently ill. His hands and feet looked too large for his spare body. His ears seemed abnormally large under his military haircut. He was around thirty years old, though the lines running down from either corner of his mouth should have belonged to an older man.

"I'm Keely Preston Williams," she said by way of introduction. "You wanted to see me?"

"Yes, Mrs. Williams. I'm Lieutenant Gene Cox."

The name struck her right between the eyes and she staggered back a step or two before she clutched the back of a chair for support. Her ears rang so loudly that she almost didn't hear Nicole's gasp of concern. She warded off her assistance, however, and tried to pull herself together. "Won't you please sit down?" she said hoarsely.

The soldier was obviously distressed that he had brought on such a drastic reaction. Keely's face had drained of color and her lips looked blue. He sat down, fearing that if he didn't do as she asked, she might fly apart altogether. Keely collapsed on the chair and leaned forward. "Why did you come to see me?"

He glanced fleetingly toward Nicole as if seeking her advice about talking to this deranged woman, but at her nod he brought his honest, open eyes back to Keely's strained face. "Well, I've known about you since Paris. I was in the hospital, but we were kept informed about what was going on. I think it was the chaplain who told us about PROOF and all." He looked down at his hands, which were still twisting the cap. "Everything happened so fast, I get confused about who told me what."

"I'm sorry," Keely said gently. "I don't mean to rush you. Take your time and tell me what you came for."

"Well as I said, I knew about your work in PROOF and that you were in Paris. Excuse me, Mrs. Williams, but didn't Congressman Devereaux tell you what I told him in the hospital? I mean when he left that day after we figured out that it was probably your husband I went down with, I felt sure that he'd go straight to you and tell you."

Keely ignored Nicole's soft cry of dismay. She nodded her head. "Yes, he told me, but—"

"Well, I saw him in Washington last week. I finally got to come home five days later than everybody else. I was pretty sick," he said bashfully. "I'm sorry, I'm off the track again. I saw the congressman in Washington and asked him how you had taken the news. He said you weren't convinced that it was really your husband who was flying that chopper. 'Course I can't be certain either, but I brought something today that might clear it up for you."

He was digging in his breast pocket and Keely's heart began to thud. It couldn't be! But it was. Gene Cox was taking a medallion on a silver link chain out of his pocket. She recognized it immediately.

"The Mark Williams I went down with was wearing this with his dog tag. Just before he—he...uh...died, he asked me to get this back to you if I ever made it out. When I got captured by the Cong, they took my dog tag and his, but they weren't interested in this, so they gave it back to me. I've kept it all this time. I didn't know if I'd ever have an opportunity to return it to you or not, but I hung on to it. I never bartered it for food or anything. I promised that GI I wouldn't." He was attacked by self-consciousness again when he extended the oxidized medallion toward Keely.

Her fingers could barely close around it, they were trembling so hard. She looked at the St. Christopher medal she had given Mark on their wedding day. Turning it over in her palm, she read the inscription she had paid extra to have engraved there: "God keep you, my husband." It was also dated. Tears flooded her eyes as she stroked her thumb over the blackened silver.

"Is it his, Keely?" Nicole asked quietly from behind her.

She only nodded. Her throat was closed to speech.

Gene Cox shifted uncomfortably on the sofa and said, "I wish I could tell you he didn't suffer, but he did. His legs were broken, and he kept vomiting bl— But he died like a hero. Even with his legs the way they were and the chopper exploding and burning debris flying, he wanted to look for the other boys. I think there were three of us besides him in that chopper. I really can't remember. I only remember that I had to fight him like hell to get him out of that clearing and under the cover of the jungle. When—when the end did come, he was peaceful-like about it, you know? He said something about better this way than to come home to you a cripple."

"He was wrong," Keely said hoarsely.

"Yes, ma'am. But I guess I know how he felt." He cleared his throat loudly again. "My—my wife's been married to another guy for three years now. She came to Washington last week to see me. I barely recognized her. And she sure as hell didn't recognize me."

Keely raised her eyes to him. "I'm sorry."

He only shrugged, made a fist, and coughed unnecessarily into it. He stood up. "Well, I hope that settles things for you anyway."

She went to him and, without reserve, hugged him tenderly. "Thank you so much," she whispered in her ear before backing away.

"I'm glad I could do it. I wish I had answers for all the others. See, sometimes we thought we were the only twenty-six guys left over there. It's spooky to think there are a hundred times that many still unaccounted for. We had no idea." He turned toward the door.

"Lieutenant Cox, I have one more question."

"Yes?"

"Did you show Congressman Devereaux the St. Christopher medal?"

"Yes."

Keely's hands clasped together at her waist. "What did he say?"

The soldier's eyes darted to Nicole again then back to Keely. "He…uh…he said it would mean more if I brought it to you myself."

Before he left, he wrote down Keely's address, promising to stay in touch with her. He volunteered his services to PROOF in any way the organization could use him.

When he closed the door behind him, she laid her forehead against the hard wood. The metal was still impressed into her palm and she squeezed it tightly.

"Come sit down," Nicole said, taking her by the shoulders and turning her away from the door. She let herself be led to the sofa and sank down on it. Nicole sat beside her, smoothing her hair and rubbing her back.

"Now you know, Keely. I'm sorry about Mark, but now you know."

"Yes."

"I know it's hard right now, but in a few days you'll feel such a sense of relief that it'll be like rebirth. You can go on with your life." She continued her soothing ministrations as she asked, "Keely, did Dax tell you about Mark in Paris?" Keely nodded. "And you didn't believe him?" Nicole's voice told of her incredulity that Keely could be so stupid.

"No!" Nicole was flung back by the impetus with which Keely leaped to her feet. "I didn't believe him," she cried, anguished.

"Why would you not believe him? For godsakes, Keely, what was wrong with you?"

"I don't know," she groaned, hiding her face in her hands. "I thought he was playing a low trick."

"Trick! Dax Devereaux doesn't have to play tricks."

"I know, I know, but I was so confused. It was too incredible, too coincidental, and I was feeling so guilty—" She floundered when she realized her slip.

"Guilty? Why?" When Keely tried to avoid her eyes, Nicole went to her and clamped her hands on either side of Keely's face. "*Why?*"

"Because we had slept together," she shouted and pushed Nicole away.

"So?" Nicole shouted back.

"*So?*" She rounded on her friend, aghast that she hadn't caught on yet. "So I was still married to Mark. I didn't know until *after* I had spent the night with Dax—"

"Oh, no!" Nicole threw back her head in exasperation. "Don't stand there and tell me you're going to feel guilty about betraying a man who had already been dead for twelve years!"

"But I didn't know—"

"You already said that and I'm sick of hearing it," Nicole yelled. "You can't mean that after living the life of a vestal virgin for twelve years, you're consigning yourself to another interminable purgatory. You slept with a man you love! Your husband has been dead for twelve years. Explain to me your sin."

"You don't understand," Keely said impatiently.

"You're damn right I don't. I could overlook some senseless, unbalanced person for hanging on to grief and guilt for years as some sort of security blanket. But you're an intelligent, vital, beautiful woman, and there's something pathetic and sick in your wasting your life this way. How many crowns in heaven can one person use? Huh? Well, I'm tired of you and your self-righteous self-sacrifice. Feed on your misery, culture it until it destroys you more than it already has, but count me out. I've had it."

She spun away from Keely and, after retrieving her bottles of wine from the kitchen, stormed out the front door.

Tossing on her bed, she tried to block out the visions, turn off the sounds, erase the memories, but they refused to be eradicated. Nicole's desertion had hurt. Keely had cried herself to sleep last night after feeding all the food she had prepared to the garbage disposal. She had spent Sunday morning working up a profuse sweat repotting the plants on her patio. But the work had run out and she had been cursed with hours of time in which to brood. She had never been so grateful as when the hands on her clock indicated it was late enough to go to bed.

But sleep wouldn't come. After her mind had replayed its recording of her argument with Nicole, it switched to the morning she and Dax had awakened in each other's arms.

They had decided that before they left the small hotel they would avail themselves of the bathroom that their hostess had been so proud of.

"Let me celebrate you," he had whispered as they stood facing each other in the narrow European tub.

"I never have had very good aim with one of those," she said about the hand nozzle of the shower.

"I have terrific aim."

"You sure do," she crooned and pressed herself up against his nakedness.

One black wing of an eyebrow arched over his eyes. "Do I detect a double entendre?"

"I don't know what you mean." She fluttered her eyelashes innocently.

"Like hell you don't," he growled and bit her playfully on the shoulder before he leaned down to turn on the faucets. "How do you like it? Hotter or cooler?"

"Hotter."

"One hot shower it is," he said and then they both hollered as ice-cold water sprayed on them.

"You did that on purpose," she accused when the water temperature finally adjusted and she had her stolen breath back.

"No, I didn't. I swear," he laughed as her nails raked down his chest.

When they were properly wet, they shared the soap, lathering each other until they looked like two snowpeople. "You're going to wash all the skin off," she said when he had given his attention to her breasts, delicately rubbing them with soap-slickened fingers.

"Then I'll just have to move on to someplace else." His soapy fingers were only championed by his use of the nozzle spray when he meticulously rinsed every place he had washed.

"I need a shave," he mused aloud, running his hand over his jaw as he studied his reflection in the mirror over the basin. They had eventually quit the tub in favor of drying each other with fresh-smelling, fluffy towels.

"You certainly do. You look positively piratical."

"How do you think people would react to a bearded congressman?"

"Grow one sometime and see."

"I might just do that. But are you sure you want me to? It can get awfully scratchy."

"Oh, it would be understood beforehand that we wouldn't kiss or anything while you were growing it. How long does it take to grow a nice, soft beard? Several months?"

"Would you be impressed by my unusual virility if I could do it in a couple of weeks?" His grin was smug, a modern Tom Sawyer and his Becky Thatcher.

"No," Keely said saucily and skipped out of the bathroom.

He tackled her on the other side of the door, spun her around, and backed her toward the bed until the backs of her knees caught on the edge and she collapsed. "Then I'll have to think of something else to impress you."

His mouth was like a live electric wire that had snapped in two. It danced erratically across her stomach, striking at will, shocking each place it struck, electrifying her whole body with shooting sparks.

Then it became more tame, traversing the delta of her abdomen and leaving soft, damp kisses in its path. Her thighs knew the thrilling rough scrape of his bearded cheeks. She was burning, burning, and his lips both fueled the flame and melted against it. Her fingers burrowed through his hair. She called his name over and over, though she was never sure that she spoke it aloud.

He raised himself from his knees and made a slow climb up her body. His stubbled chin abraded her skin in a way that made her shiver. He paused at her breasts.

His tongue leisurely stroked the nipples while his hands admired the full round shape. When he was face-to-face with her, his body stretched over hers, powerfully declaring his need between her thighs, he asked, "Are you impressed?"

Now Keely buried her face in her pillow and screamed her torment. Would she ever forget? No, no. That night, that dawn, was the most precious day of her life. The night she had spent with Dax bore no similarity to the nights she had spent as Mark's bride. That passion had been furtive and under cover of clothing and darkness.

She and Dax had cavorted nakedly without embarrassment or shame. She knew his dark, muscled body by touch, by smell. He knew every inch of her intimately. She had never known what it was to love and be loved by a man until she had spent that night with Dax.

Acquainted now with all the pleasures he could give her and she could return, her body throbbed with desire for him. She longed for his fervent, passionate kisses as well as the tender ones. She craved to hear once more his rushing breath in her ear and the quiet love words he had chanted.

"I love you, Keely."

She could see his face as he had said that. Why hadn't she, at that moment when he spoke the words she longed to hear, thrown herself into his arms and begged never to be released?

It was too late now. She knew that the rigid, hard jaw and the blazing black eyes he had speared her with when she had accused him of lying meant that whatever love he had felt was destroyed by her doubt. Even if she called him to beg forgiveness, he would never love her again. He would always remember the time she mocked him when he tried to tell her something that would change the course of their future. Nicole was right, she was a fool.

*Should* she call him? Should she put down her fear and hesitation and call him, asking for his forgiveness? Yes!

She was reaching for the telephone when another thought struck her. He knew about Gene Cox bringing her the medal! What had the soldier said? *He said it would mean more if I brought it to you myself.* Dax knew, but he hadn't made an effort to contact her. He knew she was free, but he hadn't come to her seeking a reconciliation.

She was free, but he wasn't.

He was still running for the Senate. She had seen his picture with Madeline Robins in the Sunday paper. Madeline had given him a lavish welcome-home party last night after his return from Washington.

So while Keely was listening to Gene Cox's story, Dax had been partying with Madeline. While her best friend was scorning her, deserting her, he was dancing with Madeline. Laughing.

He had said he loved her. Maybe he did. But would it be the best thing for him to have her in his life right now? What would it do to his career? The name Keely Preston was too fresh on the public's mind. She would have to officially announce Mark's death soon, but people had seen her and Dax together before the MIAs returned. They would be the subjects of gossip and speculation. They weren't out from under the shadows of scandal yet.

He needed the Madeline-types in his life who could help him win his Senate seat. He didn't need Keely Preston Williams.

She felt like she might very well die without him in her life, but she knew that he certainly couldn't live with her in his.

Obligation and responsibility forced her to drag herself out of bed when her alarm went off at five. She dressed and applied her makeup mechanically. She managed to gulp down one cup of coffee before she left her house and drove to the Superdome.

The morning was warm and humid with the promise of spring. There were clouds on the horizon where the sun would soon rise, but the sky overhead was clear. She had a few minutes to ponder the deep lavender-gray sky before she heard the clatter of the helicopter blades and saw it flying over the buildings of downtown like a giant mosquito.

Joe set it down with ease. Keely locked her car and ran toward it. The terrific wind tried to tear her clothes and hair off, but she was used to that and knew that it rarely did any permanent damage.

"Good morning," she shouted over the racket as she climbed inside.

"Hi there, good-lookin'," Joe greeted her. "I brought some doughnuts this morning. Help yourself."

"Thanks," she said as she buckled her seat belt and the helicopter lifted off the ground.

The morning was routine. Her earliest report came at six fifty-five when she reported that traffic was still light and that all ramps leading onto the freeways were clear of congestion. It was proving to be a beautiful morning, so weather wasn't a consideration.

It was while she was joking with the disc jockey during her second report that she heard the loud bang that sounded like a car backfiring, then a still silence when the helicopter's motor died an instant death.

"Godamighty!" Joe cursed.

Keely spun her head around and saw that his hands were busy at the controls. She broke off midway into her sentence about an upcoming rock concert. Panic rose in her throat like scalding bile. "Joe!" she shouted, wanting him to sit back and smile and relax those frantic hands and tell her that everything was all right and under control.

"Hey, Keely, what's happened up there? Did you burst a balloon?" She heard the disc jockey's joking voice in her headpiece, but it no longer seemed real to her.

"Joe!" she screamed as the chopper began to spin crazily, like a top off its axis.

"Sit tight, Keely," he said with amazing resignation. "We're going down, baby."

# Sixteen

❧⟡❧

Keely looked out and saw that the ground and horizon were no longer level, but tilting at an alarming slant. The blades of the helicopter were still rotating, but there was no sound from the engine. Around and around the small craft was spinning, even as the ground rushed up toward it.

"No!" she screamed. "No, please." As the chopper pitched forward she felt the seat belt biting into her abdomen, but it wasn't enough to hold her. When it let go, her head struck the bubble windshield with a sickening thud and suddenly she was fighting nausea and pain.

"Help me!' she cried, but didn't know if anyone heard or if she had even said the words out loud. "Oh, no, please. *No!*" She tried to open her eyes, but couldn't against a blinding light. Out of it an image took form.

Mark! She saw him, beaming proudly, reassuringly. He was the smiling, guileless, exuberant boy she remembered. His eyes lighted up with happy surprise at seeing her and his smile was as jovial as ever. *Mark!* her mind screamed, *you're alive.* He wasn't in pain.

He wasn't a nameless skeleton in a jungle on the other side of the world. His spirit was very much alive in this sphere into which she had been hurled.

Or had she? The light was growing dimmer. His image was becoming unfocused. She wanted to speak to him, but he waved jauntily and turned his back on her. Gradually his image receded as he rushed back from where he had come. A giant drapery was being pulled closed behind him, separating them. Darkness was fast closing in and she was losing her battle with it. She longed for the warm and light place where Mark was.

But the darkness wouldn't go away. Just before it swallowed her, Keely realized with startling clarity that her heart knew a peace it hadn't known in years. In this flash of time, suspended between two worlds, she had shared, even experienced, Mark's death. Now she could lay him to rest. Seeing him living in a brilliant and shining light, she could accept his death in this world and let him go.

Peacefully, with a surrendering sigh, she let the darkness engulf her.

"Easy now, just lie back. No, Miss Preston, lie down. Everything is all right. You're in the hospital."

Strong yet gentle hands kept her shoulders anchored to the bed, though she strained to raise them. "Adjust that bandage, Patsy. She loosened it." While hands still held her, others tampered with something just above her brow. "She needs to wake up. Miss Preston, wake up. Come on. Open your eyes and say hello to us."

She struggled to obey but her eyelids felt like lead and she couldn't lift them. But the voices coming at her out of a dense fog were insistent and she kept trying until she could see a slit of light.

"Well, hello. We didn't think you were going to be a very friendly guest. Gracie gets her feelings hurt if her patients don't speak to her."

"That's right, I do. Especially if the patient is a celebrity. How do you feel?"

The nurses' white uniforms hurt her eyes. A thermometer had been poked under her tongue. Her blood pressure was being taken.

Where...when...how? The questions bounced inside her brain, jousting with the pain already there. Then she remembered the spinning helicopter and struggled against the restraining arms again.

"Joe," she croaked and didn't even recognize her voice. "Joe."

"He's fine," she was told. "He landed that helicopter on the Superdome parking lot just like he always does."

"Landed it?" The words seemed to roll around in her mouth, trying to find an exit. "But..."

"Don't worry about that now. The details will be filled in later. You were the only casualty. Now, do you think you can sip on a 7-Up without throwing it up all over that glamorous gown we've got you in?"

She shook her head no, but they brought her the cup with the bent straw anyway and she took a few obligatory sips before she fell asleep again.

The way back to complete consciousness was long and fuzzy. Confusion blurred the times she did awaken and her sleep was so heavy that she seemed never to come completely out of it. She knew she had an IV needle in the back of her hand and every time she moved it, she felt the pull of the tape.

Her parents moved in and out of her dreams until she realized that they were actually there. Her mother wept softly. Her father looked uncomfortable and awkward, but he kissed her on the forehead when she managed to smile at him in a moment of lucidity.

Once she awakened to see a man's face bending over her. It was a comical face with frizzy blond hair ringing it like a wreath.

"Hi," he said cheerfully. "Just looking at my handiwork."

She stared up at him in confusion and he must have read the question in her eyes. "Dr. Walters. Call me David. Your friend called me in when she knew you had to have your forehead stitched. I'm a plastic surgeon. You'll have a tiny scar right at your hairline, but I'm so damn good, it will hardly be visible to the naked eye."

She smiled.

"Are you feeling all right otherwise? Need anything?"

She shook her head and closed her eyes and went back to sleep.

Then, as if by magic, the cobwebs had been swept away, and when she awoke, everything was clear. Her head ached abominably, but that was understandable. A debilitating weakness made her limbs tremble, but the nurses made her get up and walk around her room before allowing her to fall dizzily back into bed. She managed to drink a whole can of apple juice and keep it down, so the nurses took the hateful needle out of her hand. It left a blue bruise.

The rest of that day she napped intermittently and her sleep was no longer heavy and drugged. By nightfall she was able to read the accounts of the near-disaster in the newspapers the nurses had saved for her. Her room was filled with flowers she hadn't been cognizant enough to appreciate before. The nurses oohed and aahed over each bouquet and hovered nearby as Keely read the cards aloud to them.

One card wasn't signed and the nurses mourned over that fact since it went with the largest and most beautiful bouquet of yellow rosebuds. Keely didn't think the unsigned card was an accident. She plucked off one of the perfect blooms and kept it on her pillow. It caught her tears as it would dewdrops.

The next morning she was able to get up, shower, dress in her own negligee, and make up her face. A small bag with her things in it had miraculously appeared in her room overnight. When asked, her mother denied knowledge of it.

Both the doctor who had first treated her at the hospital and her own physician examined her and agreed that she could receive visitors. The manager of KDIX came in and she was touched by his concern and relief that she was still among the living. He brought her cards from the rest of the staff that were generally ribald and irreverent. They made her laugh until her head ached.

Joe Collins came in later. Tears made him look watery as he leaned down and hugged her tight. "Joe, thank you," she said. After his concern about her condition had been eased, he explained what had happened.

"Something, a tiny particle of something, blocked the fuel line and the engine conked out. Luckily I stabilized the chopper and managed to land with what is called auto rotation. The blades keep rotating for a while, you see. We were almost directly over the Superdome when it happened, so…" He shrugged modestly. "I was busy trying to keep us up and at the same time I was worried as hell about you. All I could see of your face was covered with blood."

"You saved my life, Joe."

He seemed suddenly shy and embarrassed so she switched subjects. She rested after he left and the nurses persuaded her other waiting visitors to come back later.

After dinner that evening she was propped up in bed watching television when there was a timid knock on her door.

"Come in," she said. Nicole and Charles walked in. Nicole looked meek and anxious. When Keely held out her arms to her, she lunged across the room and flung herself at her friend.

"Keely, I'm so sorry. Did you do this on purpose to pay me back for the terrible way I talked to you? Oh, God, when I heard you up there screaming, I thought I'd die."

"You heard?"

"Yes, we all did," Charles said. "Remember, you were in the middle of your conversation with the DJ. I'm afraid he didn't react with the quick skill he should have and cut your mic. Your radio audience heard the whole thing."

Keely covered her mouth and closed her eyes. "I didn't realize. How awful that must have been."

"Well, it made you a heroine," Nicole said with resilience since she knew she had been forgiven.

"Are you responsible for the plastic surgeon and my bag being here and everything?"

"Charles and I."

"Thank you." The women locked hands and stared at each other with understanding.

"About the other night, Keely—"

"It's forgotten. About many things you were exactly right."

"And many things were none of my damn business too."

"Yes, they were. You're my friend."

"That I am." They were both perilously close to tears. Charles saved them an emotional scene.

"Darling, you haven't told Keely your news," he said in a bland voice.

Keely was so shocked by Charles's calling Nicole "darling" that for a moment she stared at him before turning to Nicole and asking, "What news?"

Nicole twisted around from her seat on the edge of Keely's bed to glare at him. "You just love to gloat over it, don't you?"

"Yes," he said, rocking up on his toes and smiling broadly.

"Well, I don't think it's funny. Not one damn bit."

"Would the two of you please let me in on the mystery," Keely interrupted. "What news?"

"I'm pregnant," Nicole mumbled.

Keely looked at the top of Nicole's bowed blond head as she picked at the covers of the bed. Keely's eyes then moved beyond Nicole to Charles, who was managing to look both sheepish and smug at the same time. Her gaze came back to Nicole. Had her friend just announced that she was going into a convent, she couldn't have been more stunned.

"You're *what*?"

Nicole vaulted off the bed, jarring Keely's aching head. "You heard me. Pregnant. Knocked up. With child. Whatever the hell you want to call it and *he*—" she pointed an accusing finger at Charles "—did it."

Keely began chuckling softly, then the laughter built until she was convulsed with it and tears were coursing down her cheeks. It made her head throb, but the laughter felt good and she milked it for all it was worth. The corners of Nicole's mouth quirked until she was smiling and then she too was laughing.

"I can't believe it," Keely said, wiping the tears from her eyes. "When did—"

"The night we went with you and—and Dax to the Café du Monde. Charles took me home, remember? I used every feminine wile I have and finally lured him into bed. He got his revenge!"

Charles winked at Keely. "You're not too upset over it, are you, Nicole?" she asked intuitively.

Nicole bent down and whispered loudly, "Who would have thought it to look at him? Keely, he's hell on wheels in bed."

That started Keely's laughter all over again and she was weak by the time it subsided. Nicole had finally met her match and neither of them looked unhappy about it. Charles had pulled her against his chest, his arms folding across her midriff. "Well, are you going to let this child be born out of wedlock?"

"Oh, Keely," Nicole began on a wail and turned her face into Charles's shoulder.

"I'll tell her, darling, since I was the one who insisted." He kissed the tip of her nose. "We were married yesterday, Keely. Of course we would have loved to have you there, but I didn't feel it was proper for us to wait any longer."

Keely smiled at them and tears of a new kind came to her eyes. "I'm so happy for both of you. I couldn't be more pleased. I've always thought the two of you belonged together."

"So did I," Charles said. "*She* took some convincing."

"You have a most convincing manner," Nicole purred and turned into his embrace.

"May I at least kiss the groom?" Keely said impatiently when their kiss lengthened with no sign of letup. Charles pulled himself out of Nicole's possessive arms and bent down to kiss Keely's cheek with his usual reserve. When he straightened, he said, "I'll be out in the hall. Don't hurry, darling." Tactfully he withdrew, giving the two women some time alone.

"Nicole," Keely said, catching her friend's hands. "You love him, don't you? And the baby? You're happy about it, aren't you?"

"Keely, I'm so happy, I feel I'm about to burst. There will never be a mother more loving or attentive. Not a day will go by that this kid doesn't know he's loved. And Charles. Charles," she said wistfully, lovingly. "I was afraid to love him, afraid of his rejection. But wonder of wonders, he loves me, Keely. He truly does. For myself, not for— Well, you know. Despite all the—the other men and my reputation, he loves me."

"I knew he did. I'm glad he finally convinced you."

"So am I." She smiled the smile that melted the

hearts of thousands of television viewers every night. But the classic smile faded when she looked down at Keely's wan complexion and saw the haunted, lonely expression in her eyes. Her taut body couldn't hide the tension within. "What about you, Keely? How do you intend to solve your affair of the heart?"

"I think it's been solved for me." She looked sadly at the yellow roses, then back to Nicole, who was watching her closely. "I realized when that helicopter was going down that Mark is dead. He belongs in the past. Dax is the present, could have been the future, but…I love him, Nicole. I love him more than my life. But he will never forgive me for mistrusting him."

"How do you know? Have you asked him?"

"No, of course not."

"Then why don't you? He's right outside."

Eyes that had been dulled by weariness and despair flew to Nicole's face to see if there was any deceit there. "He's…Dax is…"

"Outside. He beat the ambulance to the hospital, Keely. He was listening to you on the radio. He's not left the hospital since you got here. I've seen raving maniacs with better dispositions than his, snarling at anyone who— Keely, what do you think— Get back in that bed!"

"No." She pushed off the covers and swung her legs to the side of the bed. "I'm going to him."

"Keely, for godsakes, let me—"

"No," she said, using her last strength to shake off Nicole's helping hands. She had to go to him on her own.

Halfway to the door she stretched out her arms in

an effort to keep the room from reeling, but she wasn't about to give up. She had to see Dax, to tell him….

The door was too heavy for her, so she did allow Nicole to pull it open. Her bare feet on the cold tile floor were silent as she stepped through the door and looked down the hallway.

He was sitting in a chair, his knees wide-spread, his hands clasped between them, his head bowed. He had assumed that position the night he had told her he was on the subcommittee. Dejection was evident in the slump of his shoulders, the mussed hair, the stubbled cheeks, the rumpled clothes. He had never looked more beautiful to her. He was speaking softly to her parents, who shared a short sofa in front of his chair.

"Dax."

His head snapped up at the sound of her voice and swiveled around to look down the sterile length of the corridor to where she stood, so frail, yet so courageous.

Shakily he rose to his feet. He stumbled on a small magazine table as he took a step toward her. Then he was rushing, his long strides eating up the distance between them. His eyes, always compelling, were even more so with the shine of tears glossing them. Fiercely he gathered her to him and wrapped his arms around her as though he'd never let go.

The power of his embrace robbed her of breath, but she gave it up gladly. Her arms folded around his waist. "Keely, Keely," he repeated into her hair.

They were unaware of the spectacle they were creating in the corridor, but Nicole wasn't. To protect them she placed a hand on each of their shoulders and backed them into the room, closing the door behind them. Dax and Keely were unconscious of ever moving.

He combed through her hair with frantic fingers. Anxiously he scanned her face. Lovingly he touched her features. "I thought you were going to die. I was listening to you on the radio, loving the sound of your voice, loving you, wanting to see you. Then I heard that engine die. I've been in too many helicopters not to know what happened the instant it did. My heart stopped beating. My screams matched yours, my darling. I thought you were going to die. Oh, my God, Keely…"

"Shh," she comforted him, stroking his hair as he nuzzled his face in the hollow of her neck. "I didn't. I didn't. I'm alive. Here with you now. Shh."

Her fingertips fanned across his lashes and picked up the moisture clinging to them. "When you learned the St. Christopher medal proved Mark was dead, why didn't you come to see me, Dax?"

"Did you really want me to?"

She laid her cheek against his chest and groaned softly, "Yes, I wanted you. I cried for you, but I was afraid. After what I said to you I didn't think you'd ever want to see me again. Will you forgive me for doubting you, Dax? I'm sorry."

Now he comforted her. "I was a fool, Keely. I shouldn't have blurted out Mark's death to you then. I was just so anxious that you know." He held her head between his hands and tilted it back to look into her eyes. "When you knew that what I told you was the truth, you didn't call me." His face looked pained. "Why, Keely?"

"Because I didn't think you'd ever forgive me for

not believing you. Because you still have your career and campaign to worry about. Because you don't need any problems in your life just now. Because I saw your picture with Madeline."

A smile tugged at his lips. "Is that all?"

Her own lips tried to smile, but they were trembling too much. "Because I love you and didn't want to do anything that would hurt you."

"Keely." He reached for her again and smothered her against him. "I didn't come to you because I didn't know what you were thinking or feeling. I thought you might be grieving over Mark. I had come on too strong and too soon once before, and I didn't want to risk doing it again."

She smoothed the collar of his wrinkled shirt with her fingertips. "No. I was relieved that Mark hadn't suffered years of imprisonment and pain. When I was in the helicopter and it was going down…"

"Yes?" he prodded when she hesitated.

"Well, I said goodbye to him, Dax. He'll always be a very fond memory, but he's been dead for a long time. I've been granted a second chance. I can't afford to waste one day of living."

He kissed her then, long and hard and earnestly. When at last they pulled part, he said huskily, "You need to be in bed."

He led her back to the high bed and eased her onto it. When she was propped onto the pillows, seemingly having suffered no ill effects for having got up, he took her hand and pressed it between his. "Keely, will you marry me?"

"Do you want me to?"

"Very much."

"I'm a recent widow."

"Twelve years? Once Mark's death is officially announced, people will understand your wanting to marry again."

"Oh, my darling," she said, smoothing her hand over his rough cheek. "I'm not thinking of what people will think of me, but of jeopardizing your campaign."

He turned his head far enough to kiss her palm. "You let me worry about that. Tomorrow, with your consent, I'm calling a press conference to announce our engagement. Van Dorf will be the first one I call."

"Van Dorf! Dax, he'll—"

"He'll be here with bells on and will probably give us a glowing write-up." He chuckled.

Her eyes narrowed suspiciously. "What aren't you telling me?"

"Lie back. You're sick, remember? I'll tell you for now that Al and I have reached an understanding." He dropped a silencing kiss on her mouth. "Enough of him. Will you marry me?"

Her brows knit in worry. "Dax, the voting public still might frown on us. Our names have been bandied around for weeks."

"Keely," he whispered, leaning over her to kiss her just beneath her jaw. "I think you'll be an asset. The public will love you. They already do. And if they don't vote for me because of the woman I married, or for any other reason, I'll serve my country as a farmer and businessman. I've never meant anything more than I mean this. I'd rather have a life with you than hold any office. I'd rather have you than anything."

"Dax." His name was a sigh before she brought his head down to kiss his lips.

"Do you think you can handle the campaign trail? I mean, with your job at the radio station and all?" His nibbling lips stopped when he heard her soft laughter.

"You're always the diplomat, the politician, aren't you?" He had the grace to grin abashedly. Tangling her fingers in his hair, she shook his head. "I think loving you will be a full-time occupation."

The ebony eyes liquefied with love. "I like the sound of that," he said roughly. Light kisses were brushed across her brows.

"Dax?"

"Hmm?"

"Madeline."

"What about her?"

"What about her?" she repeated.

He lifted his head. "Absolutely nothing, Keely. There never was, even before I met you. There certainly never will be now. She wanted it. The press wanted it. No one consulted me. I took advantage of the publicity she attracted. That was wrong, perhaps, but I'm all done with it now. If she wants to contribute to my campaign, then she'll have to do it through proper channels."

"Stay with me tonight." Her ready acceptance of his explanation was a pledge of trust, of love. She reached up and switched off the light over her bed. When he glanced cautiously toward the door, she laughed. "Anyone who tries to come in would have to get past Nicole, and I don't think that would be possible."

Even in the shadowed darkness she saw his smile. He slipped off his shoes and lay down beside her, cradling her body along the length of his. Without another word his lips found hers, fused with them, opened. His tongue glided over her teeth, past them, into the hollow of her mouth, probing, a reminder of the times he had loved her.

One hand lay along her cheek, tenderly, possessively. The other coasted down her chest to slip inside her negligee and cherish her breast. Lightly his thumb swept her nipple.

"Dax," she murmured, rolling to face him, pressing her body to his.

"Oh, God, Keely," he groaned and pushed away from her. "This isn't going to work. I've got to go."

"No," she cried, clutching his shirtfront.

"We can't make love, Keely. You've got to rest, to sleep—"

"I will, I promise, only please don't leave me."

She found herself in a swift, sudden embrace. "Never, never," he vowed. "I love you, Keely. I'll never leave you. Never."

He pressed her head against his heart and with its strong, steady beating she felt her old anxieties fading away. This was a beginning. Yesterday's heartache was gone; today was splendored; and they could still look forward to the promise of tomorrow.

\* \* \* \* \*

## New York Times Bestselling Author
# BELLA ANDRE

### A story of fame, fortune and falling in love...

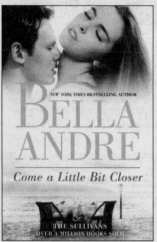

Movie star Smith Sullivan can't afford any distractions. He's staking his entire reputation on his new film…but he can't stop thinking about Valentina Landon and the fire he sees smoldering just beneath the surface of her cool exterior.

Valentina isn't averse to sensual pleasure, or even to the idea of finding true love, but as a Hollywood business manager, she's watched too many smart women fall for actors…only to be torn apart when the fairy tale comes to its inevitable end.

Smith knows he has to find a way to convince Valentina to let him get a little bit closer. Close enough to completely steal her heart…the way she's stolen his from the beginning.

### Come a Little Bit Closer

## Available now, wherever books are sold!

**Be sure to connect with us at:**
Harlequin.com/Newsletters
Facebook.com/HarlequinBooks
Twitter.com/HarlequinBooks

www.Harlequin.com

MBA1608